Jane stood perfectly still, allowing the sounds and sights to touch her, to pull from her the energy that she knew would send the public into an even greater state of adulation.

In her black dress and jewels she looked regal and elegant. She was what all the young girls from all over America wanted to be. She was them and she belonged to them. Jane Turner was theirs and they owned her. Lowering her head, Jane lifted her eyes and looked out across the crowd, drawing from inside herself the magic that they had come to see . . .

But the world didn't matter. Now only Jane Turner existed. There was nothing else. She was everything. Jane Turner was a star.

Berkley books by D.C. Richardson

ALL THAT HEAVEN ALLOWS
SHADOWS AND DREAMS

SHADOWS AND DREAMS

D.C. RICHARDSON

BERKLEY BOOKS, NEW YORK

For Harvey Klinger

SHADOWS AND DREAMS

A Berkley Book/published by arrangement with
the author

PRINTING HISTORY
Berkley edition/September 1988

ISBN: 0-425-10974-7

A BERKLEY BOOK ® TM 757,375
Berkley Books are published by The Berkley Publishing Group,
200 Madison Avenue, New York, N.Y. 10016.
The name "BERKLEY" and the "B" logo are
trademarks belonging to Berkley Publishing Corporation.

PRINTED IN THE UNITED STATES OF AMERICA

10 9 8 7 6 5 4 3 2 1

CHAPTER *One*

EVEN BY HOLLYWOOD STANDARDS the evening had been spectacular. But then, Greta Stewart was Global Films's biggest star, and the opening of her latest movie, *A Long Road*, at Grauman's Chinese Theatre, naturally created excitement. Everyone expected it to be one of the major pictures of 1938.

Jane Turner was one of the first guests to arrive at Terrance Malvey's house for the after-premiere party. Terrance was the producer of *A Long Road*, or as he called it when not being quoted, A Long *Rode*, which, when listeners considered Greta's sexual history, made considerable sense.

Terrance had an enormous estate in Beverly Hills, surrounded by a high fence with great iron gates capped by gold-painted spears opening onto the circular drive. Chauffeured limousines pulled up at the main entrance, which was brilliantly lit and manned with a platoon of handsome male attendants. To the left of the house was a tennis court, and behind it a large swimming pool, festooned with garlands of flowers and lighted by dozens of oil lamps strewn through the trees and placed on poles which had been plunged into the ground.

Jane nodded at the butler, handing him her wrap, and then found herself a seat in the back of the large drawing room.

In a few moments she was joined by Elizabeth Hudson, a

young woman from Toledo, Ohio, who had just been signed by Global Films. Elizabeth had never been to a premiere before, and she was in considerable awe of the arriving stars.

"Isn't this incredible?" Elizabeth bubbled, her voice full of wonder. "All these stars in one room. Imagine! And wasn't the premiere exciting? I've never seen anything like it. All the lights and the press and everything. And wasn't Miss Stewart's picture marvelous? I do think she's the most beautiful person I've ever seen. And *so* kind. Why, in the picture you could just tell that she was really feeling all the pain and sadness of giving up her lover. She was so touching. I *had* to cry. I just couldn't stop myself. Are my eyes red? I've never seen anything like it before in my life. Oh! Look over there. Isn't that Spring Byington? *It is!* Oh, I just love her." Elizabeth stopped for breath, and Jane took the opportunity to kindly point out several other famous faces in the crowded room, including Greer Garson, Gary Cooper, Walter Slezak, and Joan Crawford.

"But they're not with Global," exclaimed Elizabeth. "Why are they here? I thought this was a party for the Global people to celebrate Miss Stewart's opening."

"When Terrance Malvey gives a party, everyone shows up," replied Jane. "He produced pictures for almost every company in town before coming to Global, and he has a lot of friends."

"Oh, look, there he is now," said Elizabeth, nodding her head toward a short, slim, young-looking man who was hurrying toward the door. "I wonder who he's going to greet?"

She got her answer very quickly as Terrance reappeared, graciously leading Louella Parsons, talking and laughing with her. Miss Parsons didn't look very happy even though she was smiling.

Elizabeth sat mesmerized, staring at the powerful columnist. "Imagine, Louella Parsons," she said, almost to herself.

Miss Parsons looked idly in the girls' direction and nodded absently at them.

"She sees us," said Elizabeth excitedly. The two girls smiled brightly as Miss Parsons passed by them. They followed her with their eyes until a commotion at the front door drew their attention.

With as much noise and fanfare as possible, Greta Stewart swept into the room surrounded by her agent, publicity man, and a few assorted friends. She was a striking woman, closer to forty than thirty, with blond hair and very sharp eyes that never stopped taking in the room.

Everyone stood and applauded while Greta bowed and smiled and blew kisses. Two of her companions lifted off her full-length, ermine cape, revealing Greta's gold lamé evening gown. A long string of orchids cascaded down over one breast, and diamonds glittered blindingly at her throat, wrists, and ears. A man leaned forward and whispered something in her ear, and Greta laughed affectedly as she stretched out one heavily gloved hand toward her host. "Terry, darling," she drawled. "How nice of you to have this little party."

Mr. Malvey was within his rights to be insulted by Greta's description of his full house as a little party, but he knew Greta very well, and as he took her hand and bowed slightly, he smilingly answered, "I decided to only invite the people who could stand you, dear."

Greta, who never listened to anyone else speak if she could possibly help it, smiled at him and leaned forward. "Now, tell me the truth, Terry. Did you like our picture? Did I give you the performance you wanted? Was I a good girl?"

Considering that Greta had driven everyone else on the set to distraction, brought the script girl to tears on four separate occasions, thrown a large vase at her hairdresser, and held up production for three weeks due to an unsuitable romantic entanglement with one of the grips, Terrance couldn't possibly have thought of her as a "good girl." But she had given the kind of morose performance that her fans loved, and so he was lavish in his praise.

Miss Stewart, who usually chose to listen to compliments for her beauty, talent, taste, and acting ability, leaned forward and paid close attention as the producer recited the usual meaningless superlatives Greta required and expected. In fact, so absorbed was Greta in hearing her praises sung, she was a little disturbed when Murry Edson, president of Global Films, came up and interrupted with his congratulations.

"You were wonderful, Greta girl," said Mr. Edson, a short, heavy, balding man who looked as if Global had sent him from central casting to act as a studio head. Waving his cigar around, he continued, "Yes, Greta girl, really great. Gonna make a lot of money with this film. Just you wait and see." He also knew what Greta wanted to hear. "Maybe even get you an Academy Award. What do you think about that, Terry?" he asked, turning to the producer.

"It's impossible to know what the academy will do next," said Malvey.

Greta didn't understand Terry's comment, but Murry looked at him suspiciously and plunged forward into the subject of Greta's next picture. "Now, Greta, we must get you back into harness as soon as possible. After all, if this picture's a hit you'll want to capitalize on it by announcing a new role immediately."

"Oh, but Murry, *darling,*" intoned Greta, throwing her arms wide and flinging back her head. "I'm absolutely *exhausted. Drained!* I simply must have a rest. I must go somewhere and find my true self again. I put so much into this role that now I'm lost, simply lost. Completely . . ." Her voice trailed off as she noticed a particularly handsome waiter nearby. Greta was always more at home in the locker room than the living room, and her taste in men generally ran to construction workers, football players, or beach boys, with an occasional horse jockey thrown in for variety.

Murry followed her gaze. "Would you like a drink, Greta?"

"Oh, yes. I'm perishing."

Murry pointedly selected a different waiter and, after giving the head of the studio a dirty look, Greta ordered a double whiskey, no water, no ice. Murry and Terry escorted Greta to a centrally located chair where she could receive congratulations and dispense graciousness. In a few moments she was surrounded by co-workers and admirers.

"Isn't she beautiful?" whispered Elizabeth, whose eyes had never left Greta since her entrance. "She is absolutely the loveliest thing I've ever seen in my life. Imagine."

"She looks very nice," said Jane flatly. "Why don't we go outside? It's getting very stuffy in here."

Elizabeth looked wistfully around the room, then reluctantly followed Jane onto the patio around the swimming pool. It was a beautiful early spring night. A gentle breeze moved through the palm trees, and the tiny lights sparkled across the well-tended landscape. The two women walked about the pool for a few moments, greeting other guests and chatting with friends. When they were alone again, Elizabeth sighed. "Isn't this amazing," she said. "It's always so warm here. I can't believe it's January. Back in Toledo we have snow everywhere now."

"It's too hard to judge the seasons out here. In New York things change. Here it stays the same."

"Perpetual spring," said Elizabeth with wonder. "What a wonderful idea. Imagine!"

Jane couldn't think of any reply and suggested that they sit down on one of the iron benches that lined the pool. Elizabeth continued her artless chatter as she seated herself and kept exclaiming over the yard, the house, the guests; she was totally absorbed by her surroundings. Jane sat quietly, rarely answering, thinking her own thoughts.

"But, of course, this is all old hat to you, isn't it?" asked Elizabeth. "After all, you've been here longer than I have."

Jane nodded absently, her attention directed toward the French doors which led into the drawing room. Elizabeth looked in the same direction and saw Terrance Malvey standing alone in the doorway, smoking a cigarette. "Oh, it's Mr. Malvey," said Elizabeth. "He's very handsome, isn't he? Well, maybe not handsome . . . but distinguished and all."

Terrance turned in the girls' direction and stared at Jane. She returned his gaze but didn't move.

"He's looking at you, Jane," whispered Elizabeth. "Oh. He's coming over here." She quickly adjusted her skirt and nervously patted her long, dark hair.

"This is a very nice picture," said Terrance as he joined Jane and Elizabeth. "Did this just happen, or did you plan it?"

Elizabeth giggled and looked embarrassed.

Jane smiled at Terrance. "We just thought it would be nice to get some fresh air." Her voice was soft and whispery, but her eyes held a challenge to the producer.

"It is getting a little close in the house. These things are always too crowded." He kept his eyes on Jane.

"Your house is absolutely beautiful," exclaimed Elizabeth.

Terrance finally turned and looked at Jane's companion. She was a pretty girl with rosy cheeks, bright brown eyes, and perfect teeth. She had a voluptuous, healthy figure clad in an unsuitable dress of blue satin with lots of ruffles and flounces. She appeared to be on her way to a beauty pageant in Toledo rather than a chic Hollywood party.

Terry turned back to Jane. The comparison between the girls

was striking, and he gave Jane full, if uncalculated, credit for having picked Elizabeth as a companion. Elizabeth made a perfect foil for Jane's beauty. Jane had almost white blond hair, beautiful skin, a perfectly made-up face, and was wearing a low-cut simple dress of white crepe with a long, black silk scarf draped around her throat. Her eyes were gigantic and blue, and her voice was breathy and quiet.

"I haven't seen you for a while," said Terrance, speaking to Jane.

"I've been around. But you've probably been too busy with *A Long Road* to notice."

"I don't think I've ever been *that* busy," said Terrance.

"I *do* think your garden is wonderful," gushed Elizabeth. "And the swimming pool looks so clean and fresh."

"Perhaps you'd like to go for a swim," suggested Terrance.

"Oh, no." Elizabeth was confused and embarrassed. "I didn't mean that. Not with all these people here."

"Then you must come over sometime when it's less crowded."

"Th-thank you," said Elizabeth quietly.

Murry Edson came to the doors and called to Terrance.

"I guess I'd better go back in," said the producer. "Will I see you later?" he asked Jane.

"Perhaps."

He looked at her once more and then left.

"Oh, Jane. I do think he likes you," gushed Elizabeth. "Imagine."

Jane shrugged. "Don't get all excited for me. Terrance Malvey would have said the same things to anyone who happened to catch his eye. It doesn't mean a thing."

Elizabeth only half understood. "I think I'll go back in and see if any more stars have arrived," she said. "Do you want to come in?"

"Not right now. I'll join you in a few minutes."

"All right."

Jane watched Elizabeth hurry back inside the house, then reached into her bag and took out a small mirror. She checked her makeup and returned the mirror to her purse. A loud laugh from the house indicated that Greta Stewart was still holding court. Jane's face tightened. She disliked Greta more than she disliked any of the other female stars who had achieved fame and success in Hollywood. Jane was honest enough with herself to realize that her dislike was partially rooted in jealousy. But Greta incited a special hatred in Jane. The woman's vulgarity and rudeness simply fueled Jane's disgust toward her. Besides, thought Jane, Greta wasn't giving the motion picture public anything she, personally, couldn't do better. But so far, Jane hadn't been able to convince any of the executives at Global of that idea.

Jane's hands tightened around her bag as she thought about her lack of success in the film capital. She had originally arrived in Hollywood in the summer of 1936. An ambitious, young girl, sure of herself and of her future. Things hadn't worked out as she'd planned, even though she'd done all the right things and met all the right people. A slight, sad smile crossed Jane's mouth. She'd even married to help her career.

Everyone had said that Kurt Von Grau was very important— destined to be a major power in the movie business. Hollywood was very excited about the arrival of the famous Austrian director.

He had been smitten by the lovely young Jane Turner, and she had been sure that marriage to Kurt would secure her a position in films.

Jane hadn't thought much about the man himself, then. He wasn't repulsive looking, although he was considerably older than she, and it was obvious that he admired her beauty. But Kurt hadn't been as easy as Jane thought he would be. And instead of Jane using him, he had used her.

She had been a Global Gal, one of a group of girls who traveled around Europe and America promoting the studio. Kurt had gone along, using Jane's tours as a means of gathering information to send to the German government.

And at night . . . Jane shuddered as she remembered the nights she had spent with Kurt. His horrible and sadistic needs had first surprised, then terrified her.

Kurt was dead now. Jane had never said a word to anyone about the night Kurt died. Never told how her mother, discovering Kurt's sexual practices and his real goals in the United States, had struck out at him with a fire poker, killing him. There had never been a scandal or even much of an investigation. It had been an accident. A terrible accident. And the only way Jane would ever have been free of Kurt.

She had stayed at home for a while, but then returned to California to find herself starting all over again.

That had been almost two years ago. Since being back, she had done publicity events, some glamour girl photographs, and been an extra in a few movies. But nothing had clicked.

She was only twenty-two years old, a young woman with her whole life ahead of her. But she felt old. And she was convinced that if something didn't happen for her soon, she wouldn't have a chance at the career she wanted. Jane knew how quickly the Hollywood community devoured the young, soaking up their innocence and then tossing them aside. And each day a fresh shipment of newcomers arrived, eager and confident of success. Ready to be or do anything to get ahead.

Elizabeth was one of those, thought Jane. Only nineteen, Elizabeth had been in Hollywood two months. She was a contract player for Global and was supposed to have a nice singing voice. Jane wondered how long it would take the young girl to wise up.

Jane stood up. Maybe it's time I wised up myself, she thought.

She looked about her at the lush estate. Elizabeth had been so impressed with all the trappings of wealth. But they didn't mean much to Jane. Her family was comfortable and often sent her extra cash so she could live easily. It wasn't the money or the houses or the cars that attracted Jane to the movies. She realized that she wasn't sure what it was that made her keep trying to reach the top. But Jane knew she couldn't quit. She couldn't stop until she had achieved her dream.

Another burst of noise drew Jane's attention back to the party, and she walked toward the house. Inside, the rooms were still full of guests, although the big names from the other studios had mostly gone, leaving the Global people in full control of the party. Greta Stewart was still very much the center of attention, talking and laughing while keeping a sharp eye on the waiter she had picked out earlier.

Jane went into the drawing room and, as she passed Greta, the famous actress lurched out of her chair, attempting to stand. It was obvious Greta had had a lot to drink.

"Careful, Greta," laughed one of her companions.

"Careful, yourself. I'm fine. Perfectly fine . . . but I need another drink." She turned abruptly and bumped into Jane.

Jane fell back, maintaining her balance, but Greta slipped sideways and fell flat on the floor.

At first Jane was mortified. But then, looking down and seeing the star floundering around on the floor, her face covered by her orchid corsage, Jane started to giggle. She quickly took a deep breath and controlled her laughter. Bending over, she reached out to help the actress off the floor.

"Are you hurt, Miss Stewart?" asked Jane.

"Get your hands off me," snarled Greta. "You tripped me."

"But Miss Stewart . . ." began Jane, "you . . ."

Greta pulled away from Jane and allowed one of her companions to give her his arm. When she was finally on her feet, she looked down at herself. Her dress was rumpled and the flowers that had not been pushed up into her face were completely crushed. She looked more like a Mack Sennet heroine than a great tragic actress. Again, Jane had difficulty controlling her amusement.

Greta was not so drunk that she missed Jane's inclination to laugh, and this made her even more furious. "It's nice," snarled Greta, "to see that it amuses you to try and hurt a professional actress. I know you contract players are consumed with jealousy, but it seems to me that you could at least try to look where you're going. After all, you don't really have anything else to think about, do you? I mean, like roles or pictures or anything important. Well, let me tell you," she continued, her voice rising, "that you nobodies are just so much dead weight around Hollywood. I can't imagine where the studios find you in the first place."

Jane stood silent as Greta continued her attack, the star's voice growing more and more shrill and her language coarser as anger along with the drinks she had had rapidly overcame her. A thin stream of saliva slipped out of one corner of Greta's mouth as she lost what little control she had over her emotions.

Finally, Jane felt she had had enough. She had stood passive throughout Greta's abuse, but now she looked the woman straight in the eye and smiled slightly. "You're spitting on yourself, Miss Stewart," said Jane in her whispery voice.

Greta gasped. Then her breath came rapidly as, with a growl of rage, she reached out to slap Jane. But Terrance Malvey was too quick for her. He stepped between the two women and grasped Greta's outstretched arm.

"Now, now, Greta," he said gently, "you don't want to do that."

"The fuck I don't. Get out of my way. I'm going to kill this little bitch."

"Language, language," said Terry, placatingly. "Try to remember who you are, Greta. And if that doesn't do any good, you might try remembering who *I* am."

Greta turned her anger on Terrance. "You're nobody without me. None of you are. I carried that stinking picture of yours all by myself. How dare you interfere with me? You . . . nothing! Producer! Hell, you can't even produce an acceptable guest list for a fucking party."

"My, you do have a way with words," said Terrance.

Greta continued her assault on Terrance, and he turned slightly toward Jane and suggested that she leave while Greta was busy with him.

Jane nodded and, after gathering up her wrap, headed for the front door. She passed Murry Edson, who looked idly in her direction as he headed toward Greta's scene.

Outside, Jane stood confused for a few moments. She had come alone to the party in a taxi, sure she would meet some friends who would give her a lift home. But everyone was still inside. It was possible that after the confrontation no one would want to be seen with her. Greta's influence was too great for any of Jane's friends to run any risks. Well, the hell with them all, thought Jane. She hadn't been really angry listening to Greta's insults. She had been fascinated by the star's inarticulate vulgarity. But now she was mad, and her thoughts were filled with the things she would like to say to Greta Stewart.

Presently, Elizabeth came rushing out of the house. Two young men were with her.

"Jane, Jane, are you all right?" asked Elizabeth anxiously. "What a terrible thing to have happen. I just can't imagine what came over poor Miss Stewart. That language! Imagine! She must be ill. I'm sure that's what it must be. Perhaps she has some terrible disease that nobody knows about. The poor, poor woman."

"That was quite a scene," muttered one of the young men.

"Jane, do you know Ralph and Taylor?"

"Yes, of course. But are you all sure you should be seen with me right now?"

Taylor, the younger of the two men, had blond hair and was boyishly handsome. He looked nervously over his shoulder, but Ralph kept his eyes on Jane, his dark face betraying no emotion. He would have been the better looking of the two, thought Jane, except that his handsome features seemed devoid of any animation.

"I mean," continued Jane, "if I had leading man ambitions, I don't think I'd want to be seen with someone who'd just insulted Greta Stewart."

"Then let's get out of here," said Ralph.

Elizabeth turned to Ralph, delighted with his masterful statement. "Oh, yes," she said, "let's go now."

"How?" asked Jane simply.

"I have a car," said Taylor.

"All right," said Jane. "Which way?"

Ralph and Jane sat in the back seat of Taylor's battered 1931 Ford. Ralph leaned forward to Taylor and suggested that they all go to Pete's.

"Do you think we should?" Elizabeth asked Jane. "I mean it is late and . . ."

"If you don't want to go," answered Jane, "we don't have to."

"Oh, I want to go," said Elizabeth, "but . . ."

"Enough said," replied Ralph. "On to Pete's."

Taylor turned the car on Encino and headed down Sunset Strip. Pete's was popular with the young contract players and many of the local musicians. He served cheap liquor and cheap food. The place wasn't very clean, but you could usually find a small card game in the back room, and Pete would place a bet on a horse for you. There was a booth with a private telephone Pete would let his customers use occasionally, and he would even extend a small amount of credit if he knew you. A lot of musicians used Pete's to meet other musicians and find out about possible jobs or just talk about music. Late at night, after work at the fancy nightclubs, they liked to bring their instruments and play their own music.

Jane and her friends didn't feel out of place in Pete's in their evening clothes, as most of the patrons had been somewhere else and quite a few of them were dressed up. When the group walked in, they recognized several of the other customers.

"You girls want a drink?" asked Ralph.

"Oh, dear," said Elizabeth. "I had a glass of champagne at Mr. Malvey's." She leaned forward and confided, "I'd never had champagne before. But I just sipped it."

"Well, I don't think this is the place for champagne," said Taylor dubiously.

"Oh, I didn't mean that I wanted more," said Elizabeth in some confusion.

"Why don't you have a whiskey?" suggested Ralph. "It'll keep the cold out."

"Cold?" asked Elizabeth. "I'm not cold. I'm from Ohio, and there the winters get really bitter."

"It's just a saying," said Jane.

"Oh."

"And what about you?" Ralph asked Jane.

"Nothing thanks," she answered. "I'm fine."

"Yeah, I'd say so," smirked Ralph.

"Stop talking like a movie script," said Jane. "I'll just have a ginger ale. I don't like the taste of liquor very much."

"Maybe that's what I should have, too," piped Elizabeth. "After all, I did have that champagne."

Ralph turned to Elizabeth. He was sure he was striking out with Jane. "No ginger ale for you, baby. I think you'd like something sweet and smooth."

"Oh, I don't know," said Elizabeth, confused.

"Sure," urged Ralph. "I think . . . a Brandy Alexander."

Taylor looked surprised. "Do you think Pete can make one?"

Ralph shrugged. "He can get close." He called the owner over and ordered whiskey for himself and Taylor, a ginger ale for Jane, and a Brandy Alexander for Elizabeth. Pete looked a little surprised by the last order, but he didn't object. He simply grunted and walked away.

A group of musicians gathered on the little bandstand and started to play loudly, each taking a solo turn with the melody. Jane and her group sat and listened, Elizabeth particularly delighted by the talented performance. She moved slightly with the rhythm and watched the players closely.

When the music was finished, the small audience applauded

and Pete arrived with the drinks. Elizabeth tasted hers and exclaimed over how smooth and good it was. Then the band began again. Elizabeth took another sip of her drink and looked eagerly toward the musicians.

"Oh, I know that song," she gushed.

"Maybe you ought to join them," suggested Ralph with a slight smile.

"Do you think they'd mind?" asked Elizabeth. "I mean, I wouldn't want to intrude, but they are awfully good." Elizabeth took another sip of her drink.

"Sure, go ahead," urged Ralph. "They're just fooling around."

Elizabeth smiled brightly, got up a little unsteadily from her chair, and walked over to the bandstand.

Jane watched her go and then turned to Ralph. "Did you do that to be funny?"

Ralph shrugged. "It might be time she grew up."

"The same might be said about you," breathed Jane.

Elizabeth stood next to the piano player and watched the band for a few minutes. Soon the pianist saw her, nodded at her, and moved slightly on the bench to make room for her. Shyly Elizabeth joined the musician and, as the soft strains of "Night and Day" filled the little club, she quietly hummed the melody. After listening for a few bars, the piano player smiled and said, "You take it."

Elizabeth nodded, and began singing softly. As the song continued, she gained confidence and soon stood and moved gracefully to the center of the band. When they had finished the chorus, the piano player signaled for another and Elizabeth turned toward the audience and sang.

Her voice was pure and smooth, ringing clear on every note with a slight throbbing quality that brought listeners to the edge of their chairs. When the song finished and the last note died away, there was complete silence in the room. Then the instrumentalists tapped their feet on the floor in approval. Elizabeth looked at each band member, smiling her thanks, and returned to her table as they started another number.

"That was wonderful," said Taylor as Elizabeth sat down. "Absolutely wonderful."

"Thank you." She seemed totally unaware of her companion's amazement.

"I didn't know you could sing like that," said Jane. "It was really beautiful."

Again Elizabeth just said thank you as if her performance was the most normal thing in the world. She suddenly seemed older and wiser. It was obvious that when it came to her music, Elizabeth was not the innocent and unsophisticated child she was about her new experience in Hollywood.

Elizabeth looked around at her three friends who were still staring at her. She smiled. "Well, after all, it *is* what Global hired me for," she explained.

"Imagine," breathed Jane.

CHAPTER *Two*

THE NEXT MORNING, Jane was awakened by the sound of the telephone ringing next to her bed. Untwisting herself from the sheets, she reached out to answer.

"Hello?" she muttered.

"Jane? Is that you, Jane? Is it true?"

Still foggy from sleep, Jane looked at the phone, puzzled. "Who is this?"

"Jane, wake up, damn you. This is Mable, Mable Cramer. Is it true that you ripped Greta Stewart's dress right off her back and then threw her to the floor and kicked her last night?"

"Wh—what?"

"It's all over town about how you grabbed hold of the old bitch's dress, which I hear was really tacky, and stripped it right off her. And then you threw her to the ground and—"

"Mable," interrupted Jane, now fully awake, "this is ridiculous. None of it's true. Where did you hear this story?"

"*Honey*, it's all over town. I heard it late last night and called you immediately, but there wasn't any answer. And then Gary came over and stayed and stayed . . ." Mable's voice was suddenly muted as if she'd turned away from the phone. "Stop that right now, do you hear me? I'm on the telephone." Jane thought that Gary must still be there. "And so," continued

Mable, "I'm not giving up until I hear all about it . . . blow
by blow. The whole story."

"There's nothing to tell. It was nothing at all."

"Nothing! That's not what I hear. Why—"

"Let me call you back, Mable."

"Promise? I have to be at Warner's at noon. But I'll be here
until then, and I'm dying to hear all the dirt."

"I promise. Good-bye."

Jane hung up and reached for a cigarette and a match from
the bedside table. Lighting up, she picked up an ashtray and
settled back against the pillows. Damn, she thought, now
what? Obviously some inspired press agent or rumor monger
had seen the incident at Malvey's and decided to make some
points out of it. Jane stubbed out her cigarette and got out of
bed. She was naked, and even first thing in the morning her
incredible face and lovely body were stunning. She crossed the
room and gathered up a lightweight robe, which she pulled on
as she went into the kitchen.

Jane made coffee and went out and collected her mail,
carrying her cup with her. Returning to the kitchen, she looked
through the small collection of mail, tossed it on the table and
walked out onto a small back porch and stood for a minute. She
went back inside and sat down at the kitchen table.

But she couldn't stay still. She got up again and moved
aimlessly through the rooms of her apartment. It was a small
place, selected more for its convenient location near Global
Studios than its charm or attractiveness.

With a living room, bedroom, bath, large kitchen, and small
back porch, it was considerably better than what most of the
young players in town had. But with help from home, Jane was
able to live comfortably, if not ostentatiously. The apartment
furniture was an eclectic collection chosen quickly when
necessity had demanded, and the cleaning was handled by an
elderly woman named Mrs. Evans, who was very kind,
motherly, and amazingly inept except at dusting, which she did
relentlessly, to the detriment of the dishes which piled up in the
sink and the bed which was usually left unmade. Jane rarely
noticed her surroundings, concentrating any domestic impulses
she possessed on clothes. She spent lavishly, with a total
disregard for her budget, but with an unerring eye for garments
that would accentuate and flatter her beautiful figure.

Returning to the porch, Jane stared out at the blazing California morning. The sun swept over the low buildings and glinted through the palm trees, drenching the whole scene in bright, glaring light. There were moments when Jane was sure that she hated everything about Hollywood. But she also knew that she would stay there and keep working as long as she could.

She was hopeful that the whole thing about Greta would blow over quickly, but she needed to see how things stood. She could call the studio, but that might look as if she were overly concerned about the situation. She went to the bedroom telephone and called her agent, Constance Steiner. Constance had signed Jane right after the young actress had married Kurt Von Grau, and despite the fact that Constance had made very little money out of Jane, or gotten Jane any good parts, the two were still legally linked.

"Constance? This is Jane Turner."

"Oh, yes," replied Constance, as if she had more important things on her mind. "I understand you had a busy night."

"Not nearly as busy as the gossips would have people believe," Jane replied, telling Constance the simple facts about the night before.

When Jane had finished, Constance sighed, then said, "When are you young kids going to realize that when it comes to stars there is no such thing as a small scene. Jesus! I don't know why I keep you contract players on my list." Actually Constance knew very well that she, like many of the other agents, had a few young players who showed promise and kept them on in the hope of being in on the ground floor if they made a hit. It didn't cost the agent anything and, besides the outside chance that one of their young actors might make it big, having them on the roster was good public relations. Constance conveniently forgot all this when she was angry, and now she sighed again before continuing. "You can't win when you get into a confrontation with an established star. Why couldn't you have just kept your mouth shut?"

"And let her insult me over and over again?"

"Forever if she wanted to. For Christ's sake, she's a *star!*" Constance said the word as if she were announcing the second coming.

"I see," said Jane, quietly. "But what do I do now?"

"Well, my advice is to just lay low. Go on with whatever you have scheduled, and if anyone asks you about it, just appear stupid." Constance privately thought this wouldn't be a difficult task for anyone dumb enough to get involved in such a situation in the first place. "Don't make any waves at the studio. Do what you're told."

"All right," answered Jane.

"And don't give any interviews," Constance went on. "If you're lucky, this whole thing will die quickly. Don't think you can expand it into some kind of publicity thing for yourself. You can't do it. Did you see the reviews of Greta's picture?"

"No."

"Well, they couldn't have been worse if Greta had been Judas Iscariot. So all the sympathy's going to be on her side right now. If she chooses to stay around and milk it a little, it might help her film. If she goes away, you can count yourself very lucky."

"She looked like she was very interested in a waiter at the party last night."

"Well, if she got laid that might help. Greta could be in a benevolent mood and be gracious. But the best thing that could happen is if she and that waiter really hooked up and she takes him away for a few weeks with her."

"I see," said Jane.

"Just keep your mouth shut. Talk to you later." Constance hung up and Jane sat looking at the dead phone for a few seconds before replacing the listening arm.

Jane got up and went about selecting her outfit for the day. She dressed with her usual care, and skillfully applied her makeup. Her car, a small, 1936 Ford, was parked at the curb in front of her apartment house, and soon she was driving the short distance to the studio.

As she went through the large gates and headed toward the open parking lot, she got the same thrill she had experienced her first day at work. She loved coming to the studio, the nod of the gatemen who recognized her, and the sight of all the activity and confusion which made up the daily life of the movie business at Global. Jane drove past the private parking area where the studio heads and leading players had their special spaces. As always, she looked at the carefully marked section longingly. She wanted her own parking space just like

Murry Edson and Greta Stewart and Ken Holt, the western star, and Vivian Redson, an aging character actress who had recently won an Oscar. But for now, she had to keep driving around the open lot until she found a place to put her car.

As Jane walked across the lot, she passed friends and acquaintances, all of whom appeared to have heard about the events of the previous night. A few called her slugger, and one of the grips called out, "Hello, champ," to her, while others merely nodded knowingly. Jane smiled at everyone, never uttering more than a polite hello, and hurried into a large building where the contract players were sent for acting, dancing, and voice classes. Today she was to have a voice lesson.

Because of Jane's whispery vocal production, the Global coaches had decreed that she would spend a great deal of time learning how to project her voice and make it heard. So Jane had started voice classes her first few weeks with Global, and as soon as she had returned to California from New York, the schedule had been continued. Jane's friends had not noticed any particular increase in volume when Jane spoke, but she still went faithfully to each class. She breathed, spoke, recited the alphabet and the vowels, and read a short scene from an old Global movie. The teacher, an aging, taciturn, old gentleman brought out from New York at great expense, considered Jane and all the rest of the contract players a waste of time, and simply went through the motions, collecting his substantial paycheck at the end of each week.

After class, Jane reported to the management office to find out if she had any assignments. The office staff stared openly at Jane as she walked in, and one of the girls giggled. Opal Walters, the woman in charge of all contract girls, came out of her office when she heard Jane had arrived.

"Well," said Opal, "I understand you had quite an evening."

"That's what I hear, too," said Jane. "Although to be honest, it didn't seem all that exciting at the time."

"These things have a habit of growing sometimes," said Opal mildly. She had been in Hollywood too long to get upset about anything.

"Have you heard anything from the front office?"

"Not much. Mr. Hawkins, head of publicity, would have

liked to do something with it, but since Greta's away for a few days, he can't seem to get anywhere." Opal noticed Jane's interest in Greta's departure. "Miss Stewart says she needs a rest," finished Opal.

"What did Mr. Hawkins say about me?"

"Nothing much. Just the usual stuff. I don't think he knows who you are."

"That figures," said Jane.

"Well, all I know is that no one has said anything about your not doing the things that have been arranged for you to do. So as far as I'm concerned, you should get to work. They need some girls to show around some visiting dignitaries this afternoon, and tomorrow you have a photography session with David Granoff at his studio."

"Who?" asked Jane.

"David Granoff. He's a new photographer out from the east. Global just took him on."

"And they're trying him out on me, is that it?"

"You got it. If I were you I'd just keep on doing whatever is on the schedule. This other thing will blow over soon . . . if Greta doesn't come back too quickly. And from what I hear, she's not likely to."

"The waiter?" asked Jane innocently.

"I don't know *what* you're talking about," said Opal.

After lunch, Jane went to Studio B where she found several other young starlets waiting together. Elizabeth was one of them.

"Jane," said Elizabeth quickly, "are you all right?"

"Yes, of course. Why?"

"Well, everywhere I've gone today, I've been hearing about what happened last night. But somehow I think I must have missed something. It all sounds so different to me."

"The story changes depending on who's telling it," said Jane. "You were there. You saw exactly what happened."

"I thought so," said Elizabeth. "And except for Miss Stewart's language, I didn't think she was hurt."

"She wasn't. And I hope everyone will forget it soon."

Elizabeth patted Jane's arm as Mr. Olsen from publicity arrived, along with three heavyset men in Panama hats and crumpled suits. Mr. Olsen first introduced himself and then each of the men carefully. They were congressmen from southern states and were visiting Global to see just how movies were made. Mr. Olsen was sure that the girls would be happy to show the gentlemen around and explain everything to them.

The visitor assigned to Jane and Elizabeth looked them over carefully and let his tongue slide over his lower lip as he greeted them. Jane led the way, and the threesome took off to explore the world of movie-making, despite the fact that neither Jane nor Elizabeth knew very much about the technical side of the business.

Jane led them around at a brisk pace, not liking the idea of walking too slowly near the congressman's all too friendly hands. Elizabeth was probably more excited about the tour than the guest was; even though she'd been there for several weeks, she was still starry-eyed about her surroundings. And Jane had to admit to herself that her love of the studio made walking about it a lot easier. All of the structures at Global were of the same pink stucco and, while the studio grounds covered over twenty acres of land, the major buildings were concentrated in a central area along with the offices and leading players' bungalows.

They walked past the executive building, and Jane pointed out the windows of Murry Edson's and Terrance Malvey's offices and the publicity and financial departments, along with the assorted vice-presidents and other officials who ran the company. They crossed the narrow street and passed through the workrooms for the costume designers, set designers, makeup artists, hairdressers, and the rest of the company's creative force.

The visitor wasn't interested in the executive offices, having already been in them to have his official welcome. And the artistic area seemed to make him feel that his manhood was in imminent danger, but he perked up as they neared the private dressing rooms of Global's leading stars and major directors. Even though each bungalow had a name on the door, Jane mentioned the occupant as they passed the row of beautifully decorated dressing rooms. There was a small garden in front of each, and all the windows were heavily curtained. The congressman was very interested in the bungalows of Ken Holt, Vivian Redson, Greta Stewart—Elizabeth laughed nervously when Jane mentioned her name—Wanda Carver,

Global's second-string leading lady and her usual costar, Wayne Marshall, often called the poor man's Scott Mack, who was Global's leading man and one of the most popular matinee idols in the movie business. Baby Susie Tucker's cottage was made up to look like something out of a fairy tale, which was appropriate, as Grimm was the best description Jane could think of to describe the child's vicious temper and her alcoholic mother.

From the star area, Jane took them to a sound stage where Baby Susie was doing her stuff. The scene was not going well, and it was obvious to Jane that the little angel was building up to one of her celebrated temper tantrums, so she hastily took Elizabeth and the congressman to the next sound stage.

Here, Wanda Carver was rehearsing a scene with Wayne Marshall. They went over it again and again, but the director didn't seem to be getting what he wanted. After a few moments, both Elizabeth and the guest were getting bored by the repetition and were anxious to leave. But Jane asked them to wait for a few moments. She was interested. The scene was not particularly well-written, and the actors were obviously having trouble with the lines. Jane watched carefully, ignoring Elizabeth's indications that they should move on.

They just can't do it right, Jane thought to herself. Damn it, I could do it better with my eyes closed and my hands tied behind my back. Finally, disgusted, Jane turned abruptly and they went outside, where the congressman, now bored with seeing the studio, suggested that they all get out of the hot sun and go have a drink together at his hotel. Jane quickly explained that she had an appointment in a few moments and that Elizabeth had to go with her. Elizabeth didn't understand what Jane was talking about at first, but before she could object, Jane laughed quickly and took them to Mr. Olsen's office. When the visitor announced that neither Jane nor Elizabeth was willing to join him for a drink, Mr. Olsen looked surprised and took Jane aside to reason with her, suggesting she might like to change her mind.

"No, I don't think so," replied Jane. "I have a lot to do this evening, and I have a photography session in the morning and I want to look my best."

"Yes, of course, but I know the studio would take it as a personal favor if you could manage to spend a little time with our guest. After all, he is an important person, and Global likes to make their visitors feel at home."

"This visitor has been trying to feel *me* since we met."

Olsen shrugged. "He obviously finds you attractive."

"Well, I don't find him attractive. Sorry, Mr. Olsen, you're going to have to find a different girl for your guest."

Olsen gave Jane a dirty look, but he knew when he was beaten and returned to the congressman as Jane and Elizabeth walked away together.

"Did Mr. Olsen want us to do what I think he wanted us to do?" asked Elizabeth.

Jane was surprised that Elizabeth had figured it out. "Yes," she answered, "he was hoping we'd find his sweaty friends perfect companions."

"But why?" asked Elizabeth.

"Good public relations," said Jane. "It happens all the time."

"Have you gone out with these men before?" asked Elizabeth hesitantly.

"Not these particular ones. But I have been on several studio-arranged dates."

"I see," said Elizabeth.

"Don't look so glum," said Jane. "It's all part of the business. I just didn't happen to like this one."

"It doesn't sound very nice," said Elizabeth.

"No one said movie-making was nice," replied Jane, heading for her car. "Do you need a lift?"

Jane dropped Elizabeth off at the small hotel in which she had taken a room and then drove home. It was late afternoon and the sun, glowing in the western sky, made all of Hollywood look subdued and romantic. At her apartment, Jane found that Mrs. Evans had done her usual job and that the sink was still filled with this morning's dishes. She was starting her bath water when the phone rang. At the other end of the wire, Mable Cramer was bellowing at her.

"I thought you were going to call me back," exclaimed Mable. "I waited as long as I could, then I had to go to Warner's. I *still* don't know the whole story. Are you going to be home for a while?"

"Yes."

"Good. I'll be right over. I can't wait to hear. I'll bring something to eat. What do you want?"

"Nothing fattening."

"I know what you mean. I'm on a diet, too. That son-of-a-bitch dresser over at Warner's said I was too heavy to fit into my costume. Shit! I know he just wanted it for himself. I'll be there in about thirty minutes with some celery."

Jane hung up and undressed, had her bath, and was wearing a pair of shorts and a halter when she heard the doorbell. She pulled her hair back and tied it with a ribbon and went to answer the door.

"Hi, honey," said Mable happily as she stormed through the door carrying two heavy bags. Jane had known Mable since her first days in California. She was a brash girl who spoke little about her life before coming to Hollywood. She had golden blond hair, brown eyes, and a large mouth. As she strode into the room, her firm buttocks and breasts strained against the tight one-piece playsuit she was wearing. Mable had been in movies since she was sixteen, usually cast as a showgirl, an extra, one of a group of the star's friends, or a gangster's short-term girlfriend. She had never had over two lines in a picture, and never seemed to care one way or the other about her career.

Mable had brought celery, and she had also brought a large selection of foods from a nearby Italian grocery store. She spread it out on Jane's kitchen table with anticipation.

"Mable!" exclaimed Jane. "We can't eat any of this. It's out of the question. Neither of us will be able to fit into any costume."

"Oh, the hell with it," said Mable. "You never gain any weight, and I never liked working for Warner's, anyway. Besides, I know from experience that it takes at least two days for the fat to show, so I can eat now and still get through tomorrow."

"What are you doing?"

"It's some gangster picture. *Not* with anyone whose name you'd recognize. Jesus what a bore. They've got Cagney, why the hell do they want to do the same thing with somebody else."

"Is it a good script?"

Mable looked at Jane with disdain. "Shit! I wouldn't know

if it was. I only have one line after my boyfriend is killed. I get to say, 'Oh, Tommy, no, no.'" Mable spoke the line in a monotone voice. "If you could smell Tommy's breath, you'd say, 'no, no,' too."

"Why don't you try and get a contract with one studio like I have instead of going around from studio to studio to get work?"

"Because I like my independence," said Mable. "This way I work when I want to and can stay in bed the rest of the time." Mable looked at Jane. "But all this isn't important. I want to know all about what you've been doing. What *did* happen last night?"

Jane took a deep breath and once again related the events of the night before.

When she finished, Mable stared at her and stuffed a large piece of salami into her mouth before speaking. "Is that all? Hell. I was sure you'd really let her have it. So what happens now?"

"Nothing, I hope," said Jane. Her voice became arch. "*Miss* Stewart has gone away to rest . . . with a waiter, I imagine."

"I personally am all for being served in bed," said Mable between bites.

"You know what bothers me the most?"

"Did *you* want the waiter?"

"No, of course not. What bothers me the most is that I've been on tenterhooks all day about what the studio was going to do or what Greta was going to make them do, and it makes me furious that both of them have that kind of power."

Mable shrugged. "Well, I know if I were in her shoes I'd probably be just as bad. After all, she does have her image to consider."

"Yes, I know. My agent already told me that Miss Stewart is a *star*. That bitch," muttered Jane.

"Which? Greta or your agent."

"Both, probably." Jane was silent for a few minutes and watched Mabel eat.

"Why don't you have some?" asked Mabel, looking up from the food and catching Jane's eye on her. "It's really very good. What else happened today?"

"Not much. Elizabeth Hudson and I had to escort some southern bigwigs around the studio."

"Who is Elizabeth Hudson?"

"A new contract player. She's from somewhere in the Middle West and sings."

"Hmmm," said Mable through her food.

"Seems nice enough, but not very bright," continued Jane.

Mable almost choked. Jane Turner was, in most people's opinion, the ultimate dumb blond. It was a little strange to hear her commenting on the intelligence of someone else. "How was the tour?" asked Mable, deciding against a discussion of brains.

Jane shuddered. "Horrible! The old guy tried to get his hands all over us and then invited us for drinks. God. He was just a politician."

"And you didn't go?" Mable was stunned.

"Of course not. Why would I want to go out with some old politician?"

"Because, honey," Mable answered sweetly, "they have lots of filthy money and usually take you to the best places. As long as a politician is in power, he's the king of the hill. They can do a lot for you."

"Oh hell," said Jane. "Olsen the publicity man tried to convince me to go, but I refused."

"Honestly, Jane, you need a keeper. First you have a run-in with Miss Bitch of Global, and then you turn down a chance to gain a few points with publicity and possibly help yourself in the bargain. You are the limit. And don't try and tell me you're saving yourself for Mr. Right. I *know* that isn't true. After all, I knew you when you married Kurt Von Grau." Mable's voice became sarcastic. "Or have you suddenly gotten religion and decided to reach the top on your own merits?"

"I never said I was holding out for either Mr. Right—or becoming a prude. I just didn't think it would do me any good to be seen with some shoddy politician."

"Honey, nothing's shoddier than the movie business. And it doesn't make any sense to try and play the game unless you follow the rules. Believe me, the ones who got there on their backs are just as rich as the ones who got there on their feet. And they're a lot more rested," she added thoughtfully. "*After* you win you can talk about ideals and talent and integrity and all that other stuff. But right now, your object is to get on top and stay there."

"I'll be more careful next time," said Jane. "But I still can't promise you I'll go out with every V.I.P. the studio aims in my direction."

"No one's asking you to. Just make sure you don't ignore the important ones."

"All right."

Mable stopped eating and looked about the kitchen. "Do you have a lease on this place?"

"No. I just took it when I got back. But I only have it month-to-month. Why?"

"It seems nice. I'm thinking of moving. I need more room and the apartment I'm in depresses me."

"Maybe we could find a larger place together. I don't like living alone," suggested Jane, "and if it's big enough, maybe Elizabeth could come and live with us, too."

"All right with me. She doesn't *act* like the Middle West, does she?"

"Well . . . sometimes. But I'm sure she'll change."

The next morning Jane went to the address she'd been given to meet photographer David Granoff. He admitted her himself and led her into a large studio full of lights, scene paper, and equipment.

"This is a very nice studio," said Jane.

Granoff had stopped to adjust a light. "What?" he asked.

"I said this was very nice . . . the studio, I mean."

"Oh, yeah. Global found it for me. Have you got a cold?"

Jane smiled. "A lot of people ask me that. I'm fine. I just don't speak very loudly."

David shrugged. "I guess I'll just have to listen closely." He was a nice looking man with brown hair and eyes, and an easy grin.

"What about wardrobe?" asked Jane.

"Oh, the studio sent over some things for you to wear. They're behind that screen," he added, pointing to one corner of the room. "There's a makeup table and stuff back there, too. You can do your own, I suppose."

"Naturally. It was one of the first things I learned when I

found out that contract players didn't always have people to take care of them."

David laughed, and Jane left him and went behind the screen. In a short while he called out to her to see if she was ready yet.

"Just a few more minutes," she answered.

Granoff made some last-minute adjustments to his lights, and then went to a chair and lit a cigarette. Shortly, Jane appeared wearing an evening gown of midnight blue satin. It was cut very low in the front and had long sleeves and a skirt which fit snugly over her hips. Jane had swept her hair up, pulling it tightly back from her face, which was carefully made-up. She looked radiantly beautiful.

She moved in front of the camera and stood quietly, waiting for directions.

Granoff blinked once when he saw Jane. When she had arrived in her shorts, with her hair casually pinned back, he'd thought she was attractive, had good bone structure, and would probably photograph well. But he hadn't been prepared for what was now facing him. He gave her a few simple instructions and went to the camera.

For the next four hours, Jane twisted, turned, smiled, and moved her body and face about for the relentless eye of his lens. She stared sexily at the small circle, luring it, drawing it toward her body with her eyes. David was delighted with her work.

And Jane was loving it. She loved the warm feel of the lights on her body and the complete and absolute attention of the photographer and the camera on her. There was music playing in the background, and Jane could feel the sounds washing over her, helping her move and direct her energy. Photography sessions were always Jane's favorite appointments, and she found that Granoff, with his short, easily understood directions, was a joy to work with, drawing out her sensuality and making her feel more and more attuned as he clicked the camera.

"You look great," he called out. "I have to change film." Jane stretched. "Thanks. Do we have much more to do?"

"Just one more roll and then you're finished. Would you like to do another session later this week?"

"Fine with me," said Jane. "Just let me know when. I have

my regular classes at the studio, and I have to show up at a supermarket opening this week. But other than that I'm not exactly overcome with demands."

Granoff laughed. "Well, you never know what those supermarket openings can lead to."

"Yeah, sore feet and a sunburn. You'd think they could put up a tent or something in those parking lots."

"Well, speaking of supermarkets, why don't we go have something to eat?"

"Sure. Just let me get out of all this. I'll be right with you. But what about that last roll of pictures?"

"I'll save it for later."

Jane laughed and disappeared behind the screen.

Seated in a small café on Santa Monica Boulevard, Jane and David were enjoying each other's company. Jane was wearing the shorts and shirt she had worn to David's, and Granoff had thrown an old alpaca jacket over his shirt and slacks. They had large plates of pasta and a bottle of wine before them. It was late for the lunch crowd, and the place was almost empty.

"How long have you been in Hollywood?" asked Jane.

"About a month. Global asked me to come out after they saw a spread of mine in *Women's World* magazine."

"*Women's World*?"

"Yeah, that's right."

"Did you meet Margaret Turner?"

"Sure did. She's quite a powerhouse."

"I know. She's my mother."

"Really?"

"Yes. I'm surprised that she was around when you were there. Since she's the foreign correspondent, she's usually traveling."

"She was on her way to England, as a matter of fact. I only met her for a few moments. There was another woman there . . . a Dawn, something. Is she any relation?"

"No."

"Good. Because Dawn is a real terror."

"I know. But mother says she does know her job."

"Yeah. But what a pain in the ass."

Jane laughed.

"But what about you?" continued David. "Why aren't you

a big star? You said you've been here quite awhile. You certainly have the looks. When is the studio going to give you the big star-building treatment?"

"I wish I knew," said Jane. "I'm afraid they're getting used to me as just a contract player. If this keeps up, I'm going to be a second-stringer forever."

"Sometimes studios can't see what's in front of them. They have to be pushed."

"Yes. But I haven't figured out how to give them a shove before they give me one. As you may not know, the life-span of a contract player is very short. If I don't get something soon, they may just decide they don't need me anymore." Jane's face tightened. "And I won't let that happen."

"Well, we'll just have to think of a way of getting them to notice you."

"We?"

"That's right. Oh, don't misunderstand. I'm not totally altruistic. I happen to think you've got something, and I want to be on the bandwagon when you're a success."

"Don't you mean *if*?"

"No. I mean *when*."

CHAPTER *Three*

ELIZABETH HUDSON WAS RUNNING DOWN THE STREET between the Global Studio buildings when she ran head on into Ralph Mason, who was walking in the other direction.

"Oh, I'm sorry," sputtered Elizabeth. "I'm so clumsy."

"Are you hurt?" asked Ralph.

"Oh, no. Not at all."

"What's the hurry?"

"I'm supposed to meet Jane and a friend of hers to look for an apartment. We're going to share one together. Isn't that exciting?"

"Yeah, I guess so," answered Ralph. "I haven't seen you around very much. How've you been?"

"Fine. I've been practicing and everything. Are you working today?"

"Just some extra stuff."

"Oh. Well at least it pays the bills," said Elizabeth, who was becoming increasingly reliant on platitudes and clichés.

"Yeah, sure. Look, I've got to go. I'll see you around."

"I hope so," said Elizabeth. She watched Ralph leave, and then continued to the front gate where she was to meet Jane and Mable. Her thoughts lingered on Ralph Mason. She had been intrigued by the arrogant and often rude man, and she hoped he

would find her again soon. She was so wrapped up in her
thoughts of Ralph that at first she didn't see Jane's little
convertible waiting outside the gate.

Jane honked at her, and Elizabeth ran to the car. "I'm
sorry," she exclaimed, "am I late? I just finished a dance
lesson and then I had to go by publicity and see about some
pictures, and then I ran into Ralph Mason . . ."

"Ralph Mason!" snorted Mable. "That's a bad one if I ever
saw one."

Elizabeth looked at Mable as Jane introduced the girls to
each other. "I thought he was very nice," said Elizabeth,
shaking hands with Mable.

Mable shrugged. "It's your funeral."

Elizabeth settled herself in the back seat and leaned her arms
on the front seat so she could continue talking to the other two.
"Where are we going?" she asked.

"I thought we might find something near Beverly Hills,"
said Jane.

"Beverly Hills," said Elizabeth. "Imagine! I never thought
I'd be living in Beverly Hills."

Mable turned and looked at Elizabeth as if she'd come from
another planet. "She said *near*, not *in*," she emphasized.

"Don't expect to find yourself in a big house with a pool and
tennis court and all," said Jane. "But if we combine our
resources, we ought to be able to find something big enough
for us. I think it'll be great having roommates."

"Oh, so do I," said Elizabeth enthusiastically. "Of course, I
shared a room with my sisters back in Toledo, but they were
much younger than me and were always in the way. But we did
have some good times. It'll be wonderful having people my
own age around me. We can sit up late at night and talk and
share clothes and everything. Imagine!"

Mable looked as if she'd rather die than be seen in
Elizabeth's little outfit, but before she started explaining just
how little time she expected to sit up late talking to Elizabeth,
Jane broke in. "I'm sure it'll all be fine," she said with a
warning look at Mable.

Within two weeks the three girls had selected a place on
Ventura Boulevard, moved their things in, and settled into their
new home. Jane liked having company around, Elizabeth was

delighted, and Mable, after having decided that Elizabeth was real, was resigned to the whole thing.

At their first dinner together in their new home, Mable put down her dessert spoon and called for everyone's attention. "I think we had better establish some ground rules," she said.

"Oh, you mean like what time we have to be in and picking up after ourselves in the bathroom?" asked Elizabeth.

Mable, who meant no such thing, gave Elizabeth a quelling look. "No," she said, "I doubt that Jane cares what time you come home, and I'm sure that I don't give a damn. I'm talking about important things like having guests here and—"

"Guests?" asked Elizabeth.

"I mean men," said Mable in measured tones.

"Men?" Elizabeth still didn't catch on.

"Yes," Mable continued. "Now, I don't happen to be seeing anyone at present, but that doesn't mean that I won't be. There's an absolutely adorable man in the production department over at Paramount who's been giving me the eye. I figure it'll take him another week to ask me out and then things'll pick up."

Elizabeth stared at Mable, confusion and embarrassment combined on her face. "I don't think I understand," she said finally.

"Oh, I'm sure you do," said Mable sweetly. "But if you'd really like me to spell it out, I'm talking about fucking."

"Oh."

"What about you, Jane?" asked Mable. "Are you seeing anyone now?"

"No. I haven't met anyone for a long time. But there is . . ."

"Yes?" prompted Mable.

"Really, nobody. It's just that David Granoff, the photographer, is very nice."

"Have you been dating?"

"Not really. We had dinner after the first session, and I've been at his studio since then and stayed and talked to him each time after we finished work. But it hasn't amounted to anything."

"Maybe he's gay," suggested Mable.

"I don't think so," answered Jane.

"Look, honey," said Mable. "If he's had you around his

studio for several sessions, changing clothes and twisting your body around in front of his camera, and he still hasn't made a move, he's either gay or has something wrong with him.''

Elizabeth only understood part of what Mable was saying. "Perhaps he respects Jane," she suggested.

Mable broke into a loud laugh. "Sure, honey," she said. "That *must* be it. Women get so much respect out here.''

"I don't know," said Jane. "He's very nice, and has done some wonderful pictures of me. I like him . . . but—"

"But nothing," said Mable flatly. "Mark my words. He likes boys.''

"Boys?" asked Elizabeth, stunned.

"Some guys do, honey.''

The conversation had already held so many shocks for Elizabeth that this latest one was more than she could handle. She quickly got up and volunteered to do the dishes. Picking up their plates, she hurried into the kitchen.

"Mable, you shouldn't be so hard on Elizabeth," said Jane. "She just doesn't understand everything.''

"Everything! She doesn't understand *anything*. Jesus! She's the dumbest kid I've ever seen. And believe me I've seen some dumb ones. She makes Pickford in all those silent movies of hers look like a cheap hooker. The girl has got to grow up, Jane.''

"Yes, I suppose so. But do you have to try and educate her all at once. You didn't have to bring up your affairs *and* gay men all at the same time.''

"*My* affairs? I'm not the one who married an old Austrian just to help my career. At least when I go to bed with a man, it's because I like him.''

"Well it seems to me that you like an awful lot of people.''

"I'm the friendly type. And you haven't always been Miss Pure yourself, you know.''

"We are not discussing me," said Jane. "Besides," she said, getting up and walking across the large living room, "this is a big apartment. We each have our own room, there are two bathrooms, we even have a patio outside the kitchen. You could have had a guest here overnight and Elizabeth might not even know about it.''

"Oh, sure. I can see it all now. Little Miss Goody Two-Shoes gets up in the morning to take a pee and finds a naked man in the bathroom. Then we would really have a scene. It's better for her to know what to expect."

"I have to admit that I wouldn't relish finding a naked stranger in the bathroom first thing in the morning. Do all of your men spend a lot of time in the bathroom?"

"No, they spend a lot of time in bed with me. But that's neither here nor there. Enough about me. I want to know more about this photographer. What did you say his name was?"

"Granoff. David Granoff. He's a wonderful photographer and a very nice man."

"And that tells me exactly nothing."

In the following week, the three girls got used to each other and living in their new surroundings. Neither Mable nor Elizabeth had a car, so when Jane wasn't going their way they had to find out the right buses and how to get around town. Elizabeth and Mable learned a little more about each other, which Elizabeth would have preferred to remain ignorant of. Mable continued making the rounds of all the studios, picking up extra jobs and bit parts, while Jane and Elizabeth attended their classes at Global, which were beginning to depress Jane but were still exciting to Elizabeth. Jane's most enjoyable time was spent with David Granoff. She went to his studio often, sometimes having pictures done and other times just visiting with the photographer. She and David got along well, and Jane didn't know when she'd been so comfortable with a man. She was enjoying the friendship, although she couldn't understand why he hadn't made a move toward her.

Jane had always enjoyed the attention of men. And she had had several affairs since living in Hollywood. But none of them had been important to her; the men had been too caught up in their own careers to give her the attention she demanded, or not strong enough to make her pay attention to them. She hoped David was different. She liked his manner and his slow, sexy smile. Soon, she thought, something was bound to happen between them.

"Hello, Ralph." Elizabeth was standing just off camera on the set where Ralph was working. He was an extra in a gangster movie and looked the part almost too well.

"Hi, Elizabeth."

"I hope I'm not interrupting."

"It's all right. We're on a break. What's going on?"

"I have to sing for Mr. Grandison and Sam Withers."

"Who?"

"Mr. Grandison. He produces all of Global's musicals, and Mr. Withers is a special voice coach."

"Maybe they'll do something for you."

"I hope so, but I'm very nervous."

"That's bull. Nothing to be afraid of. They're the ones who have to listen. You just have to stand there and sing."

Somehow his reasoning cheered Elizabeth, and she looked at him gratefully. "Are you going to be on this picture a long time?"

"No. Just today. Tomorrow I'm the fourteenth cowboy being chased by what's-his-name."

"You mean Ken Holt?"

"Yeah, he's a real prick."

Elizabeth stiffened.

Ralph laughed. "Don't get all upset, Elizabeth. Jesus, that name's long. Don't you have a nickname?"

"No. I've never been called anything except Elizabeth."

"I'll have to think of something." The callboy summoned the extras, and Ralph started to walk away. He turned back to Elizabeth. "I'll have to think of a name for you."

"All right. And I'll let you know what happens with my audition."

"Sure." Ralph walked away, and Elizabeth watched him for a few moments before starting to leave. As she left the set, she heard him calling her. She turned back.

"I've got it," he called out. "The name, I mean. I heard one once . . . Lilly. It's a lot easier than Elizabeth. I'll call you Lilly."

"All right." Elizabeth smiled happily.

"See you." Ralph went back to work.

Elizabeth left the stage, thinking to herself that she liked the name Lilly.

"Jesus, Jane. Where the hell is she? We can't wait all night. That guy from Paramount said he might be over at Mike's later. And I want to casually just drop in."

"I promised Elizabeth we wouldn't eat until she got home.

She had to sing for Grandison today, and she was very nervous. She'll either come home on cloud nine or down in the dumps. Either way, we've got to hold dinner for her."

"I hope she doesn't audition a lot if that's the case. I could starve to death while I'm waiting."

"I'm sure you'll be just fine," said Jane. "Besides, didn't you once tell me you could live on love?"

"Sure. But I can't live on it until I get it. And I won't get it if little Miss Goodness doesn't get her ass home so I can eat and get out and get it." Mable moved her body around provocatively and lifted the lid off one of the pots in which Jane was trying to cook dinner. "What *is* this stuff?" she asked after dipping a finger into the pot and tasting the food.

"That happens to be beef stew."

"Jesus. I hope you act better than you cook. This is terrible."

"Good. Then you won't be in a big hurry for it."

"Oh, I am always in a big hurry for it, except for the times when I like to take it slow and easy."

"Mable, honestly. You embarrass me."

"That doesn't surprise me. I've always thought you were a lot more innocent than Elizabeth. She's just dumb. And mark my words, one of these days that sweet thing from Toledo is going to be in trouble. But you never will, because you're truly innocent."

"I don't think I know what you're talking about."

"No. You probably don't. But you do understand what it takes to get ahead in this business. You know how terrible it can be, and how rough it is. Yet you still manage to look forward to the future and plan ahead. You know what you want and can't imagine not getting it. And that, honey, is innocence. Elizabeth is just plain dumb. No matter what happens to her, she'll never know what's going on."

"You're so knowing. And so sophisticated."

"And so honest."

Just then they heard the front door open, and Elizabeth rushed into the kitchen. She grabbed Jane. "They liked me. I could tell they liked me. I sang four songs. Imagine! *Four.* And then they talked very nicely to me and asked about my family and everything. I thought they knew all about me before. I mean, I've been a contract player for a long time now."

"The big shots don't know about you until they discover you for themselves," said Mable.

"Well, it was wonderful. And I sang well. At least I think I did. Oh . . . and Ralph Mason is going to call me Lilly. Isn't that funny?"

"What's Ralph got to do with the audition?" asked Mable.

"Oh, nothing. It's just that I saw him this morning. He was so kind. He wished me luck and told me Elizabeth was too long a name to say all the time—"

"He probably can't manage all the syllables," interjected Mable.

"And he is going to call me Lilly," finished Elizabeth, who was rapidly learning to not listen too closely to Mable. She stretched out her arms. "Oh, it's been a wonderful day. *Mr. Edson* came into the audition, and he shook hands with me and called me dear. And Mr. Grandison wants to hear me sing again, real soon. It never rains but it pours. He gave me some songs to learn—"

"Do you think we could eat soon?" asked Mable.

"Just as soon as Elizabeth is finished," said Jane. "Be fair, Mable. You know that if Murry Edson called you dear, you'd be on top of the world."

"With my luck, I'd have to be under his belly for him to call me anything but 'you there.'"

Jane laughed.

"Well, I don't care," said Elizabeth. "At least I got the chance and it was wonderful. I'll never forget this day. Can we eat soon? I have to get up early tomorrow and start practicing."

"*What* a good idea," said Mable. "Funny, we never thought of dinner."

"I'll bring it in. You two go ahead and sit down."

Jane began to remove pots from the stove, but when her hands began to shake, she abruptly set down a dish and grasped the edge of the counter. I'm happy for her, thought Jane. I truly am happy. I'm glad she's getting a chance to get ahead. She deserves it. She has a beautiful voice. Jane again began putting the food onto platters, but tears obscured her vision. This is ridiculous, she thought. I don't cry. I never cry. But it isn't fair.

Damn it, it just isn't fair. I've got to have my chance, too, she thought, angrily. Somehow, I've got to get my chance.

Elizabeth's announcement of her meeting with Grandison and Edson had the effect of making Jane nervous and irritable. She became constantly aware of the passage of time and her own lack of advancement, although she tried hard not to express any action that would make her jealousy of Elizabeth's good fortune evident to her roommates. But no matter how much Jane liked Elizabeth, the young singer's progress was a constant reminder to Jane of her own desperation.

She spent long hours thinking about her future. She knew she couldn't sing or dance, but she was sure she looked good in front of the camera. She was also aware that her beauty was a transitory thing. There were a lot of beautiful women in Hollywood, and even more women whose beauty had faded along with their ambitions. Now, all that these once-hopeful starlets had left were a few names they could drop at parties and dim memories of nights spent with men whose faces were now blurred past recognition. Some of them had become hookers; others, the luckier ones, had returned to their hometowns where they lived on forgotten glory. But Jane occasionally saw the ones who remained at parties. A few were still hoping for their big break and dressed and made themselves up as well as their limited money would allow. But nothing they wore on their faces could hide or cover up the fear that showed in their eyes. Jane was terrified that she might become one of these women.

She stared at her reflection in the mirror, searching for tiny lines, imagining imperfections.

Each day she went through her usual appointments and classes at the studio. And each night she tossed and turned in her bed as she tried to think of a way to capture the chance she wanted so badly.

The girls were becoming increasingly fond of each other. Even Elizabeth was beginning to get used to Mable's strange conversation. And there was a feeling of security and comfort in the apartment.

One night as they were sitting together after dinner, Jane looked over at Mable, who was stretched out on the sofa painting her toenails a particularly toxic shade of pink. Mable looked up and noticed Jane's interest.

"It is a bright color, isn't it?" said Mable, smiling. "I wasn't sure at first, but now I'm positive that Larry will like it."

"Larry?" asked Elizabeth. "Who's Larry?"

"Oh, he's the guy from Paramount I told you about. I knew I'd get him. But he's big into toes, so this is a special treat for him." She reached over and dipped the brush back into the paint.

"Toes?" asked Elizabeth.

"Stop it, Mable," said Jane automatically, aware that the older girl was about to give Elizabeth another fact of life.

To change the subject, Elizabeth asked Mable a question. "Mable, I know it's none of my business, but you've had a great deal more experience than I have . . ." Her voice trailed off as she encountered a dirty look from Mable. "I mean," she began again, "you've been in Hollywood a lot longer than I have . . ." She stopped again.

"I suppose if I'm ever going to hear this question, I might as well put away my pride," said Mable. "Go on, Elizabeth. Out with it."

"Well, I was wondering about *your* career. I mean, you go around to the casting calls and all. But what do you want to do?"

Mable looked thoughtful.

"I don't mean to pry," said Elizabeth hurriedly. "But we all know that I want to sing, and Jane wants to be an actress. But you've never said much about your ambitions. Don't you want to have a career?"

"Look, honey," replied Mable, "you and Jane have enough ambition for this whole town. Besides, I already have what I want."

"What's that?" asked Jane.

"I'm out of Oklahoma City . . . *and* I have plenty of men. Anything else is just gravy." Mable laughed. "I admit, when I first got here the idea of making it big interested me. But it's too much work. Jesus. I hate to get out of bed in the morning. And sometimes these creeps want you at the studio at five or six A.M. I had to do that in Oklahoma to feed the pigs. No. I'll do enough work to make a living, and the rest of my time I'll do what I like best."

"But what's that?" asked Elizabeth, stupidly.

"Honey," drawled Mable, "I like to fuck."

"Mable," Jane interposed before Elizabeth could faint, "I know you're being funny, but there's no reason to be vulgar."

Mable shrugged. "Sorry, honey," she said to Elizabeth. "But you should know by now that I'm not a very cultured person." She looked at the clock. "Jesus! I've got to get out of here. I'll be late for my date with Larry." She waved her toes madly in the air to dry them. "Jesus, if this stuff doesn't dry, I'll stick to my shoes, and that won't turn Larry on at all." She hurried out of the room, walking on her heels to avoid smudging her polish.

Jane looked over at Elizabeth. "Don't let Mable upset you. You know how she is."

"Sure." Elizabeth smiled. "What are you doing tonight?"

"I'm going to see David. We're going to take some pictures."

"Again? He must have a lot by now."

"I guess so." Jane shrugged. "What about you? Are you staying home and working on your music?"

Elizabeth colored slightly. "Well, Ralph said he might call or come by later. I saw him at the studio today, and he said if he wasn't busy, he'd let me know."

"Oh." Jane couldn't understand Elizabeth's fascination with Ralph Mason. He had a terrible reputation around town for his dealings with women. But Elizabeth seemed to be attracted to him, and Jane didn't want to interfere. Besides, it wouldn't do any good to say anything, anyway. Elizabeth would only get angry at her.

Elizabeth looked away from Jane. "I know you and Mable don't like Ralph. But he's really nice. Honestly he is."

Jane smiled at her friend. "Sure," she said, and went to get ready to leave for David's.

David was waiting for her and called out as she came into the studio. "Hello, beautiful. I thought you weren't coming."

"Am I late? I thought I was right on time."

"You probably are. It's just that I have something special to ask you tonight, and I've been a little nervous about it."

Jane stopped on her way to the dressing room and looked at David. He was dressed as usual in slacks and a sloppy sweater.

His dark hair was mussed, and there was a smudge of something dark on his cheek. She thought he'd probably been working in the darkroom. She moved close to him and smiled.

"You are a mess," she said kindly, wiping his face with her handkerchief.

"Oh?" He seemed embarrassed. "Sorry. It's just that I have something on my mind."

"Do you want to tell me about it?"

"Not yet." He grinned at her. "Go on and change. I put some bathing suits in the dressing room. There's a white one that should look good on you."

"All right." She touched her finger to her lips and then placed it on his cheek.

In a short while Jane came back. She was wearing a one-piece white bathing suit with a short skirt. Her hair was pulled back and held with a white ribbon, and her makeup was subdued. She looked sweet and virginal, and very lovely. Jane took her place on the set, sitting on a white bench which had been placed in front of a bright blue backdrop.

David had the equipment all set up, and for a while they worked companionably, David moving quickly about, changing lights and adjusting Jane's poses to catch her best angles. After about an hour, he stopped. When Jane didn't hear the click of the camera, she looked up toward him.

"Is there something wrong?" she asked.

"Yes," he answered thoughtfully.

When David didn't elaborate, Jane looked questioningly at him. "Are you going to let me in on it?" she teased.

"I don't know if you'll want to be in on it."

"Well, try me."

David came over and sat down beside her. He didn't look at Jane, but stared out across the studio. "I think I've figured out what I've been missing in the shots we've been doing. Don't get me wrong. You look great. But I want something more. I want to get *you* on film. A special quality you have. And I haven't been able to get it. I know what I'd like to do . . . but . . ."

"What do you have in mind?"

David was very serious. "I want you to pose nude for me," he said finally.

"Nude?" Jane was startled.

"That's right. With your hair down and slightly disheveled. No more makeup than you're wearing now. Simple, direct . . ."

"It sounds direct," said Jane.

"Well," asked David, finally looking at her, "what do you think?"

For a few seconds Jane was silent. Then she looked at David. She liked him, and she felt very comfortable with him. "Sure," she said. "I'll just get a robe."

Jane slid off the seat and went into the dressing room. She removed the bathing suit and stood nude before the mirror. She looked down at her body. Nothing to be ashamed of, she thought, smiling slightly to herself. She touched her lips with a light pink lipstick, pulled on a white terry cloth robe, and returned to the set.

David had removed the bench and changed the background. Now there was only a shiny black backdrop, the cloth extending over the floor.

He waited until Jane was standing in the center of the set, and then began adjusting lights and moving equipment about. When he had everything set to his satisfaction, he went behind the camera and told Jane he was ready.

She hesitated briefly, then dropped the robe off her shoulders, letting it fall almost to the floor before tossing it aside with one hand.

Jane stood perfectly still, her body bathed in the warm shadows and lights. Reaching up with one hand, she loosened the cloth band that held her hair in place, and the blond tendrils fell softly about her shoulders.

Looking about, she saw the lights directed toward her, the camera focused on her, David watching her. Suddenly it seemed that the whole world was looking at her. And she loved it. She basked in the attention. She wanted to bring the whole world close, to draw it to her. To let it see and feel her.

The heat of the lights was like a sensuous caress at the start of love. And Jane loved in return.

After several seconds, David spoke. "You are truly beautiful," he said softly.

Jane's perfect mouth moved into a smile. She felt totally in control and completely free. She loved the feeling of the heat from the lights caressing her skin and the absolute attention of the camera on her.

There was tenseness and excitement in the dull air of David's studio, a feeling of sensuous anticipation. Jane reached up, mussing her hair slightly with her hands. Tossing her head slightly, she boldly faced the camera, absorbed by the picture she knew she was creating. She had never felt more desirable or more beautiful.

David called out brief instructions to her, but he didn't need to say much. Jane moved instinctively, her body appearing to have a mind of its own as she slid gracefully from one pose to another. She lifted her arms high, stretching her body taut, then dropped her arms, running them over her breasts and her hips. She lowered her head and shook her hair over her face, and in one movement suddenly threw back her head, exposing her eyes to the brightest light. Her face was at once tense, then relaxed, then alluring.

David reached behind him and raised the volume on the record player. The crashing sounds of a Beethoven symphony filled the studio as Jane continued her breathtaking movements. Jane slipped down onto the black floor and lay perfectly still. All around her was black, nothing distracting from the perfection of her body. Sitting up, she pulled her knees up to her chin and hugged them close to her, looking out at the lens, her gaze challenging. Stretching out, she lay on her stomach and pushed her upper body up with her hands and lifted her chin, defying the camera to capture her. She loved the feel of the drop cloth on her body. Its smooth surface made each movement a caress, and she felt heat course through her. She wanted to entice, to lure the camera. She wanted the lens to penetrate her body. Jane looked up at her mechanical lover, her face filled with hunger and desire. Small beads of sweat ran down between her breasts as she lay back on the drop cloth. She raised one leg slightly and placed her hands on the floor behind her head. Her hair was spread out around her face. Jane briefly closed her eyes, and David moved the camera slightly toward her. She looked up and her eyes caught the light.

David gasped involuntarily. The woman who stared up at him, at his camera, was not loving or sweet or gentle. She was consumed by lust, and her goal was to control, to have power over anyone she could touch with her remarkable sexuality. She was wantonly magnificent.

David had said little throughout the shooting, allowing Jane to interact with the camera on her own. Finally, after almost an hour, he moved away from the tripod and sat down on the sofa. "Wrap," he said quietly. There was sweat on his forehead, and his hands shook slightly as he lit a cigarette.

He reached out and lowered the volume on the record player as Jane stood up and gathered her robe around her. She was still in the throes of the experience, and her movements were slow and studied.

She walked over to David and reached down and took the cigarette from his fingers. Taking a deep drag, she tilted her head. "Was I all right?" she asked.

"You were amazing," David said softly. "Exciting . . . beautiful." He smiled at her. "I just hope I did you justice with the camera."

"I'm sure you did." She sat beside him. "David . . . I wanted to be good."

He didn't answer.

"I wanted to be good for you," she continued. "I wanted to be what you wanted."

David was still silent, and Jane leaned forward and crushed out the butt of his cigarette in the ashtray. She turned toward him, her robe falling open slightly. "Did you hear me?"

David didn't look at her. His face was closed and his eyes were fixed on some distant point. "Yes. I heard," he answered.

"David, is there something wrong? Have I done something?"

David's lips twisted into a sad smile. "No, Jane. You haven't done anything. Nothing at all."

"But you seem different somehow . . . distant."

He looked at her and smiled brightly. "Nonsense. You were great. It was a great shooting. We should be very proud of ourselves."

She reached out and touched his arm, running her fingers up to his shoulder. "David . . ."

He turned away again and pulled slightly away from her.

"David!" Her voice grew angry. "David, pay attention to me. I'm trying to talk to you."

He looked back at her. "All right. I'm paying attention."

"David," Jane fought to control her voice. "I don't understand. I thought we worked well together. I thought we were friends."

"I hope we are."

"I care about you, David. I care very much."

"And I care about you, Jane."

"Then what's wrong. Is it *me*? Have I done something? Look at me," she ordered. "What's wrong with me?"

He covered his face with his hands, sighed deeply, and then raised his head. "It's not you, Jane. It's not you at all. You're a very beautiful and desirable woman."

"Then what is it? I don't understand."

"I'm afraid I don't have the answers. It isn't you, Jane. It isn't any woman." He smiled at her. "Don't get me wrong. It isn't men, either. It's . . . nothing."

"You mean you've never—"

"Oh, I've tried several times, with both women and men. But nothing happens, Jane. Nothing ever happens."

"Perhaps if we—"

"No!" His voice was rough. "I couldn't, Jane. If we tried and I couldn't make the grade, I'd never to able to look you in the eye again. And I want us to be friends. I don't want to lose you."

"I see." Jane's voice was quiet.

David looked at the camera still sitting on the tripod. "Please don't hate me, Jane."

"No . . . of course not."

"You're an amazing woman. And you probably have a brilliant career ahead of you."

"That doesn't seem very important at this moment."

"Don't say that! Don't *ever* say that. You have a right to success. You've got magic, the quality that sets apart the real stars from the rest of us." He shrugged slightly. "And I have . . . that." He nodded at the camera. "It's hard to explain. I really don't understand it myself. But everything I have, everything I feel is right there. I can appreciate all the things you are and the way you look and the wonderful energy that comes from you. But I see it and feel it all with the camera between us. Never any other way. Can you understand at all?"

Jane smiled at him. "Haven't you heard? I'm a dumb blond. I never understand anything."

"Well, understand this. I'm on your side. I want you to reach the top. I want you to be a great success."

"You only talk about business."

"There isn't anything else for me, Jane. I'm sorry. Truly sorry. I wish with all my guts it was different. But it's not."

Jane nodded and stood up. "I'd better get dressed."

David didn't answer, and Jane left him sitting alone staring at the black backdrop, his face as expressionless as the empty set.

CHAPTER *Four*

AS JANE DROVE AWAY from David's studio, she was confused and hurt. She didn't really understand his problem at all. It didn't make sense to her. The only reality she recognized was that she had offered herself to a man and been rejected. She felt embarrassed and angry . . . and very lonely. Men had always adored her. Ever since she was a child, she had been the center of male attention. And suddenly, a man didn't want her.

Coming on top of her concern about her dead-end career, David's lack of interest frightened her. Grasping the wheel, she began to imagine that no one wanted her. She saw no future ahead of her. No career. No love. Just endless days and nights, of loneliness. She couldn't live that way. Somehow she had to prove to herself that she was still valuable, still wanted.

Jane drove aimlessly for a while, unwilling to go home. Finally she decided to drive to Pete's.

It was midnight, and there were just a few people in the club. Some jazz players from the Copa were messing around on the bandstand, starting and stopping various tunes. A couple in evening clothes were leaning close together at a back table, and at a table near the door were two local girls—probably hookers taking a break. Against one wall five men and one incredibly ugly woman were seated together. The group was arguing loudly about something. Jane went to the bar and was greeted by the owner, who looked surprised when she ordered scotch and water. He didn't remember her ever having anything stronger than ginger ale.

"Not very busy tonight," Jane said as she sat down at the bar.

"No," said Pete, setting her drink down in front of her. "The late crowd'll be in soon. Actually, I like it best about this time. I get a chance to take a breath. Early it's always full, and later it's always full."

"Who comes earlier?"

"Tourists!" Pete spat out the word. "They like to come in here and think they're seeing what life is really all about. Stupid bastards. Everything all right with you?"

Jane shrugged. "Sure, Pete. I'm on top of the world. Can't you tell?"

"We all got problems, baby. Look at those guys over there." He pointed to the table where the argument was still going on. "That bunch has been here for five hours, bellyaching about some political thing. What do they think they're going to do about anything? I'll tell you what they're going to do. Nothing! But they'll still stay here half the night arguing."

"Who are they?" asked Jane.

Pete shrugged. "Writers mostly, I think. The ugly broad's sold a couple of stories, but the rest are just trying to get started. They sleep all morning, write and hustle their stories all afternoon, and sit in here and drink all night. Nice life ain't it?"

One of the men looked up and saw Jane and Pete staring at his table. He looked at Jane for a moment before turning back to the conversation.

"Who is that?" asked Jane.

"Name's Wilson . . . something funny, Wilson. Morning. No that's not it. Morgan—Morgan Wilson."

"Is he a writer?" Jane didn't really care, but she liked talking to Pete and wanted to keep the conversation going.

"Wants to be. Hell, you never know. I may have the next Fitzgerald over there. But I understand *he* does most of his drinking at home. At least he's never been in here. Neither has Dorothy Parker, and from what I hear she can really put the stuff away. But they've never done it in here."

"They probably just never heard of your place."

"Yeah, that must be it." Pete laughed. "I'll take out an ad in *Variety*. 'Drunk writers welcome at Pete's.' Might work, you never know."

"No," Jane said to herself as Pete moved away, "you never know."

Jane sat alone, nursing her drink. She wasn't really thinking about anything. She had resolutely put the scene with David out of her mind, and now she simply sat, not even sure what she was waiting for.

"Drinking alone is supposed to be very bad for you."

Jane turned around on the barstool and found the man from the writer's table standing behind her.

"Haven't I seen you around?" he asked.

"Pete says you're a writer. Surely you can come up with something better than that."

"Maybe. But I like to know who I'm writing for."

"Jane Turner."

"Morgan Wilson. Do you mind if I sit down?"

Jane shrugged and Morgan quickly seated himself on the next barstool. "What are you drinking?" he asked.

"Scotch."

He signaled to Pete to bring another round, and while he ordered and then carefully counted out the money to pay for the drinks, Jane was able to study him.

Morgan Wilson wasn't particularly good-looking. He was tall and thin, with light brown hair which needed cutting; his nose was large and his eyes were brown and narrow. He had beautiful hands. He wore an old tweed jacket, nondescript trousers, and a checkered shirt, open at the collar.

"How come you're all alone?" asked Morgan, after Pete had brought the drinks.

"I just finished work and stopped in for something to drink," Jane answered.

"What kind of work?"

"Tonight I was doing some still photography. I'm a contract player at Global."

Morgan grunted. "I tried to sell those bastards one of my stories, but they said it wasn't right for any of their stars. Did they mean you?"

"No," said Jane, "I'm not a star."

"Shit, baby. I knew that. I know every star in town, at least by name. I meant are they going to give you the big buildup and all to *make* you a star?"

"If they are, they haven't started yet."

"See what I mean. I try to sell them a great story, and they don't even read it all. And you're sitting in here instead of getting a big role. Shitheads, that's what they are."

Jane laughed. "Sure. Here we are. Two great, undiscovered talents."

Morgan's friends suddenly got noisier.

"What's wrong with your buddies?" asked Jane, looking toward the commotion.

"Politics. We all belong to a writer's club."

"Is that what writer's clubs are for . . . to discuss politics?"

"Well, along with our work, we're naturally concerned about the state of the world."

"Are you involved in politics?" asked Jane.

"I'm interested in the way things should be. Communism is the only real kind of government for today. Capitalism is over, finished. If America was communist, there wouldn't be any Murry Edsons who can barely read or write over at Global telling people what's wrong with their stuff."

"I never thought of it that way," said Jane.

"Naturally. You're too involved with the system. One of these days there'll be a revolution, and everything will change."

"How?"

"It'll be just like Russia. They have the right idea over there. They know how to do things. Everyone works for the common good; none of this big-boss stuff."

"Oh." Jane didn't know what to say or how to answer Morgan. She honestly didn't much care about the topic of conversation, but she liked the way his eyes never left her. And she was attracted to him. Beneath his surly manner and lofty talk, Jane could feel the sexual energy that he projected. He was frightening in a way. He created tension around him like a tightly strung wire. Jane thought he was probably ruthless and dangerous. But she also thought he was very exciting.

For the next hour, Jane sat and listened as Morgan expounded his theories on the ideal state of the world. He

illustrated his points with examples of decadent capitalism
versus the utopian communist state. He talked and talked, his
flow of conversation seemingly endless. And Jane, only half
listening and understanding, was mesmerized by the vibrant
web he spun around her.

His friends came by to say good night, and shortly afterward
the club began to fill up with the late-night crowd. Morgan
suggested they leave.

"I don't have a car," he said, "so I can't offer you a lift."

"I have one. Can I take you somewhere?"

"I live over near Melrose."

"I can take you," said Jane.

They didn't talk much on the ride, and when Jane pulled up
in front of the old building in which Morgan had his apartment,
she stopped the car and turned and looked at him.

"You wanna come up?" he asked casually.

Jane didn't answer immediately. She knew she should say
no, let him out, and go home. But she needed someone
tonight. She needed someone who wanted to be with her. "All
right," she said.

Jane followed Morgan into the building and up a battered
staircase to his apartment. He opened his door, flicked a switch
inside, and stood back for her to enter.

Jane found herself in a tiny room, messy beyond belief. A
table held a typewriter and a collection of papers which
cascaded over the edge onto the floor. A closed curtain hung by
only a few hooks; a large armchair covered with dirty clothes
sat next to a tiny table which supported an ashtray filled with
cigarette butts. Through an open door, Jane could see a small,
not very clean bathroom, and turning, she noticed an unmade
studio bed against the wall.

Morgan dropped his keys on the table and asked Jane if she
wanted a drink.

"No. I don't think so," she answered. She had had three
drinks at Pete's, and that was a lot more than she was used to.
She didn't feel drunk, however, just a little off-center in a
comfortable sort of way.

"I think I will," said Morgan. He pushed open the curtains,
revealing a small sink filled with dirty dishes, a hot plate, and
some open containers of food. He grabbed a bottle of rye and
an almost-clean glass and poured a drink.

"Sit down," he invited. Jane looked around for a place, and Morgan grabbed the clothes on the chair and threw them onto the floor. "There," he said.

Jane smiled at him and sat down. Morgan stood leaning against the table, staring at her.

"You know, you're pretty good-looking," he commented.

Used to being called beautiful and stunning and lovely, Morgan's offhand compliment came as a surprise to Jane. Strangely, she found that she liked it.

"You can listen, too," Morgan continued. "Most women can't stop talking."

"Thank you."

Morgan leaned down and ran his hand along Jane's leg, pushing her skirt up slightly. She didn't move. The electricity she had felt from his voice earlier had transferred itself to his fingers as they touched her skin.

Morgan leaned close to her. His lips brushed her cheeks, her eyes, then moved down to her lips. He kissed her gently at first, then more demandingly, forcing his tongue into her mouth. His hand continued to move over her leg as he pushed her body back against the chair.

Suddenly he stood up. Walking to the door, he switched off the light, plunging the room into complete darkness.

"Too dark," he muttered to himself. He went to the bathroom and turned on a light, closing the bathroom door most of the way, allowing only a pinpoint of illumination into the room. He returned to Jane and took her hand, drawing her out of the chair.

Slipping his hands under her sweater, he ran his fingers over her stomach, moving up until he touched her breasts, teasing and toying with her nipples. Jane moaned slightly.

She stood perfectly still, neither encouraging nor rejecting his advances. He pulled her sweater up, and she raised her arms to allow him to lift it over her head. She was naked beneath it. Morgan tossed the sweater aside and leaned forward, his tongue nibbling and licking at her breasts as his hands quickly released her skirt and pushed it to the floor. Jane stepped out of the skirt and moved back from Morgan. Clad only in her white panties, she looked beautiful, and Morgan simply stared at her for a few seconds. He walked over to the bed, and, after pushing various articles off, he lay back and looked at her. The dim light threw shadows across her body, at once revealing and concealing her perfect figure.

She was really something, he thought. His eyes were riveted on her.

Jane saw in his face the look that she had been waiting for. The look that most men had when they saw her. The look of hunger and lust and desire. As she felt his gaze, she began to feel her power.

She reached up and released her hair from the ribbon which held it. She shook her head, and her hair fell gracefully about her shoulders. She raised her chin slightly, her eyes challenging Morgan. Wanting him . . . daring him to take her.

He started to stand, and she held up her hand for him to stop. Walking over to the bed, she placed her hands on her breasts. Her fingers moved around her nipples, making them harden with excitement. She leaned forward, letting her breasts slide over his jacket. She began removing his clothes, and he sat up to help her. In a few seconds, Morgan lay back down, clad only in his shorts.

Jane climbed onto him, sitting astride his body, rubbing herself against his hardening penis. Morgan reached out for her, but she moved away, slipping down over his body until she was kneeling on the floor. Her hands moved over his legs and touched his crotch. He was hard, and Jane began ripping at his shorts, pulling them away from him. When he was naked, she ran her fingers along the shaft, touching it gently, teasing it.

Morgan lifted himself toward her. "Yeah," he whispered hungrily. "Take it. Take it."

Pushing her hair back with one hand, Jane leaned forward and placed her lips on his cock. Her tongue touched the head, moving around it in small circles, licking, caressing. Her eyes never left his as her lips continued to taunt him.

Suddenly she slipped her mouth over his penis, letting it sink down into her throat. She sucked and licked him, letting her teeth skim along the sensitive surface.

Morgan reached down and grasped her hair with his hands, guiding and encouraging her. "Get it, baby," he ordered. "Get it all."

Jane worked on him, bringing him to the edge several times before releasing him. Then she stood and slipped out of her panties and crawled onto the bed next to him. He started to reach out for her, but she quickly moved, twisting her body until she was lying opposite him, her face and hands reaching hungrily for his dick.

He reached behind her and pushed his face against her cunt, spreading her legs wide for him to reach her. Together they explored each other, licking, touching.

"Eat me," whispered Jane, her breath shallow and hard. "Lick me, touch me."

Their bodies pushed together, their hands and mouths grasping for the feel of each other. Morgan pushed Jane's legs down and forced her to lie on her back. He moved up over her, his mouth sinking between her breasts as he licked her soft skin. Over and over he moved his face across her body. Jane whispered words of wonder and desire, her body moving around in an agony of lust. She wanted him. She wanted him to want her. She wanted him to need her and desire her above everything else.

Morgan raised his head and looked down at her. A slight smile crossed Jane's lips as she saw the completely hypnotized expression on his face.

He raised himself up fully and slowly lowered his body and entered her.

"God, yes," she moaned. "Yes." Her voice was harsh and demanding. "Take me. Put it in me. Do it. Do it now."

Their bodies were drenched in sweat and as Morgan lay on Jane, their bodies rubbed and slipped together. Deeper and deeper, he pushed into her.

"Fuck me," screamed Jane. "Fuck me. Fuck me. Fuck me. Fuck me." Her voice was a cry that shattered the air.

Morgan's breath came rapidly, and there were low, animal sounds from his throat as he moved faster and faster. Jane's legs captured his body and tightened around him. Her hands grasped at his back, her nails digging deep into his flesh.

He cried out in pain and surprise, and then again as he began to come. Feeling him inside her, Jane immediately had her own orgasm, and they clutched each other wantonly, almost brutally, as they pulsated to their climax.

As they slowly slipped back to reality, Morgan kissed her lightly, and ran his fingers over her face. "You're very beautiful," he whispered. "Very beautiful." Jane smiled down at him, and they drifted off to sleep.

• • •

Jane spent the night at Morgan's. In the morning when she was ready to leave, she leaned over to kiss him and he woke up.

"See you tonight?" he asked.

"Sure."

"Pete's then . . . at seven." He fell back asleep.

Jane drove home feeling wonderful, if a little guilty. She had had affairs before, but she had never succumbed so quickly to a man. But it had felt perfect. She felt so good, she was even able to forgive David.

She entered the apartment quietly, not sure whether or not Mable and Elizabeth were still sleeping. She found them both up, drinking coffee in the kitchen.

"Well," said Mable. "How *nice* to see you. I guess I was all wrong about the photographer. It must not have been boys after all."

"You weren't wrong. But then you weren't right either."

"What?"

"I'll explain later. I have to shower and get dressed. I have a class at the studio this morning."

Elizabeth hadn't spoken, and Jane looked toward her. "Good morning, Elizabeth."

Elizabeth nodded.

"Is something wrong?" asked Jane.

"Oh," answered Mable, "it's just that Mr. Mason didn't see fit to be free last night."

"It doesn't matter," said Elizabeth. "He probably had something important to do."

"Yes," agreed Mable. "I've noticed how much in demand he is." Her voice was sarcastic.

"Well, he might have been busy," interjected Jane. "Maybe you'll see him at the studio today, Elizabeth."

"Maybe," said Elizabeth. "At least you two had a good time. Mable only got in a few minutes before you." She started to leave the room. "I guess I'd better go and dress."

Jane watched her leave. "It's a shame about Mason," she said.

"I always said he wasn't any good. But that isn't all that's bothering her. I don't think our Toledo miss approves of our later hours. She looked at me like I was the whore of Babylon when I walked in. But I don't think she was surprised. You, on the other hand, are something of a heroine to her, and I think she's just disappointed in you."

"Well, she's very young . . ."

"I wish to hell people would quit telling me how young people are. Jesus. You'd think I came over on the ark."

Jane laughed.

"I want to hear all about your adventures last night. What *did* happen?"

"Well, it wasn't at all what I expected." Jane told Mable about her evening.

Mable was fascinated. "Wow!" she commented when Jane had finished. "That's some story. So the magic photographer couldn't get it up, huh? I knew there was something wrong."

"Don't pick on him, Mable. He's still a nice guy and it isn't his fault."

Mable shrugged. "So what about the writer? When are you going to see him again?"

"Tonight at Pete's. At seven."

"Seven! You'll be the only people there who aren't tourists. I don't even think Pete shows up that early."

"We're not going to stay there. Last evening when we met he mentioned some political meeting, so I imagine he wants to take me there. It might be interesting."

"About as interesting as a tour of Greta Stewart's bath-room," said Mable. "Jesus! Politics, no less."

"You can come along if you want. You might learn something."

"No thanks. I have better things to do with my time than go to political meetings."

"Like what?"

"Like painting my toenails."

"You just did that last night."

"I know. And they were such a hit that I thought I might try another color. What do you think of green toenails?"

"It'll look like your feet are moldy."

"Just because you got laid doesn't mean you can be rude to your friends."

Jane was nervous about going to Morgan's political meeting. She hadn't had much experience with the intellectual set in Hollywood, and she was afraid she might do or say the wrong thing. She had dressed carefully for the meeting, choosing a simple skirt and sweater. Her hair was pulled back, and she wore only a little makeup.

The apartment was filled with people, cigarette smoke, and noise. It seemed to Jane that everyone was talking at once.

Morgan took her arm and led her through the crowd. "We can get seats over there," he shouted above the din.

Jane nodded and followed him to an empty sofa. When they were seated, Jane asked who the people were.

"Mostly writers and technicians," he answered. "There's a few actors, but not many."

"But what kind of organization is it?"

"It's not really an organization. Most of the people here belong to one of the guilds, you know, the unions. And they're active in politics. This is just a casual gathering. The people in this room care about what's happening in the world. We get together and talk about events that are important. And we discuss what can be done to make the world better. The group doesn't have a name. It's probably better that way."

"Why?" asked Jane.

"Oh . . . ." His voice was casual. "If you establish a real organization, then you attract attention. We want to avoid that."

"Oh."

"Just listen and you'll learn a lot tonight. Esther Bright is going to talk."

"Who's she?"

"You must know Esther Bright. She wrote *A Generous Man* for Paramount, and was up for an Oscar for *Always Be True* when it came out from Metro. She's quite a writer and one of the few established people in this town who pays any attention to what's going on. Most of the jerks out here, once they make a few bucks, they're more interested in keeping the bosses happy and getting to the bank than they are in what really matters. Esther's different. She doesn't give a shit about the studios or the bosses. She's got guts."

Someone tapped on a glass, and the room gradually grew silent. A man spoke a few words of welcome, and then mentioned that the bucket at the doorway was for contributions to offset the cost of the food and drink. He hoped everyone would be generous.

"Can't he afford to entertain?" asked Jane very quietly.

Morgan looked at her with disgust. "In the first place, he's not entertaining. This is a *meeting*. And in the second place, most of the people here are just getting started in the business, and they have all they can do to pay the rent."

The man introduced the guest of honor, Miss Esther Bright.

The room exploded in applause as the ugly woman Jane had seen the night before stood up. Esther Bright was large-boned and, despite the summer heat, wore a heavy tweed suit and felt hat. She used no makeup and smoked constantly, waving the cigarette around as she made her points. And she made many. For the next two hours, with only brief pauses for applause, Miss Bright told her audience about the evils and injustices in the world. She talked about China's incursion into Manchuria, and the horrors in Spain that were allowing Franco to destroy democracy. She pointed out the plight of the homeless in America, and the inequality of wealth that permeated the United States, citing J.P. Morgan as an example of all that was bad and wasteful.

Jane tried to listen, but couldn't help wondering why it was that people who had a mission in life were usually so very boring.

"And you," Miss Bright finally seemed to be finishing, "the artistic and creative forces of this celluloid wasteland, must make your voices heard. Daily you go about your tasks, writing, producing, and manufacturing the tripe that the American public downs like maple syrup. Eighty-five million people in this country go to the films to which you contribute your genius. But only a few listen and look around them at what they must know in their hearts to be wrong, unjust, and inexcusable. We must make all people aware of what is happening around them. We must support our labor unions and our fellow creative artists in their fight to expose the horror in the world, in their striving to right the wrongs and oppressions that surround us."

Esther sat down to tumultuous applause. Morgan joined in the ovation, standing and cheering. Jane stood with him. His face was alive and filled with excitement. He was almost good-looking swept away as he was with enthusiasm.

Morgan introduced Jane to a few people in the group, and Jane was welcomed heartily. She was sure she wouldn't remember anyone's name, but she smiled and said what she hoped were the right things. Soon Morgan suggested they leave, and Jane was grateful they weren't going to stay for the group discussions which were beginning.

As they walked to her car, she asked, "Is all that really true?"

"What do you mean?" Morgan was obviously still thinking about the meeting.

"I mean about all the injustice and poverty and everything."

"It sure is. You should see some of the people who come out here from the Midwest. They've lost everything. All they have is the clothes on their backs. They don't have anything left."

"I know about the dust storms," said Jane quietly.

They had reached Jane's car, and Morgan leaned against it and lit a cigarette. "Oh, yeah? What do you know?"

"I was born in Kansas. My family lives in New York now, with my Aunt Maud, and they're all doing very well. In fact," Jane smiled slightly, "I suppose Miss Bright would classify them with the decadent rich. They send me money, and that's why I'm more comfortable than a lot of the contract players. But a few years ago we lived on a depleted farm. My father died on that farm, and my mother took us to New York for a fresh start."

Morgan looked at her speculatively. "Then you know what it's all about, don't you? You must be able to understand what we're fighting for."

"I guess I do," said Jane. "But I always thought that the only way to change things was to work hard; get on top."

"Some people can't do that. And it shouldn't be necessary, anyway."

"I see," said Jane, who really didn't understand. She got behind the wheel, and Morgan went around to the passenger side.

"Where shall we go?" Jane asked.

Morgan ran his hand over her leg. "Do you need to ask?"

CHAPTER *Five*

MORGAN AND JANE CONTINUED to see a lot of each other. They spent long evenings together talking about Morgan's writing and the causes he thought were important. And they spent much of their time making love. They constantly experimented, exploring each other's bodies in search of new and different thrills. Jane was fascinated by Morgan's ability to expound endlessly on his ideas and still never stop projecting a sexual energy that captured her entirely. No matter how serious his conversation, he never lost his desirability. In fact, Jane found that his sensuality was enhanced by his intellectual awareness.

Morgan never talked much about his life before coming to Hollywood. No matter how often Jane asked about his past, Morgan kept their communications directed toward his work or his concerns.

Jane's career didn't interest him any more than his background. There were times when she wished that her ambitions would elicit half as much energy from him that the starving people around the world did. But then she would assure herself that Morgan was working for things that were considerably more important.

In her imagination, Jane saw Morgan as a lonely man,

fighting to survive in Hollywood, while still working to help the oppressed.

Despite her fascination with Morgan and his mission, Jane could never completely take her thoughts away from her own ambition. But her time was more and more taken up with her new lover. Often she worried that she wasn't doing enough for her career, but then thoughts of Morgan would push into her mind, alleviating her guilty conscience.

Each afternoon, when she finished work at the studio, she rushed home to get ready to meet him. They would often join his friends, and Jane would sit quietly and listen as the men and women discussed the world and made plans for demonstrations or sending out pamphlets.

The unremitting earnestness of Morgan and his friends occasionally depressed Jane, and she wished that once in a while they could talk of something light, or even just laugh at something silly. But frivolousness was frowned on, and anyone not interested in changing the world was not welcome around Morgan or his companions.

One evening as Jane was driving to meet Morgan to attend a meeting, she thought about the night ahead. They would drink cheap wine and crucify the ruling classes. Jane's only contribution would be to help address envelopes.

But then, she and Morgan would go back to his place and make love. Jane felt herself grow warm at the thought of his touch. They would lose themselves in each other, forgetting all about the horrors in the world. It was always wonderful between them, always new, always exciting. But first, Jane thought wryly, they had to make their contribution to society.

Jane wished they didn't have to go to the meeting. It would be nice to see some people who didn't take either themselves or the world around them so seriously.

Suddenly she turned the car and headed in a different direction. In a short time, she pulled up outside David Granoff's studio. She turned off the engine and sat looking up at the building. It had been awhile since she and the photographer had seen each other, not since that night when he had taken the nude shots of her, the night she had met Morgan.

Jane wondered if David would want to see her. He hadn't called, but perhaps, she thought, he had been waiting to hear from her. She got out of the car and walked to the door of his studio.

David was there, alone, working in his darkroom. He came out to meet her, and their first few minutes were awkward, neither knowing what to say.

"I've been wanting to come and see you, David. I wanted to tell you that I hope there are no hard feelings. *I* don't have any."

"Neither do I. . . . Friends?"

Jane smiled. "Friends."

"Good," said David. "I've had something I've wanted to show you. In fact, I was just making a present for you. If you can be patient for a few minutes, I'll bring it to you."

"All right. But I don't have much time."

"It won't take long."

Jane sat down and idly leafed through a magazine that featured a picture layout of Greer Garson and her preparations for *Mrs. Miniver*. In a short while, David came back carrying a large print still damp from the developing tank.

Jane started to reach for it.

"Careful, it's still wet," said David.

She moved behind him and looked over his shoulder. It was one of the nude shots. Jane stared at it for several seconds. She couldn't believe it was actually her. The camera had captured and intensified all of the emotions and sensuality she had felt that night.

Jane didn't speak. She couldn't take her eyes from the photograph.

"It's amazing, isn't it?" asked David. "And if anyone can take their eyes off your incredible body and look at your face, they'll see something so sexy they'll come in their pants."

Jane laughed.

"I mean it. At first it looks like the pictures are sexy because you're nude. But that's not it. I've seen nudes that still look like Rebecca of Sunny Brook Farm. But that look in your eyes . . . the way you're holding your mouth. That's what does it. That's what makes the picture sizzle. Watch." David moved his hand to cover her body, leaving only her face visible.

"See what I mean?"

David stared down at her face in the picture. Her eyes

looked back at him, sensual, challenging. Her mouth lured men to the destruction she held in her eyes.

"Even with the body covered, that damned Catholic Legion of Decency will hate it. And the Hay's office would go crazy."

"Who?" asked Jane, still looking at the picture.

"Hay. The man responsible for keeping the movies pure."

"Oh, sure," said Jane. "I've heard of him. I just haven't done enough for him to notice me."

"You will after I show this around."

"Show it?" asked Jane, stunned. She looked at the photographer. "But you can't, David. I can't have a naked picture of me out there for everyone to see."

"Not everyone. Just a few, well-chosen executives at Global. I think you'll be hearing from them after they see this picture."

"Sure. But will they want me for a movie or a date?"

David laughed. "Promise them anything. But just don't come across until you have a role."

"Try it again, Elizabeth. One more time."

"Yes sir." Elizabeth moved around the piano and stood facing her voice coach, Sam Withers. They were in a rehearsal room working on an arrangement he had done for her. She looked toward the piano player and nodded, and he started the opening bars of Cole Porter's "Night and Day."

As always, when Elizabeth sang she seemed to lose contact with the rest of the world. The only thing that existed for her was the music, as she submerged herself in the mood and the melody.

Withers sat watching her, and when she finished he smiled slightly. She really had a voice, he thought. She reminded him a little of the Garland girl over at MGM. Elizabeth had the same kind of throbbing quality that could tear your heart out. But Elizabeth had something of her own, as well. A special tone to her voice that set her apart. He'd seen a lot of singers and he always knew deep inside when they had something. Elizabeth Hudson had it. Aloud he said, "Very nice."

"Thank you," she answered.

"You'd better come back tomorrow. I want to work on this song a little more."

"All right."

"I have something to tell you. Murry Edson wants you to test for a part in a new musical. It's not much of a role. It's the part of a nightclub singer. You wouldn't have any lines, but you'd get to sing one song. It's a good start."

"It would be wonderful," Elizabeth said excitedly. "Imagine."

"There's one thing I ought to warn you about, though." Elizabeth looked expectantly at him.

"Well, this doesn't have anything to do with me. But if I were you, I'd take off a little weight. The camera is going to add a few pounds, and you're not exactly petite."

Seeing Elizabeth's look of embarrassment, Sam was quick to console her.

"Oh, I don't mean you're fat. If it weren't for the camera you'd probably be just right. But . . . well, there's no sense in not having everything going for you at the test."

"How soon do you think they'll want to do the test?"

"Probably in about two weeks."

"Then I guess I'd better get on a diet, quick," she said.

"But don't let it hurt your voice. You have a lot to do in the next two weeks. I want you to work very hard on your song and keep your voice in shape. And if you can lose a little weight, then you'll look even better in front of the camera. But, whatever you do, don't neglect your voice."

"I won't."

"Good. Then I'll see you tomorrow."

Elizabeth left the rehearsal room full of anticipation. A test in two weeks, she thought. She could hardly wait. Elizabeth walked over to the commissary. Singing always gave her an appetite, and although she knew she couldn't eat much, she needed something to take the edge off her hunger.

As she walked into the commissary, she saw Ralph Mason sitting at a table with another man. She walked over to them and said hello.

"Oh, hi," answered Mason.

The other man got up and said he had to get back to work.

"Do you mind if I sit down?" asked Elizabeth after the man had gone.

"No," said Ralph. "What have you been doing?"

"I've been working with Sam Withers. I'm going to have a

test in two weeks, for a musical. He said it wouldn't be a big part, but that I would get to sing a song."

"Congratulations," said Ralph, without any particular enthusiasm.

"Unfortunately, I have to go on a diet, too. Sam thinks I would photograph better if I was a little slimmer."

"Probably right."

They didn't speak for a few moments. Then Elizabeth said, "I haven't seen you for a while. I missed you that night."

"What night?"

"I mean, awhile ago when you said you might come over."

Ralph tried to remember and then gave it up. "Yeah, well I must have gotten busy."

"I thought you probably did," agreed Elizabeth.

"I have to go," he continued. "I'm in some goddamn biblical epic this afternoon. I carry a spear."

"That sounds exciting."

"See you." Ralph started to leave.

"Ralph?"

"Yeah?"

"I just thought that some night you might like to come over for dinner."

"Don't you live with a couple other girls?"

"Yes."

"Well, if I'm not too busy, we'll go for a drive soon. I have a friend who loans me his car sometimes."

"That would be wonderful," said Elizabeth.

"We'll do it later this week." Ralph saluted her and walked away, leaving Elizabeth completely happy.

"This is a very special occasion," announced Elizabeth as she and Jane and Mable seated themselves around their dinner table that evening. "After all, we haven't eaten together for a very long time. Jane, you've been out with Morgan working on your projects, and Mable's been with her friend, doing . . ." Elizabeth's voice trailed off as she hesitated to say what she was sure Mable had been up to. "Anyway," she continued gaily, "I've been home alone most evenings, studying my music, and it's nice to have you both here for a change."

"It's not as if we've been separated since birth," said Mable. "How come you're home, Jane?"

"I'm going to pick up Morgan later. He's at a meeting of the writer's guild."

Mable nodded and looked at Elizabeth. "Anything new with you?" she asked.

"Well," began Elizabeth hesitantly, "yes, there is."

"Are you going to tell us about it," pursued Mable, "or do we have to ask twenty questions like on that radio program?"

"Oh, I'll tell you." Elizabeth took a deep breath. "In two weeks I'm going to be tested for a part in a musical," she blurted out.

"You don't say," said Mable. "Well, go on. Tell us all about it."

"It's not a big role. I mean, I won't have any lines. But I'll get to sing a song in a nightclub."

"Congratulations," said Mable cheerfully.

"Yes," agreed Jane. "It sounds wonderful."

Mable looked at Jane suspiciously, and she immediately brightened up.

"Do you know what you're going to sing?" asked Jane.

"For the test or the movie?" asked Elizabeth.

"The movie," said Mable.

"No. Not for sure. But I'll be all dressed up in a nightclub and . . ." She stopped.

"What's the matter?" asked Mable.

"Oh, it's just that Sam Withers told me that I should lose some weight."

"Then you'd better start now," said Mable, reaching over and removing Elizabeth's filled plate and replacing it with the salad bowl.

Elizabeth looked mournfully down at the lettuce in front of her. "It's just so hard for me to stay on a diet. I'm always hungry, especially after I sing. I've always had a big appetite. My whole family—we're all big eaters."

"That makes them sound like they should live in a cave somewhere," commented Mable.

"But what am I going to do?" asked Elizabeth, who hadn't understood Mable's comment at all.

"Obviously you have to do something about your weight. I've thought for some time that you were looking a little heavy."

"Do you have to lose a lot?" asked Jane.

"Just a few pounds."

"Well, that should be easy."

"It's going to be terrible," moaned Elizabeth. "What am I going to do?"

"I think you should get help," said Mable.

"What kind of help? You mean go to a doctor?"

"In a way," continued Mable. "I have to watch my weight sometimes, too, and I got one of the studio doctors to give me some pills that cut down my appetite. They work beautifully, and you don't have to worry about being hungry."

"Really?" asked Elizabeth. "They sound wonderful, but are they dangerous?"

"Do I look as if I were in danger?" asked Mable. "You're not going to live on them. You're just going to take a few for the next couple of weeks so you'll stop eating like a farmhand."

"What do you think, Jane?"

"I don't suppose they'll do you any harm, if Mable takes them. I wouldn't make a habit of them, though."

"Of course not," said Elizabeth virtuously. "Do you have some now, Mable? Or do I need to go to the doctor first?"

"I can let you have a few. But you'll have to get your own. Just go see Dr. Hicks at Global. He'll fix you up with all you need."

"Mr. Edson, there's a Mr. Marvin Coats here to see you."

"Who?" Murry Edson spoke into his desk intercom.

"Marvin Coats. He's says he's from publicity."

"What does he want?"

"I'm not sure," replied the voice of the long-suffering secretary. "He only asked me to tell you that it was important."

"Tell him to wait," said Edson, snapping off the intercom and swiveling around in his chair.

Terrance Malvey sat across the desk from Murry. "What was all that about?" he asked.

"Some fool. You ever hear of Marvin Coats from publicity?"

"Never."

Murry sighed and stared down at the script in his hands. Terry knew that it would take his boss a few minutes to get his

mind back on the business at hand, so he amused himself by
looking around the opulent office.

Murry's large desk sat in front of a big window that gave a
view of the entire studio. At the other end of the room was a
fireplace, which had never been lit, a sofa, and two leather arm
chairs. Murry sat in this area when he wanted to impress
someone or needed a favor. A door on the far side led to a
private bathroom, which contained a small steam room. The
wall-to-wall carpeting was a soft gray, matching the color of
the walls, which were full of the awards and citations Murry
had managed to collect over the years, along with framed
posters of Global films that had been nominated for Academy
Awards, and the studio's most famous personalities.

Murry cleared his throat, and Terry turned back to their
conference.

"So," asked the studio head, "what are we going to do
about this?" Murry waved the script.

"Get Greta back and put her to work, I suppose."

"You'd think that after *A Long Road* she would be here
already, eager to try and redeem herself."

"Greta doesn't blame herself for the bad response to *Long
Road*, she blames me."

"You only hired her. *She* did the acting. Or as *Variety* said,
'the lack of acting.' Jesus! The critics killed the film and the
audiences can't get out the theater fast enough. What the hell
happened?"

"Well, this is just a guess," said Terry, smiling. "But it is
just possible that the public is a little tired of Greta Stewart."

"You think you're so smart," snarled Murry. "All right, big
shot. Then tell me why they're not tired of Davis or Garbo?
Tell me that?"

"Davis and Garbo don't do the same movie over and over
again. Or at least if they do, they try to change the script.
Greta's been playing the same part for ten years now. The
world keeps changing, and Greta stays the same. I might also
mention that both Davis and Garbo have talent, which is a
commodity that Miss Stewart is noticeably without. In *A Long
Road*, Greta's clothes worked harder than she did."

"We still got her under contract . . . with another year to
run. We got to put her to work. See if we can't salvage

something out of her. Do you realize how much we're paying her a week?"

"I can imagine."

"Well? What about this?" Murry indicated the script again.

"Murry, it's the same old thing all over again."

"But what the hell else are we going to do with her?"

Terrance shrugged. "I guess you're right. Maybe if we surround her with a good cast—"

"Scott Mack was the only one in *A Long Road* who got even passable reviews. And all the women love him."

"And he loves the men," Terry commented.

Murry gave Terrance a dirty look. "He's all right, isn't he? I mean, he isn't out of control or anything."

Terry smiled. "Scott Mack may be the gayest actor God ever invented, but he's also the most stable one we've got. He's perfectly content up in the hills with his boyfriend. The only thing you have to worry about as far as Mack is concerned is if he gets an offer to go back to Broadway. He really likes working on the stage, and if someone showed him a good play, he'd take it."

"Broadway!" spat out Murry. "Shit! He's going to give up ten thousand a week here for two hundred and fifty a week there? That's a laugh."

"Laugh all you want. But he's been here two years now and made a lot of money. The last time I saw him, he was hinting that it would be nice, for a change, to play something other than Greta Stewart's long-suffering costar."

"I tell you what," said Murry, leaning his arms on the desk. "Suppose we give him a big publicity buildup in this next film and promise him that we'll find something more interesting for his next movie. He'll like that. Of course, we'll have to find somebody for him to have a romance with."

"What about Ken Holt?" asked Terry. "He ought to be tired of his horse by now."

"Very funny. Incidentally, keep your eye on Holt. He's been whoring around with a lot of women recently. I hear he likes them young, too young. We don't want any trouble like that."

"I'll watch him. But what about Mack?"

"Well, it wouldn't make any sense to try and make something between him and Greta. After all, they've done several pictures together, and if they didn't click before—"

"It would look stupid if they suddenly found each other," finished Terry. "But you could do something with Mack and whoever plays the part of the other woman in the picture."

"Who do you have in mind for that role?"

"No idea," answered Terry. "I've looked at about everybody we have, and haven't seen a thing yet."

"Maybe we could borrow someone from Metro or Paramount."

"No good. If we borrow a big name, Greta'll have a kid all over the place. No. This is a good chance for us to bring along someone new." Terry looked thoughtful. "Actually, this could work out well."

"Go ahead."

"You've been complaining that you need someone new around here. What do you say to finding a fresh face . . . someone with potential. We start her in this part, and then publicly pair her off with Mack. That way you take care of the publicity for both of them, and get the girl on the screen at the same time."

"Jesus! That's great. We get double the exposure everytime they do something. We'll start with—"

The buzzer on Murry's intercom interrupted him. He flicked the switch.

"Yeah?"

"Excuse me, Mr. Edson, but I was to remind you that you have to leave early today."

"Oh, yeah."

"And that man from publicity is still sitting out here."

"What man from publicity?"

"Mr. Coats."

"Oh, hell. Send him on in." Murry turned off the intercom. "Just let me get rid of this guy. Now how are we going to find the girl? She's got to be something special. . . ."

A soft knock on the door was immediately followed by the appearance of a short, prematurely balding man with large glasses and the start of a potbelly.

"Excuse me, Mr. Edson," began Mr. Coats.

"Yeah. What do you want?" asked Murry impatiently.

"Excuse me, Mr. Edson, but I thought this was important enough for you to see personally. When I first came here a few months ago, they told me downstairs to always be on the lookout for anyone special and—"

"Why didn't you show it to Hawkins? He's head of publicity," said Terrance.

"Mr. Hawkins is away, and I thought—"

"You thought you'd just sneak up here and get a little plug in for yourself," finished Terry.

Mr. Coats looked offended. "It's just that these pictures came in and I thought you should see them, Mr. Edson."

"Leave them on my desk. I'll get to them later," said Murry.

"Yes, but—" began Marvin.

"Leave them," said Murry dangerously.

"Yes, sir." Marvin set the envelope down on Edson's desk, and after another hopeful look at the head of the studio, he left the room.

Murry ignored the folder and turned back to Terry. "Now about this idea of ours. I think it's good. But we have to find the right girl."

"Naturally," agreed Terry. He got up, walked over to Murry's desk and idly picked up the envelope. "Of course, it's a good idea." He opened the folder as he spoke. "That's why I'm such a great producer. Jesus Christ!"

Murry looked up at him, startled. "What's the matter?"

Terrance didn't answer. Instead he simply lowered the contents of the envelope until they were in Murry's view.

Both men were silent for several minutes.

"Who is she?" asked Murry quietly.

"Jane Turner," answered Terrance.

"Who?"

"Jane Turner. One of your contract players. She's done a couple of little things, nothing important."

"I don't think I know her."

"Yes you do. She was married to that Austrian, Kurt Von Grau."

"He's dead."

"Yes, but you've seen her since then. As a matter of fact, she was at the party I gave for *Long Road*. She had a little difficulty with Greta."

"Oh, sure. I remember that. Is this the same girl?"

"I always thought she had something . . . but I never—"

"Missed one, huh?" Murry laughed. "Well, if she looks this good on moving film, you've lost your chance."

Terrance was staring at the pictures, not listening to Murry. "You know," he mused, "it's not just the body."

"Hell, that's enough."

"Yeah. But look at her eyes, her face. Jesus! She looks like she wants to fuck everything in sight." He moved his hand over Jane's exposed body, just as David Granoff had done. "Look at that."

Neither man spoke for a few seconds. Finally, Terry broke the silence.

"Are you thinking what I'm thinking?"

Murry was never quick to commit himself. "Well. Just what do you have in mind?"

Terry smiled. "Do you think Miss Turner might be right for the part?" He picked up the script. "What do you think? Greta Stewart and Scott Mack in *Dawn to Dusk*, introducing Jane Turner."

Murry didn't look convinced.

"Come on, Murry. We both agreed we need someone new. Jane might be the right one."

"Then why haven't we done anything with her before?"

"You could ask almost any studio in town that question about one of their stars." Terry got a gleam in his eye. "Or about one of their contract players who became a star at another studio."

Murry looked frightened for a second. But he still wasn't ready to commit himself. "Just because she looks good with her snatch showing doesn't mean she should be in pictures."

"It's worth a try." Terrance suddenly laughed.

"What's so funny?"

"Can't you just see Greta's face when she finds out that Jane Turner is in her next picture? After that scene at my house, it could be very interesting."

"Be careful. I don't want any trouble on the set. You know how bad that reads in the columns."

"Don't worry. Greta always behaves herself around the press. But underneath, she'll still be hating the Turner girl. Not just because of what happened, but because Jane is a lot younger and better looking. And Greta's hate and Jane's looks will all show up on film. In fact . . ." Terrance looked thoughtful. "It might be worth some rewriting."

"Now what are you talking about?"

"Just let me think a bit." Terrance walked about the office for a few minutes, still carrying the photograph of Jane. He stretched out on the sofa and tapped his forehead with the picture. Murry watched him settle down and then went to his bar and mixed himself a drink. He sat down in one of the leather armchairs and waited patiently for Terry to talk. He'd worked this way with his best producer before, and knew that the results were usually worth the wait.

Finally, Terry looked up and smiled at Murry. "It'll work," he said.

"Do you mind letting me in on it?"

"Look. We both know Greta's too old to play the sweet, little wife anymore. *Long Road* proved that. But she's not too young to play the hard bitch whose got her claws into her husband and won't let him go. Say we rewrite *Dawn to Dusk* a little. Make Greta's part the heavy, the bitch. Then the other role can be sympathetic. The good girl. Greta can drag her husband and the girl through all kinds of hell. Greta could do it blindfolded."

"She won't like it. She thinks her screen image is sweet and gentle. She isn't going to want to play a bitch."

"She will, if we tell her she might cop an Oscar by doing it."

Murry frowned at Terrance.

"Don't look so concerned. She *might* do it. Greta may not be much of an actress. But she *is* a great bitch. Other women have won awards for playing themselves."

"If this woman is such a bitch, why has her husband stayed with her so long? What's wrong with him?"

"Nothing. He's just honorable. The guy has gone through life miserable with this terrible woman. Then one day he meets this sweet, gentle, and beautiful woman with great tits, and crash, there he goes. She resists him at first, but then realizes that she loves him. But Greta won't give him a divorce, and at the end the sweet young thing is all alone, having insisted that he go back to his wife. I can see the ending now. She's sitting in a cafe. She tells him good-bye, and the camera pulls away with her sitting by herself . . . waiting for every man in the audience to climb all over her. It'll be dynamite."

"It sounds risky to me."

"Anytime you've got Greta on the set it's risky. But what have you got to lose? Another Greta flop isn't going to go over too well with the New York financial boys."

Any mention of New York always made Murry nervous. "Have we got any film on this Turner girl?"

"Probably. We must have done some stuff when she first got here. And she's had a couple of bit parts."

"That's not much to go on."

"I'll call down and get them to gather up anything we've got. We can look at it tomorrow. If it's not enough, we can always do some more."

"What about that?" Murry pointed at the photograph.

"Yes. I've been thinking about this. I think we should find a good job for this photographer, and incidentally, make sure we pick up all the prints he has . . . along with the negatives. We don't want this floating around, in case Turner starts to take off."

"It looks to me like she's taken off quite enough," said Murry, removing the picture from Terrance's hands so he could study it a little more.

CHAPTER *Six*

JANE SAT UP AND LOOKED AT MORGAN, still sleeping beside her. She climbed out of bed and went into the bathroom. When she came back, Morgan still hadn't moved.

Jane looked around the tiny apartment with disgust. The place was filthy. She had started to clean it several times, but Morgan had ordered her to leave everything alone, particularly the area around his typewriter. He didn't like anyone messing with his papers.

She sat down on the bed next to Morgan. Reaching out one hand, she touched his shoulder gently.

"Morgan," she whispered. "Wake up. I've got to go home."

Morgan rolled over to face Jane and grunted.

"Morgan . . . Morgan," she continued. "Wake up."

"All right. All right. What is it?"

"I have to go home. I have an appointment at the studio today."

"Good for you," he snarled. Rising up slightly, he reached for a cigarette. Lighting it, he coughed and lay back on the bed.

"You smoke too much," said Jane, leaning close to him and taking the cigarette from his fingers.

"Uh-huh."

"Listen, Morgan. I have to go to the studio today. Are you going to write?"

"Sure."

"Good. I'll see you tonight. What are you going to do?"

"We have to go to a meeting. We're going to send letters to government officials about the situation in Spain."

"All right," agreed Jane wearily. "But do you think the letters will do any good?"

"We have to make people aware of what's happening."

Jane shrugged and leaned over to kiss him. He didn't respond at first, but then as Jane touched his face with her fingers, he reached up and slipped his hand under her skirt, gently caressing the smooth mound between her legs.

"I've got to go, Morgan," said Jane.

"Sure," he answered. But he didn't remove his hand. His fingers probed gently between her legs and with his other hand he pushed her skirt up to her waist. He looked up at her and smiled, then jerked off her panties, ripping them from her body, and pressed his face down between her legs.

Jane moaned and tried to pull away. But her resistance was slight—she was already falling into the rhythm of desire that Morgan's touch always created in her.

He pulled her down beside him and began unbuttoning her blouse. When she was naked, he covered her body with his and entered her immediately.

Jane cried out once, then held him close as he came inside her.

When Jane reached her apartment, she found Mable and Elizabeth rushing around in confusion.

"What's going on?" asked Jane.

"Oh, Jane. Isn't it terrible?" giggled Elizabeth. "Ralph took me for a drive last night and we parked out on Mulholland and talked and talked. I was so late when I got home that I over-slept this morning. I have to work with Sam at ten, and I know I'm never going to make it." She hurried off to finish dressing.

"What about you, Mable?" Jane asked her other roommate. "You're not usually up this early."

"*I* am working," exclaimed Mable in a dramatic accent.

"Really?" asked Jane.

"Yes. I am on my way to MGM to appear with the great Norma Shearer in her latest film epic, *Marie Antoinette*."

"Why, that sounds wonderful," said Jane.

"Along," continued Mable, "with several hundred other extras. Apparently, Miss Antoinette liked a lot of people around her. Or if she didn't, then Miss Shearer certainly does. Rumor has it that there are almost twelve hundred of us taking part. And if the crowd isn't big enough, the set will be. According to the columns, the ballroom for the picture is actually bigger than the one at Versailles. So obviously, you're going to have to look quickly, if you want to see me in the final cut."

"Well, it all sounds very exciting," said Elizabeth, coming back into the room.

"You're home early, Jane," said Mable. "Anything going on?"

"Even *I* have an appointment at the studio today."

"What's it for?" asked Elizabeth.

"I don't know. I just had a message from Constance that I was to be at Building A this morning at eleven."

"We'll keep our fingers crossed for you," said Elizabeth.

Building A held the executive offices of Global Films. When Jane first got the appointment, she thought that Global was going to cancel her contract. But then she realized that the top brass wouldn't be bothered with anything so unimportant.

After going through several receptionists, Jane found herself in Murry Edson's office with Mr. Edson and Terrance Malvey.

"Good morning, Jane," said Edson, coming from behind his desk and taking both of her hands in his. "It's very nice to see you. Won't you sit down?"

"Thank you," said Jane.

She seated herself and smiled at Terrance. He nodded.

"Now Jane," said Murry, "I think I should come right to the point. We've seen some pictures of you done by Mr.—er—"

"Granoff," supplied Malvey.

"Yes. David Granoff."

Suddenly, Jane was afraid. "Mr. Granoff has taken a lot of pictures of me," she said weakly.

"I'm sure he has. But these were a little more . . . revealing."

Damn it, thought Jane. Damn it to hell. I should never have let David take those pictures.

"They were very exciting," said Terrance, intruding on Jane's thoughts.

"Yes," continued Murry. "So exciting that we decided to buy them all up, including the negatives. And we were even able to find a place for Mr. Granoff at Global. He has a great future, we think."

Jane didn't speak.

"And he's not the only person whose future we're interested in. We've been thinking about you for some time. We think you might have a real quality. And so," said Murry, finally getting to the point he had intended to reach immediately, "we have decided to have you tested for a role we have in mind for you. Terrance will pick a director to work with you and rehearse you in the scene. Can you be ready a week from today?"

Jane was so stunned that it took her a few seconds to find her voice. Finally she answered, "Yes. Of course."

"Good. Report to wardrobe. They'll want to pick out a costume for you. And check at the front desk for your test schedule. Naturally, we'll let your agent know all about it."

"Thank you," said Jane. She stood up and walked toward the door. Terrance's voice stopped her.

"By the way, Jane."

"Yes?"

"Did you enjoy posing for the pictures?" he asked with a smile.

She returned his smile. "It was very interesting," she said.

After she closed the door behind her, Terry leaned back in his chair. I bet it was, too, he thought to himself.

"You're late," said Morgan as Jane pulled up at his apartment.

"I know. And I'm sorry. It's just that it's been a hectic day. You'll never guess what happened."

"What?" asked Morgan as he climbed into the car.

"I'm going to be tested for a role," she said excitedly as she pulled away from the curb.

"Oh yeah?"

"Yes. Mr. Edson himself talked to me today. And the test is next week."

"Good," he answered briefly. "This should be a good meeting tonight," he continued, already forgetting Jane's news. "We turn here and then go two blocks."

The apartment for the meeting that night was like all the other apartments Jane had visited since meeting Morgan. The same people were gathered around tables on which there were piles of mimeographed copies of letters and stacks of envelopes.

For the next few hours, the group discussed their causes, the movies, and the lack of social concern in current films. They folded letters, stamped envelopes, and planned future events that would rivet the attention of the American public.

But Jane couldn't keep her mind on the business of the committee. Her thoughts were back at the studio. Over and over again, she privately relived the meeting she had had that morning. She tried to remember everything Edson and Malvey has said to her and the tones of their voices. Each time she thought about what had been said to her, she felt a shiver of excitement.

Toward the end of the evening, the host got up and announced to everyone that they should be sure and attend the rally in Griffith Park in two weeks. It was to be a big demonstration, and everyone would be needed.

When Jane dropped Morgan off, she didn't get out of the car.

"Aren't you coming in?" asked Morgan.

"I really want to," said Jane. "But I've got to go home and get some rest. I've got to be at the studio early in the morning to pick up my script and start getting ready for the test."

"Sure," he replied casually. "I've got some work of my own to do. I've had an idea playing around my mind that I want to get down on paper."

"That's wonderful," said Jane. She reached out and touched his arm. "If it's as good as the other writing you've shown me, I'm sure it'll be fabulous."

"Sure," said Morgan. "And like my other stuff, it'll just sit on my desk."

"Don't worry," said Jane encouragingly. "You'll sell something real soon. Just wait and see."

Morgan shrugged, saluted her casually, and walked into his building.

• • •

Both Elizabeth's and Jane's tests were scheduled for the same morning, and the two girls got up at four A.M. to prepare themselves. They had to be at the studio by six.

Jane had worked slowly and carefully on her face, doing several treatments before applying ice cubes to make her skin tight and glowing.

Elizabeth had roamed about the apartment, doing scales and warming up her voice. Her hands trembled so much she could barely hold a cup of coffee.

"I don't know what's the matter with me," Elizabeth had said as she put down her cup. "My hands just keep shaking."

"Maybe it's those pills Mable gave you."

"Maybe. But at least they worked. I've lost five pounds. Can you tell?"

"Of course. You look great."

Elizabeth sighed and stared at Jane. "I'll never look like you," she mused. "It must be wonderful to be so beautiful."

"Are you nearly ready?" asked Jane. "We can't be late."

Jane had dropped Elizabeth off at the music department, and then rushed into the makeup rooms where she was met by a crew of five who would combine their talents to prepare her for the camera.

The head makeup man, Roger Todd, was an elderly man who looked more like a comfortable grandfather than a creative artist. But he knew his business. Holding a copy of one of Granoff's photographs of Jane which had been cropped to show only her face, he alternately looked at Jane and then back at the picture. Finally, he put it down and said, "Let's go to work."

For the next two hours, Jane's face was measured, studied under a large magnifying glass, and touched with a variety of creams. Then, with quick, careful fingers, the gathered artists began applying foundation and colors. They lined her eyes and tinted her lashes and lids, and with a tiny brush, they carefully painted her mouth.

The hairdresser, Paul Grimes, arranged Jane's hair in a number of styles before finally selecting one he thought best.

When they were all finished, Jane was beautiful. Her skin seemed completely without pores, while her eyes were bright and luminous. And her hair framed her face perfectly.

Jane thanked the crew and went over to wardrobe. An aging woman helped Jane into a simple white evening dress as

Charles Dupre, Global's leading designer, watched carefully. Paul Grimes had come with her to touch up anything that might be disturbed as Jane dressed, and after he had checked her over carefully, she was pronounced ready.

The preparations themselves had been a wonderful experience for Jane. She was amazed to find that Dupre, Grimes, and Todd, all tops in their fields, had been assigned to work on her.

She walked over to the set alone. The excitement she had felt on the day Murry Edson had told her about her chance had continued to build over the past two weeks. Being groomed by the top people on the lot had added to the anticipation. Now, as she neared the actual test, Jane was completely enthralled. She couldn't wait to get started.

Crossing the lot, Jane didn't feel there was anything strange in being fully made up and gowned at nine A.M. on a hot July morning. It was all part of the life she had wanted for a very long time. She reveled in it.

When Jane reached the sound stage, she found a great deal of activity going on. The set wasn't extensive. An abbreviated terrace had been constructed with French windows and a fake stone bench set in front of a low wall. It was built to resemble the back of a great mansion.

Another contract player had been asked to feed Jane the lines, and he was standing off to one side, looking as if he'd rather be in bed.

Terrance Malvey was also there, and he greeted Jane and took her to meet the director, Earnest Kahn. Mr. Kahn informed her they would start shortly. The men left her alone. Jane, remembering that she had heard how the cameraman could make or break a performer, went over to him. He stood with several other members of the crew. Jane introduced herself and smiled at them all, thanking them for being there, even though they all knew it was just part of their job.

They nodded at her professional behavior, and she stood chatting with them until Kahn announced that he was ready to begin.

Jane went onto the set and stood waiting for instructions. The director placed her where he wanted her, asked if she knew her part, and explained the scene to her. She was to be a beautiful orphan visiting the home of an unhappily married couple. In the dialogue, she realizes that she truly loves the married man.

She was quiet as Kahn explained what he wanted, and when he asked if she was ready, she nodded without speaking. The actor assigned to feed her her lines took his place off camera, and Kahn called for a rehearsal.

They ran through the scene several times. Once the cueing actor lost his place in the script, and during another run-through, Jane's dress caught on a rough edge of the fake bench. But finally, Kahn felt ready to do a take.

Terrance came over to Jane, gave her a few words of encouragement, and then walked back behind the director.

Jane looked out over the studio and caught the eye of the cameraman. He smiled at her, and she smiled back. She felt wonderful. God, how she loved it all. The careful attention from the cosmetic artists, the great, vacuous studio, the intense heat of the lights, the casual attitudes of the crewmen who went about their business, totally unimpressed by what was going on. Even the fake set with its battered paint job. She loved every bit of it. She didn't want it to ever stop. She wanted the camera to start rolling and go on forever.

One of the assistants called out, "Take one," slammed the box, and Kahn yelled, "Action." The actor gave his first cue, and Jane spoke her lines for the rolling camera.

From within, once again the feeling of power and command began to take hold of her. Just as it had in David Granoff's studio. Jane let the energy created by her surroundings and her internal emotions combine to create the magic that was uniquely her own.

When the scene was over, Kahn said they would do it again, and gave Jane some minor directions about movements and inflections. When he went back to his chair, Malvey leaned toward him.

"What do you think?" asked Terry.

"There's not much to say to her. She does the whole thing naturally."

"She looks incredible, doesn't she?"

"That will tell the tale," said Kahn, nodding at the camera. "I've seen a lot of beautiful women who look like dogs on film. But I think she's got it."

"She's got a lot," replied Malvey. "And I wouldn't mind having a little of it."

"Well, you'd better get to it quick. If this test looks like I think it's going to, none of us will be able to do anything except work with her . . . if that."

"Stars," spat out Malvey.

"It's your own fault. You create them. Then we all have to live with them."

Elizabeth was going through much the same kind of morning as Jane. She had been groomed, and then taken to the stage assigned for her test. But it wasn't as easy or as exciting for Elizabeth. She was nervous and dreading every moment of the ordeal; unsure of herself, of the way she looked, and even if she could remember the words of her song.

Sam Withers and Mr. Grandison were on the set when she got there, and she tried to smile at them, but she was too frightened.

She stood slightly apart from everyone, chewing off her lipstick, as the crew made their final preparations. When she took her place, she looked distraught and upset.

Her voice was weak at first, and her manner was hesitant as she started to sing. But as she worked her way into the melody and forgot about what was happening around her, her voice gained strength and her presence improved.

She had been told that if she were actually filming a sequence, she would simply be mouthing the words in front of the camera and her voice would be taped in a recording studio. But for the test, she had to sing and look good on film.

There were several takes, Elizabeth growing alternately more nervous and then more resolute each time they started. Finally, the director felt he had enough.

Relieved that it was over, Elizabeth was finally able to smile. But she left the stage convinced that she had been terrible.

That night Jane picked up Morgan and insisted on taking him out for dinner to celebrate the day's filming. As they ate, Jane couldn't stop talking about how exciting the test had been.

"Well, I hope you'll still have time for the rally," said Morgan, leaning back in his chair and lighting a cigarette.

"Of course I will. I'm looking forward to it. I hope it does something constructive."

"It should. There are going to be a lot of speakers and we hope to get some attention from the newspapers, maybe even radio. It would be great if Winchell would pick up on it, or Kaltenborne."

"That would be good," agreed Jane.

They finished dinner and returned to Morgan's apartment, in its usual state of disarray.

"I really wish you'd let me clean up this place," said Jane, as they walked in. "I'm not much of a housekeeper, but all this dirt—"

"It's fine as it is," said Morgan. "I don't like a lot of fussing. I know where everything is, and I don't want to have to go looking for stuff when I need it."

Jane walked over to the bed and sat down. "Just what kind of stuff are you looking for?"

Morgan smiled at her. "What do you think?" he asked.

"I wouldn't know," she replied innocently.

"Then I'll have to show you."

"Yes. Why don't you show me. Show me everything."

Morgan smiled again and removed his shirt. He kicked off his shoes and pushed down his pants. Standing in his undershirt and shorts, he reached out to Jane.

"No. You haven't shown me everything yet."

Morgan looked her directly in the eyes and stripped off his undershirt and pushed down his shorts. When he was naked, he grinned at her.

"God, you're so big," she said. "I don't know how you're able to fit in me."

"I'll show you," offered Morgan.

"Don't rush me. I like to look at you. I like you to look at me. Do you like to look at me?"

"Sure. But not with all those clothes on."

Jane stood up and quickly pulled off her dress and underclothes. Then she lay back on the bed, opening her legs slightly.

"Do you like me?" she asked.

"Sure, baby, I like you." He reached out his hand and ran one finger around her vagina. He brought the finger back to his lips and slipped it into his mouth. Jane watched, fascinated as he licked his finger.

She reached out and placed one hand on his semi-erect penis and rubbed it gently.

For a long time they explored each other's bodies with their fingers, touching, probing. Their excitement grew and their movements became more frantic, their touches more demanding.

Jane drew Morgan down onto the bed and knelt over him. She kissed his face and ran her lips down to his neck and over his chest, biting, nibbling on his skin. She covered his body with her mouth, moving about, sucking and licking his legs and crotch and arms.

Morgan's body writhed on the bed, his arms reaching out for her, trying to pull her closer to him. But she held back, teasing and taunting him. She wanted him to want her more than anything else in the world. She wanted him to desire her alone, above all things.

Jane stood up on the bed, one leg on either side of Morgan's body. She ran her hands over her breasts and down between her legs. She stroked herself, challenging Morgan. He sat up and pushed his face between her legs, licking and exploring with his tongue.

"Want me," she whispered. "Want me!"

Morgan reached up and grasped her arms, pulling her down on top of him, impaling her on his erect cock. He pushed up hard inside her and she gasped with excitement as she rode his body, forcing herself onto him, harder and harder.

Morgan raised his head, running his tongue over her flat belly. His eyes suddenly widened and his breath was rapid.

"Now," he moaned. "Now. Push now. Push hard!"

Jane threw back her head, her eyes glazed in passion as Morgan pumped into her again and again.

Two days later, Jane was once again in Murry Edson's office along with Terrance Malvey. It was ten in the morning, and Jane had been up for some time getting ready for the meeting.

"We've seen your test, Jane," said Murry. "And we've decided to cast you in a part."

Jane sat up straighter in her chair.

Seeing the look of excitement on her face, Murry continued

quickly. "It's not a leading role. You only have a few scenes. The film is called *Dawn to Dusk*. Perhaps you've heard about it."

Jane had. She knew it was to be Greta Stewart's next movie. Jane assumed it was to be a standard Stewart vehicle: happy couple threatened by another woman, but Greta stands resolute and wins in the end, wearing an expensive and opulent wardrobe.

"We think you can play Sadie Eversleigh," said Murry. "She's the woman Greta's husband really loves."

Jane looked surprised. Greta was always the sympathetic character.

Terry understood the expression on her face. "We've changed the story a little," he said. "You'll understand it better when you see the script."

"Well, what do you think?" asked Murry.

"It's wonderful," breathed Jane.

"Good. We'll talk to your agent about terms. Constance Steiner, isn't it?"

"Yes," said Jane.

"Oh," Murry went on, "there's something else. We think it might be a good idea for you to have some publicity. Go see Hawkins and give him your background. He'll be expecting you. Also, Scott Mack will be co-starring with Greta and we think it might be a good idea if you were seen with him."

"Scott Mack?"

"Yes. We think it might stir up a little excitement if you and Scott have a rather public relationship."

"I see," said Jane.

"Publicity will set everything up. It's nothing for you to worry about." Murry looked at Terrance and then back at Jane. "I guess that's everything," he said.

Jane knew she was being dismissed and got up. "Thank you very much, Mr. Edson, Mr. Malvey," she began. "I—"

Murry took both of Jane's hands in his. "My dear," he said. "We have high hopes for you. So be a good girl and you can expect great things."

Jane smiled, nodded at the men, and left.

Terrance looked over at Murry. "Well, there goes another future monster," he said caustically.

• • •

The afternoon of the rally, Jane and Morgan walked across the bright green lawn of Griffith Park to the area designated for the meeting. A lot of people were already gathered, and they worked their way into the throng.

In addition to the participants, there were several policemen on foot and horseback around the area, and a few reporters standing near the temporary speakers' platform.

"It's a great turnout," said Morgan, looking about him.

"It's very exciting," said Jane. "I wonder how many people there are."

"Several hundred, I imagine."

In a few moments the speakers arrived and began a series of speeches which encouraged the audience to maintain their ideals and values.

Despite the fact that she'd heard it all before, Jane found herself caught up in the group emotion and excitement. Around her the faces of the listeners were alive and very involved, listening carefully to each speaker and cheering loudly at every opportunity.

But despite the electricity in the air and the lucidity of the speakers, Jane still privately wondered if anything said or done here today would make any real difference in the long run.

She supposed she was naïve. But speeches didn't feed people; food fed people. And Jane couldn't help thinking that the group would accomplish more if they worked directly with the people they insisted needed help.

The speakers finished and a march down Griffith Boulevard was to begin. The police had made an aisle through which the crowd was to pass. But many people ignored the directions shouted at them, both by the police and from the podium, and took off toward the street on their own. It was at this point that tragedy struck.

Several of the policemen were alarmed when the crowd surged around them. They tried to push the people back in line. The demonstrators pushed back, and there was confusion on both sides.

Police whistles blew, and the tumult caused some of the officers' horses to rear nervously above the heads of the crowd.

The line broke down entirely, and people began running in all directions, pushing and shoving each other. The excitement created by the speakers turned to panic as the tension started to break, releasing fear across the gathering.

Individual arguments between policemen and participants caused additional officers to wade into the mob, their night-sticks out, ready to protect their coworkers. The sight of the nightsticks further alarmed the crowd, and as they became increasingly frightened, their movements grew more chaotic.

The newsmen who had been standing idly on the sidelines sensed a good story, and added to the confusion by rushing forward to take pictures and get as much information as possible.

Jane clutched Morgan's arm. "Morgan, what are we going to do?"

"I think we'd better get out onto the street before this gets really bad."

They tried to move through the crowd, but found themselves hemmed in by the throngs of people, all pushing each other in an attempt to get away from the police, who were now closing in to try and restore order.

"Morgan. I'm frightened," said Jane. "We can't move."

"Don't worry. We'll get out all right. Just keep close. These goddamned policemen were hoping for something like this. They want to hurt us. They hoped that something would happen to give them a chance to move in on us."

Jane turned and saw a reporter bearing down on her, camera in hand. My God, she thought. If he gets a shot of me and it turns up in the paper, I'll be finished at Global. Just a few hours earlier she had been planning her future. And now, one photograph could destroy the whole thing. No film company wanted an actress who showed up in demonstrations and brawls. She had to get out of here.

The situation was getting worse. Many of the policemen were now actually using their clubs, hitting the heads and arms of the demonstrators. Women screamed and tried to protect themselves. Jane saw two policemen drag a man she recognized off to a wagon, and she stood horrified as another was beaten to the ground. A woman stumbled and fell before Jane, and she reached down to help her up only to be pushed down herself by a man trying to get away from the police.

Fighting back to her feet, Jane momentarily lost sight of

Morgan. When she found him, she cried, "Morgan! Get me out of here. Get me out of this. I can't stand it!"

He grabbed her arms and tried to calm her as the crowd surged around them. It was a scene of complete chaos as the demonstrators and the police fought brutally, all of their fears and frustrations erupting into violence.

"Come on," said Morgan, grabbing her hand and dragging her along. Jane stumbled beside him, just missing being hit by a policeman's upraised hand as he attempted to subdue a man near her. In a few moments, Jane and Morgan were in a stand of trees, out of the main part of the confrontation.

Jane thought she had stopped breathing. For a few seconds she couldn't catch her breath. There was a smear of dirt on her cheek and a scratch on her arm, but otherwise she was unhurt. Morgan's shirt was torn, and he had a large gash above one eye.

They looked at each other, and Jane fell into his arms, crying. He ignored her, staring back at the carnage on the lawn.

"Those dirty bastards," he whispered. "Those dirty bastards. They were hoping for this. They wanted it. They wanted us to panic so they could move in and beat us. Jesus Christ! I hate all policemen. Shit! This really messes up the march."

"The march," exclaimed Jane, pulling away from him. If she hadn't been so frightened, she would have laughed. "There are injured people out there. I could have been hurt, and all you care about is the goddamned march."

Morgan grabbed her shoulders. "You fool. Don't you understand. It's not us. We don't matter. None of these people matter. It's the cause . . . the reason we met here. That's what's important." He turned back to look at the park. His face was suffused with rage, wild and uncontrollable. "The cause," he shouted over and over again. "Nothing matters but the cause."

CHAPTER *Seven*

MORGAN CALLED EARLY the morning after the horrifying scene in Griffith Park. He wanted her to come over. But Jane told him that she had to be at the studio.

Actually, she only had to drop by and pick up her script. But she was sure that Morgan would spend their time together vilifying the authorities and complaining about the rally. And Jane just didn't want to relive that terrible day.

After she finished at Global, Jane stopped and picked up a copy of every local paper. She searched through them for any mention of the conflict, fearing she would find a picture of herself illustrating the articles.

She had several tense moments as she quickly scanned the papers, but then she leaned back and sighed with relief. The photographers had missed her. She'd been very lucky this time, thought Jane. But she'd be damned sure she was more careful in the future.

Pushing the papers aside, her thoughts turned to Morgan. Now that she was actually doing a picture, Jane knew she wouldn't be able to spend as much time with him as she had, and attending the meetings was impossible. Jane was honest enough with herself to realize that she was doubly grateful to Murry Edson. Not only was he giving her a chance at the career she wanted so badly, but he was also freeing her from politics. Her schedule would require her to pull away from the committee meetings and political discussions she had been attending. And after the rally, Jane wanted very much to be away from revolutionary concerns.

For the rest of the day, Jane read her script. She was delighted to find that she had so many scenes and thought about how it would be when she really started shooting. Her imagination lifted her away from the frightening memories of the rally and took her into a dream world where she could see thousands of people sitting in darkened theaters, staring up at her image on the screen.

That evening Morgan called again. Again he wanted her to come to his apartment. He sounded a little depressed, and Jane thought that perhaps he'd want to talk about something other than the day before. She finally agreed to go.

Morgan let her into the apartment, and then slumped down in the chair and lit a cigarette. It was obvious that he'd been drinking.

"It was good of you to drop in," he said sarcastically.

"You asked me to come."

"Yeah. Well, we've got a lot to do. There're some folders over there that need mailing out. We have to get started planning another rally and—"

"My God, Morgan. Wasn't yesterday enough for you? We could have been really hurt, or even killed. To say nothing of what the publicity could have done to us."

"That isn't important."

"It may not be to you. But it is to me."

"Always thinking about yourself, aren't you? Just because you got a part in a movie doesn't mean that the world is any better off."

"Couldn't we just forget about the world for one night?"

"Sure. It's easy for you, isn't it? The hungry and poor don't mean anything to you. You're going to be a movie star—"

"Morgan!"

"I've told you before, Jane. You're not important. No one is important. It's the ideals that matter. We have to change the whole world."

"*From this room*? Good God, Morgan. You can't even wash your dishes."

"You just won't understand."

"Can't," exclaimed Jane. "*Can't* understand. I can't understand how some obscure idea can mean more than a flesh and blood person standing right in front of you. That can't be right."

"I get it. You're sore because I didn't coddle you yesterday, because I didn't worry enough about *you*. Well, welcome to the real world, baby."

"I'm not so sure I like your reality."

"Well, that's just too fucking bad."

"Then I think we ought we call it quits." Her statement surprised both of them.

He looked up at her, a slight smile twisting his lips. "That's right. When you get a glimpse of what it really takes, then you dump everything."

"I'm not a coward, Morgan. I agree with a lot of what I've heard from you and your friends. Not all of it, maybe, but some. I just don't think I can help anybody else until I've helped myself. I want to make something of this chance that Global's given me. I want to see what I can do. And I can't work all day and shoulder the burdens of the oppressed all night. I'm not that strong."

"You just don't care enough."

"That's not true."

"I suppose you've been sitting all day practicing this little speech. Well you've given it, and we both know that all you care about is getting your ass in the movies."

"I haven't been practicing a speech. I hadn't even thought of these things until just now. But I'm glad I did. I'm glad I'm finally starting to understand."

"You don't understand anything."

"Oh, yes I do, Morgan. I understand a lot more than you give me credit for. Than anyone ever gives me credit for. I know there are people who need help, and I know there are individuals who really care about them and truly try to help them. But you're not one of them."

"You're crazy. Just look at the work I've been doing."

"I have looked. And all I've seen are some stupid letters to congressmen that will never be read, and a lot of slogans that nobody remembers. You're supposed to be a writer. Then why don't you write something that will actually make a difference?

Where are all those lofty thoughts? Why aren't they a part of a story that people everywhere will see and understand?'' She walked over to the table and began picking up papers and hurling them at him. "What are these, Morgan? All I see here are leaflets and lists of meetings. Is this what your important work is? Are you going to write an Academy Award-winning leaflet? Is that your great amibition now? Or have you just realized that you don't have what it takes to actually finish anything that anybody would want to read.''

"Shut up." Morgan was on his feet, his face contorted with rage.

"I won't shut up. Would you like to tell me all about your ambitions again? All about how you were going to write scripts and stories that would make a difference in the world, that would express your ideals and thoughts. Well, where are they? Or is it that talking about yourself is your only talent? Talking about what you want to do and what you want to change and how terrible everything is. Talking, talking, talking. Morgan, I've heard nothing but talk from you . . . and I've *seen* nothing at all.''

"I care about the suffering of humanity.''

"You make it sound like something you write on a grocery list. You don't give a damn about anybody or anything. You love suffering humanity because it makes you feel important. You think that because you shout slogans about the wrongs in the world, that makes you right.'' She picked up a picture of striking steelworkers in Pennsylvania. Pointing at it, she waved it in Morgan's face. "You're no better off than these people. They're at least involved in their own lives. And you only live through their pain, their grief. You don't have a life of your own. You don't write—''

"I'll start writing again as soon as I'm finished with—''

"With what? With the war in Spain? The homeless in China? The Nazis? But then there'll be something else, won't there? There'll be a new tragedy to fill up your time so you don't have to face yourself, don't have to accomplish anything. Don't have to come to grips with what a miserable failure you really are. You talk about exploitation. You're exploiting these people more than J.P. Morgan ever could. Because you're using them to hide from yourself.''

Morgan's hand shot out, slapping Jane hard across the

mouth. "You bitch," he screamed at her. "You fucking, cheap bitch. I should kill you."

"Careful, Morgan. That doesn't sound very humane," she answered. Jane wiped her hand across her mouth and found that her fingers were sticky with her own blood. She looked at it, and then stared at Morgan. "Where's your compassion now?"

"You don't deserve any. You don't deserve anything."

"That's fine with me. Because I don't want anything from you."

"Yeah? You're wrong there, and you know it. You'll always want what I've got. You came here the first time with hot pants, and you've stayed because you loved it. You'll always love what I've got."

"I think I can even get over that."

Morgan grabbed her hand and pushed it against his crotch. "Sure you will." He laughed. "Feel it. Feel it, baby. You know you want it. Go on, make it hard.

"Don't stop, baby. I like it. Feel it, touch it." His grip tightened on her wrist as he rubbed her hand up and down the front of his pants. "Keep it up, baby."

"Morgan . . . I don't want—"

"Yes, you do, baby. We both know you want it."

She pulled her hand away. "I'm leaving now."

"The hell you are," he shouted, reaching out and grabbing the top of her blouse. With one movement he ripped it open, exposing her naked breasts. "Do you think I'm cruel, Jane? Well, let's just see how cruel you think I am."

He grabbed her head between his hands and began kissing her, hard. His teeth bit into her lips as he forced his mouth onto hers.

Jane pushed him away and tried to cover herself with the torn blouse. "Stop it, Morgan."

She reached out to slap him, and he grabbed her hand. "Fight me." He smiled. "Go ahead and fight me, you cunt."

"You son of a bitch. *Let me go!*" screamed Jane as Morgan picked her up and walked over to the bed. He threw her down onto the sheets and stood over her.

"You're going to like this a lot, baby," he whispered.

Jane was suddenly very calm. She knew she couldn't win if she fought him. And there was no one to help her. The whole thing seemed to be happening to someone else. It was as if she weren't even really there. She looked up at Morgan, his face hard and brutal. But she wasn't frightened of him. Instead, she almost pitied him.

Morgan reached out and pushed her skirt up to her waist, and then pulled her panties away from her body.

Undoing his pants, he lowered his body onto hers and entered her quickly, driving hard into her.

Jane didn't move or utter a sound.

"Do you like it, baby? I knew you'd like it." Morgan kept talking until he came, and then he rolled off her onto the bed.

Jane looked over at him with disgust. "Are you finished?" she asked, her voice emotionless. "Because if you are, I'd like to go home now."

Morgan didn't answer.

Jane stood up and adjusted her clothing, pulling the torn blouse together and tucking it tightly into her skirt to hold it in place. She opened her bag and carefully repaired her makeup. She looked down at her former lover.

"Strange, isn't it," she said lightly, "that you can care so much for so many . . . and so little for one."

Morgan turned his face away from her.

"I don't expect you to look at me, Morgan. You can't even face yourself."

"Get out of here," he said. "Just get out!"

"I'm going. And I'm not coming back."

Jane walked to the door. Glancing back at Morgan, she smiled slightly. "Oh, about those leaflets . . . stuff them yourself."

She left the apartment, quietly closing the door behind her.

Greta Stewart stormed into Murry Edson's office without a glance at the receptionist or secretary. Banging the door shut behind her, she marched directly to the desk and faced her boss.

"You dirty son of a bitch," enunciated Greta carefully. "How dare you?"

"Greta," exclaimed Murry, standing and coming around his desk to greet her. "How nice. You look lovely this morning. You start rehearsals tomorrow, right? And then you'll be making another picture. Naturally, I'll come down on the first day of shooting to wish you luck."

"You're the one whose going to need luck if you don't explain just what the hell you think you're doing by putting that little bitch nobody in *my* picture."

"Greta," replied Murry, sitting down again behind his desk, "I don't know what you're talking about."

"I am talking about," Greta said with horrible slowness, "the fact that in two weeks, I am to begin a new picture. *In* a role that you and that bastard Malvey talked me into against my better judgment. And this morning, quite by accident, I discover that the little tramp who knocked me down at Terry's party is to be in the film. I am talking about deceit and lies. I am talking about your total lack of sensitivity toward me as an actress, a person . . . *and a star*." Greta threw her arms out dramatically.

"Now, Greta, dear," consoled Murry. "You can't possibly mean that harmless little actress—"

"Actress!" screamed Greta. "Whore is more like it."

"Now, Greta. Jane Turner is a nice little girl who has a small, almost insignificant part in your new picture. She can't possibly—"

"You're goddamn right she can't. She can't possibly be in my new film. She can't possibly be on the same set with me. How dare you hire her without asking me first?"

"Greta—" Murry tried again.

"You listen to me," continued Greta, mowing him down. "If that little bitch comes anywhere near my picture, I'm walking."

"Now, Greta. You wouldn't do that. You're a great actress. Everyone knows that. You certainly have nothing to fear from a beginner."

"Fear!" Greta almost strangled on the word.

"After all, you're an established star. And we think it would be good for you to have Jane Turner in your next film."

"For *me?*"

"Yes, you. Jane's role, small as it is, is a pivotal part of the plot. And with Jane in the part, you don't run the risk of working with an established actress who *just might* take some of the spotlight away from you. If Jane even slightly succeeds in the role, *you* get the credit for having the courage to work with a new talent. If she fails, then everyone will say that she simply couldn't match your performance. You can't lose."

"I can't lose because it's not going to happen," said Greta flatly.

Murry Edson was used to temper tantrums. In his business, he had learned to listen impassively through accusations, pleas, and threats. Nothing upset him very much, except the possibility of losing a dollar. His calmness was based on his knowledge that he always had the final word. And when he chose to utter it, no one at Global Films dared to oppose him. Now he felt it was time.

"I must remind you, Greta, that you have a contract with us."

"Bullshit!"

"A very strong contract that will hold up in any court."

"*Bullshit!*"

Murry thought that at least Greta was consistent in her choice of words.

"Greta, I think you had better stop being hysterical and listen to me," said Murry softly.

The tone of his voice made Greta shut up and look at him closely.

"As painful as it would be for me—for us—if you were to walk off the set of *Dawn to Dusk*, I would have to put you on suspension. You know what that means, don't you? We would have to cast someone else in your role. And who knows how long it would be before we found something else for you? And while you're on suspension, you don't receive *any* money. If I were you, I'd think about that."

"I don't know how much this most recent—uh—romance, cost you. But I do know that the two minor episodes during *A Long Road* were very expensive. As a matter of fact, that stagehand is still driving his new car. I saw him last week."

"The son of a bitch," said Greta.

"And, of course, there is that little matter of taxes . . ."

Greta didn't answer. She stared out of the window at the Global lot. Murry gave her a few moments to think things over, and then walked up to her and put his arms around her comfortingly.

"Now, Greta girl, don't you worry about Jane Turner. You're

a big star, and this film will make you even bigger. You'll see. We know what's best for you."

Greta gathered the last shreds of her dignity. "Very well," she said quietly. Then, lifting her chin, she looked defiantly at Murry. "But I want my dressing room redecorated, no visitors on the set, and Edith Head to do my costumes."

"I can do it all for you—except Edith. She's under a strict contract at MGM. There's nothing I can do for you there. But just wait until you see what Charles Dupre has created for you. You're going to look incredible. Why, there's real—uh—fur on some of the dresses . . . *mink*."

"Really?" asked Greta.

"Absolutely. The New York office didn't want to spend the money. But I said there was nothing too good for Greta Stewart."

She looked at him suspiciously, but didn't speak.

"Now go home and relax. Tomorrow you start rehearsals. In two weeks, we'll be shooting. You'll want to be at your best."

"Naturally," said Greta, as if nothing else had ever entered her mind.

Murry saw Greta to the door, and then returned to his desk and sat down. Wiping his forehead with his handkerchief, he reached out and pushed his intercom button.

"Tell maintenance to paint Greta's dressing room. And call Charles Dupre and tell him to stick some goddamn fur on one of Greta's costumes."

"Fur?" asked his confused secretary.

"Yeah. Tell him to use monkey if he has to," snapped Murry. He turned off the intercom, leaned back in his chair, and went on with his work.

Hawkins was delighted. He had introduced Jane and Scott Mack to each other, and they seemed to be hitting it off beautifully. And on the first day of rehearsals, too. A time that was usually very tense.

Hawkins liked Mack, as all his friends called the star. Of course, there was that little sexual problem, but Hawkins considered himself broad-minded. After all, he thought, if he had ever had any inclinations in that direction, Mack would be the man he was sure he'd be most comfortable with. But, naturally, Hawkins never thought about doing anything like that.

Jane and Mack sat in canvas chairs, waiting for Greta Stewart to arrive. Jane was having a wonderful time. It seemed that she and Mack, as she'd started calling him almost immediately, had known each other for years. She listened attentively as he told her about his ranch out in the valley.

Jane had already heard a lot about Mack from Mr. Malvey. It seemed that Mack lived on the ranch with a male friend. He had a herd of pure-blooded horses, which he rode superbly, an extravagant collection of Chinese pottery, and an extensive library.

Mack had come to Hollywood five years earlier from the New York stage. Tall, dark, with romantic good looks, he had been virtually an overnight sensation. He was inevitably cast as the steadfast, boyish, and often perplexed leading man.

Virtually everyone in the business was aware of Mack's lover of seven years, Bill Tremont. A few giggled about it, others were intrigued, while most simply didn't give a damn. As far as Global was concerned, as long as Mack kept his private life to himself, they didn't intend to interfere with a sure-fire box office favorite. Besides, as Terry Malvey often pointed out, it was much better to have Mack comfortably settled with a boy than out behaving like Ken Holt, combing the streets for young girls.

Scott Mack was a perfect choice for a public romance with Jane Turner. He always got good press coverage, and they would look spectacular together. An added benefit was the fact that since there wouldn't be any real entanglement between the two personalities, the studio could control and arrange events the way they wanted.

In the past, Mack had gone out on studio-arranged dates, but he had continually resisted any efforts of the publicity department to link his name with any of the starlets they were trying to promote.

But today, Hawkins was very hopeful. The couple seemed to like each other, and Mack appeared to be very comfortable with Jane Turner.

Greta still hadn't made her appearance, so Hawkins decided to see what he could do about making some arrangements for them.

He walked over to where Jane and Mack were sitting and suggested that they might like to go to a premiere the following evening. Then he held his breath and waited for Mack's reaction.

Mack looked at Jane for a long moment, then replied, "That sounds like a good idea. What do you think, Jane?"

Jane smiled at him. "I'd be delighted to go."

"Fine, fine," gushed Hawkins. "Jane, after rehearsal, you go by wardrobe and pick out a dress. I'll take care of the car and everything else."

"All right," said Jane.

Hawkins continued making plans for the couple, but was interrupted by the arrival of Greta Stewart, only one hour after the time she had been called. She was followed by the director, Earnest Kahn, who immediately apologized to everyone for being late.

Greta didn't bother with manners and went directly to Scott Mack.

"Mack," she intoned, holding out her hand, "how nice to see you again. And how glad I am that you're to be in my picture." The emphasis on "my" was almost too slight to be noticed.

"Greta," returned Mack, "it's always nice to costar with you. Do you remember Jane Turner?"

Greta had been carefully ignoring Jane since walking onto the stage. "Who?" she asked, while waving hello to the propman.

"Jane Turner," repeated Mack carefully, as if Greta was hard of hearing. "She's going to be in the picture with us. I'm looking forward to working with her."

Greta finally turned toward Jane. She silently looked her up and down, taking in every aspect of Jane's clothes, hair, and makeup. "I think you're going to be wearing some of my old costumes," she said.

"Oh?" said Jane.

"Yes. Are we ready to start the rehearsal?" asked Greta. "Earnest. I would like to get started."

"Right away, Greta. Let's begin with the scene in the nightclub."

Greta nodded and moved over to the improvised set.

"Don't let her get you down," whispered Mack.

"I won't. Do you suppose I'll really be wearing her old costumes?"

"Not unless they decide to pad your hips," replied Mack as they went to work.

The next night the girls' apartment was a scene of complete chaos as Mable and Elizabeth attempted to get Jane ready for the premiere.

Jane had selected a black sequined gown. With it she wore a long, black chiffon scarf along with diamond earrings and a bracelet given to her by her mother. She had arranged her hair onto the top of her head, and her makeup had taken hours to complete.

Elizabeth continually ran to the window to see if the car had arrived yet, while Mable attempted to calm Jane down.

"I simply don't understand why you're so nervous," complained Mable as Jane rushed to the mirror for the tenth time to check her hair. "After all, you've been to premieres before."

"*Not* with Scott Mack. And not as an actress working on a picture. We're going to be introduced and interviewed by the commentator. You'll be able to hear me on the radio."

"Well, if you don't lean toward the microphone, I doubt that anyone will hear you."

"Oh, that's right," moaned Jane. "I'll have to bend close to the microphone." She practiced bending.

Mable caught a glimpse of the deep décolletage of the dress. "Well that should certainly make you popular, at least with the front row," she commented.

"Oh, God," said Jane. "Maybe I should change."

"You look beautiful," exclaimed Elizabeth, returning from the window. "Imagine going out with Scott Mack. Back in Toledo I never missed one of his movies. My mother said he was the handsomest man she'd ever seen."

"Had your mother known a lot of men?" asked Mable.

"Why . . . I—"

"Never mind," said Mable. "You do look nice, kid," continued Mable, returning her attention to Jane. "When is Miss Mack coming to get you?"

"Really, Mable," said Jane. "There's no reason to be snide."

"I'm not being snide. I was an extra on one of his pictures, and he was a doll to be around. That sound you hear in my voice is simply envy directed toward whatever he's got hidden away up there in the hills. I bet if I could get Mack alone for about an hour, I could change his whole life."

"I doubt it," said Jane. "He seems very happy the way he is."

"Why would you want to?" asked Elizabeth innocently.

"Mable is talking about the fact that Mack is gay," explained Jane.

"He is?" asked an astonished Elizabeth. "Well . . . imagine! I never knew that."

"That would make you the only human being in the movie business to be in ignorance," said Mable.

"Well, I still think he's very handsome," said Elizabeth. She looked defiantly at Mable. "And so does my mother."

Jane laughed. "Well I guess that puts you in your place."

"Wherever that is," muttered Mable.

Since she'd been talking, Elizabeth had missed the arrival of the enormous Packard limousine which drew up outside, and the doorbell surprised them all. Elizabeth opened the door and nearly fainted when Mack smiled down at her.

Mable was left equally speechless when Mack remembered her from the film she had been in with him. After a few moments of idle chatter, Jane and Mack left for the theater.

On the way, they talked about New York and their favorite places in the great city. Jane felt the conversation was just getting interesting when the car pulled up at the entrance to the Roxy Theater.

The premiere that night was for Ken Holt's latest western movie. There was a gigantic blowup of Ken on horseback over the entrance, a red runner was spread from the sidewalk to the door, and red velvet cords blocked off the crowds that had come to see the stars.

Hawkins had been very wise in selecting a Ken Holt picture for Jane's first public appearance. Westerns never got the attention afforded the romantic dramas of Greta Stewart, Bette Davis, or Mary Astor, or the great biblical epics favored by DeMille.

But Ken Holt was popular, and since he usually drew a good-sized crowd anxious to see him arrive on horseback wearing his white and silver costume, Hawkins was reasonably sure of a decent turnout for Jane and Mack.

The couple's arrival had been kept a complete secret from everyone but the press and the announcer at the Roxy, and when Mack stepped out of the car, the crowd went wild. He smiled and waved, and then reached back into the car and helped Jane out.

At first she blinked at the lights, then smiled and waved with one hand while with the other she released the long scarf from around her throat, giving the audience an ample view of her décolletage.

Hand in hand, they walked up the runner to the announcer whose voice was amplified over the area as well as being broadcast over live radio.

"Why, look everybody," he exclaimed. "It's Scott Mack. Good to see you, Scott." They exchanged a masculine handshake.

"This is certainly a surprise," lied the announcer.

"Good evening, Paul," said Scott. "It's nice to see you."

"And *who* is this lovely young lady?" asked Paul, who had read a complete press release on her earlier.

"This is Jane Turner. She's going to have a featured role in *Dawn to Dusk* with Greta Stewart and me."

"*Isn't* that something," boomed Paul. "*Jane Turner*. What a lovely young woman. I'm sure that'll be one picture we won't want to miss."

"Thank you," replied Jane, leaning forward to the microphone.

"We all should have known that you would steal a march on us," said Paul, looking slyly at Mack. "You *would* find her first. Ha-ha-ha. Well, thank you for stopping by. And we'll be looking forward to seeing more of you, Miss Turner. *Scott Mack and Jane Turner,* ladies and gentlemen," he shouted as Jane and Mack went into the theater. "Aren't they a perfect couple?" Paul leaned close to the microphone. "And just between you and me, I hear they've been together almost all of the time since they met," he whispered conspiratorially.

Standing just inside, Jane and Mack looked at each other and laughed.

"Well," said Jane, "I suppose that's true. We met yesterday, spent a long time together at rehearsal, and then we worked again today and we're out tonight. We *have* been inseparable since we met."

"Darling," intoned Mack.

"Dearest," whispered Jane.

They laughed again.

When the car reached Jane's house, Mack got out and walked her to the door.

"You're going to be all right, kid," he said, smiling at her. "You're a good sport. I've had a good time, which, believe me, ain't easy when you have to sit through a Ken Holt western."

"Thank you," said Jane. "You've been very kind. I appreciate it. I hope . . ." She stopped.

"What do you hope?" asked Mack.

"Well, it's just that I know the studio talked you into all this. I hope it's not going to be too boring for you."

"In the first place, the studio can't talk me into anything I don't want to do. And in the second place, I think we're going to be good friends. I'd like you to meet Bill."

Jane realized this was a great compliment, and took it as such.

"And," continued Mack, "if you have any problems or questions, just ask me. I've seen or been through practically everything they can throw at you out here, and I might be able to help. Just don't start believing your own publicity. Take your work seriously, but never yourself. You don't want to become another Greta Stewart."

"No," said Jane thoughtfully, "of course not."

CHAPTER *Eight*

FILMING ON *Dawn to Dusk* began on a hot July morning. Jane woke up early that day, dressed casually, and tiptoed out of the house so as not to awaken her roommates.

After hair, makeup, and costuming were completed, she was driven to Stage Four, where most of the film would be shot. Scott Mack was already there and welcomed her heartily.

"I guess you're nervous," said Mack. "Well, just stop for a minute and listen to me."

Jane wasn't allowed to sit, but there was a standing board, slightly slanted, with armrests she could lean against. She eased herself against this apparatus and turned to Mack.

"I hope you know how ridiculous you look," he commented.

Jane and Mack had become good friends and traded barbs without concern about his star status.

"Not any more ridiculous than I feel. But if I sit down in this dress, Mr. Dupre will kill me. And may I say that you don't exactly look your best this morning. Just what did you and Bill do last night?"

"That is none of your business. And if you were a lady, you wouldn't ask."

"If I were a lady, I wouldn't be trying to get into the movies."

"But you are. And that's what I want to tell you. There are certain things you must always remember. And today is one of them. This is the first day of your first real part. I want you to remember it fondly. There will be other times, the premiere of your first film, the Academy Awards. But today is very important to you. Not just for what it can bring. But for what it is. Don't miss out on what's happening or lose the day because you're frightened. Everyone here knows what they're doing, including you. Just let the experts guide you and you'll be fine. You have nothing to worry about."

"Thank you," whispered Jane. "I—"

A commotion at the door interrupted her. Greta Stewart, only a little late, had arrived. And almost immediately behind her were Murry Edson and Terrance Malvey.

"We just came down to wish everyone luck," boomed Murry. "It's going to be a great picture. With Terry producing and Earnest Kahn directing, and our dear Greta and Mack," continued Murry as if he were playing a role, "along with the newest member of our family, Jane Turner, I feel this picture is going to be great. I can feel it in my bones."

"Really?" asked Greta, unimpressed. "I won't have any champagne," she went on, ignoring the traditional bottle being circulated. "I think I'd better go and rest. I feel this picture is going to take everything out of me. Working with inexperienced people is so tiring. I only hope I don't exhaust myself." She smiled wanly and went to her on-set dressing room, moving as if she were on her way to the gallows.

"Whew," said Murry, after Greta was gone.

"Well, that was a nice bit of preparation," said Terrance.

"What do you mean?" asked Jane.

"Well, in so many words, the divine Miss Stewart was telling us that if there were any problems, they wouldn't be her fault. They would be due to Jane's lack of experience, or the fact that our star had to work too hard in the role and was weakened. Of course, that would cause her to be sick—a great excuse in case she gets lucky some night and doesn't want to come in the next day. I just hope she can give as good a performance when the cameras are rolling."

"Don't you worry," said Murry. "Greta's a pro. Everything will be fine. Just you wait and see."

"The eternal optimist," said Terrance. "I hope you can handle her, Earnest."

"Don't worry," said the director. "I've worked with Greta before. I know just what she needs."

"We *all* know what she needs, or at least what she wants," said Terrance. "But Global doesn't make that kind of picture."

Elizabeth was having trouble balancing the positive and negative aspects of her life. Her picture had been postponed, and that was depressing to the young singer. But the studio had promised her that it would begin production soon, and they had increased her salary and extended her contract. But other than study the same music over and over again and watch her diet, Elizabeth didn't feel that she was doing very much as far as her career was concerned.

Ralph Mason was paying more attention to her. She saw him often. They rarely went out, but Ralph would come to the house and sit in the kitchen while Elizabeth cooked for him. And because she was making more money, she was happy to lend him some from time to time, since he wasn't working much.

Each time Ralph left, Elizabeth found herself looking forward to the next time they would be together.

Her fascination with Ralph was a complete mystery to Jane and Mable. Jane just couldn't understand how a talented and sweet young girl could be interested in someone like Ralph, while Mable simply thought that Elizabeth was dumb. The worst part of her roommate's relationship, as far as Mable was concerned, was the fact that Ralph always seemed to be around the apartment.

One morning, Jane and Mable met in the kitchen at their usual time and found that Elizabeth wasn't in the apartment. And it didn't look as if she'd been there all night. Jane was immediately worried about her friend, but Mable was convinced that Elizabeth had finally gotten what she'd wanted all along from Ralph Mason.

In a few moments, Mable was proved right as Elizabeth walked into the house looking a little tired and slightly hung over.

"Good morning," she said bashfully. "Are you both up?"

"No," answered Mable. "We're both on a desert island playing with ourselves. Jesus!"

"Are you all right?" asked Jane.

"Of course I am. At least, I think I am. I mean—"

"You don't have to talk about it if you don't want to," said Jane.

"Oh," began Elizabeth, "it's just that it was very private and I . . . Well, I think you ought to know. After all, you are my best friends. Ralph told me last night that he loved me."

Neither of her roommates expected to hear this, and Mable sat and stared at Elizabeth. Jane walked to her and touched her arm.

"That sounds very . . . nice," she said.

"It was wonderful." Elizabeth sighed. "We were driving around in his friend's car, and we stopped near the beach and the waves were just coming in. We sat on the sand for a while, and then got back in the car and watched the ocean for the longest time." Elizabeth giggled. "Ralph had a little bottle of scotch. I've never had scotch before. It's kind of bitter."

"So what happened?" asked Mable ruthlessly.

"Well, we had a few drinks from the bottle and then he kissed me, and, well . . . touched me, you know—"

"I know. I just wonder if you do," said Mable.

"But it was very romantic, and we had another drink and he said he loved me."

"Well, go on," said Mable.

"We stayed in the car all night." Elizabeth looked slightly ashamed. "I know I shouldn't have let him . . . but we *love* each other. So it must be all right. I mean, it's not as if I was just with someone I didn't really care about."

"Was that directed toward me?" asked Mable.

"Oh, no, of course not. You and I are just different. I couldn't ever have anything to do with a man I didn't love. And I really love Ralph."

"I see," said Mable.

"Are you all right?" asked Jane.

"You asked that before," said Elizabeth. "Of course I'm all right. We'll probably be married soon."

"Married!" Mable was stunned.

"Of course. I have to go shower and get dressed. I have a voice rehearsal today."

Elizabeth left the kitchen, and Jane and Mable stared at each other.

"Married," said Mable in an awed voice. "Jesus! How stupid can that kid be?"

"Well, you never know. He might marry her."

"Shit! He said he loved her last night when he got so hot he couldn't stop. He isn't going to marry her. And if he did, it'd be even worse."

"But what can we do?"

Mable shrugged. "Nothing. It's none of our business."

"But we can't let her go on thinking—"

"Thinking! Hell, it's obvious that she can't think."

"Listen, Mable. Right now she's in there lost in a dream of wedding dresses and organ music and a little house somewhere for just the two of them."

"Could be the three of them, if she's as dumb as I think she is."

"God, Mable. Don't make it any worse. We can't sit by and let her throw herself away on this bum."

"When did you become the little mother?"

"Oh, Mable—"

"Oh, nothing. You have a career to think about. And *I* have a life of my own. Besides, there's nothing either of us can say or do that will make the slightest difference. The poor kid's hooked on that bum."

Jane looked defeated.

"Jesus, Jane, don't take it so hard. It's not your responsibility."

"I know. It just seems so sad."

"We've all got sadness, honey. Every goddamn one of us."

But sadness didn't appear to be a part of Jane Turner's life. It seemed that things couldn't be better for her.

Having only been an extra in the past, Jane had never experienced the pressures or responsibilities that comprised having a feature part in a motion picture. And she fluctuated between exhaustion, exhilaration, and confusion.

Each morning she was at the studio by eight, and usually stayed until near six. And several evenings a week she and

Mack would make the rounds of the nightclubs. They were seen by the press at the Trocadero and the Mocambo. They lunched on the same salad at the Brown Derby. They had dinner at the Pineapple Room and Chasens and Romanoff's, and attended parties given by Murry Edson, Mr. and Mrs. Charles Coburn, and Lewis Stone, who was enjoying a lot of public attention as Andy Hardy's father. They even double-dated with Clark Gable and Carol Lombard. It was a strenuous and demanding schedule, but Jane found that she enjoyed every minute of it and was enthusiastic about the greatest and least important event.

She admitted to herself that she did miss Morgan. But then she realized that it wasn't the man himself she wanted, but the remarkable sexual release he had provided. There were times when she was tempted to call him, particularly after a long day at the studio. She would think about his touch, but then her mind would focus on their last night together, and she would turn away from the telephone, resolutely putting Morgan out of her mind, and concentrate on her performance in *Dawn to Dusk*.

Her dedication to the part was paying off. Jane had completed most of her scenes in the movie, and Murry Edson, Terrance Malvey, and the director, Earnest Kahn, had seen the rushes and were very happy about the way things were looking.

But the real test was yet to come. Even though a film was always shot out of sequence, it turned out that Jane's biggest scene was to be her last one.

So far, Jane's part had only required her to be sweet and romantic. But in her final scene with Greta, she had to be something more than just a pretty young girl. She had to be a woman, forced to give up the man she loves to a woman she despises. Her face and her every action had to display a wide range of emotions. The camera would be placed on a dolly so that it could move around and catch Jane and Greta from every angle. And Jane knew that Greta was going to try and completely dominate the scene. The conflict was important to the film. But it was more important to Jane. For her own sake, for her future, she had to present more than just a dumb-blond image.

She had studied her lines and moves carefully, but she was still nervous and frightened.

Greta had been her usual self through most of the film. In fact, she had behaved a little better than she usually did. She was having a fling with one of the scenic artists, a man who was a step above her usual choice in men, and it had apparently given her confidence. She had thrown a few hair brushes at the hairdresser and screamed at the costume designer. But it seemed that she was doing these things more to keep in practice than out of any real malice. Murry was delighted with Greta. But Terrance cautioned him to hold in his exuberance. The movie wasn't over yet.

Terrance was right. The morning Jane and Greta were to shoot their big scene started badly. It was raining, and Greta's hair, never her best asset, was practically impossible to control in the humidity. Surrounded by huge fans the hairdresser labored over her, but it didn't help. And Greta took out her frustration about her appearance on the hairdresser, making his life hell throughout the session.

Greta's temper wasn't quieted when she walked onto the set and found that Jane was not yet ready. Greta filled the time by making snide comments about inexperienced actresses.

Jane's appearance did not make Greta any happier. The younger woman was wearing a soft, white gown with no jewelry. Her hair was simply styled and her makeup was restrained. She looked virginal and innocent. Greta, in her opulent sequined gown and paste jewels, looked hard and experienced by comparison—exactly what the movie required. But Greta didn't approve of it.

It was a long scene, set in a ballroom after the party was over. There were to be a lot of artistic touches, such as a burned out match in an ashtray and an upended bottle of champagne in a wine cooler. Earnest Kahn had worked hard with both of his players independently. He had high hopes and yet expected the worst.

Earnest called for a rehearsal and silently moaned as he watched the disaster unfold before him.

Despite her hatred of Jane, which Earnest had been counting on to make sparks fly, Greta was playing her part as gently as possible, attempting to create the impression that she was the victim. She was quiet, sad, and totally wrong. And since Jane's character was also quiet and gentle, the scene looked ridiculous.

After the run-through, Earnest made several suggestions to both women and then called for a take, hoping that once the cameras were actually rolling, Greta would let loose. But it didn't happen. Every intonation, every move from both women was slow and studied. It appeared that the four minute scene was going to last as long as *Ben Hur*. As the scene continued, Terrance Malvey slipped into the sound stage and stood behind Earnest's chair. When it was over, he leaned forward.

"Jesus Christ, Earnest. What the hell was that?"

"*That* was Greta being sympathetic."

"If it'd been any slower, she could have played it from her bed."

"She sees the character differently than we do."

"Shit. This is supposed to be the big confrontation. She has to dominate Turner."

"Greta doesn't see it that way. She wants the audience's sympathy."

"Well, they'll have to send her get-well cards if she keeps this up, because I'll personally put her in the hospital."

"I'll think of something."

"Well, you'd better. Unless you want us all to be laughed out of town." Terrance looked toward the set where the two actresses had gone to opposite sides and were waiting for their next instructions. Both were surrounded by makeup and hair technicians, making slight adjustments.

"Well," said Terry. "They've gone to their corners. Now if Greta will only come out fighting. Jesus! You have to admit Turner looks good. She could almost carry this scene alone if her dress were a little lower. No wonder Greta hates her."

"How do you feel about taking a chance?" asked Earnest, a gleam in his eye.

"At this point I'd try anything. And that doesn't exclude the possibility of murdering Greta Stewart."

"All right. You asked for it." Earnest got up from his chair and, with a bright smile, approached the set. Greta looked up at him expectantly, but he walked past her and went directly to Jane, his arms outstretched.

"Jane, Jane," he said. "I think you're doing beautifully. But when you say, 'I'll let him go,' make sure that you turn your face to the camera. We don't want to miss those wonderful blue eyes of yours.''

"Th-thank you," said Jane, sounding a little confused.

"But other than that, you're doing fine. And you look beautiful. Absolutely beautiful." He leaned forward and whispered something in her ear and then stood back and laughed. Jane laughed, too, but her eyes still showed confusion.

Earnest turned to go back to his seat and, as he passed Greta, he waved casually. "Doing fine, Greta."

The star stood silent, watching Earnest sit back in his chair and turn to the cameraman. She couldn't hear everything he was saying, but she was able to make out that Earnest was suggesting that the camerman move in tighter on Jane.

For a few seconds, Greta was overcome with surprise and depression. Then she looked across the set toward Jane. The young woman was smiling, joking with her makeup man. Slowly, Greta was filled with rage. She wanted to rake her nails across those wonderful blue eyes. She was so angry she couldn't think properly. All she wanted to do was jump up and down on Jane Turner's face.

"Let's try it once more," called out Earnest.

The two women took their places, Greta's eyes so filled with hate that Jane involuntarily took a step backward and had to be moved back to her mark by one of the assistants.

A man ran forward and snapped the box marked *Dawn to Dusk* with an unreadable scene number and the take number on it. The set quieted down and Earnest, now sitting on the edge of his chair, called out, "Action."

Greta took a deep breath and spoke her first line. She had intended to continue playing the character as she had all day, but it took all of her control not to reach out and slap Jane. Her voice was tight, hard. Over Jane's shoulder, Greta could see Earnest Kahn, his eyes fixed firmly on Jane, ignoring Greta entirely.

Jane spoke her first line, and Earnest nodded, smiling.

Greta was almost out of control with anger. She barely waited for Jane to finish her speeches before she hurled her lines back at her.

Jane was actually a little frightened of the woman before her. But she knew that she couldn't let Greta walk away with the scene. Her character was desperate, and so was Jane. She spoke with quiet control and looked helpless before the torrent of abuse being thrown at her.

At the climax of the scene, Greta almost screamed her final line: "'You could never take my place!'" and then broke into hysterical laughter as Jane collapsed into tears.

Earnest called out, "Cut, print," and came forward to his stars.

At the end of the series of unconnected scenes that constituted the final yet unedited rushes from *Dawn to Dusk*, Murry ordered the lights up and leaned back in his chair and lit a large cigar.

"Well, ya gotta admit that Turner's hotsy-totsy."

Terrance nodded, but didn't answer.

"I mean," continued Murry, "that the knockers on her alone could hold up a picture. Jesus, she's something. And that sweet little ass of hers, bouncing around the set . . . Every man on the crew must've been hard all the time."

"If they were, you can be sure that Greta took care of them," said Terry.

"You're probably right. Did you think Greta was looking a little old?"

"Greta *is* old for this kind of role. And it's about time she realized it. Us, too."

"Hmmm," murmured Edson. "Hard for a woman. Not young enough to do the sexy stuff and too young to do mothers."

"Can you imagine Greta as anyone's mother? Of course, if you decide to do a remake of Dracula—"

"But Greta's good in this film."

"You're right. She played the bitch just like we hoped. She might even cop an Oscar for this part."

Murry appeared to think this over. Then he turned his mind to other things. "Now, about this Turner girl. She's obviously no Greer Garson, but she *does* look good."

"She did a nice job," agreed Terry. "But, of course, the lines gave her all the sympathy. That scene with Greta is good, although Greta walks away with it."

"Do you think she's got anything?" asked Murry, bored with Terry's ramblings.

"Hard to tell if she'll ever be an actress. But she does have a cetain magic all of her own. The camera loves her, really loves her."

"In the right part, that's enough," said Murry.

"Yeah, I know. Wait a minute . . . I think I've got it."

"What?"

"You remember that Broadway play we bought a few years ago, *On Duty*?"

"Hell, yes. I remember. You wanted it for some reason. I didn't see it, still don't. But you had to have it."

"And now you're going to thank me."

"Yeah?"

"Sure. Look, it's a comedy about some rich people, stuffy old ladies and hard-boiled old men. Young man with an acceptable fiancée falls for a sexpot and invites her out to the country estate for the weekend. The sexpot doesn't have to do anything but wriggle around in low-cut dresses. We might even be able to stick in a pool scene and get the sexpot in a bathing suit."

"The story, the story," moaned Edson. "What happens in the story?"

"Nothing much." Terrance shrugged. "Turns out the sexpot doesn't really want to marry the rich guy, but was only playing him along so she could meet his father and get him to invest in her boyfriend's factory. The girl has to be dumb, but sweet. She walks around the estate making all kinds of mistakes and attracting attention."

"Doesn't sound very funny to me," said Murry.

"Don't worry about it. It'll be great. Of course, we need someone like Preston Sturgis to direct—"

"We don't have Preston Sturgis. And you're crazy if you think I'm going to borrow him from Jack Warner. It'd cost a fortune."

"We can do it without him."

"And where does the Turner girl come into it?"

Terry looked at Murry, exasperated. "The sexpot, of course. She's a natural. She won't even have to act. All she has to do is strut around the set, pushing those tits of hers at the camera and looking vacant. The audience will love her."

"Sounds good. Who for the other woman, the one the guy is supposed to marry? And don't suggest Greta. The strain of those two together this time was enough to last me forever. You'll have to find somebody else."

Terrance thought for a few moments. "It's not a big part. How about Esther Mahoney? She's dark, the right age, and her pictures haven't done badly."

"Might be all right," mused Edson. "And what about the guy?"

"No sense throwing away good publicity. Keep Mack with Jane for another picture. The columns will love it, and they do photograph well together."

Murry nodded. "All right. I guess Turner's agent is going to want more money. We can talk to her tomorrow. I don't want to waste any time on this. We've got a lot of good press going on this supposed affair between Turner and Mack, and if the audiences like her in *Dawn to Dusk*, I want something on her ready to release quick. I suppose Mack won't mind going on with the romance."

"They like each other. Seem to have a good time."

"Good time," spat Murry. "Hell, he couldn't get it up for her if we put a gun to his head."

"Well, as long as the press is happy and the public likes it, I don't care if privately he's getting it up for sheep."

"Sheep," said Murry, shocked. He looked at Terry suspiciously. "Do you know something I don't?"

"Jesus," moaned Terrance. "It was a joke."

"Oh. Well, this new picture of yours better be funnier."

Jane was invited to see some edited scenes from *Dawn to Dusk*, and was so excited and embarrassed about seeing herself on the screen that she was unable to make any kind of objective criticism of her own work.

But everyone around her said she was great, and she could only hope they were right. She wasn't so sure herself. The other actors seemed to know things of which she was completely unaware, and Jane didn't know how she could learn them. She decided she would watch everyone very closely on her next picture.

Jane had been given her assignment in *On Duty*, and she was eager to go to work. But she hoped the film would be finished before Christmas. She hadn't been back to New York for a long time, and had been thinking that it would be nice to spend the holidays with her family.

There was a happy crew on *On Duty*. Esther Mahoney was Global's answer to Mary Astor, always a lady, often with a sense of humor but never vulgar or out of control.

In her private life she lived with her quiet, bookish husband and two cats in a sequestered part of the valley, and rarely took part in the Hollywood social life. She had been one of Mack's friends for a long time and took Jane in on his recommendation. The three got along very well.

But as filming started, the production had its share of bad luck. Esther was ill for several days, which effectively closed down the set, and Mack sprained his ankle when he was thrown by one of his horses, which again delayed production.

As November approached, *On Duty* showed no signs of being anywhere near completion, and Jane resigned herself to spending the holidays in California.

Mack invited Jane to his place for Thanksgiving, but Jane thought she should stay with Elizabeth and Mable. Naturally, Elizabeth had invited Ralph to join the girls, and Mable had added a few friends of her own, so Jane thought it would probably be a full, if not particularly exciting day.

The three girls cooked all morning, Elizabeth taking over the kitchen and running it with complete authority, insisting that in Toledo things were done properly on holidays. Jane and Mable scurried around doing as they were told until Elizabeth pronounced everything ready. It was an excellent dinner causing all three women to swear they wouldn't eat anything for days. When the kitchen was cleaned up, Jane excused herself and drove to Mack's.

"I hope you don't mind," said Jane, as Bill let her in. "Both my roommates have dates, in fact, Mable has several, and after dinner I felt like I was in the way. If I'm in the way here, too, I can leave again," she finished anxiously.

"Of course not," said Bill. "Glad to have you. We've finished dinner and the Movie Star and the rest of them are out at the barn staring at the horses. I don't know what they expect them to do." Bill often referred to Mack as "the Movie Star." It was always said as a joke, but privately Bill hoped that the nickname would keep his lover's ego under control.

Jane laughed.

"Come on out and have a drink. Or would you rather join the hayloft crowd?"

"No. I'll stay with you. I don't know anything about horses, although we used to have one on the farm in Kansas. But I never thought it liked me very much."

"They're not supposed to be very bright animals," commented Bill.

"Thank you," said Jane as she followed him out onto a tree-shaded patio which faced a large swimming pool. Off to one side was a tennis court, and farther away Jane could see the barn where Mack and his guests had gone. Jane sat down and Bill brought her a drink.

"It's nice here," she said. "Peaceful."

"You should see it when the Movie Star decides that all of Hollywood is bunk and that he must go back to New York and do real theater. It isn't so quiet then."

"Why doesn't he go?"

"Don't you start encouraging him! I quit my job in New York to follow him out here, and now I've got a nice little real estate business going, and he's making a lot of money. In a couple of years, when the bank balance is big enough, we'll go wherever he wants. But we've got to get things set first."

"I see. But if he isn't happy—"

"Mack suffers from the same thing all of you acting people have. He's insecure about his talent, his looks, and his career . . . everything. So the minute something looks strange or unusual, he thinks he must be in the wrong place."

"You seem to understand him so well."

"I don't have much choice. After all, I have to live with him."

Bill told Jane all about real estate, a subject she didn't understand at all, then the others came back. Mack welcomed her warmly and introduced the guests, who included several young married couples who had nothing to do with the movies, three startlingly handsome men whose names Jane never got right, Lucille Evans, an aging character actress who had made a fortune portraying outraged matrons, and Madam Olga Brinski, an elderly and severe-looking acting teacher who had had to leave New York and come to California for her health. She now took a few, carefully screened pupils for coaching.

Madam Brinski glanced at Jane without interest and devoted herself to Lucille.

At first Jane couldn't understand why the young married couples were there, but eventually she learned that they were people to whom Bill had sold property, and in the process, became friends. They were charmed by Bill, in awe of Mack, terrified by Olga, confused by the young men, and madly in love with Lucille. The married men eyed Jane when their wives weren't looking. Everyone talked at once, and Jane relaxed in a large chair and listened.

She had been at the ranch before, and although she wasn't very interested in the great outdoors, she enjoyed being with Mack and Bill. The property covered a number of acres, but the house was small. It had three bedrooms, a massive kitchen, a small dining room, and a living room decorated with natural wood, comfortable overstuffed furniture, and modern paintings. Books were everywhere.

After the married couples, two of the young men, and Olga had gone, they moved inside. Mack sat on the floor next to Jane's chair, sipping from a brandy snifter, while the group talked about the movies.

"Mark my words," said Lucille, "nothing is going to be important for the next year except *Gone With the Wind*. In fact, it could be longer before people finally get tired of it all."

Mack smiled. "Well, since I'm not playing Rhett Butler, I can't say that makes me feel very good."

"You don't have to worry," said the remaining young man, "you'll always be a star."

Bill choked and Mack gave him a dirty look.

"Has anyone met Vivian Leigh?" asked Jane. "I haven't even seen her."

"She is spectacular," said Mack. "I met her at the Derby not long ago. She has the most incredible green eyes I've ever seen."

"Well, here's to her," said Bill, raising his glass in a toast. "It ain't going to be easy for her to live in this town when you think about all the women who wanted that role. Everyone of them is going to be out for her blood."

"She's got Selznick," said Mack. "She doesn't need anybody else."

"From what I hear," said Lucille, "she's got Larry Olivier, too."

"Really?" asked Bill, impressed. "That is something."

"Well, they've spent enough money on that picture," said Lucille. "And I can't believe that everyone's going to Georgia for the premiere."

"It's a great publicity gambit," said Mark. "Actually, I'm looking forward to seeing the film. And as far as the money's concerned, the studios have made plenty this year. From what I hear it's been the biggest in the history of the movie business."

"Well, they're spending it, too," said Lucille. "There's *Dark Victory* for Bette over at Warner's, and Metro's doing the *Wizard of Oz*, and I hear Global wants to do *Salome* . . ."

"And *you* want to go back to New York," said Bill, leaning over to Mack.

"I didn't say that . . . today," replied Mack, grinning at him.

Bill called out to Jane, "See what I mean?"

Jane laughed.

"What secrets have you two got?" asked Mack.

"Nothing, just talk," replied Bill. "And, by the way, I hate to break this up, but several of you people have to get up early in the morning."

"I don't," offered the young man.

"Pity," said Lucille, "probably do you a world of good if you did."

Mack walked Jane to her car. "I'm glad you came," he said.

"Thank you. I felt so silly just barging in here, but I'm glad I came, too."

"You're always welcome. Always. Bill likes you, and so do I. And after all, we *are* sweethearts, you know. At least that's what Louella said in her column last week. I personally hope it's going to be true for a very long time."

CHAPTER *Nine*

HOLLYWOOD WAS PREPARING FOR CHRISTMAS, but Jane Turner and her coworkers were still laboring on *On Duty*. One morning during a costume adjustment, Jane was called to the front office. The messenger seemed to think it was very important, and as Jane rushed across the lot, thoughts of instant dismissal or an accident in New York plagued her mind.

When she reached the executive building, Jane found her Aunt Maud standing at the receptionist's desk, surrounded by several suitcases.

"Aunt Maud!" exclaimed Jane.

The elderly lady turned, beaming at Jane. Maud Watson was in her late sixties, had married wealth in New York, and lived there in considerable style and comfort for over forty years. She had graying hair, piled insecurely on top of her head, a plump figure which was always perfectly and expensively dressed, and bright, mischievous eyes. Now a widow, Maud had been the mainstay of the Turner family after they had left Kansas, dedicating enormous amounts of time, energy, and a considerable portion of her bank account toward making Jane's family happy and secure. She was charming, motherly, imperious, and slightly mad. Jane couldn't imagine anyone she'd rather see.

"Darling!" said Maud, throwing open her arms. "Dear me, what have you got on?" she asked, looking down at Jane's flowing robe which inadequately covered a skimpy bathing suit. "Is that what you wear all the time?"

Jane hugged her aunt, then explained, "It's a costume. A messenger came for me, but he didn't say what it was about. *What* are you doing here? I mean I'm glad to see you, but—"

"Didn't you get my telegram?"

"No."

"I wonder if I sent it," mused Maud.

"It doesn't make any difference," said Jane. "Why don't you just tell me."

"How clever of you," said Maud. "I believe I remember exactly what I said. 'Your mother and sister off to Europe again, so I'm coming to California to see you.'" Maud smiled, impressed with her total recall.

"Mother and Mary went to Europe?"

"Yes, dear. I'm sure your mother wrote you about it. They left very quickly, and since they seem to go back and forth so much—"

"But why didn't you go along as usual?"

Maud looked disgusted. "They were going to Germany. And there are the strangest people over there now. That dreadful Hitler and all those blond men marching about. They say there's going to be a war. I don't know about that, but Maggie wanted to see for herself just what is happening so she can report it in her magazine. And, of course, Mary wasn't about to let her go alone. But I just didn't feel like it."

"So—"

"And it's so dull and cold in New York right now that I decided to come and pay you a visit." Maud suddenly looked alarmed. "You don't mind, do you?" she asked anxiously.

"Of course not. I couldn't be happier. It's wonderful." Jane looked down at all the bags. "But I'm afraid we don't have room in our apartment for—"

"Oh, dear. I'm not going to move in on you. I have a reservation at the Beverly Hills Hotel."

"But where's Maria?" asked Jane, knowing that Maud would never leave New York without her faithful maid.

"She's such a sissy. *I flew here*. And she absolutely refused to get on the plane. So I sent her along on the train with my trunks and just brought these few things with me. I'm sure she'll be along soon, and then I can get organized and find a house."

"A house?"

"Why, yes. I thought it would be nice to stay several months, and then when your sister and mother get back from Europe they can come out and join me for a vacation. You know your mother's marrying Laurance Austen?"

"Yes, of course. Mother wrote me."

"Well, this would be a perfect place for a wedding. After all that dreadful publicity about Laurance's first wife going insane in that hospital and taking all those nasty drugs and things before she died, I'm sure your mother would like a very private ceremony. Out here she's not so well-known. And, of course, this is so much closer to Hawaii—so nice for a honeymoon."

"Do they want to go to Hawaii?"

"I haven't the slightest idea, but it's good to know it's there if they want it."

As usual, Jane was overwhelmed by her aunt's ability to maneuver things. "It's wonderful to have you here," said Jane, impulsively hugging Maud again.

"Thank you, dear. Can you have dinner with me tonight? We'll go wherever you want. I suppose you know all the best places."

"We can go to Chasen's or Romanoff's. Oh, I forgot, I have a date. But it's all right, you can come along."

"On your date? How very interesting."

"I'll explain it all later. I have to go back to work now, but I'll meet you at the hotel at eight."

Jane asked the receptionist to get Maud a taxi and, after seeing her off, she returned to the set happier than she had been for some time.

When Mack picked Jane up that evening, she told him they were going to be joined by a relative of hers from New York. He sighed and reluctantly agreed. Mack didn't mind company, but he knew about relatives. Most of the successful movie community had someone from back home on their payrolls or an extended visit, living off their famous family member.

Mack and Jane went to the Beverly Hills Hotel and walked into the lobby. They were dressed for dinner, Mack wearing black tie with a white jacket which set off his tan, and Jane in a silver-gray evening gown with a gray scarf around her throat. They made an impressive couple, and several of the hotel's guests pointed and nudged each other as they passed.

Jane asked for Maud Watson, and a harassed hotel clerk looked wildly at them for a moment, then recognizing Mack, became very gracious. He personally called Mrs. Watson's suite and returned with the information that she would be with them shortly.

Mack suggested they sit down, and they took a table in the lounge and ordered drinks. Within ten minutes Mack had signed four autographs and finished his cocktail, but there was still no sign of Maud. Jane was starting to apologize when an unmistakable voice interrupted her.

"My dear, my dear," cried Maud, floating up to them. "*Do* forgive me. I had every intention of being on time, but I'm afraid everything takes twice as long without any help around. Do I look all right?"

Maud was wearing an evening gown of purple satin that was obviously Mainbrocher. With the dress, she had on diamond earrings, bracelets, pins, and an impressive necklace. In case it should turn chilly, an ermine scarf was casually thrown over her arm.

"You look wonderful," said Jane. "Aunt Maud, this is Scott Mack."

"Mr. Mack," said Maud, holding out her hand. "How nice to meet you. Your face is terribly familiar to me. Perhaps we've met before."

"Aunt Maud," said Jane, horrified. "Mack is a major star."

"Of course. How stupid of me. I think it's very nice of you to allow me to go on your date."

Scott had met a lot of visiting relatives, but he had never come across someone like Maud Watson. He was delighted with her.

"It will be a pleasure, Mrs. Watson," said Scott, turning on his irresistible grin. "I didn't realize that Jane had such a lovely aunt."

Maud simpered and batted her eyelashes at Mack.

"Well, I'll tell you a secret," she said, causing Jane to wonder madly just what Maud was about to reveal. "You see, Jane is not *really* my niece. Her grandmother was a cousin of mine, but we were never sure just how many times removed.

So that makes Maggie, Jane's mother, a cousin, too. But, of course, I'm not sure what relationship I am to Jane. But I always think of her as my niece," she finished, looking at Mack as if he knew all about such things.

Grinning, Mack bowed to Maud. "I didn't think you could really be Jane's aunt. You look far too young," he whispered.

Maud beamed delightedly at Mack, and the threesome left for Romanoff's.

The famous restaurant was crowded with Hollywood's elite and a large number of its leading personalities, many of whom stopped by Mack's table to say hello. Maud met Irene Dunne, Robert Donat, and James Mason.

Hedda Hopper was there, and she pulled up a chair and gushed over Jane and Mack. When she was introduced to Maud, Hedda remembered her from a charity ball in New York for which Maud looked on as the two ladies discussed the city, common friends, and the importance of finding the right hat. Miss Hopper was well-known for her often amazing and unusual headgear, but Maud had worn a few peculiar hats in her time as well, so they had a lot to talk about.

Eventually, Hedda got down to business. "And they say that Mrs. Watson is your aunt?" she asked Jane, taking out a note pad.

"Actually, an honorary one," said Jane. She started to explain, but Scott pinched her under the table. Hedda was busily taking notes and didn't notice Jane's slight squeak.

"Yes," said Maud. "Jane is my dear, dear niece. She's just made a movie and—"

"I know all about Jane," said Hedda. "I hear very good things about your first film," she continued, turning back to Jane.

"Thank you," said Jane. "It was very exciting for me."

"And how was working with Greta Stewart?"

"Miss Stewart was . . . uh, very professional."

"I'm sure she was," said Hedda dryly. "And, of course, Mack is in your next picture."

Jane was visibly confused. "Oh, no," she said anxiously.

"You mean you're not working together on *On Duty*?" asked Hedda.

"I didn't mean that he wasn't in the picture," explained Jane. "I just meant that he's not in *my* film. I'm in *his*. His and Esther Mahoney's."

Hedda looked approvingly at Jane. "I understand." Turning back to Maud, she put her notebook away and kept talking. "Now Mrs. Watson, I hope you're not going to leave town before we have a chance for lunch."

"Not unless you're booked up for the next several months," replied Maud. "I'm taking a house here and plan to stay at least until the spring."

"How lovely. Then I'll call next week and we'll have a good time talking about all our friends in New York."

Maud grinned wickedly. "I always think enemies are so much more interesting," she said.

Hedda laughed delightedly and left them.

As the powerful writer walked back to her own table, Maud said, "I seem to remember her from New York. But I thought she wanted to be an actress."

"She did," replied Mack. "Still does, occasionally. But her real talent seems to lie in that column of hers. You certainly made a hit with her."

"How nice," said Maud who, having been presented at several courts, was not particularly impressed with a gossip columnist.

Later, after dropping Maud off at her hotel, Mack leaned back against the car seat and laughed loudly. "I don't believe her," he exclaimed. "She's too good to be true."

Jane looked affronted. "Don't make fun of Aunt Maud. She's a very special person."

"Jane! I'm not making fun of her. I love her. Besides, if I'd known that you were that well connected, I'd probably be taking you out in earnest."

"Bill would like that."

"Bill," said Mack. He smiled slightly. "What do you want to bet that he and Maud get on like mad?"

Jane thought for a moment, then smiled back at him. "You're right," she said. "They're going to love each other."

Elizabeth rolled over in bed and touched the pillow next to her. It was cool, and bare. She sat up, looking about the room. There was no sign of Ralph Mason. She got out of bed, grabbed a robe, and went into the kitchen. Ralph was sitting at the table, a cup of coffee before him.

"Good morning," said Elizabeth cheerfully, picking up his cup. "Oh, this is cold. I'll make some fresh."

"Don't bother."

"I don't mind. I'd like some myself." She busied herself about the sink and stove while she continued talking. "I must get some groceries today. We're almost out of everything. I'm going to have to move in here in order to keep things organized. You never remember to buy anything," she finished playfully.

Ralph Mason lived in an apartment house in an old area of Los Angeles. The neighborhood and the building had seen better days, but the apartment was cheap and large, and since Elizabeth had started spending time there, she took care of it and stocked the icebox.

"Why the hell do you keep shopping all the goddamn time?" he asked irritably. "Why don't you just leave things the hell alone?"

"You won't say that tomorrow morning when you don't have any coffee. You certainly are grumpy this morning," she teased, leaning over him and linking her arms around his neck. "Did you get up on the wrong side of the bed?"

"I'm fine," he answered abruptly.

Elizabeth returned to the stove. Still keeping her voice light, she asked, "Are you working today?"

"Sure. This morning I'm doing a big love scene with Claudette Colbert, and this afternoon I'm having lunch with Sam Goldwyn." His voice was bitter.

Elizabeth looked at him with compassion. "Don't worry," she said. "Things will get better."

Ralph didn't answer her. He got up from the table and walked into the living room. He stood in front of a small bar and poured himself a drink. When he looked up, he noticed Elizabeth staring at him.

"Isn't it awfully early?" she asked.

"Not if you don't have anything better to do all day."

"I—I guess I'd better get dressed. I have an early call."

"Good for you," said Ralph sarcastically.

Elizabeth left him and returned shortly, dressed for the day. "Shall I get some things for dinner?" she asked.

"Whatever you want."

"Do you need any money?"

"No."

"Are you sure? I have some extra."

"*I said no*!" Ralph yelled at her. "Jesus! Why the hell won't you listen?"

"I'm sorry," said Elizabeth meekly. She went to him and kissed him, but he didn't respond. "I'll be back early. It shouldn't be a long day."

"Yeah, yeah."

Elizabeth left the apartment and walked to the bus stop. On the way to the studio, she thought about Ralph. She was sure she must love him. She had gone to bed with him, let him make love to her. It must be real love, she thought.

But it wasn't easy. Ralph was so unhappy much of the time. Elizabeth knew that sometimes men took their unhappiness at work out on their families. Her father had been like that.

She remembered how much she had dreaded it when he came home angry from the factory. But her mother always said that that was the way men were. And it was a woman's job to try to make life easy for them. Women had to do what men wanted them to. Elizabeth's mother had always tried to please her husband. Elizabeth didn't remember them having a very happy life.

She and Ralph would be different, thought Elizabeth. He just needed a break, then he would be happy and they could be happy together. She was sure of it.

At the studio, Elizabeth went through her wardrobe test and then joined Sam Withers for a rehearsal.

Sam was in a terrible mood and picked her performance apart note by note until Elizabeth thought she was going to cry. Finally, he called it quits and let her go for the day. But as she started to leave, he called her back.

"You look tired, Elizabeth," he said.

"It's been a rough day."

"That's not it. Something wrong at home? One of your roommates giving you trouble?"

"No, of course not."

"I hear good things about Jane. She seems to be going somewhere. Is that what's bothering you?"

"No. I think it's wonderful that Jane's getting her chance. She deserves it."

"So do you. Don't let things get you down. You'll see. This may be only one scene, but it's gonna be important to you. The camera is staying on you through most of your song, the only cutaway will be to the principals, once. That's really something the first time out. So keep yourself together. Are you still watching your weight?"

"Sure. Don't I look all right?"

"Your shape is fine. But your eyes look a little tired."

"I've been having trouble sleeping. I think those pills I take to lose weight must have something in them that keeps me awake."

"Probably do. You could always take something to help you sleep."

"If I don't start to rest soon, I'll look into it."

"All right. Just take care of yourself." He leaned over and kissed her cheek, and then went back to his work.

Before returning to Ralph's apartment, Elizabeth stopped at the grocery store. Carrying the bags, she walked the last few blocks. Letting herself in, she called out to Ralph, but there wasn't any answer.

She went into the kitchen and found a note from Ralph saying that something had come up and he wouldn't be back until late that night. Elizabeth put the groceries away and then took another bus home.

"How does it look?" asked Murry.

"Good. I think we got a winner. You ought to see Turner in that bathing suit scene. I don't think the Hay's office can touch us, but Jesus, it's dynamite."

"Good, good," said Murry, smiling and nodding his head. "When do you think the whole thing will be finished?"

"Well, we're a little late, you know. But we ought to be done by mid-January."

"Oh, great," said Murry sarcastically. "That doesn't help the budget any. Can't you get it to move faster?"

"Christmas," said Terrance.

"Christmas," spat out Murry. "When are we releasing *Dawn to Dusk*?"

"First of March."

"All right. That means that we'll at least have something in the can in case she's a hit. Does she look good enough to start her in something else right after *On Duty*?"

"Yeah. I think so. I'm thinking about *Salome*."

"We'll have to think about that a lot. Anything else?"

"You might want to take a look at Baby Susie's latest work of art."

"Bad?"

"Stinks like a dirty diaper. She's *too* old to be a baby anymore. And she can't act at all. By the way, her mother's being a real pain in the ass again."

"What's bothering her now?"

"Aside from all the usual stuff about more money, Mrs. Baby Susie is all up in the air because her darling daughter's doll is not the hottest item this Christmas. She blames the studio for the slow sales."

"How the hell can she blame us?"

"Not enough publicity for babykins. According to Mother, if the public doesn't see baby, they won't buy baby's doll."

"What the hell does she expect us to do? If we send Baby Susie out on tour at her full height, dressed up as a six-year-old, she'll get laughed off the stages. Hell. Why do kids have to grow up? I guess it's time we got rid of her. I'll get legal on it."

"They're going to fight."

"Let them fight. It won't do them any good."

"Means we need a new child lead."

"We got plenty of kids under contract."

"Sure. But none of them can match Temple or Moore."

"Temple isn't getting any younger. She must be twelve or so now."

"Yeah." Terrance's voice was noble. "But America still loves her."

"Hell. Why couldn't they still love Baby Susie?"

"Love her? I'd be grateful if people would just stop hating her."

Maud Watson was installed in her furnished Beverly Hills house within two weeks of her arrival. She immediately sent for her butler and cook—Mr. and Mrs. Hardgrave—from New York, hired additional servants, rearranged the furniture, decorated for Christmas, and invited Jane to move in with her.

Jane loved the idea of living with her aunt. She adored Maud, and the large, beautiful house with its pool and tennis court would be a lot more comfortable than her little apartment. But Jane worried about deserting her roommates. She knew her share of the rent would be missed, and the idea of leaving Elizabeth and Mable alone together didn't seem very kind. Jane didn't know what to do.

The decision was happily removed from her hands when Mable announced she was going to Las Vegas with some friends and wasn't sure when she'd be back.

Almost immediately after Mable's news, Elizabeth hesitantly told her roommates that she was going to live with Ralph. She seemed happy about it, and Jane and Mable were glad to see her excited, even if they didn't think it was a good idea. Ralph hadn't thought much of the plan, either. It had taken Elizabeth several days to convince him to accept the arrangement. But Elizabeth first convinced herself and then him that things would be better between them if they were living together. She was sure she loved Ralph, and hoped they would be married soon.

Jane moved in with Maud almost immediately. But she didn't have much time to enjoy the house or her aunt's company. She was busy all day filming *On Duty*, and in the evening, she either had publicity dates to go on or her lines to study.

During her few, rare moments of leisure, Jane joined her aunt in entertaining all of Maud's new friends.

Mrs. Watson had arrived in California with letters of introduction to the older California families. But in a very short time, she had extended her acquaintance to include a wide range of people. Many of Maud's guests were complete strangers to Jane, while others were famous personalities. Billie Barnes, Louella Parsons, Gary Cooper, and even the hermitic Greta Garbo dropped in to see Maud. In addition, there was a constant stream of contract players from practically every studio in town. Maud didn't know MGM from Paramount, but she was a perfect hostess to all her guests, treating the starlets from Fox with the same graciousness that she extended to the matrons from Oakland. They all soon fell under her spell.

Jane's public romance didn't make any sense at all to Maud. But she took Mack and Bill's relationship as a matter of course and, as Mack had expected, Maud and Bill hit it off immediately.

Bill was a constant guest at Maud's, and he rarely missed stopping by for a drink on his way home from work.

• • •

Dawn to Dusk was previewed at a theater in the valley in the beginning of February. Maud, Jane, Mack, Murry, and Terrance went together, and as they exited after the show, the two film personalities were mobbed by fans. The cards put out for audience comments looked favorable. The women were delighted to see Scott Mack in any role, while their husbands appeared to take particular notice of newcomer Jane Turner. The movie would go into general release in a few weeks, and Global had high hopes.

Jane had finally finished *On Duty* and was taking a week off from work, lying around the pool at Maud's house. Elizabeth had also completed her scene, and she often dropped in to see Jane during the afternoons.

The two women sat in the sun and talked about the movies in general, and Elizabeth's concern that she had been terrible in her picture in particular. Jane tried to reassure her, but the young singer was very worried about her performance.

One day she showed up at Maud's in a very good mood.

"Guess what," she said happily.

"What?" asked Jane.

"Sam and Mr. Grandison tell me that everyone loves my scene in the movie—including Murry Edson. *And* they're planning another picture in which I will actually have a speaking part and play a character and everything. And I'll have three songs. Imagine!" Her face turned serious. "But I'll have to dance, too."

"It'll be easy for you," said Jane. "What wonderful news," she continued. "I'm so excited for you. You must be thrilled."

"I am. I came right over to tell you. I haven't even told Ralph yet."

"Sit down and tell me all about it."

"Oh, no. I can only stay a minute. I have to hurry home. I haven't even shopped for dinner yet."

"But we should celebrate."

"Later. I must run. But I just had to tell you."

Jane walked Elizabeth to the front door and watched her leave for the bus stop. Jane was happy for Elizabeth. This time, she thought, her delight in her friend's accomplishments wasn't dimmed by her own lack of success. They could enjoy their triumphs together.

• • •

Elizabeth rushed into the apartment, her arms full of groceries, and called out to her lover. He wasn't home, but Elizabeth was sure he'd be back soon and began sorting the food. As she worked, she thought about her morning at the studio. It had been wonderful. All those people around her telling her how well she'd done and how pretty she'd looked. And the plans they had were just as exciting.

Publicity wanted to take her picture again, and she was to sing at a lot of events, along with appearing on several radio shows where she would be heard by people all over the country. Elizabeth could just imagine the expression on her mother's face as she sat next to the old radio box in the living room and listened as her daughter's name was announced.

As Elizabeth moved about the kitchen, her hands began to shake and she dropped a pan on the floor, making a loud noise. Startled, she clasped her hands together and took several deep breaths.

Honestly, she thought, I have to get control of myself. Too much excitement in one day. She sat down and rested her arms on the kitchen table, staring at her hands as she gripped them tightly to stop the trembling.

She hadn't eaten all day. The studio had stressed the importance of her keeping her weight under control, and she didn't want to have anything until Ralph and she were together for dinner. Elizabeth got up, went to the sink, and took down her bottle of pills. The label recommended only one a day, but she reasoned that if hunger was making her shake, another pill would remove the hunger and let her relax.

She swallowed the pill and turned back to her chores. In a few minutes her hands were steadier, but she felt strange. Inside her, it seemed that she could actually feel her blood coursing through her veins. She became horribly aware of the functioning of the organs of her body. Suddenly, she was frightened. She looked around her at the shabby kitchen. Everything seemed to be larger than she remembered it. She stared at the stove for a few seconds as if she had never seen it, then turned her attention to the icebox and then the sink, fascinated by the porcelain whiteness and the small crack that ran across one side.

Her heart beating fast, Elizabeth found that she had trouble catching her breath. She was sure she could hear her heart pumping the blood that she felt moving through her body. It was terrifying to be so completely aware of herself.

Elizabeth didn't know how long she stayed standing in the peculiar condition of separateness from herself. When Ralph came home, he found her still staring at the sink.

"What the hell are you doing?" he asked.

Elizabeth turned to him and looked at his face as if she'd never seen him before.

"Hey," he said, giving her arm a shake. "You all right?"

Elizabeth finally was able to remember who he was. She smiled slightly. "Oh, hello," she said.

"What's going on?" asked Ralph.

"Oh, oh nothing. I just got overexcited, I guess."

"Excited? About what?"

"The studio. They liked my picture. They want me to do another one."

"Well, that's great. But you don't look very happy."

"I was hungry . . . I took another pill. Do you think it could hurt me?"

"I doubt it. What you need is a drink."

Elizabeth didn't answer, and Ralph went into the living room and returned with two glasses of straight scotch. "Here," he said. "This should make you feel better."

Elizabeth took the glass and held it for a second. "Drink it," ordered Ralph. "It'll calm you down."

Elizabeth drank obediently and did feel a little better. She smiled at Ralph. "I meant to have dinner all ready for you."

He shrugged.

"But don't you worry," she continued in a bright tone. "It'll only take me a few minutes. You go on in and sit down in the living room. I got us something special . . . steaks."

"Good. I'm hungry."

"Did you have a good day?"

"All right . . . nothing unusual."

"Well, you go rest. I'll have everything prepared real soon."

"All right. Do you want another drink?"

Elizabeth looked at her half-full glass. "Maybe just a small one," she replied.

Ralph got her drink for her and then returned to the living

room and sat down, holding his glass tightly in both hands. It *had* been an unusual day for him. But he didn't think Elizabeth would understand it. He had gone by Global, looking for work, and run into Ken Holt. The western star was finished shooting and was bored. He had invited Ralph, along with two of the studio's showgirls, out to his house. They had to be the youngest girls on the lot, Ralph thought. One of them, a blond, couldn't be over sixteen. But it seemed that Holt liked them young and looked at the two girls as almost mature. They'd certainly gotten some experience somewhere. They'd been all over the star.

Jesus, but that bastard knew how to live. Ralph had been a good sport all day, even smiling obligingly when Ken suggested that both women might want to join him in the bedroom, leaving Ralph all alone. But Ralph had just laughed and made himself useful, mixing drinks and keeping the drugs that Holt enjoyed on his day off ready for him.

As the afternoon wore on, Holt told Ralph that he was a good friend and that when he went to Mexico to film in a couple of weeks, he'd like Ralph to come along. He'd repeated the offer later, before Ralph left.

Ralph knew damn well what the trip meant. After work, Ken would want some young broads around, and it would be Ralph's job to find them and make sure they were all right—no diseases or anything. It wouldn't be much fun to be at the beck and call of Ken Holt all the time. But the trip might be interesting.

Ralph took a swallow of his drink. And there was something else. He needed to get away from Elizabeth. She was suffocating him with her cooking and her cleaning and her concern. He liked her all right. But she wasn't much fun anymore, and she'd never been much of a challenge. And she just didn't know when to quit and leave him alone.

She would take his departure hard, so it might be better to just not tell her. Just leave quietly some morning after she'd gone to work. She'd get over it, he thought. After all, he was getting over not having a career. Everybody always got over everything.

CHAPTER *Ten*

THE GREAT SEARCH LIGHTS snapped and popped into action as the crowds pushed against the barricades that lined the front of Grauman's Chinese Theatre. It was a warm California night, and many of the sightseers were eating ice cream as they craned their necks to see what was happening at the entrance to the movie house.

As yet, nothing major had taken place. A few lesser known personalities had arrived at the premiere of *Dawn to Dusk*, but the important stars had yet to make their appearance. According to movie protocol, actors who were guests at the opening would show up first, followed by the stars of the film being honored.

In a short while, excitement swept through the crowd as Bette Davis and George Brent arrived in an enormous limousine. Waving and smiling, they walked up the red-carpeted entrance. Then Ginger Rogers with her mother, Lela, arrived, followed soon by Gene Autry. Joan Crawford escorted by Franchot Tone, and Norma Shearer with her husband, Irving Thalberg, showed up at almost the same time and smiled hatefully at each other. Sylvia Sidney looked stunning in a red dress, and Miriam Hopkins was sweet.

Murry Edson and his wife, a plump woman wearing a

beaded black dress, a cascading orchid corsage, and too much
jewelry, were briefly interviewed by the master of ceremonies.
Murry said it was a great night and a great picture. He was sure
that all of the great Greta Stewart's fans were going to enjoy the
picture. When asked about newcomer Jane Turner, Murry
responded that she was a great little actress, and Global had
great hopes for her.

A loud cheer went up from the crowd when Sarah Miller, the
elderly character actress who had played a small part in *Dawn
to Dusk*, arrived on the arm of Terrance Malvey. Terrance was
also interviewed and said virtually the same thing Murry had.

When Mack's car drew up, he quickly leaped out, and the
crowd was beside itself, shouting and cheering him. He
smiled, waved, and shook hands with the people nearest him,
then leaned back into the car, offering Jane his hand.

Jane was nervous as she stepped carefully out of the car,
holding Mack's hand tightly. She was wearing a shimmering,
black silk dress, cut almost to the waist in the front and with no
back at all. Her chiffon scarf was also black, and her only
jewels were a large diamond ring and earrings borrowed from
Maud.

The couple stood on the sidewalk together, Scott waving
while Jane smiled shyly, accepting the crowd's adulation. Then
Mack turned back to the car and helped Maud alight.

At first, Hawkins had been against including Maud in the
opening, but had changed his mind, deciding that it might
make a nice homey touch for the young actress to be
accompanied by her beloved aunt, who also happened to be a
leader of New York society.

Maud was also in black. Her dress by Worth had a high
neckline and long sleeves. With it she wore a startling diamond
pin, several ropes of pearls, and diamond and pearl earrings.
On the hand with which she casually held a black fox stole was
a huge, blindingly beautiful, square-cut diamond ring.

She looked at the crowd briefly, somewhat dismayed by all
the sticky faces thrust forward toward her, but recovered,
smiled, and raised her head slightly. Mack stepped back for the
two ladies to precede him, and then whispered in Jane's ear.

"You're doing fine, sweetheart."

Jane smiled at him, and then she and Maud walked toward
the entrance.

During the crowd's reception of Mack and Jane, the announcer extolled upon the greatness of Scott Mack, the beauty of Jane Turner, and the charm of Maud Watson. He was virtually drowning in a sea of superlatives and was only rescued by the arrival of Mack's group at the microphone.

Scott said it was a pleasure to be with someone destined to be a major star, and Jane thanked everyone for everything.

Once inside the theater, they heard the crowd roar again.

"Greta must have arrived," said Mack.

"Who will she be with?" asked Jane.

"I'm not sure. I hear that RKO was willing to lend her King Kong," replied Mack.

Jane giggled. "I guess we'd better take our seats."

"Couldn't we wait?" asked Maud. "I want to see Greta Stewart."

Mack agreed, and they watched through the door, out of sight of the crowd, as the leading lady of *Dawn to Dusk* regally marched up the red carpet with Hawkins, head of Global's publicity, in tow.

"I guess they wouldn't let her bring her latest jock," said Mack.

"What?" asked Maud.

"Nothing," said Jane firmly.

Mack whispered to Jane that Greta was dispensing graciousness with the same abandon that Roosevelt gave away money. Jane privately had to agree that Greta was almost overpowering in her studied kindness and charm. Dressed in green, with an enormous collection of jewels dotted about her person, the lady smiled, waved, blew kisses, extended her arms, and, Jane thought, generally made a complete ass out of herself. The crowd adored it.

"My God," moaned Mack, "she's done everything but go down on the first row of fans."

"Hush," said Jane.

Greta swooped up to the microphone and started talking. The poor announcer found that the interview had been totally taken out of his hands and that Greta was in full charge. Gently moving him aside, Greta spoke of her great appreciation of her fans, and her devotion to work. She casually mentioned Scott Mack's able assistance in *Dawn to Dusk*—at which point Mack whispered "bitch," under his breath—and the great joy she'd had in playing her role in the movie. She hoped her following would enjoy the picture. "After all, I've done it just for them."

Managing to push his way back to the microphone, the announcer loudly thanked Greta for stopping by and saying a few words. She then allowed Hawkins to escort her into the theater.

When she found Mack and the others in the lobby, she walked up to him.

"Hello, dear," said Greta, checking her makeup in the wall mirror behind his head. "Shouldn't you be in your seat? I'll wait for you to get settled."

Mack knew full well that Greta would stand in the lobby until the following morning in order to insure that no one interfered with her entrance into the movie. He smiled at her, bowed slightly, and said, "Of course, Greta. But if I were you, I wouldn't follow Jane too closely."

Greta looked over at the beautiful young actress, then back at Mack. "Thank you, dear," she said sweetly. "And fuck you."

The next morning, Jane Turner woke up to find that her name was in every major column in America. Her much publicized affair with Scott Mack, her breathtaking beauty in *Dawn to Dusk*, and her incredibly glamorous appearance at the premiere the night before had culminated in her almost instant elevation to the rank of a household word.

Maud spent the morning clipping the articles and comments from the columnists, exclaiming over what Hedda Hopper, Louella Parsons, Adela Rogers St. John, Walter Winchell, and all the rest had to say.

The critics who wrote about *Dawn to Dusk* were less enthusiastic than the feature writers, about both the film and Jane Turner, dismissing them individually and collectively as so much cotton candy. But as far as the public was concerned, Jane was beautiful, had a superb figure, dressed provocatively, had a rich family, and was dating Scott Mack. They couldn't ask for anything more. She was a star.

At Global, Murry and Terry were very happy with the response.

"Goddamn," exclaimed Murry. "She's on her way."

"I'll say," agreed Terrance, tossing aside one of the newspapers. "The critics hated the picture, though."

"Fuck the critics. Who reads them, anyway? They don't even pay for their seats. The moviegoers read Winchell or Parsons. And you've got to admit, they love Jane."

"That's true."

"We'll release *On Duty* next month," Murry went on, rubbing his hands together, "but we'd better get her to work right away on something else. In fact, it wouldn't be a bad idea to line up several properties. Constance won't be any problem. She'll be happy to see that Jane has work coming along."

"I agree. When's Turner coming in?"

"I made an appointment with her for later this morning. You'd better be here."

"All right. Uh, I guess you noticed that our Greta didn't fare too well with either the critics or the columnists. Miss Hopper came right out and said that it might be time for a younger woman to play her roles, and that it wasn't fair to expect Greta to compete with someone who looked like Jane Turner."

"I know, I know. . . . What do you think we ought to do?"

"Well, I guess we—you better talk to her. If she doesn't see her way clear to maturing on screen, then we'd better think seriously before her next option comes up."

"We'll worry about Greta later. Right now, I want to make sure everything's under control with Turner. She's a real blond bombshell, and I see a great future ahead for her."

"What you see are dollar signs."

"Is there a difference?" asked Murry innocently.

Within a week after the premiere of *Dawn to Dusk*, Jane's career had gained considerable momentum. She had captured the public's interest and imagination. They wanted to see more of her. Murry Edson had worked out a new five-year contract with Constance Steiner, and in conference with Jane, Murry and Terry had outlined their plans, which included completing three pictures in the next seven months. She was to go to work immediately.

The publicity department swung into full gear and began churning out a series of new releases about Jane. Few of them bore any resemblance to the truth, but they were all effective in keeping her name before the public. It was decided that her relationship with Scott Mack would be discontinued and Jane would be another of Hollywood's "bachelor girls," who was saving herself for the right man. She and Scott were "just friends."

On the lot, technicians, contract players, and other actors went out of their way to say hello to Jane. Fans at the gate asked for her autograph, and she was given her own dressing room bungalow next to Global's other leading players.

Mack had told her to remember everything. But perhaps, she thought, even he wouldn't understand one of her most perfect moments when, one morning, after greeting the guard at the gate, he had directed her to her own parking place where the words "Miss Turner" were painted on a small sign.

Jane enjoyed it all, even though she worked very long hours. One evening after a hard day of fittings, interviews, and rehearsals, Jane returned home. It was almost nine in the evening, and her mind was occupied with the idea of buying a new car.

As she drove up the long drive from the road to the house, she could see a figure sitting on the front steps. At first she thought it was probably a fan who had found out where she lived and wanted an autograph. But when she pulled up at the front door, she realized it was Elizabeth sitting alone in the dark.

Jane jumped out of her convertible and called to her friend. "Elizabeth! What are you doing out here in the dark? Isn't there anyone home? Why didn't you go in and make yourself comfortable?"

Elizabeth looked up at Jane. Her face was closed and filled with sadness.

"Ralph is gone," she said flatly. "I went home after work today and found a note. He's gone off with Ken Holt to Mexico."

"Oh."

"He doesn't have a part in Holt's new picture. I checked on that."

"Then what will he be doing?"

Elizabeth shrugged. "I don't know. His note just said that Ken Holt had offered him the trip, and he was going to take it. He said he didn't know when he'd be back in Hollywood . . ." Elizabeth's voice cracked.

"Then he'll be back soon. You know they never stay on location long for westerns."

"Yes. But they're not coming right back. When I called casting to find out if Ralph had a part in the picture, the man said that Ken Holt was going to stay down there for a long vacation. I guess Ralph probably plans to stay with him." Elizabeth started to cry.

Jane sat down next to her and put her arms around the sobbing girl's shoulders. Elizabeth looked at Jane, tears streaking her face. "What am I going to do?" she asked in a soft voice.

Jane didn't answer. She continued to hold her friend for a few more moments, then suggested that they go inside. Elizabeth nodded without speaking as they walked through the hall and found Maud sitting in the drawing room with her embroidery spread out around her.

"Jane dear," said Maud looking up absently from her work. "You have had a long day. I was wondering when you . . ." Maud stopped when she caught sight of Elizabeth's face.

"Why, what on earth has happened?" she asked, dropping her materials and coming to the girls. "Elizabeth, dear. What's wrong? Can I help? Is there anything I can do?"

"Elizabeth's had a bad shock," said Jane. "I'm sure she'll be all right."

"Poor dear," murmured Maud. "Perhaps something to eat, or some coffee."

Elizabeth shook her head.

"I know," suggested Maud. "Brandy. Thomas always said that brandy was the best thing for shock." She rang for Hardgrave and sent him for brandy, then helped Jane seat Elizabeth on the sofa. Elizabeth didn't seem to pay much attention to what was happening around her.

Hardgrave returned with the brandy and, after giving Elizabeth a large swallow, Maud suggested that she had better stay overnight. Elizabeth didn't object, and Jane took her away to a guest room, got Maria to take care of her, and returned to Maud.

"Is she all right?" asked Maud as Jane came back into the room.

Jane smiled. "I think you gave her too much brandy. She was almost asleep as Maria was trying to undress her."

"The poor girl. Whatever happened?"

"Ralph," answered Jane flatly.

"Ralph? You mean that dreadful young man she's brought here a few times?"

"Yes."

"But what about him? He isn't dead or anything, is he?"

"I wish he were," said Jane vehemently. "He walked out on her." Jane told Maud Elizabeth's story, and then leaned tiredly back in her chair.

"How very sad," said Maud. "Of course, one hopes that she'll get over him soon, particularly since he wasn't very nice. But a lot of women do have very strange tastes in men."

"Yes, I know," said Jane, thinking of Morgan.

"Well . . . we'll keep her here with us for a few days. I suppose she must go to the studio."

"Yes. I hear they have high hopes for her. She's starting a new picture soon. In fact, she may have already started. I haven't talked to her much recently." Jane leaned her head back against the chair.

"You look absolutely exhausted, dear. Are you hungry?"

"Not very."

"You must eat something. I know. Why don't you go up and take a nice hot bath. I'll have Mrs. Hardgrave make you a tray, and you can have it in your room. I'll come and sit with you if you like."

"That sounds wonderful," said Jane, pulling herself up from the chair. "I hope Elizabeth will be better tomorrow."

"I'm sure she will be," said Maud. "Now, you go and get into your bath. If I know Maria, she's already prepared it. I'll be up in a little bit."

"Thank you, Aunt Maud." Jane left the drawing room and started up the stairs.

Maud watched Jane carefully until she was out of sight.

The next morning Jane had breakfast alone as usual at six A.M. She was surprised to see Elizabeth walk into the dining room just as she was finishing up.

"Good morning," said Jane.

"Good morning," answered Elizabeth, her voice subdued and controlled.

Jane was determined not to mention the night before. "Do you have an early call?" she asked.

"Yes. I've got a costume fitting and a makeup test both this morning. And a rehearsal this afternoon."

"Have you started filming yet?"

"No. We're supposed to start next week, but I don't think anything will be ready."

"It never is." Jane sighed. She hesitated, then continued. "Aunt Maud and I thought it would be nice if you stayed here for a while."

Elizabeth looked up from her untouched food and smiled. "Thank you. But I don't think so. Ralph said in his note that I could take over the lease of his apartment if I wanted." She shrugged. "Nice of him, wasn't it?"

Jane didn't answer.

"I might as well stay there for a while. It's cheap, and I can afford it. I haven't spent much money. Of course, I loaned some to Ralph and I paid for the household bills, but I haven't spent anything on clothes. I didn't want to show off when he was doing so badly. But now I guess I can get some new dresses. Maybe I'll even buy a car." Elizabeth's voice was deliberately light. It was as if she had decided to put on a brave face regardless of what she was feeling.

Jane thought it was worse to see Elizabeth's studied calmness than it would be to witness her in a complete breakdown. It can't be right, Jane thought. Not for her to keep all of her feelings bottled up inside. But Jane didn't say anything aloud, and Elizabeth continued with a list of her plans for the future.

"Won't you mind living alone?" suggested Jane when Elizabeth had stopped talking and gone to the sideboard for coffee.

Elizabeth shrugged. "I don't know. It might be nice for a change."

"You know you can come here anytime you want," said Jane.

"Thank you," said Elizabeth, smiling. "But I'm sure I'll be perfectly fine."

"Turner costume test, take four," announced the callboy as he snapped the block before the camera started rolling.

Jane stood in a nightclub set wearing a glittering evening gown. Following instructions, she faced forward, turned to the right, then to the left, then turned her back to the camera and walked upstage a few steps. Turning back, she returned to her original position and stood still.

"Once more to the right," called the director.

Jane complied, and then he called, "Cut!"

"Beautiful, Jane," said Terrance Malvey, standing off to one side. "It's a great costume, and you look sensational."

"Thank you," said Jane. "It's very tight, don't you think?"

"It looks wonderful. It's going to make this scene."

Jane nodded and stood still, waiting to be told what to do next.

She was tired. It was four-thirty on a Friday afternoon in May. Jane was preparing for the second of Murry Edson's three projects for her. She had completed her third movie, *Handle With Care*, in six weeks and was now finishing off the costume tests for her next picture, *When Midnight Comes*, which was scheduled to begin shooting in a few days. She had one more costume to try out, and then she hoped that everyone would be through with her for the weekend. She was looking forward to a couple of days off.

"Jane. Jane!"

Hearing her name, she turned and saw Murry Edson bearing down on her, accompanied by a distinguished-looking man.

"Who's with Murry?" she asked Terrance.

"That's Warren Harris. Big shot from the Midwest. Owns something like twenty theaters."

Jane sighed. "Oh."

In a few seconds Murry and his guest had crossed the sound stage and joined Jane and Terrance. Murry came close and took both of Jane's hands in his. Then, leaning forward, he gave her a big kiss.

"You look radiant, my dear. Absolutely radiant," he said.

Jane nodded and looked toward the other man, whom Murry quickly introduced as Warren Harris.

"Warren is an *independent* theater owner," said Murry, as if the idea were appalling. "He has been visiting Hollywood this week to select movies for his theaters. I'm sure that there will be a Jane Turner picture among them."

"How do you do?" said Warren, staring at Jane. He was tall

and slim, with gray at the temples and deep blue eyes. His skin was smooth, despite the fact that Jane figured he must be in his forties.

She smiled, putting forth her best star manner.

"Yes, sir, Warren," continued Murry, "I don't know what they showed you over at Metro or Warner's or any of the rest of the studios, but let me tell you that Global makes the best family films on the market. And little Jane Turner here has just finished a picture that's bound to be a winner. It's called *Handle With Care*. Catchy title, isn't it?"

Jane smiled automatically as Murry continued extolling the glories of Global Films and Jane Turner. At one point Jane looked at Warren, and he winked at her.

She was a little surprised and disconcerted by the twinkle in Warren Harris's eyes as he stared at her and ignored Murry's discourse. Jane was used to being looked at, but Warren appeared to be enjoying a private joke behind his steady gaze.

When Murry finally realized that no one was listening to him, his voice trailed off and the four people stood silent for a few seconds.

Clearing his throat, Murry began again. "Now, Warren," he said, putting his arm about the man's shoulders. "I think you will want to see the next studio. We're doing a biblical epic over there. Amazing how adaptable the bible is to films."

"I'm sure," agreed Warren. "But could I join you there in a few minutes?"

Murry looked at Warren, then at Jane, and back at Warren again.

"Yes, yes, of course," he said. "Take your time. Terry, why don't you come with me? I want you to see how we've brightened up Palm Sunday."

"Glad to," said Malvey.

The two men looked at Jane and Warren like a couple of satisfied duennas, and then walked away, leaving them alone except for the dozens of workmen and studio people who rushed back and forth, trying to finish for the day.

"It's rather noisy in here," said Jane, as a loud crash sounded behind them.

"Excuse me, I can hardly hear you," replied Warren.

"Sorry," said Jane, raising her voice slightly.

"Is that your usual voice?"

"Why, yes, of course it is."

"You sound louder on film. I thought maybe you had a cold. I didn't mean to insult you."

Jane smiled. "I'm not insulted. Everyone asks me that."

A workman came perilously close to hitting Warren in the head with a large piece of wood, and Jane reached out instinctively to pull him away.

"I guess I'd better get out of here. Do you have to stay?"

"Yes. Unfortunately, I have another costume test before I can quit for the day."

"I know the hours. I've been out here before. I just thought you might be lucky today."

"No, I'm afraid not. I imagine they're going to come and get me any second."

"Then I'd better not waste any time. Would you like to have dinner with me this evening?"

Jane looked disappointed. "I'd love it, but—"

"But . . . ?"

"I live with my aunt, and she's taken a little house on the beach at Malibu for the hot months. We just started going there last weekend. We're going to try and spend weekends there all summer. She's probably at home waiting for me right now, all ready to go."

"Well, it sounds like an ideal plan. It does get hot around here this time of year."

"Yes, it's pretty miserable in California during the summer," agreed Jane, mentally cursing herself for letting the conversation sink into a discussion of the weather.

"Perhaps some other time?" suggested Warren.

"All right," said Jane. "Maybe next week?" She didn't have any idea why she felt it was important to go out with this man, but she knew she wanted to.

"Now it's my turn to be sorry. I have to leave for Kansas City tomorrow."

"Kansas City?"

"That's where I live."

"Oh."

He held out his hand, and Jane took it as Warren said, "I think I'd better catch up with Murry and hear all about the bible and the rest of his sales talk." He grinned at her. "It was a pleasure meeting you, Miss Turner. I hope we see each other again."

"So do I."

Warren started to leave, and Jane watched as he walked away. Without thinking, she called after him, raising her voice to make him hear. Warren turned back to her.

"Mr. Harris," said Jane slowly. "I don't suppose you'd like to drive out to Malibu for dinner with Aunt Maud and me tonight? I could give you directions."

"That sounds very nice," said Warren. "I'd like it very much."

Jane smiled at him as he walked back to her side.

Maud's departure for the weekend was an impressive sight. Two cars were used. The first, a new Pierce Arrow limousine, purchased in California and driven by Hardgrave, conveyed Maud, Jane, a container of martinis, several road maps in case they got lost, Jane's scripts, the two women's makeup kits, and Maud's jewel box. The second car, a little Ford driven by Louise, Jane's new personal maid, was filled with food and luggage, along with Mrs. Hardgrave and Maria, who usually made the trip with her eyes closed as automobiles terrified her.

The beach house, which Maud referred to as a cottage, had an enormous living room, one wall of which was covered by a massive fireplace. There were six bedrooms in addition to the staff quarters, indoor and outdoor dining areas, and a large porch facing the ocean. The house was done completely in natural wood paneling and filled with light wood furniture and masses of bright cushions. Maud thought it a sweet little place.

The weekends so far had been quiet. Maud worked on her embroidery and listened to her favorite radio programs, which included Burns and Allen, Fred Allen, Fibber MaGee and Molly, and Amos and Andy. Jane rested, learned her scripts, took solitary walks along the beach, and ate the excellent food Mrs. Hardgrave prepared.

That afternoon as they left the city, Jane smiled and turned to her aunt. "I hope Mrs. Hardgrave has something good for dinner tonight," she said.

"She always does. Are you particularly hungry, dear?"

"Starved. But I've invited a guest as well."

"Really? Who? Or do I mean whom?"

Jane ignored Maud's sidetrack into grammar and answered her first question. "A man."

"A man?" exclaimed Maud. "My dear, why didn't you tell me? Who is he? Is he handsome? Where did you meet?"

"We met at the studio. His name is Warren Harris. He's probably in his early forties. He's tall, slim, and has dark hair with flecks of gray. Oh, and blue eyes and a wonderful smile." Jane sounded like a teenager describing a football hero. "He's visiting from Kansas City—"

"Kansas City?" asked Maud, stunned. "How very peculiar. I suppose he has his reasons."

Jane explained Warren's connection with the movie business while Maud listened avidly. When she had finished, Maud asked, "Dear, I don't mean to pry. But do you think he's married?"

Jane laughed. "Do you know I never even thought of asking."

"I will," replied Maud complacently, settling back in her seat.

They sat down to dinner a little after nine that evening. Warren had arrived on time, and after two cocktails, during which Maud charmingly found out all about him, they moved to the dining room.

He was a widower with two children: a boy, fifteen, named David, and a girl, twelve, Susan. Both children went to private schools while Warren lived in the family home with an old housekeeper, in the exclusive Country Club section of Kansas City. In addition to his theaters, Warren was involved in a number of businesses. Warren asked Maud about some people he knew in New York.

"Oh, yes, the Andersons," said Maud. "I haven't seen them in ages. But if you know the Andersons, you must know the Tuckers."

"Beefy man, wife looks like a hungry basset hound?"

"That's her exactly," agreed Maud.

"The last time I saw Tucker, they were leaving for Europe. I doubt that they're still there now."

"Jane's mother is abroad . . . and her sister, too," said Maud. "I do wish they'd come home. Things are so unsettled over there."

"Where is Mrs. Turner?" asked Warren.

"In her last letter, she and Mary were in France. But they were leaving for Germany again the next day. So they must be in Berlin by now." Maud shuddered. "I hate the thought of Maggie and Mary in the same country with that awful Hitler."

"He is terrifying," said Warren. "I just hope *this* country is prepared for the worst."

Jane looked confused. "Do you think Hitler has any designs on America?"

"He says not. But once he's gotten everything he wants in Europe . . ."

"Oh, dear," said Maud. "I do wish that Maggie would come home."

"Just what is Mrs. Turner doing there?" asked Warren.

"She's the foreign correspondent for *Women's World* magazine."

"If she's a member of the press, you don't have to worry about her. Most governments are very careful with reporters."

"I don't care," said Maud. "I just want them away from any possible danger."

"I wish I knew more about what was happening in Europe," said Jane. "I try to read the papers, but I just can't seem to keep up."

"Poor Jane," lamented Maud. "She goes to work so early and then comes home absolutely exhausted. You have something to do with the movies, Mr. Harris. Why don't you tell that studio they're working Jane too hard."

Jane and Warren laughed at this suggestion as they all left the table.

"Perhaps you and Mr. Harris would like to go for a walk," suggested Maud. "I must see to it that the servants have everything they need for the weekend. They always manage to forget something." She smiled and left them.

Warren glanced at Jane. "Shall we take a walk?"

"All right."

They went down the stairs to the beach, and Jane kicked off her shoes and tossed them back onto the porch. She was wearing a full-length hostess skirt of blue and white checks, with a white, off-the-shoulder blouse. Her skirt swept along the sand as they moved toward the ocean.

"It's a very beautiful night," said Jane.

"Yes," agreed Warren. "And it's particularly nice to be away from all the craziness in town."

"You don't sound as if you like Hollywood very much."

"I don't," he answered flatly.

"Then why do you come here?"

Warren smiled. "In one word, money. A few years ago a business partner offered me a chance to invest in a group of theaters. Then he dropped dead, and the whole thing fell into my hands."

"But you could sell the theaters, or find someone else to run things, or send someone else out here to take care of the business."

"You seem anxious to be rid of me," he said, smiling.

"Of course not. But I just don't understand someone doing something they don't like. Particularly when it takes so much time. You have other businesses, so I don't suppose you have to be involved with the movies."

"No," he agreed. Warren looked thoughtful. "Well, I guess I get a little restless alone in Kansas City. Don't get me wrong, it's a great town. But since I've been alone—"

"What was your wife like?" asked Jane, changing the subject.

"Caroline?" Warren stopped. "Caroline was a very beautiful woman who came from a very wealthy family."

Jane looked over at Warren, expecting him to continue. But he was silent. Apparently, she thought, he'd said everything he had to say about Caroline Harris.

"Do you travel a lot?" she asked.

"Quite a bit. I go around to the theaters every now and then. And, of course, I have business in New York." He grinned at her. "But I'm afraid I'm getting a little old for all the running around."

"Aunt Maud says that age is a state of mind."

"It's also a reality."

Jane began walking again. "I'm very glad you could join us this evening."

"Thank you for inviting me. Do you entertain a lot?"

"If you mean, do I invite Murry's business people to dinner, no, I don't. You're the first."

"That's a nice compliment. And it's been a charming

evening. It's not often a man my age gets to have dinner with a young, beautiful movie star."

"Age again? I'm not a child, you know. I'm twenty-three."

"And I'm forty-seven." They stopped again and looked at each other. Warren moved slightly toward her, then hesitated.

"Jane . . ."

"Yes?"

He didn't move for a few seconds, then looked away from her and said, "I guess we'd better be heading back. It's getting late."

"All right," said Jane. She felt a little hurt, a little rejected. And she wasn't exactly sure why.

Eleven

JANE WORKED CONSTANTLY the entire summer, and by the end of August, Maud began to be seriously worried about her niece's health. One night, when Jane had returned later than usual from the studio, Maud waited until after she had eaten and then sat down to talk to her.

"Jane, dear, I'm very worried about you," began Maud.

"What about?" asked Jane.

"Your schedule. You simply can't go on working day after day in this fashion. It's inhuman. I, for one, think it's ghastly."

"But, Aunt Maud," said Jane. "It's just part of the business. Everyone works hard."

"Nonsense!" snapped Maud. "It was just this kind of work that killed my poor Thomas. He could never stop, either."

"Aunt Maud, I can't explain it, but it's something I have to do."

"Nonsense," said Maud again. "There is nothing you have to do which wears you out and actually threatens your health. It's bad enough that you work all day, but to have to do all those publicity appearances is just ridiculous. I think you should speak to the studio. And if you don't, I will."

"Aunt Maud, you can't! The studio would think I was out of my mind. There's nothing you can do about my schedule or the way things are done. Don't worry about me. I'm fine, really I am. Actually, I enjoy everything. I get a little tired, but it's fun and interesting . . . and it's what I want,'' she finished.

"Very well, dear," said Maud with resignation. "But I don't mind telling you that I don't like it one bit. And I don't know *what* your mother would say."

"Where is mother now?" asked Jane, grateful that Maud had given her a chance to change the subject.

"She's in England. I thought she'd be home long ago, but she insists on staying."

"What about Mr. Austen?"

"Your mother says that he's joining her in a few weeks. But she hasn't mentioned the wedding for some time. I do hope there's nothing wrong."

"I'm sure everything will be all right," said Jane. She put her arms around Maud and patted her shoulder. "You worry too much," said Jane.

"It's going to be the most marvelous party," said Elizabeth enthusiastically. "Everyone's going to be there. You must come."

"But Elizabeth, it's in the middle of the week. I have rehearsals the next day."

Elizabeth shrugged. "But it's going to be so exciting. We're all to be in costume. I'm dressing as the queen of Sheba."

"I'm sure you'll be lovely, but I just can't. I promised Aunt Maud that I wouldn't go to anything not ordered or arranged by the studio. I've got to get some rest. Do you realize that I've done two pictures this summer?"

"Yes, yes, yes," said Elizabeth impatiently. She took out a cigarette and lit it with a gold lighter. "I've been working, too," she said petulantly.

"I know you have. That's why I can't understand why you've been going out so much. Every time I pick up a paper, the columns say that you were at the Trocadero or Ciero's or the Mocambo. I don't know how you do it."

"Why not?" asked Elizabeth gaily. "What do you think I'm working so hard for, anyway? It doesn't make sense not to have a little fun out of it all."

"But your voice. Doesn't it get tired?"

"Of course not. My voice is fine. I'm having a wonderful time and I think you should, too."

"I'm sorry. But I can't just now."

"Well, I don't really see why not," said Elizabeth snidely. "After all, your pictures can't be all that hard to do. I mean, you just have to *be* there, and the camera does the rest."

Jane looked angry, her eyes blazing at Elizabeth. "I see you read the reviews of *On Duty*," she said quietly.

Slightly abashed, Elizabeth leaned over and stubbed out her cigarette. "No one pays any attention to critics," she muttered.

"That's very easy for you to say," returned Jane. "I noticed they called you another Judy Garland. And I know that the reviews all said that my looks were a lot more impressive than my acting talent."

"I'm sorry," said Elizabeth. She smiled at Jane. "Well, if you won't go to the party, you won't," she continued, getting up to leave.

"Are you working this week?" asked Jane.

"Oh, yes. I've got dozens of rehearsals with Keith Barrows. Honestly, he seems to think that the whole world revolves around his stupid dances."

"Well, they are important, aren't they?"

Elizabeth looked disgusted. "Actually, I'm sorry that I ever danced in that last movie. I'm a singer. Just because we did a few steps, Mr. Edson thinks he has Global's answer to Astaire and Rogers. I'll never be able to dance like Ginger, and between you and me, Keith is certainly no Astaire, regardless of what he thinks."

"I hear you two are doing three more films together."

"We'll see about that," said Elizabeth.

"Well, I hope you take better care of yourself," said Jane, unintentionally parroting Maud's warning to her.

"And I wish you'd have a little fun out of life. After all, we only go around once." Elizabeth did a little two-step and hurried out to her new car as Jane returned to her script.

But Jane's thoughts were not on her work. She was concerned about Elizabeth. The young singer was considerably thinner and more sophisticated now. Her hair and makeup were professionally slick, but under the artfully applied cosmetics, Jane had noticed tiny lines etched on Elizabeth's youthful face.

And Jane was afraid of the toll that the diet pills, alcohol, and late nights were having on her friend.

After Ralph had gone, Elizabeth had been depressed for a while, then suddenly hurled herself into the Hollywood party circuit, rarely spending an evening alone in Ralph's old apartment.

And she never mentioned Ralph.

Jane turned her thoughts away from Elizabeth's problems and concentrated on her own, particularly the one Elizabeth had so unkindly pointed out.

Jane supposed everyone had read what the critics had written about her. Their opinions had all been unanimous. Jane Turner was a lovely young girl with a superb figure, a beautiful face, and a sexual quality. She also had absolutely no talent. Jane had worried so much about the reviews that Murry Edson had sat her down and explained that critics weren't important. What mattered was what the public thought. And from the reaction in the theaters, the public liked Jane Turner.

Her picture had been on the cover of *Photoplay* magazine, and she was constantly being discussed in the columns. Her clothes, her hair, and her makeup were the topics of endless articles. There were constantly pieces instructing the average woman in how to achieve the Jane Turner glamour.

Most of it was pure fabrication, but the readers loved it. When Jane appeared in public, she was inevitably surrounded by mobs of people, and there was now a guard at the gate to keep out the noisy tourists who daily trooped by the front of the house in hopes of a glimpse of the star.

But despite all the public acclaim and Murry's comforting words, Jane was still worried about the critics. But she kept her fears to herself. Besides, she thought, sighing and looking down at her script, she didn't really have time to think about the critics. She had to learn her lines before the next morning.

On September 3, 1939, a few days after Jane and Elizabeth had had their talk, Jane came home from the studio to find Maud sitting in the living room with tears running down her face.

"Aunt Maud? What's wrong?" Jane rushed to her aunt's side. "What happened? Are you ill?" she asked.

"No," Maud answered sadly. "I'm all right." She looked up at Jane. "But the world isn't."

"But what's happened?" pursued Jane.

"England's at war," she said softly. "How sad. How very, very sad. I don't understand how it could happen." She shook her head. "I thought last time we had settled it all. I thought it would never, never happen again."

Jane knelt beside Maud's chair. "It'll be all right," she said, trying to comfort the woman. "What exactly happened?"

"The Germans pushed their way into Poland and Mr. Chamberlain, the prime minister of England, declared war. My lovely England." She started to cry once again. "Thomas and I always had such wonderful times in England."

Jane looked up at Maud, suddenly alarmed. "But Aunt Maud, what about Mother and Mary? They're over there."

"Oh." She looked stunned. "I'd forgotten. Of course, Maggie'll come home immediately. I'm sure she will. I wonder if I should leave for New York?"

"Why not wait and see if she cables about her plans."

"Perhaps you're right. Oh, dear, and Laurance just went over to meet them a week ago. How terrible for them. But they must all come home. Mark my words. If England goes, all of Europe will fall. It would be terrible if they were trapped."

"I'm sure they'll leave on the first boat," said Jane. "But why don't you wait here until we know for certain? Maybe she and Mr. Austen will want to come out here for a while."

"Perhaps you're right, dear. I'll wait to hear from Maggie." Maud got up and left the room, her thoughts still on the conflict facing the British Empire.

A long cable arrived from Maggie the next day. In it she told Maud and Jane that she had convinced her publisher to let her stay in London, and that Mary had decided to stay with her. Maggie informed her family that there was nothing to worry about at present. There had been an air-raid alert within minutes of Chamberlain's declaration of war, but it had turned out to be only a drill. Unfortunately, the officials in charge of the practice had neglected to inform anyone of the rehearsal, and there was confusion all over the city. In a postscript, Maggie had somewhat embarrassedly announced that she and Laurance Austen had been married at the American Embassy that morning. Maggie apologized for depriving Maud of a wedding, but offered a large party when they returned as a consolation.

"But what about Joel?" asked Jane, reading over Maud's shoulder.

"He's fine, dear. I called him long distance this morning. He's at school. He had a cable from Maggie, too. And other than wanting to join the RAF, he's all right."

"Aunt Maud," said Jane.

"Yes, dear?" asked Maud, rereading the cable for the third time.

"I know you're thinking about going back to New York. I suppose it's probably a good idea. But, but . . . but if you could stay a little longer . . ." Her voice trailed off. The night before, Jane had become terribly aware of what it would be like in Hollywood without Maud. Her aunt had only been with her for a few months, but Jane had come to depend on her, both as a companion and as a bulwark against the outside world. Maud had created an environment of comfort and hominess, and even the thought of her departure made Jane feel a little frightened and lonely.

Maud turned from her reading and looked at Jane. She knew immediately what was on her niece's mind. It was nice to be needed, she thought. Patting Jane's arm, Maud gazed at Jane affectionately. "Well, I don't think I have to go right away, after all. If you don't mind," she continued casually, "I'll stay out here awhile longer."

Jane smiled at Maud.

"And dear," she went on practically. "I think we'll keep the Malibu house. It's so nice to get away. What do you think?"

"I think that's a wonderful idea," said Jane.

"And," said Maud emphatically. "I hear Lady Rippon is in California. I've known her for years. Frankly, I've always thought she was a little dreary. But she's always doing good works. I wonder what she's planned for the British war effort. I must give her a call and see what she has in mind. There must be hundreds of things the English people will need. I do wish I'd learned to knit instead of embroider," she lamented. "I haven't the faintest idea how to make a scarf or a pair of stockings. And I can't imagine them needing sofa pillows right now."

Maud looked so crestfallen that Jane, forcing back her laughter, put her arm around her. "I'm sure you can learn to knit in no time," she said reassuringly.

"I hope so, dear," said Maud. But she didn't sound convinced. "But, no matter. I'll find some way of helping. I must contact my English bank and make some money over to the British Red Cross, and then I'll call Lady Rippon. I'm sure she'll be delighted to hear from me."

Jane noticed that the social and political climate in Hollywood changed almost immediately after the war in Europe began. It was a reasonable change, she thought. After all, many members of the film colony had only been in America a few years; they had important ties to and relations in European countries. For a number of the movie people such as Murry Edson, whose mother still lived in Poland, the policies of the Third Reich had been a constant source of concern. With the conflict actually beginning, he was frightened for the safety of his parent and other relatives caught in the center of the gathering storm.

For a few, the war was simply an inconvenience, limiting the travel plans of individuals who had expected to vacation in England or France. Their casual dismissal of the terrifying events happening across the ocean and their constant reiterations that America would never be involved were voiced disparagingly against the fears of wiser people who feared the complacently peaceful were wrong.

Most studios immediately began thinking about pictures that would inspire the free world without breaking America's neutrality. Regular work continued as usual.

Jane was on the set of her new film when Warren Harris arrived. He had asked for her at the front office and been directed to Stage Six. He was in time to watch her completing a scene.

Wearing only a revealing white bathing suit, she lay seductively next to the leading man, Wayne Marshall. As she spoke her lines, she ran her fingers over his chest.

When the director called for them to cut, Jane casually got up from her position.

"Was that what you wanted, Earnest?"

"Perfect. You look beautiful. Now why don't you take a break while we set up the next shot?"

"Fine." Jane sank into a chair marked with her name, and signaled to her maid.

Louise hurried to Jane's side, helped her into a robe, and handed her a glass of iced tea and a cigarette.

"Thank you, Louise. I'll come to my dressing room in a few minutes."

"Yes, ma'am."

Warren walked over to Jane and stood beside her.

Absently, Jane looked up and saw him. "Well, hello," she said, smiling. "I didn't know you were back in town."

"I just got in this morning."

"Please, sit down with me. I have a few minutes." She looked around for a chair, and then called out to Louise to bring one. The maid obediently hurried over with a chair, and Warren sat down.

"Did you see the scene?" asked Jane.

"Yes."

He didn't seem very enthusiastic, and Jane pursued the subject.

"Did you like it?" she asked.

"You looked very beautiful."

"Thank you." She grinned at him. "That wasn't so hard now, was it?"

"What wasn't?"

"Giving me a compliment."

"I would have thought that you heard it enough without my small voice."

Jane looked at him curiously and decided to change the subject.

"Will you be staying long?"

"I'm not sure. I have some business to attend to."

"I see."

"Would you like to have dinner with me tonight?" he asked.

"All right," said Jane. "No . . . wait. I've got a very early call tomorrow. I have to get some sleep."

Warren looked disappointed.

"But," she continued, "if you'd like to have an early dinner at the house, I'm sure Aunt Maud would love to see you."

"How is Mrs. Watson?"

"She's fine. Very upset about the war in Europe. But she's very busy organizing things for the British war relief."

Warren smiled for the first time. "I'm sure she'll be very

helpful. And yes, I'd like to come to dinner . . . and see Mrs. Watson."

"I'll call Aunt Maud and let her know. Six-thirty?"

"Fine." Warren stood up. "I guess I'd better get on my way."

"I'll see you tonight," said Jane.

Louise appeared and informed Jane that her hairdresser was waiting for her. Jane got up, smiled at Warren, and quickly walked away.

Instead of attending to business, Warren returned to his hotel and sat on the small terrace outside his room. The Hollywood panorama was spread out beneath him, but he wasn't interested in the sights. He wanted to think about Jane Turner.

She was a beautiful woman. More like a beautiful girl, he mused. Less than half his age, she had her whole life ahead of her. At forty-seven, he suddenly felt very old.

The whole thing was ridiculous. It was stupid for him to come back to California. He could have handled his business by telephone or mail. He knew why he had come back. He wanted to see her again, to be near her.

Like a lot of other guys, he thought. All of whom had fallen under the spell of her looks in darkened theaters across the country. But Jane's on-screen personality didn't really touch Warren. He wasn't interested in Jane Turner, movie star. He was intrigued and fascinated by the vulnerable and almost childlike person under the glossy and glamorous image.

Warren's face grew angry. A gentle girl caught in a world of make-believe and unreality that he found decadent and irresponsible.

All his life he had lived by a certain set of rules. He had worked hard, been honest in his dealings, and lived an exemplary home life, never giving his wife cause for concern or worry. But that had been easy. He had never really loved Caroline, any more than she had loved him. But they had had a satisfactory marriage based on propriety and mutual respect. After her death, he had found that he sometimes missed a woman whose face he couldn't always remember.

At those moments, he would walk into the living room of his house and stare up at the uninspired portrait of Caroline which hung above the fireplace.

He would look at her as an interesting stranger, and realize that he had never known this woman who had shared his bed, attended parties with him, given birth to his children, hired and fired their servants, played golf and bridge, gone on vacations, and cleaned her face carefully each night before bed.

Not one single moment of their married life had been out of the ordinary. No brilliant or tragic event had set Mr. and Mrs. Warren Harris apart from their friends in Kansas City.

And now, he was intrigued by a young woman whose life and ambitions were alien to him. He had visited Hollywood often enough to become familiar with all the types the movie industry produced. He had seen the con artists and the crooks, and watched them manipulate the ambitious young actors. He had seen the ruthless stars, wrenched with agony that they would lose their foothold on success, and the desperate and tragic women whose time in the spotlight was over.

And he didn't want Jane Turner to be a victim of the users or a pained has-been. He didn't want her to become a "type" to be manipulated, produced, and then discarded by a world of which he disapproved and was, if he could be completely honest with himself, slightly afraid.

She was better than that, he thought. There was something different about her, something distinctive and special. She deserved better than what Hollywood offered. She should have a home, a life like other women, secure and protected.

He could take care of her, thought Warren. He could give her all she should have. With devastating insight, Warren Harris realized that he was in love with Jane Turner.

At dinner Warren often found himself staring at her, but he quickly turned his attention back to Maud and they discussed the war. He rarely spoke to Jane and left soon after the meal.

Jane walked him to his car and watched him drive away.

Damn him, she thought. He'd hardly even noticed her all evening. He simply sat and talked to Aunt Maud. She could have gone to bed or studied her lines without even being missed. He had to be one of the most irritating men she'd ever met.

Jane sat down on the front steps and rested her chin in her hands. She remembered how Morgan had tried to be casual about her effect on him the first time they met. But Warren wasn't pretending, thought Jane. He really didn't seem to be impressed or awed by her looks. And he hadn't made any effort to be alone with her. He was so stuffy and dignified, always correct and polite. Damn him. She couldn't imagine why she even bothered talking to him.

Jane smiled to herself. Then again, there was something intriguing about Warren Harris. Just once, she thought, it would be nice to see him with all his defenses down. There was something very sexy about him. His tall, slender frame exuded a quiet sensuality, and his bright blue eyes seemed to mask a private joke that he had never shared with anyone. Comfort and security surrounded him. Jane knew that he would never be cruel or dangerous, either in life or in love.

She tried to picture herself in bed with him. His hands touching her, his face pressed against her body . . . the image created a feeling of warmth through her body. Standing, Jane started into the house. She didn't understand Warren. But she knew she wanted him.

Maud was in the living room, sorting a collection of clothes recently gathered by one of her committees when Jane joined her.

"Aunt Maud," began Jane. "Do you like Warren?"

"Why, of course I do," she said, looking up at Jane from her place on the floor. "I think he's very nice. *And* he's a gentleman, which seems to be getting rarer and rarer in the world today. I wonder why anyone would send a shirt without any buttons on it to a charity. What do they think we can do with it?"

Jane ignored Maud's meanderings. "Warren's different, isn't he?"

"Different from what, dear?" asked Maud, her attention still claimed by her work.

"You know. Most of the men here—"

"Are not very nice," finished Maud. "You see, dear, Warren isn't different to me at all. In fact, he's much like most of the men I've known all my life. He sometimes even reminds me of Thomas. But I do see what you mean. Warren is different from actors and directors and all those people."

"I don't think I've ever known anyone quite like him," mused Jane.

Maud was astonished. The world was certainly coming to a pretty pass when Hollywood people were the norm in a young girl's life, and men like Warren Harris were unusual.

"I mean," continued Jane, "he's very conservative. He doesn't like the movie business very much."

"Really?"

"No. But he seems very nice. Sort of comforting," finished Jane lamely.

"Yes. I can see where you might think that. Of course, he's not very exciting, but then none of the men I've known have been very exciting. But do you think he's dull?"

"Oh, no. Not at all," said Jane vehemently.

Maud stared at Jane. Was it possible that Jane was truly interested in Warren Harris?

"I'd better go to bed." Jane kissed Maud's cheek and left the room.

Maud sat on the floor, holding a particularly unattractive blouse. But her mind was not on her task. I wonder, she thought. It might be a very good thing. He's years older than she is. But that could be just what Jane needs. Sort of a father and lover in one. Maud shuddered when she remembered that Warren lived in Kansas City. That would have to be changed, she thought. Naturally, Jane wasn't ready to give up her career. But Warren could move to California. That would work out perfectly. He could do his business out here, and at the same time, create a safe, secure home for Jane.

He *does* have children. But they weren't really young, and they'd probably adore Jane. On the whole, Maud decided it was a good thing.

I think I'll invite him to Malibu for the weekend, she decided. I'm sure that Jane would like that. I wonder how large a house they should have? Maud continued planning Jane and Warren's future as she turned her attention back to her work.

"Come on, Lizzie, sing for us."

"No!" said Elizabeth, turning her back on the young man prodding her. "I don't feel like it."

"Jesus, honey. You used to be willing to sing every time someone hit a downbeat. Look up there." He pointed to the band. "The Mocambo is famous for its orchestra. And they'll be glad to play anything you want. They know everything, honey, really they do."

"I said I don't want to sing," Elizabeth snapped.

"All right, all right. Jesus, a couple of pictures and you're a big shot. Excuse me, Big Shot," he said, bowing and backing away.

Stupid man, Elizabeth thought. Every time she went out now, someone always asked her to sing. God, didn't they realize she got tired of singing?

She slipped around on her barstool and surveyed the crowded nightclub. What a bunch, she thought. Tourists everywhere. It looked like an Elks convention.

Elizabeth got up and walked a little unsteadily toward the hatcheck counter, pushing her way through the mob on the dance floor.

Grabbing her stole, Elizabeth hurried outside and then stopped. Where now? she wondered.

The attendant brought her car, and she drove to the Mocambo's exit. But she didn't leave the drive. Looking back and forth at the street in front of her, she couldn't make up her mind which way to go.

Someone honked at her from behind, and she pressed the gas pedal and leaped out into the traffic, barely missing another car. She pushed the car up to fifty in the thirty-mile zone, still without any destination in mind.

She could always go to Ciro's, thought Elizabeth. There were usually people there she knew. Or the Orange Room. Anywhere but home. She couldn't go back and sit alone in that apartment where she had lived with Ralph. Yet at the same time, she couldn't convince herself to move to a new place.

Elizabeth turned off onto a side street and in a few moments found herself at Pete's. Sitting behind the wheel, she looked at the weathered entrance. This was where she had first met Ralph. It wouldn't hurt to go in. She'd just have one drink and then go home.

Inside the bar, her eyes scanned the room, involuntarily seeking Ralph's face. She recognized a few faces, but his wasn't among them. Several acquaintances called out to her to join them for a drink, and Elizabeth accepted. In a little while she was the life of the party.

CHAPTER *Twelve*

IT WAS LATE SATURDAY NIGHT. Maud had gone to bed early, leaving Jane and Warren alone in the living room of the Malibu house.

Jane stretched, raising her arms high above her head.

"Tired?" asked Warren.

"Not at all. Actually, I feel wonderful. It's been a nice day."

"You slept most of it."

Jane smiled. "I know. I guess that's why I feel so good now." She got up and walked to the door. "I love this place." Pushing back the curtain, she looked out at the ocean. "It's a beautiful night. The water looks so calm." Suddenly Jane turned back to Warren, her eyes bright. "Let's go for a swim."

"Now?"

"Of course. It'll be wonderful. Come on," she said coaxingly.

Warren shrugged. "Sounds a little strange . . . going swimming in the middle of the night, I mean. But all right."

In a short time they were in bathing suits, running across the sand to the water. Jane splashed in immediately, but Warren held back, feeling foolish about their late-night excursion.

Jane called out to him to join her, and slowly he waded into the ocean. As soon as Warren was close enough, Jane cupped her hands and sent a shower of water splashing over him, covering his head and face. Warren looked astounded, and Jane laughed delightedly before diving beneath the surface of the water.

Warren seemed confused for a moment, then dived after her. And soon, he found that he was enjoying their childlike games. Warren and Jane played together, laughing and teasing each other, and Jane was surprised by Warren's ability to disappear underwater for long periods of time.

"All right. I give up," she said, giggling after Warren surfaced and unceremoniously dunked her. She ran out of the water and sat on their blanket, grabbing a towel and rubbing her skin dry.

Warren joined her, and she handed him a towel as he knelt beside her.

Warren took the towel, but didn't bother drying himself. His attention was totally captured by the picture before him. The pale moonlight reflected off the water and created a glow around Jane's blond hair and white bathing suit. She looked breathtakingly beautiful, and he couldn't take his eyes off her.

Jane looked up and saw Warren's expression. A slow smile crossed her lips, and she lifted her face to him.

He kissed her gently on the mouth, and Jane reached out and encircled his neck with her arms, drawing him down, bringing his body close to hers. A slight breeze moved across them, brushing Jane's hair against Warren's face. It was soft and still damp from the ocean. He ran his hands through the silky texture of her hair as they kissed again, and Jane slipped her tongue between Warren's lips, probing his mouth.

Warren pulled away and looked around him at the deserted beach.

"What are you looking for?" she asked.

"I know this is a private area, but you never know who might be wandering around."

"You worry too much," said Jane. "If anyone else is out here, I'm sure they have their own concerns to think about."

"It doesn't hurt to be careful."

"There's such a thing as being too careful," said Jane. She ran her hand over his thigh, making small circles as her fingers moved toward his crotch.

Warren didn't move as Jane's hand traveled over his hip and

to his flat belly. She could feel the taut muscles move beneath her touch as Warren's breath grew quicker.

He grasped her hand and kissed the palm. Then his lips gently moved up her arm as he slowly slid down next to her, stretching out full-length on the blanket. Over them, blindingly bright stars created a diamond-studded umbrella of protection.

Warren looked at her face. He'd never seen anyone so beautiful. He kissed her eyes, her mouth, her throat, his lips hungrily devouring her soft skin.

Jane pushed her body closer to him, her arms moving over his back. She slipped her hands into his trunks, pushing them down as she caressed his buttocks, feeling the smooth muscles. She slid the trunks down along his muscular legs. Warren lowered the straps of her bathing suit, and then reached under her to unfasten the zipper. She released her hold on him to help, and in a few seconds she was naked.

He spoke her name softly and she looked at him, her eyes full of desire.

"I love you, Jane," he whispered.

She smiled and lay back on the blanket, bathing her body in the rich, muted colors of the night.

"Yes, Warren," she breathed. "Love me . . . love me."

Taking her in his arms, Warren held her tightly to his body. It was as if they were becoming one person, one human creature whose whole survival depended on the other. There was nothing between them, nothing separating their bodies.

Warren slipped his face down to her breasts, brushing them with his tongue. Jane moaned slightly, her lips parted. She reached down between his legs and grasped him, her face intense and excited as she felt him grow and harden beneath her touch.

Jane released him and pushed herself away from their embrace. Warren looked at her, startled, confused, as she raised herself up to a sitting position.

She smiled. Her eyes never left his face as she traced her fingers down her body, lingering on her nipples before moving down over her stomach, each touch an invitation, a dare. Warren was fascinated by Jane's movements. She was compelling, sexual, desirable. Warren reached out for her, and she lay back on the blanket, exposing her body to his view, luring him, demanding him to come to her.

She lifted her hands to Warren, and he moved into her embrace, covering her body with his.

Slowly, gently, he entered her. She twisted under his penetration, pushing her body up to meet his, as her hands pulled him closer to her. Their movements grew stronger and faster as their need for each other blotted out everything else. The dark night covered the lovers as the crash of the silver waves buried their cries of passion.

The next morning Jane walked into the dining room for breakfast and found Warren already in his place. He jumped up and helped her to her seat. Throughout the meal he was very solicitous of her comfort, making sure she had enough to eat and insisting she finish her eggs. Maud looked curiously at him, but didn't say anything. When the meal was over, she excused herself and Warren suggested a walk to Jane.

It was a bright day with a slight nip in the air. Jane had thrown a plaid cape over her light dress, and Warren, in his usual coat and tie, turned up his collar and jammed his hands into his pockets.

"Are you sure you're warm enough?" he asked.

"I'm fine. It feels nice. Yesterday was so hot, and now it's actually chilly."

"If you want real weather changes, wait until you see Kansas City."

"I'm afraid that'll be awhile," said Jane with a smile.

"Why? We'll have to go there so you can meet my children and friends. Of course, you probably won't want to get married until your mother's back. I understand that. But it won't hurt for you to get acquainted with the people I hope we'll be spending a lot of time with."

"Married?" asked Jane, stunned. "Warren, what are you talking about?"

"Us, of course. I'm sorry we can't go to Europe for a honeymoon, but we might try the Bahamas or one of the islands."

"I think you're moving a little fast for me," said Jane.

Warren looked over at her and smiled. "Oh, I'm sorry. I guess I should make things official." He stopped and turned to Jane. Taking her hand, he smiled at her. "I love you, Jane. Will you marry me?"

Jane simply stood and stared at him. Finally, she spoke. "Warren . . ."

He laughed. "Don't tell me it's too sudden. I won't believe you."

"I'm not sure—"

"Oh, I know it'll take awhile to settle things at the studio. But I can help with that. I have some influence with Murry Edson. And soon, you'll be Mrs. Warren Harris." His voice grew serious. "I'll make you happy, Jane. I swear I will. No more getting up in the middle of the night to go to work. No more publicity events, or greasy fans chasing you around. I'll take care of you, Jane . . . and protect you."

Jane took a deep breath. Everything seemed to be out of control. "Warren, stop this," she said. "Please stop."

"But Jane—"

"Listen to me, Warren. I care for you. Very much. But I'm not ready to get married. And as for giving up my career, that's out of the question. I've worked hard to get where I am, and I'm not going to drop everything now that it's going well."

"But last night—"

"Was wonderful. But it wasn't a commitment for either of us. We shared something beautiful. We can share many things, Warren. But not marriage, not yet."

"I see." Warren turned away from Jane and looked out at the rolling water as it plunged and hurled itself toward the shore. "I guess I jumped to some wrong conclusions. Funny, I always thought that if a girl made love to a man it meant she loved him."

Jane reached out and touched Warren's sleeve. "Perhaps I do love you, Warren. I'm not sure. But I do know that I'm not ready for marriage or to give up my life here."

"Last night didn't mean a thing to you, did it?" asked Warren angrily, turning to her and brushing off her hand. Hurt and confused, he struck out at her with words. "What was it? Just another fling? Did the famous movie star suddenly feel the need for a man? How many times have you laid on this beach, Jane? Did it matter that it was me this time—or would anyone have done as well?"

Jane slapped him hard across the face. "How dare you?" she exploded. "How dare you accuse me? You sound like some high school girl who's lost her virginity behind the

gymnasium. Just because I won't marry you, your super male
ego is damaged. You can't stand the thought that I could make
love to you and not want to marry you. Last night was
beautiful, but it doesn't mean that I belong to you. I *don't*
belong to you or any other man."

"I understand," said Warren sarcastically. "You can care
about someone as long as they don't interfere with your selfish
plans. I love you and want to take you out of this phony life-
style. And you're too stubborn to realize what's really
important."

"To you, Warren. Important *to you!* My career is important
to me. My life *here* is important to me."

"And I'm not."

"Yes, you are, Warren. But don't make me choose."

"Well, I am asking you to choose. I want to marry you and
take you away from this whole Hollywood trap. Will you do
it?"

"No."

"Then I guess I'd better leave." Warren looked at Jane and
then turned and walked back to the house.

Jane stood watching him, her feelings a complex mixture of
anger and loneliness.

For the next several weeks, Jane was a very difficult person to
live with. She worked harder than ever, and came home
alternately angry or exhausted.

Maud didn't know what had happened between Jane and
Warren. He had come back to the house, quickly packed his
bag, and left immediately, barely stopping long enough to say
good-bye. Jane would not discuss the situation.

Finally Maud decided that Jane needed some diversion to
take her mind off both her work and her problems with Warren.
She began planning a little dinner party. Maud had to admit to
herself that the party was also a break in her now constant work
for British war relief. At first, Jane had insisted they were both
too busy to have guests, but Maud persisted, and eventually a
date was named for the dinner.

A few days before the party, Jane was surprised by a visit
from Mable Cramer, who dropped in at the Beverly Hills house
late one afternoon and found Jane stretched out by the pool in
the fading sunlight, a script in her hand.

"So tell me everything," said Mable, settling down on a chaise longue. "I feel as if I've been away for years."

"Did you have a good time?" asked Jane.

"It was all right."

"How was Las Vegas?"

"Full of gangsters, naturally. But I've been other places as well."

"Where?"

"Around. After all, I've been away several months. You didn't think I was holed up in some casino all this time."

"How am I to know? You haven't exactly kept in touch."

"Well, I've heard plenty about you. I almost expected to be turned away at the door. *And* I've seen your cover on *Photoplay*, and your interviews in all the rest of the magazines. To say nothing of the lines at the box offices, all the fans waiting to get a glimpse of your fair beauty. You certainly have moved fast."

"I've been very busy," said Jane with a smile. "Would you like a drink?"

"Love one. I did mean to call and let you know I was back in town, but then I changed my mind and decided to just drop in."

"I'm glad you did. What do you want to drink?"

"Scotch and water would be nice. Not too light."

Jane went to the patio door and called a servant. She gave him the order for Mable's drink, requested a lemonade for herself, and returned to her guest. "Where are you living now?" asked Jane as she settled back in her chair.

"I've found a little place near MGM with a friend."

"Anyone I know?"

"I doubt it; Sadie McCoy. She's been around for a while. Not bright, but we have a few laughs together."

Jane had heard of Sadie, and knew that she was one of the highest paid hookers in town. It was obvious which direction Mable's career was taking her.

"Speaking of roommates," continued Mable, "I also hear that Miss Goody Two-Shoes is doing well."

"Elizabeth?"

"Who else?"

"She is coming along. She's finished two pictures, and the studio's all excited about her next one. She's filming it now. For some reason her films seem to take longer than mine. I've done five pictures in the same amount of time. Did you hear that Ralph left her?"

"Hear? I've seen the creep."

"Really? Where?"

"In Mexico. I was down there for a few days with a friend, and we met Ken Holt, who insisted that we come to a party he was giving. And right in the middle of the action was good old Ralph. Jesus, you should have seen him. He poured Holt's drinks, lit his cigarettes, brought girls up to him. Hell, he did everything but help him take a pee. Of course, he could be doing that, too, but I didn't get intimate enough with Holt to find out. He's also keeping Holt in drugs. Elizabeth is well rid of him. He's no good, never was. I said so from the start, but the little fool would never listen."

"I guess she didn't see him like you did."

"She didn't see *him* at all. I can't imagine what she was looking at. She chased him for whatever reason, and then couldn't handle him when she caught him."

"Well, I hope he never comes back."

"Oh, he'll be back. They always do. But it'll be awhile."

"How do you know?"

"Holt left Mexico right after we did for a vacation in Colorado. Then it's on to Paris to tout some film of his. I can just see Ralph in Paris. If he plays his cards right, he could be king of the pimps."

"Maybe Elizabeth will forget all about him."

"Sure," said Mable without conviction. "What about you?"

"Me?"

"Yes, you. What about your love life? You can't be spending all of your time in front of the camera, although God knows there's so damn many Jane Turner pictures around, you could be."

"Well, I do work long hours. Aunt Maud thinks it's criminal," said Jane, giggling.

"The old lady is no fool," said Mable. "Even though she doesn't like me."

"What makes you say that?"

"Come now. Your Aunt Maud took one look at me and saw

someone from the wrong side of the tracks and hoped she'd never lay eyes on me again."

"Aunt Maud has known a lot of people. And I don't think they've all been in the social register."

"Maybe not. But your aunt and I both know where we stand . . . with each other and with ourselves. It's only you people who still have a lot of illusions who have all the trouble."

"I don't understand."

"No. I didn't think you would. Skip it. I still want to know about your love life."

"That's easy. There isn't one."

"That isn't simple; that's stupid. You mean you haven't met one eligible man since I went away?"

"I thought there was one."

"Not that crazy writer again."

"Of course not. I haven't seen Morgan since that last night."

"And even you wouldn't try and change that photographer . . . what was his name?"

"David Granoff. We're still close friends. We see each other occasionally."

The servant appeared with the drinks.

"Is your drink all right?" asked Jane.

"Fine. Don't change the subject. What about men?"

"There haven't been any men."

"All right, *man*."

Jane got up and walked to the edge of the pool. Kicking off her shoes, she dangled one foot in the water. "There was someone. But it didn't work out."

"What happened?"

"He was too proper." Jane looked back at Mable and smiled. "He thought he could reform me. Make me a perfect wife and mother."

Mable noticed that Jane's voice was too light. "Reform you from what?"

"This," said Jane, extending one arm. "Hollywood, the movie business. You know . . . all the decadence of a film star's life."

"Oh sure," said Mable. "You're really decadent. And you took that?"

"No. That's why we're not together anymore. So I'm a free spirit, as usual," said Jane with a little laugh.

"Some freedom. You're practically married to the studio."

"Speaking of which, what do you know about Constance Steiner?"

"Your agent? Not much. I hear she's a patsy for the studios. Whatever they want, she's willing to give them. She's certainly no William Morris or one of the other big guys."

"Nothing else?"

"No. Are you having trouble with her?"

"Not really. It's just that last time she negotiated my contract with Global, I suggested she ask for better stories."

"And?"

"And she said to just take care of showing up on time and let her handle the business. I just wondered if, when the chips are down, she will really fight for me."

"Honey, in this town, no one fights for anyone else. Hell, most of them can't fight for themselves. If you really want anything from the studio, you have to make yourself so important that they can't turn you down."

"And how do I do that?"

"Money. Pure green stuff. It's the only language they understand. You make a lot of dough with your pictures, and then you can get what you want. And if Constance Steiner won't help you, then dump the bitch and find someone who will."

"You're probably right," said Jane thoughtfully.

"Well, listen, honey. I have to go," said Mable, climbing up from the chair and putting down her glass. "Sadie and I have a couple of dates this evening."

"Is that one for each of you, or two apiece?" asked Jane with pretended innocence.

"Bitch," muttered Mable. The two women smiled at each other.

"Why don't you wait a few minutes? Aunt Maud will be home shortly. She's out gathering up clothes for British relief."

"Figures," said Mable. "No. I've got to move." They walked to the front door of the house together, and Mable turned to her friend.

"Don't let them get to you. You know what you want. Just keep after it."

"Thanks."

"And Jane . . ."

"Yes?"

"I'm sorry about the guy."

Jane smiled slightly.

"But don't let it worry you. After all, what's the big deal about a man?"

"I never thought I'd hear *you* ask such a question."

Laughing, Mable gave Jane a kiss and left.

Jane went back into the house and met Hardgrave, who asked if she wanted dinner or would wait for Mrs. Watson. Jane told him she'd wait and walked into the drawing room and sat down with her script. She tried to study her lines, but she couldn't concentrate. Finally, she slapped the pages down on the coffee table and sighed.

"Dear me," said a voice, "is it that bad?"

Jane turned and found Maud looming in the doorway. She was still wearing her hat, her arms were full of papers, and her bag hung over one wrist.

"Aunt Maud, I'm so glad you're home. I was getting lonely."

"How nice to be needed," said Maud. Hardgrave appeared and began unburdening his mistress of her possessions.

"Now, Hardgrave. I want all of those papers in the den. I must go over them tonight. And please put my bag someplace where I can find it. It always seems to disappear."

"I'll give it to Maria, Madam."

"That's a good idea." Dismissing Hardgrave, she turned her attention back to Jane. "Now, dear, why are you lonely? Did you have a bad day?"

"No. It's been a normal day. Mable Cramer came by."

"Oh, is she back in town?"

"Yes."

"Did she have a good trip? Where did she go?"

"Las Vegas, Mexico, I don't know where else."

"How interesting."

"She thinks you don't like her."

"Well, I can't say that I absolutely dote on the girl. She is a little hard, dear."

"She's had a rather hard life."

"And you want to help her? How? We could include her in the dinner party."

"Thank you. I feel sorry for Mable." Jane shrugged. "I don't even really know why."

"I think we always feel sorry for the people we leave behind," said Maud with paralyzing insight.

For a woman who had been the hostess at enormous balls and supervised important social events, the small dinner party wasn't a major occasion. But with Jane's schedule at the studio and her own increasing involvement in war relief, Maud found that there was little time for entertaining friends. Consequently, she looked forward to having some friendly faces around her dining room table.

The dinner party included David Granoff, Bill and Mack, and Lucille Evans. Mable had sent her regrets, and Elizabeth had called and asked if she could bring a friend she had met at the studio.

At first Maud was concerned about Elizabeth's date, but was pleasantly surprised to find that the young singer's escort was Senator Mark Richmond, visiting California from Washington, D.C. Originally from Kentucky, the senator was a young, very dynamic personality in his second term, and considered a very up and coming politician.

Although Jane hadn't really been looking forward to the evening, as the guests gathered, she realized that she was surrounded by the people closest to her in Hollywood. Her eyes scanned the room, taking in each face. These were her friends, her family. Suddenly, she felt very good having them near her.

Dinner conversation was mostly about the movies and what was happening around the film community. The group laughed about Greta Stewart's latest conquest, a lineman for the telephone company, Baby Susie's dropped option, Joan Crawford's recent marriage, and the opening of *Gone With the Wind* in Atlanta.

Jane mostly listened to the others and was happy to notice that Elizabeth seemed to be less frenetic and more her old self around Mark Richmond.

Maud suggested that perhaps the senator wouldn't want to spend the whole evening hearing Hollywood gossip.

"Oh, I don't mind at all," said Richmond. "It's all very interesting. Washington scandals don't have nearly as much glamour."

"I'm sure Washington is just as peculiar," said Maud, and then wondered what on earth she was talking about.

"I was supposed to go to a dinner with Murry Edson tonight," said Mark. "But then Elizabeth invited me to come here. I don't know if I'm more grateful to her for rescuing me from a boring business dinner or for introducing me to such nice people."

"How charmingly said." Maud smiled. "I do like a man who can give a compliment well. My husband could always do that."

"Thank you. My wife says I'm often a little heavy-handed." He smiled. "Particularly in my speeches."

"Do you have a family?"

"Yes. Two children. They're in school outside Washington."

The conversation moved to the situation in Europe and was just getting interesting when Jane was called to the telephone.

She excused herself and went into the study to take the call.

"Jane?"

"Yes."

"It's Warren. I hope I'm not interrupting you."

"We're having a small dinner party. Just friends."

"It sounds nice." Warren's voice was stilted. "I won't keep you. It's just that I'm coming to Hollywood next week, and I'd like to see you."

"I don't think that's a good idea," said Jane.

"I just want to talk to you. No scenes."

Jane didn't answer.

"Jane . . . are you still there?"

"Yes. I'm here."

"Can we meet?"

"All right." Jane's voice was tightly controlled.

"Good. I'll call you when I get to town. I'll be in on Wednesday."

"All right. Good-bye."

"Good-bye."

Jane hung up and stood unmoving for a few moments. In a few days he would be back. She had tried to erase any thought of Warren from her mind. But inside, Jane knew that he would always be something special to her, and she couldn't dismiss him completely from her life.

Yet she couldn't imagine any future for them. She knew that her frustration over the past weeks had been caused by their conflict on the beach that day. Part of her wanted Hollywood while another part of her wanted to fall into his arms and feel the protection and love he offered.

She lived and worked in a world that created dreams, but Warren was real, and he wanted a reality that to Jane was more of a dream than all the fantasy Hollywood could produce.

She sighed and returned to the dinner party.

In Kansas City, Warren sat in the living room, beneath his wife's portrait. He had promised himself that he would never call Jane Turner again. But he had. He hadn't been able to resist the need to speak to her again, the chance to see her once more.

His thoughts continually returned to that night on the beach when they had made love. She had made love with him and had not expected or even wanted him to marry her. She was capable of passion outside marriage. In his well-ordered and controlled life, Warren couldn't understand this. And it wasn't just that she had made love with him, but that he knew she must have made love to other men, perhaps had seen other men since their night together. Marriage, to Warren, was a bulwark against the other men in Jane's life. But since she wouldn't marry him, he had come to the conclusion that it was because she wanted other men. And that thought tortured him. It was like a poison inside his gut, ripping and tearing him apart.

He loved her. Deep inside, Warren knew that Jane Turner was the woman he had loved all his life without even knowing her. She was the woman he had been waiting for, wanting. And despite the dangers of disappointment, he was going back to her.

As Elizabeth and Mark drove away from Maud's house, he turned to his date.

"Thank you very much," said Mark. "It was a charming evening."

"I'm glad you enjoyed it. Jane is a very dear friend and Mrs. Watson is really a character, isn't she?"

"Mrs. Watson reminds me of many mothers in my past," said Mark with a smile.

"Not for me. The mothers I knew all had soapsuds or dough on their hands all the time. And they always looked tired. I don't think my mother ever had a really nice dress."

"And now you have a closet-full."

Elizabeth grinned at him. "Not a whole closet, yet. But I'm working on it."

"Where are we going?" asked Mark.

"It's up to you. We could go to the Mocambo or Chasens."

"I'm afraid the newspapers would have a lot to say about that."

"Sorry. I forgot that you were a big shot from Washington with a wife and children."

Mark's voice was soft. "I like it when you forget."

Elizabeth glanced at him. He certainly was a nice-looking man, tall, aristocratic. A successful man, perfectly dressed and at ease in any situation. He was attracted to her.

Elizabeth smiled to herself. She was coming up in the world.

"We could go to my place. It's not much, but I could give you a brandy."

"That sounds very nice," said Mark.

Thirteen

ONCE A YEAR, IN DECEMBER, Murry Edson gave a party. His house was decorated by the studio design department, lavish food was provided, and the entertainment featured the skills and talents of Global players. All of the major stars, financial men, and important contacts of the studio were invited.

Warren Harris returned to California on the day of Murry's celebration, and he asked Jane to attend with him. As much as he hated the idea of the party, Warren privately thought it might be better for them to have somewhere to go where the first awkwardness of their meeting would be softened by the noise and confusion created by a large number of people.

Maud had also been invited to Murry's party, and although she only knew the Edsons slightly, she decided to go.

Jane assumed that her aunt was looking forward to seeing all the stars and personalities. But Maud had a subtler, deeper reason for attending.

Mrs. Thomas Watson was well aware of the value of her name in the society pages, and the fact that she had gone to a party given by a Jewish movie mogul would be a nice slap in the face for that man in Germany who insisted that Americans were just as prejudiced against the Jews as he was. Maud rather doubted that Hitler himself read the New York society columns, but the few Americans who seemed to have an affinity with Nazi Germany would certainly take note. We all fight in our own ways, she thought to herself.

It was to be a very formal evening, and Jane and Maud spent a few enjoyable hours trying to outdo each other in the opulence of their ensembles.

Jane had selected a white sequined gown, cut low at the bosom, and with virtually no back at all. Her scarf was bright red, and she wore long, white gloves along with diamond and ruby earrings and bracelets.

Maud chose a black gown, and covered it with a veritable jewelry shop of precious stones. Lengths of pearl and diamond chains hung from around her neck and cascaded over an enormous diamond brooch attached to her bosom. Her earrings of diamond starbursts glittered like beacons, and on her arms she had several bracelets of pearls and diamonds. In addition, she had sent to the bank in New York for her famous tiara which she wore only on the most special occasions.

The two women waited for Warren in the drawing room.

"You look beautiful, dear," said Maud, staring with complacency at Jane. "Every time I see you, I'm astonished at how truly lovely you are."

"What a nice thing to say," replied Jane, giving her aunt a kiss.

"Careful, dear," said Maud. "You never know when this headpiece of mine will suddenly decide to swoop down on you."

"It is certainly imposing."

"The last time I wore it was for your sister Charlotte's party in New York." Maud looked a little sad as she remembered the lovely girl who had been killed by a terrible fire only a short time after her marriage.

"You still miss Charlotte, don't you?" asked Jane. "I know she was your favorite."

"Oh no, dear. Not my favorite. I care for all you children."

"It's all right to have a favorite." Jane smiled. "Charlotte was a very special girl."

"Yes, but she wouldn't have been able to do what you're doing."

"What do you mean?"

"It was something Charlotte once said to me. You know, she

looked so much like your mother that everyone thought they must be alike. But they weren't. Maggie is strong and independent, like you. Charlotte saw that. She said she could never have gathered up her family and brought them to New York like your mother did. But she told me that you could have. You have the determination and strength to get what you want. She could only hope and dream about her goals, while you and your mother went out and made them realities."

"I never knew she thought that."

"Oh, yes. We talked a lot together. Just like you and I have. And I imagine Mary and I will talk, eventually." Maud preened herself slightly. "You see, we old ladies do have our purposes. It's good for you all to have someone to talk to other than your parents. Children rarely say what they really think to their parents. At least that's what I think," finished Maud with the air of someone who'd dedicated her life to understanding children.

"Well, I'm very happy you're here now to talk to me," said Jane.

Hardgrave announced Warren Harris, who walked into the room wearing white tie and tails. He looked very handsome and a little nervous. Because Maud was with them, Warren and Jane behaved very politely to each other, saying little. But Maud kept up a stream of small talk that took the trio to Murry Edson's house.

Two uniformed guards checked the invitations of the guests, after which a platoon of men in powdered wigs and the silks and satins of the French court opened the gates and allowed the cars to enter the estate.

"How very grand," said Maud, looking at the lighted drive.

"The costumes are from Global's production of the French Revolution last year. It was a big success," said Jane.

"I suppose we should be grateful that Global didn't make Ben Hur," said Warren.

Maud giggled, and the car arrived at the front door which was, if possible, even more brightly lit than the drive. Another congregation of costumed servants hurried forward and helped the guests from their cars, bowing low as they did so.

"I feel just like Madam Du Barry," said Maud, alighting from the car. She looked concerned. "She did keep her head, didn't she?"

"We'll have to ask Murry," said Warren.

"Chances are, he'll think you mean Ethel DuBarry over at Republic," said Jane, and, laughing, the group entered the house.

Murry Edson lived in the grand manner he adored and imagined the public thought he should live. His taste was ordinary and his desire for comfort constantly vied with the pageantry and opulence he both enjoyed and assumed was expected of him. Consequently, the massive stone house held a peculiar combination of rare and valuable artwork sitting cheek and jowl next to overstuffed chairs and chunky ashtrays.

Mrs. Edson, whose first name was Elsie, also had her own taste which manifested itself in fluffy doilies on the arms of the chairs, bright, overdressed dolls sitting on top of telephones, and vases with pictures of Niagara Falls set on priceless antique side tables. Pink was Elsie's favorite color.

As Jane, Maud, and Warren walked into the large entrance hall, they were greeted by additional servants. Above them on the wall were two enormous crossed swords over two complete sets of armor, poised and ready as if for battle. Between the suits of armor was a large Christmas tree decorated with pink angels.

"How very dramatic," murmured Maud as she handed her furs to one of the servants.

"It gets better," said Jane. "I was here last year for a party and had a tour of the entire house."

"Sometime I must set aside a day for that," said Maud as their host came toward them, beaming.

"Come in, come in," said Murry happily. "How nice that you could all come. And Warren, too. Glad to see you back in Hollywood. We'll make a Californian of you yet."

"Perhaps," said Warren, noncommittally.

"And Mrs. Watson," Murry went on. "We are honored by your presence in our house. My wife will be delighted to see you. She's around somewhere with our guests, but soon she'll find you."

"I look forward to it," said Maud.

Murry led the group into the main drawing room which also boasted a Christmas tree, this one decorated with traditional ornaments, and more art objects and homey touches. The room was full of Global people, all in their finest, along with representatives of the press.

Murry was called away, and in a few seconds they were joined by Mack and Bill.

"You'll be interested to know," said Bill, "that Mrs. Edson has elected to wear silver lamé with all of her garnets. It was a terrible mistake."

"I'm glad you warned me," said Maud.

"You both look spectacular," said Mack. "Maud, you, particularly, bring all of us a touch of class."

"Thank you," said Maud.

"Mack, you and Warren know each other, don't you?" asked Jane.

"Of course," said Mack. "It's good to see you again."

"I'm glad you all got here," said Bill. "The movie star here has had his eye on a chess set that he insists is valuable. I've been afraid he was going to try and walk away with it."

"What is it made of?" asked Warren.

"Pure ivory—and at least two hundred years old," said Mack.

"Really?" asked Warren, interested.

"Do you play chess?" asked Mack.

"When I get the chance."

"Would you like to see the set? It's in the game room."

"Along with several disgusting animal heads and two pool tables," offered Bill.

"Do you mind?" Warren asked Jane.

"No. Of course not. Go ahead."

The two men left and in a few moments, Mrs. Edson hove into view and made a dead set at Maud. Elsie was, indeed, in silver lamé and wearing an enormous number of garnets. But Bill had failed to mention that she was also wearing bifocals in wire frames. This final touch almost put Maud over the edge.

Elsie was happily greeting Maud when Murry announced the start of the entertainment. All of the guests hurried into chairs around the huge drawing room, where a piano and a small band were set up.

Baby Carol, Baby Susie's replacement, made her appearance in blue and silver, and sang several ruthlessly cute numbers which made most of the guests slightly ill, but seemed to delight Murry and the publicity men. Then Murry introduced Global's brightest new singing star, Elizabeth Hudson.

"How nice," whispered Maud. "I've always wanted to hear Elizabeth sing."

"She's wonderful," answered Jane.

Elizabeth took her place and stared out confidently over the crowd. Jane thought back to a few months earlier and remembered how her friend would have suffered incredible nerves at the idea of performing for such a gathering. Elizabeth had changed a lot since Jane had first met her. Her continuous dieting had made her figure slim and chic; her wrists were tiny. And her makeup, created and supervised by the studio artists, was restrained and perfect, accentuating her large eyes. Tonight, dressed in a simple red gown, her dark hair loose and flowing over her shoulders, Elizabeth was elegant and lovely— a real pro. Jane privately applauded Elizabeth's metamorphosis, but also found she missed the gentle and innocent young girl from Toledo who was now obviously gone forever.

The music started, and Elizabeth began a moody Cole Porter number. She followed it with a bright Noel Coward song, and left to tumultuous applause.

"That was lovely," said Maud. "Absolutely lovely. I had no idea she could sing that well."

"I was amazed the first time I heard her, too," said Jane.

"Where do you suppose Warren and Mack are?" asked Maud.

"Why don't we go see."

They went into the game room and found the two men seated on opposite sides of a small table. An intricately carved chess set was between them.

"Your move," said Warren.

"I know, I know," said Mack. "Just let me think."

"Oh, dear," said Maud.

"Come on, you two," said Jane. "You can't sit in here. Dinner is about to be served on the patio."

"We're not hungry," said Mack.

"That's not the point. You have to join the other guests."

"No one will miss us," said Warren.

"Of course not," said Jane. "Mack is just Global's leading male actor, and you're just one of its biggest business contacts. No one will think a thing about it."

"Bill will take you to dinner," said Mack. "Where is he?"

"The last time we saw him," said Maud, "he was talking to Greta Stewart."

"That won't last long," said Mack. "I'm sure he'll be back in a minute to take care of you."

"That's not the point," said Jane. "You shouldn't ignore the party."

"Why not?" asked Mack.

Jane couldn't think of an answer to this question and turned helplessly to Maud.

"Come along, dear," said Maud. "I suppose we'd better just leave them alone."

"Do you think it's all right?"

"Of course. Thomas often played bridge or chess at our parties. Some evenings he would greet the guests, and then we wouldn't see him again all evening. I remember going into the study on one occasion, and he told me to get out." Maud smiled, picturing her grumpy husband.

"Sounds like a good man," said Mack. "So you two get out of here."

Warren looked up at Jane and smiled. "Yeah, get out of here," he repeated. "We'll see you later."

Jane glanced back at Warren, and their eyes met. His smile grew larger, and Jane grinned at him. Despite the fact that there were other people near them, Jane felt it was probably the most intimate moment they had ever had.

Jane didn't say anything more. She just stood there, her eyes on Warren. Finally, Maud offered to bring the men some food, and she and Jane left Warren and Mack to their game.

Murry Edson and Terrance Malvey walked around the swimming pool, talking between nods and smiles at guests.

"As usual, it's a nice party," said Terry.

"Ought to be," Murry said. "It's costing a fortune."

"I thought Global was picking up most of the tab," said Terry with a grin.

"Global doesn't pay for the wear and tear on the furniture," answered Murry.

"Well, at least everyone showed up. Is that really Maud Watson with Jane Turner?"

"Sure is. Do you know her?"

"Not me. I never moved in those circles. But don't forget, I come from New York, and that Watson name is big stuff back there."

"Real society, huh?"

"Sure is. I knew Turner was connected, but I didn't realize it was this good."

"They live together out here. I think Mrs. Watson must pay the bills, because Turner isn't making enough yet to have that house and all the rest of it."

"She will in her next contract. Did you see the rushes from *When Midnight Comes*?"

"Not yet."

"She's dynamite. You won't be able to take your eyes off her."

"Good. *On Duty* is doing well, and we'll release *Handle With Care* soon. That's the first picture she gets star billing on. Should be a big premiere."

"Before I forget, just what is Maud Watson doing out here?" asked Terry.

"The rest of their family is in Europe, so she came out to visit Jane. At least, that's how I understand it."

"Europe? Hell, you couldn't get me there these days."

"Me either. But I've got some family still there I'd like to get out."

"Sorry to hear it, Murry."

Edson shrugged. "I wonder how much money is leaving here and going to England?"

"Hard to tell. Actors are always pretty cheap."

"I bet Maud Watson is sending some."

"Probably a lot. But the only thing that worries me is how much might be going from here to Germany."

Murry looked shocked. "That's not possible," he exclaimed.

"I'm afraid it is, Murry. There are some people out here with German backgrounds. Not as many as in New York, but a few."

"Son of a bitch," spat Murry. "Tomorrow I want you to find out if any of our people are sending money to Germany. I want names."

"What are you going to do about it?"

"Fire the bastards, of course."

"Do you think that's a good idea? We're still a neutral country, Murry."

"Shit! I won't have Global money going to Germany."

"I have a better idea," said Terry. "Why don't you start some kind of fund-raising benefits. You know, get the stars together to help raise money for British war relief or the Polish relief fund, or something. You have the two best people around to help you organize it right here."

"Who?"

"Maud Watson and Warren Harris. I notice he's with Jane, too. By the way, is that something?"

"Warren and Jane? I don't have any idea. If so, it couldn't be better for them or us."

"Except for publicity. Warren would never stand for it."

Murry shrugged. "I want to hear more about that idea of yours about the fund-raisers." The two men kept talking as they went back into the house.

When Mack and Warren were finally dragged away from their chess game, Warren and Jane went out to the patio.

After the special show, Murry had provided nonstop background entertainment. A trio of singers were performing while the guests moved around the massive house. As a special treat, Murry was also showing brief scenes from some of Global's major films in his projection room. Different actors hurried in to see their parts, leaving immediately after their appearance on the screen to head back to the bar.

Maud had been cornered by Elsie Edson and was pretending an interest she didn't feel in the woman's garden club activities. Mack and Bill were in a heavy political discussion with some friends.

"It's quite a party," said Warren.

Jane smiled. "Murry only does this once a year, invites everyone, I mean. He has a few smaller gatherings that aren't too bad."

"I'm having a good time."

"Are you? Of course, you and Mack didn't see anyone for almost two hours. So you haven't really been at the party, have you?"

"Sorry about that. But he's a pretty good chess player."

"I don't mind. I'm glad you're enjoying yourself."

They walked over to a bench away from the crowd and sat down.

"Being with you today is the first time I've enjoyed myself since I left Hollywood."

Jane didn't answer.

"I guess I owe you an apology, but it isn't easy for me." Still, Jane didn't answer him.

"There is something I want to explain, Jane. Something I want you to understand. I still don't like this place or anything it stands for. I don't like the glamour and the false images and all the rest of it. I don't consider Hollywood a good place to live or raise children. . . . I love *you*. But when I see you surrounded by all of this, I wonder if there's a place in your life for me."

"You were never in competition with Hollywood, Warren."

"Aren't I? Hollywood is like a rival to me—a rival I can't shake off. I can't defeat a whole way of life."

"It's not a way of life I'm working for, Warren. It's a career."

"All right. Then my rival is your career."

Jane looked at him. "Does that mean that my rival is your business?"

"Of course not." He sounded indignant.

"Oh? Then you would pick up and leave all of your professional interests for me?"

"You know I can't do that."

"Then why would you expect me to give up my career?"

Warren sat quietly for a moment. "I guess it's because you're a woman. Women are supposed to adjust their lives and their ambitions to a man."

"Really?"

"You know that's the way it is."

Jane laughed. "I know that's the way it is," she agreed. "I'm not arguing with you. I know exactly what you're talking about. I *know* what women are supposed to do. Most girls would leap at the chance to marry you and settle down in Kansas City and live the life you offer . . . but I can't do it. Maybe there's something wrong with me, something that makes me different. But, inside me, there's something that forces me to keep going.

"It doesn't mean that I don't care for you, or that I don't

want many of the things that other women want. I just want more. Much more. I won't, I can't, bury myself under someone else's accomplishments. I have to have my own."

"I see," said Warren, only half understanding.

"And you know as well as I do, that there's something else. It's not only my career that bothers you, Warren. It's my life, my past."

He didn't speak.

"You can't stop thinking about the other men that have been in my life. And somehow you seem to feel that if I married you and moved to Kansas City then all that would be wiped away, that I wouldn't be different."

"Jane—"

"Let me finish, Warren. The last night we were together, you hinted at it. And again tonight, you're attacking Holly-wood and the movie business instead of confronting what's really bothering you: who I've slept with in the past. You can't keep blaming a town for what I am."

"Jane, please. I don't think this is the time to discuss it."

"Why not? No one can hear us. No one is interested in what we're saying. Or if they are, they're not going to admit it." Warren had turned to search the crowd, hoping they weren't being noticed. "Look at me, Warren," she went on. "Would you like a catalog of the other men in my life? Would you like me to make out a list of who I've been with and exactly what I've done with each of them? Would that settle your mind?"

"I wouldn't ask such a thing of you."

"No, you wouldn't. You'd just let it sit inside and eat away at you, and at your feelings for me. You've said you love me. You've told me several times. But how on earth can you love someone you disapprove of? It doesn't make any sense."

"I never said I disapproved of you, Jane. But as long as you've brought it up, yes, I hate the thought that some other man has touched you. I hate seeing you up on that screen for everyone to look at and drool over. I've seen the way men look at you. I've seen their eyes following you, mentally ripping off your clothes. Secretly making love to you. I hate it. And worst of all is the feeling that any second you'll find someone else."

"My God, Warren. I'm not a child. I know exactly what men think when they see me. But I don't care. They can think anything they want. I've worked hard to get in pictures. And being looked at is just part of the game. And as for finding someone else, the chances are better that you'll discover some perfect little housewife in Kansas City who exactly meets your standards than that I'll run off with one of my leading men. Or did you actually believe the publicity about Mack and me?"

Warren had understood Mack and Bill's relationship almost immediately, and although he didn't really approve of it, he didn't think it was any of his business. Jane's suggestion that she might disappear with Mack broke the seriousness of the conversation, and despite himself, Warren smiled.

Jane leaned close to him. "My darling, Warren. Don't you understand? I care for you. I don't know if I love you or not. I don't even know if I can love you. But you mean very much to me." She grinned at him. "You're a very sexy man."

Warren blushed.

"And I feel warm and protected when I'm with you. I feel safe with you, Warren."

"If you need to feel safe, then why don't you come with me. Get away from this business."

"Because I need it. I need the danger and the challenges and the accomplishments it gives me. But even while I need these things, another part of me wants to be held and comforted and secure. That's me, Warren. I can't explain it any more than that."

"I see."

"I hope you do."

"Do you ever think you might change, might want to leave all this?"

"Maybe. But I can't imagine ever being away from here. And don't base your feelings for me on some remote possibility, or on a future that might never come. Isn't what we have now enough, Warren?"

He was silent for a while, looking out across the pool with its glittering lights. The guests were moving about, laughing and talking. He looked back at Jane. She was the woman he wanted, but he wanted her on his terms. For now, he would either have to give her up or try it her way.

"I do love you, Jane," he said quietly. "That's why I came back. I still hate the thought of you as a sex symbol the whole world can look at. But I hate the thought of losing you even more."

"Then stay with me, Warren. Let's make at least one of the dreams in this town a reality."

"I'd like to try."

They looked at each other, and Warren reached out and touched Jane's hand.

"Are you two going to be exclusive all evening?"

They looked up and saw Mack coming toward them with a tray in his hands. On it was a bottle of champagne and several glasses.

"I swiped this from the pantry. I thought we deserved it."

"What for?" asked Warren.

"Oh, I'm feeling a little sentimental all of a sudden." Mack smiled down at the couple.

"Anything in particular?" asked Jane.

"Just us," he said. Maud and Bill joined them, and Mack passed around the wine.

"To us." He raised his glass. "Good friends."

The others raised their glasses. Warren looked at each of the people in turn. It was a strange group: Bill and Mack, an aging dowager, and the woman he loved—a film sex goddess. Kansas City would never understand it. He smiled slightly to himself and suddenly realized that he was happy.

The thought came as a shock. He hadn't ever actually expected to be happy. And now, here it all was. He looked over at Jane and raised his glass to her. She leaned forward and kissed him. Maud sighed and smiled brilliantly at everyone.

CHAPTER *Fourteen*

ELIZABETH HUDSON AND MARK RICHMOND lay in bed, their
naked bodies covered by a sheet. Elizabeth shifted slightly and
moved closer to him.

"Hmmm," he murmured. "You feel good."

"It's my weight loss."

"Do you think all those pills are good for you? You never
seem to eat anything."

"I can't. The studio wants me to be slim and attractive.
Besides, you wouldn't be here if I was fat."

"How do you know? I've always liked my women hefty."

"Hefty? What a terrible word. Besides, I've seen pictures of
your wife, and she's thinner than I am."

"My wife is a very strict woman about her diet . . . and
everything else."

"Well, I'm not going to gain weight just to give you a
thrill."

"Does that mean you don't like me anymore?"

"Of course not." She ran her hand over his chest. "I like
you a lot. Can't you tell?"

"I was afraid you were just acting."

"I'm not that good at it." Elizabeth laughed. "All I have is a
voice."

"I wish I could have come to the party tonight and heard you sing."

"You were invited."

"Yes, I know. But I'm here for the government, remember. I have to get some work done. And if I'd gone to the party, I wouldn't be able to be here now."

"I'm happy with your choice," she said. "When do you have to go back to Washington?"

"On Monday."

"That only leaves us a few more nights."

"I'll be back soon."

"Really?"

"Yes. I'm supposed to look over some naval installations here. It'll be quite a job, and I may be here for some time."

"That sounds lovely."

"I'm glad you like it. Do you think you'll have some time for me?"

"Of course."

"Good. But in the meantime, do you think you could feed me? I know you don't eat anything, but *I'm* hungry."

Elizabeth looked at him with mock concern. "Poor baby," she said. "Well, I happen to be a very good cook, and I have a steak here that I can fix in a few minutes."

"Sounds great."

Elizabeth got up, pulled on a robe, and went to the kitchen where she began pulling out food and pots and pans. She was delighted to be cooking for him. She had always liked the idea of taking care of a man, and fixing Mark dinner in the middle of the night seemed like a perfect job to her. Better than singing or being in the movies or going to parties, or anything else she'd experienced. It made her feel needed and wanted, and she loved it.

She had tried to take care of Ralph, but he hadn't really appreciated it. Any more than her father had appreciated her mother's hard work, or any of the other men Elizabeth had known in Toledo had appreciated what their women did for them. They had all been the same, despotic, domineering. Expecting to be waited on and then left alone.

But Mark was different. Sophisticated and aristocratic, he was the kind of person all of her girl friends had longed for and never met. The kind of person that Elizabeth's mother had always insisted was too high-hat and important for the Hudson girls. They had to stay in their place.

Well, look at me now, Ma, she thought.

Of course, it wasn't all perfect. Mark was married and had a political career to think about. So they had to keep their affair a secret. But the time they had together was wonderful. Mark was funny and charming and very loving. And even if he didn't really take their relationship seriously, it was nice to have a man in her life who didn't expect her to pay his bills. She knew he liked her. And that was all she'd ever wanted.

Elizabeth picked up an old skillet and put it on the stove. Frowning, she stared at it. It looked so dingy. Glancing about the kitchen, she came to the conclusion that it was all dingy. She'd stayed in the apartment, hoping that sometime Ralph would come back. Well, maybe it was time to forget all about Ralph. Mark had shown her that she could have something better. She would look for another place. Something nice, maybe in the valley. That would be pretty, she thought. And she could afford it. She was making good money now, and there was the promise of more to come. She could have a really nice apartment or a little house, maybe with a flower garden. Happily, Elizabeth hummed softly to herself as she finished preparing the food.

"Hey, woman. Are you going to take all night?" Mark stood in the kitchen door with a towel around his waist.

She looked up at him and smiled. "Not much longer. Sit down. Do you want coffee?"

"No. Keep me awake. Just some milk."

"A healthy man."

"Once I've eaten, I'll show you how healthy I can be."

"I'll hurry."

She put a large steak in front of him, along with some vegetables, and then sat down opposite him.

"Aren't you having anything? You didn't have any dinner."

"I'm fine. I have to film tomorrow, and I don't want any bulges."

"I still don't think it's healthy."

"Maybe not. But it keeps me in shape."

"When I get back, I'm going to get you on a good diet—one that'll keep you slim and still in good health, off those pills."

When Mark had finished, he leaned back and lit a cigarette. "That was good."

"I'm glad you liked it," said Elizabeth as she gathered up the dishes.

He watched her for a few minutes, and then reached out and grabbed the end of her robe. "Can't you finish that later?"

"Maybe . . ."

He pulled her onto his lap and put his hand in her robe, stroking her breast, lightly touching her nipple.

"Oh," said Elizabeth softly, "that's very nice."

His hand explored her body, slipping down over her belly and between her legs.

Elizabeth gasped as his hand moved slowly and seductively over her. She put her face up to his and they kissed, Mark's tongue pushing inside her mouth and rubbing against hers. She slipped off his lap and, without speaking, they moved into the bedroom. The only light was a tiny sliver which shone through the open kitchen door, and their figures were like dim shadows moving toward each other.

Mark took Elizabeth's face between his hands and held it up to his. Leaning down, he kissed her, gently at first, and then more passionately. He ran his mouth over her neck, her cheeks, and then back to her lips as he slid his hand down over her buttocks. He pulled the robe up and stroked her naked body.

Elizabeth shook off the covering and pulled at his towel. Nude, they pressed their bodies together, touching, feeling each other.

Mark lifted her up and placed her carefully on the bed. In the soft light her face was young, vulnerable and very innocent. He felt it was like making love to a child. She looked up at him, trusting; she was eager to feel him next to her.

Elizabeth stretched out her arms, and Mark moved onto her body. Their lips met again and again as Elizabeth opened her legs and drew them around his body.

Slowly and carefully, he began to penetrate her. She gasped at the first feeling of him inside her, and then breathed harder as he began his rhythmic moving in and out of her body. His arms were wrapped under her, and she held him close as he pressed against her. His body moved faster, and Elizabeth matched his urgency, thrusting her hips up to him.

Desire and excitement built inside her until she suddenly felt her whole body exploding; flame after flame of passion consumed her. Seconds later, she could feel Mark reach his orgasm. He thrust harder and harder into her. He cried out once, and then suddenly relaxed and lay quietly over her.

She reached out and stroked his head as it lay on her breast. "Sleep, baby," she whispered. "Sleep, sleep." She held him close to her as he drifted off, her hands continuing to stroke him. Her voice, soft and quiet in the still night, whispered the words a mother would say to a child.

"So, Jane. How was the big party?" asked Mable, flopping herself down on the sofa in Maud's Beverly Hills house.

"It was very nice."

"Was Greta the Bitch there?"

"Of course. But she didn't speak to me."

"I can't imagine why," said Mable dramatically. "Of course, the fact that everyone in town is saying that you're replacing her on the Global lot as number one *might* have something to do with it."

"No one has said that to me."

"Maybe not. But that's what I hear."

"From who?"

"I do read *Variety*. And I still get around. I know how well your pictures have done. You're big stuff now."

"I'm glad you think so." Jane laughed. "I do wish they'd give me better scripts, though. I'm getting a little tired of playing the same part in every picture."

"That's something you'll have to work out with old Edson." Mable changed the subject and asked, "What are you doing for New Year's Eve?"

"Warren is back for a few days and coming for dinner. So are Mack and Bill. I imagine Mack and Warren will play chess. They always seem to."

"That sounds really exciting," said Mable with a yawn. "Why don't you all come to the Mocambo? They always have a good party."

"I don't think so. Warren doesn't like crowds, and I don't either. And of course, Mack and Bill couldn't go. We'll just stay here. You're welcome to come by if you like."

"Thanks for asking. But I have a big night planned. What about Elizabeth? Is she coming here tonight?"

"No. I spoke to her earlier in the week and I think she has a boyfriend."

"Really?"

"Well, she isn't going out as much as she did. And she didn't mention Ralph once in our conversation. She didn't actually say anything about a man, but—"

"But you got the impression that she was having an affair. Good for her. But you know as well as I do that if Miss Goody-Goody isn't talking, there can only be one reason . . . the guy's married."

"That thought entered my mind, too. But I didn't ask."

"I would have. I wonder who it can be," mused Mable.

"They're obviously keeping it very private."

"As long as it keeps her mind off that Mason creep, I'm for it. But she seems like the last girl in the world who could handle an affair with a married man."

"We also thought it was strange that she picked Ralph Mason."

"How is she looking?"

"Thin," said Jane. "She still won't eat much for fear of gaining weight, but she's not drinking, and she doesn't look tired or worn out. In fact, last time I saw her, she seemed more like her old self."

"That's good. What are you working on now?"

"I start filming *Wanton Woman* next week."

"That sounds inspired."

Jane laughed. "It's no worse than most of the stuff I do."

"That's one way of looking at it," said Mable as she got up to leave.

That evening, Maud walked down the stairs and went into the dining room. Hardgrave joined her, and together they inspected the flower arrangement and the table setting.

"It looks lovely, Hardgrave," said Maud.

"Thank you, madam. And may I wish you a Happy New Year and a very good 1940."

"Another decade." Maud sighed. "They do seem to add up."

"Yes, madam."

"Make sure that you and Mrs. Hardgrave and Maria and Louise and the others have champagne tonight."

"Thank you, madam."

Maud went into the drawing room where she gathered up a collection of papers and leafed through them. In a few moments, Jane joined her.

"I don't know what I'm going to do about this," said Maud.

"Committee work getting you down?"

"No, of course not. It just seems to me that we're not doing enough. England is in such a dangerous position now, and all those people will need our help. I just wish we could do more."

"Aunt Maud, you're with one committee or the other every day. And now you're helping Murry with his benefits. I think you're doing all you can."

Maud didn't look convinced.

"I'm glad we're staying in tonight," said Jane, changing the subject.

"Are you, dear? I am, too. I've always hated New Year's Eve. Thomas called it amateur night. All kinds of strange people dressed in totally unsuitable clothes out making a great deal of unnecessary noise."

"It'll be nice just having a small group here. But I do wish Elizabeth and David Granoff could have joined us," Jane said.

"Well, at least Warren will be with us. He's been away since right after Mr. Edson's party."

"He had to spend Christmas with his children. And he had some business to take care of."

"Have you missed him?"

"Yes, I have. But we've talked on the telephone almost every day."

"That's nice, dear. But it isn't quite the same as being together, is it?"

"No, it's not," she said quietly.

"Well, I hope he can stay a good long time this trip."

Jane laughed. "He'll be here for three days."

"That's not much of a visit."

"No. But then he'll be back in February or March for several weeks."

"That's much better," said Maud.

Jane smiled at her aunt's obvious enjoyment of her relationship with Warren. It was very clear that Maud had decided that they would be married and had probably already settled in her own mind where they should live and the number of servants they would need, along with the best way they could divide their time between Jane's career and Warren's business interests.

The guests arrived shortly, and over dinner the talk was mostly about the worsening situation in Europe. But after dinner, Mack and Warren sheepishly excused themselves to take a look at a chess problem they had discovered. Jane and Maud watched them go, and then settled down to talk with Bill who found himself alone with the two women.

The chess game broke up a few minutes before twelve, and the small group of friends gathered in the drawing room to have champagne.

"How very nice this is," said Maud as Hardgrave staggered into the room under the weight of a massive silver tray, on which was a huge bottle and several glasses.

"Just set it down here. I'm sure one of the men can handle it," said Maud.

Warren and Mack looked dubiously at the bottle, but Bill jumped up and offered his services. "No problem. I used to do this all the time."

"Entirely too much of the time," said Mack.

"I thought we agreed that was all in the past," said Bill, looking at Mack.

"Sorry. I just lost a good game, and I have to pick on someone." He smiled at Bill.

Bill smiled back as he opened the champagne, and he and Maud distributed the glasses.

"To all of you, and to the future," said Maud.

"To the future," echoed the others.

Warren spent the next few days in California, and he and Jane spent as much time together as possible. They went to the beach house or to Warren's hotel, although Jane didn't care for the latter arrangement.

Their nights were comforting and exciting to Jane, and virtually an awakening for Warren who, after the first shock at Jane's ability and knowledge in bed had worn off, was insatiable for her. He delighted in just looking at her perfect body, and thought her beauty was like an unbearably expensive gift that he received each time they were together.

When Warren had to leave, Jane stood at the train station and watched as his express pulled away. She then headed back to the studio.

• • •

"Miss Turner, on the set, please," called out a voice. In her dressing trailer on the sound stage, Jane stood looking at herself in the mirror.

She was currently starring in an epic set in the Roman Empire. Her character, that of a wicked siren, tempted and lured men to their doom. Murry Edson had told her that she was similar to Salome, although as she stared at her reflection, she thought she resembled a burlesque queen more than a seductress from ancient times.

"Good God," she said to no one in particular. "I barely have on any clothes at all." The slight drapery scarcely covered her breasts, pulling tightly at the waist before falling in strips to the floor and leaving her legs mostly exposed. Her hair was coiled on top of her head with a few strands dropping artistically about her face. The hairdresser continued to adjust the arrangement, ignoring both Jane's comment and the call from the set.

"I think they want me, Paul," said Jane.

"Yes, well . . ." He stood back and looked at her critically. "You'll do."

Jane stood up. "Thank you." She walked out onto the studio floor without looking behind her. She knew that Paul, along with her dresser, makeup man, and maid would follow and be in close attendance throughout the scene.

"Jane, you look lovely," said the director, Earnest Kahn, rushing toward her. "Do you know your lines? What a stupid question," he answered himself. "You always know your lines."

"Such as they are," said Jane. "I seem to purr more than I speak in this picture."

"Ah, but no one can purr like you," he said.

Jane ignored him, and he left her side and ordered everyone to take their places.

The set was monstrous. It was the bedroom belonging to Jane's character and had great stone walls draped with cloth. Cushions and pillows covered the floor. Three steps led up to an imposing bed, virtually obscured by cloth and cushions. The decorations were all of bright colors, and Jane thought what a pity it was that the film was being shot in black and white. The only people who would ever see the mastery of the set designer's art were those in the studio. She climbed the short steps and sat down on the bed.

"Positions everyone," called out Earnest's assistant.

Jane stretched out on the bed as instructed at rehearsal and assumed her provocative pose. The makeup and hair men rushed forward to repair any damage done on her trip from the dressing room, while the costume designer draped and re-draped the folds of her gown until it was exactly the way he wanted it. When they were all finally finished, they stepped back and the director began calling out commands. Once more, Jane Turner was making a movie.

The morning progressed with constant starts and stops as the cameraman, director, lighting engineer, and sound man checked their readings and changed positions and setups. By lunchtime, Jane had been alternately sitting or lying on the bed for almost four hours, and no film had yet been shot.

She was used to these delays and whiled away the time chatting with the actresses who played her handmaidens or joking with the crew. At twelve-thirty, Jane noticed Elizabeth Hudson standing on the sidelines, waving at her. Jane waved back and gathered from Elizabeth's peculiar mouthings and gestures that she intended to wait and lunch with her. Jane nodded agreement and then turned her attention back to Earnest Kahn.

In another half hour the stage manager called lunch, and Jane climbed off the bed and walked over to Elizabeth, closely followed by her creative technicians.

"I gathered that you meant you want to have lunch," said Jane, smiling.

"Yes. You don't have any other plans?"

"Not a thing. I was going to have a sandwich in my dressing room. But let's go to the commissary."

"All right."

"I'll be back in a few minutes. Just let me get out of this thing. I'm sure they'll never let me eat in it."

"You look beautiful."

"Thanks, I'll be back shortly."

Jane went into her dressing room where the costume designer helped her out of her scanty outfit. After powdering down her makeup and slipping into a pair of slacks and a shirt, she hurried out to meet Elizabeth.

"Let's eat," said Jane. "I'm starved."

"That is certainly some set," said Elizabeth, sounding more

like the innocent girl from Ohio than Jane had heard for some time.

"Isn't it awful? It's supposed to make me look and feel like a very elegant and beautiful courtesan, but frankly it just makes me sleepy."

Jane and Elizabeth walked into the studio commissary and looked around for a table. Elizabeth was an up and coming player, and Jane was virtually a star, but there was no star system in the dining room. Except for the table always reserved for Murry Edson, at which he had never been known to even sit down, let alone eat, all the rest of the tables were up for grabs. They found places at a small table and sat down.

"I don't suppose I'll ever get used to eating here," said Elizabeth, looking around her.

"Why not?"

"Well, just look," said Elizabeth, indicating the often unusual, inevitably strange, and occasionally beautiful costumes and people who surrounded them. There were actors dressed in everything from western clothes to evening gowns. Grips and assistants in work clothes played cards with hairdressers and costume designers, who had pins and clips stuck over their clothes. There was an extremely beautiful girl in a flowing eighteenth century gown who burped loudly as she gobbled down a hamburger, and a man dressed as a pirate who read *Emma* by Jane Austen.

Although Jane could now take all this in stride, Elizabeth still found herself fascinated each time she came into the restaurant.

Jane ordered a turkey sandwich, fried potatoes, and iced coffee, while Elizabeth asked for a small salad and coffee.

"You really don't ever eat," said Jane.

"I can't. I don't dare gain a pound. But don't talk about it. I'm so tired of people telling me I never eat. Besides, I have something more important to talk about. I wanted to see you at the party but you were busy, and since then I've been up to my ears in this new production of mine."

"What's it called?"

"*New York Nights.*"

"That won't last long."

"Probably not. Anyway, you were so busy at the party, I couldn't get to you."

"I know. I wanted to see you that evening, too. So did Aunt Maud. She wanted to tell you how beautifully you sang. It was lovely."

As usual when she got a compliment, Elizabeth seemed surprised. "Oh . . . thank you. They were songs I've known a long time."

"You did them really well. Warren said so, too."

"I saw you with Warren. You looked very happy."

"It was a nice evening."

"Is he still in town?"

"No. He was here for a few days around New Year's, but then he went back to Kansas City. It doesn't look like he'll be back until March. But that's all right. I should be finished with *Wanton Woman* by that time, and maybe we can take a vacation together."

"That sounds fine," said Elizabeth. "You always have things so well under control. Everything always seems to work out for you."

"Sure," said Jane, remembering all of the nights she and Warren had been separated because they couldn't agree on their future together. "Enough about me. What's going on in your life?"

The waitress delivered their food, and the conversation stopped. But after she was gone, Jane looked expectantly at her friend.

"Well," began Elizabeth. "I guess you know I was pretty down after Ralph left."

Jane nodded.

"I mean, work's been fine and the studio has been very good to me. Of course, I'm not as important as you are yet." Elizabeth smiled. "I seem to move slower. But I think everything's going in the right direction."

"I hear nothing but wonderful things about you," said Jane. "I think it's great." She smiled to herself, remembering that only about eighteen months before she had congratulated Elizabeth, and it had hurt a lot. Now she could do it without any reservations.

"But I did still miss Ralph," continued Elizabeth.

Jane didn't answer.

Elizabeth looked away from the table. "But . . . well, I just wanted to tell you that I've met someone new."

"That's wonderful," said Jane enthusiastically.

"But he's married and has a family," finished Elizabeth in a rush.

"I see," said Jane.

"Oh, don't misunderstand. He didn't lie to me. I knew all along he was married. But I like him so much, and I need someone so badly." She looked at Jane. "I'm not like you. I'm not as strong or as independent. I can't just live for my career. I need someone with me, someone I can care for. And he seems to like me. He's very good to me."

"Do I know him?" asked Jane.

"Yes. But I don't want to mention his name. He's rather well-known."

A thought Jane had held for some time crossed her mind. "I thought so," she said.

"You know?"

"I think so."

"Is it that obvious?" asked Elizabeth, horrified. "I mean, do you think everyone knows?"

"No, no. Not at all. I just had a suspicion, that's all. I haven't heard a word about it from anyone."

Elizabeth relaxed. "That's good. I wouldn't want to do anything to hurt him."

"What about you?"

"Me?"

"Yes. Does he feel the same way? Does he care for you and want to protect you?"

"I think so. I just know that I feel good when he's with me."

"Is that enough?"

Elizabeth shrugged. "I guess it will have to be."

"Have you made any plans?"

"Not many. He's in Wash—he's away now. But he'll be back soon for a few weeks, and then he'll be here most of the summer. I thought I might get a new apartment."

"That's a good idea, anyway. I've thought for a long time you should move out of that place."

"I was hoping that Ralph would come back. And I wanted to be where he could find me."

"Well, now you have a perfect reason for moving. Now you don't *want* him to find you."

"No. Maybe when I get finished with this picture I can start looking. I meant to do it before now, but I haven't had time. But certainly by this summer, I'll find something."

"Good for you. Just getting Ralph out of your mind makes this new relationship beneficial."

"I hope it's more than that," said Elizabeth.

"So do I," said Jane. "But we both seem to have to take our moments when we can find them."

Elizabeth smiled. "I knew you'd understand."

"It looks like we're both long-distance lovers for the present."

"Yes. It's a little like they're off at war. But of course, we don't have to worry about that."

"No, we don't."

"You won't tell anyone, will you? I mean, not even Mrs. Watson or Mable. But I just had to tell you."

"I won't tell a soul." She reached out and touched Elizabeth's hand. "I hope it works out for you, kid," she said in a passable imitation of Mable's voice.

Elizabeth laughed. "Thank you. By the way, how *is* Mable?"

"Fine. She's staying with Sadie McCoy."

"Who is Sadie McCoy?"

"Well, I'm not sure how to tell you—"

"Tell me what?"

"From what I hear, Sadie is one of Hollywood's higher priced hookers," said Jane flatly.

"You mean a prostitute?"

"That's another word for it."

"Then, you mean, Mable's a—a—"

"A hooker. Or she may just be visiting," said Jane, who knew very well that the latter couldn't be true. "If she is, I'm sure she's a very high-class one. Sadie only has the very best clients. And, of course, it means that Mable is doing what she likes best. I'm sure she gets to sleep all morning."

"Yes, but—" began Elizabeth.

"Oh, don't worry about Mable," said Jane. "She'll always land on her feet."

The two women caught each other's eyes as Jane's words sank in. They both started giggling and continued all the way back to work.

CHAPTER *Fifteen*

DESPITE JANE'S HOPES that *Wanton Woman* would be done quickly, she was still filming when Warren got back to California. There had been the usual problems connected with making a picture, and, in addition, production had to be halted for several days when one of the lions used in the arena scene got loose and destroyed part of the set.

One afternoon she rushed home and joined Maud and Warren by the pool.

"It's a wrap," she said gaily.

"You mean you're through?" asked Warren, surprised.

"That's right. We finished the last scene today."

"And is it a nice picture, dear?" asked Maud.

"I sincerely doubt it," said Jane, sinking into a lounge chair and casually extending her hand to Warren who grasped it in his. The couple smiled at each other, and then Jane looked back at her aunt.

"What on earth are you doing?" asked Jane, staring intently at the tangled yarns on Maud's lap.

"I think I'm knitting," her aunt answered. "For the British forces, you know. I do hope someone will be able to use this."

"I'm sure they'll appreciate it very much," said Warren.

"As soon as they discover what it is," added Jane sarcastically.

Warren looked at Jane in surprise, but Maud smiled complacently.

"Don't be alarmed, Warren," she said. "Jane is always cranky when she finishes a picture. Why don't you take her out tonight for dinner and then a drive on the beach? It'll take her mind off her work."

"That sounds like a good idea," said Warren. "Do you want to, Jane?"

"I'd love it. Just give me a few minutes to take a shower and get dressed. I don't have to get all fixed up, do I?"

"No. We'll go somewhere casual and quiet."

"You're sweet," said Jane, leaning over and kissing him on the forehead.

Jane walked to the French doors leading into the house, and then turned back. "Oh . . . don't forget, you two. The premiere of *Handle With Care* is tomorrow night."

"Of course, dear. We've known about it for weeks," said Maud. "I'm looking forward to it, and I'm sure Warren is, too."

"Absolutely," said Warren, but his voice didn't sound as if he meant it.

"White tie and everything, love," said Jane as she went into the house.

"I know," said Warren with resignation.

Maud looked at Warren over her knitting spectacles.

He grinned at her. "Surely you don't like these big events."

"Sometimes they can be very exciting. But I know what you mean . . . often the whole evening is overdone and exhausting. Sort of like the big charity parties in New York. Thomas always maintained that he would rather send the charity more money just for the privilege of staying home. But in this case, it's very important. After all, Jane has never had star billing before. *Handle With Care* is the first picture where she's not a supporting player. So tomorrow night is really hers. She won't have to step aside for anyone. I'm thrilled for her."

"Yes," said Warren, "so am I." His voice was very quiet.

"It's a beautiful night. The moon is so bright and lovely," said Jane as she and Warren drove to Malibu.

"I don't want to look at the moon. I want to look at you," he answered. "This is the first night since I've been here when you haven't had to set the alarm for five A.M."

"I know," said Jane. "It has been rough. What do you think about going away for a few days, after tomorrow night? I'm sure the studio will give me at least a week off. Maybe we could go to Mexico or somewhere."

"That sounds good," said Warren as he pulled up at the beach house. They got out of the car and walked hand in hand to the door.

"I have the key," said Jane, pulling it out of her bag and handing it to Warren.

It was very quiet and dark in the small house. Jane went to the windows and opened them, letting in the sound of the surf crashing against the deserted beach. The moon sent a faint light through the open curtains. She stood still, looking out at the restless waves. Warren joined her and gathered her in his arms. For a few moments they held each other tightly, relaxing in the warmth of each other's closeness.

"I love you," whispered Warren.

"Dear, dear, Warren," said Jane, lifting her face to his. They kissed lightly and Jane moved her mouth around Warren's face, enjoying the roughness of his slight beard against the smoothness of her lips.

Warren buried his face in Jane's hair, stroking her as he murmured soft words of love into her ear. He began to open the front of Jane's light dress.

She giggled. "I thought I'd surprise you," she said. "No underwear." She shrugged out of the dress and stood naked before him. No matter how many times he'd seen her, Warren was still amazed by her beauty. Her superb face shone with youth and freshness, and her smooth body glowed in the gentle light.

"Now you," she urged.

Warren undressed quickly as Jane tossed pillows from the sofa and window seats onto the floor in front of the fireplace.

"I wish it were lit," she said.

"I can take care of that," he answered, grabbing a couple of logs and some kindling from a basket. He made the fire and then turned back to find Jane stretched out on the pillows, her hair loose and flowing, her expression eager and inviting. She held her arms up to him.

"Wait," said Warren, his voice husky. "I just want to look at you." He stared down at her for several seconds, then lowered himself to the cushions beside her. At first they just touched each other, exploring with their fingers and their tongues, discovering each other's bodies as if they had never before been together.

Warren rolled over on top of Jane and pushed his face down onto her breasts. She moaned softly, luxuriating in his touch: the feel of him caressing her, possessing her. She twisted her body beneath him. Pushing upward, she rolled Warren off her and sat astride his stomach.

She looked magnificent. Her head up, her eyes bright, her hair tousled. She looked down at Warren and smiled slightly as she ran her hands up over her flat belly to cup her breasts, rubbing her nipples between her fingers.

Warren stared at her, his gaze locked on the perfection of the picture she created. Jane raised her body slightly so that Warren could enter her. Thrusting up, he plunged deeply into Jane, causing her to sway slightly and gasp.

"Yes," she cried. "Oh, yes. . . ." Warren continued to push upward, as Jane rode his body. She dropped forward, her breasts against his chest as they kissed. Warren held her hair tightly in his fists as he pushed upward again and again, and their mouths met hungrily.

Warren raised himself and pushed Jane over onto her back. He pushed apart her legs and plunged forward, pinning her to the soft pillows. She cried out once, then reached for him greedily, grasping his back and buttocks as she tried to devour him, to pull his whole body into hers.

Their movements became more and more frenetic until, suddenly, Warren's breathing seemed to stop completely. He crashed once more into Jane. She held him tightly and followed his climax almost immediately with her own.

As their bodies relaxed, the room was once again filled with stillness: a silence of peace as the lovers entwined themselves in the afterglow of their passion.

"Maybe we should just stay here for our vacation," whispered Jane.

"That sounds like a very good idea," agreed Warren sleepily.

The premiere of *Handle With Care* proved, if there were any doubts, that Jane Turner was now in the forefront of Hollywood stardom. The picture itself was not especially noteworthy for anything other than several scenes in which Jane appeared in evening gowns looking breathtakingly beautiful and sexy. Her part as a party girl who finds true love and happiness at the end was not particularly challenging for Jane, and the story had been done several times before. But Global knew that every secretary in America would picture themselves wearing the clothes and looking as lovely as Jane, while the men in the audience would imagine themselves in bed with Jane Turner.

She had captured the public's imagination in *Dawn to Dusk*, and in *On Duty* she had completed her journey to nationwide recognition. Everyone knew who she was. She rivaled Carol Lombard in audience polls, and the studio received at least a thousand proposals of marriage for her each week.

Recently Jane had stayed out of the limelight, remaining home or with Warren. The public was anxious to see her, and tonight was their chance.

David Granoff and Scott Mack had both been asked to Maud's house for cocktails before going on to Grauman's Chinese Theatre. They each had needed a date and had carefully selected someone who would make a good background for Jane. David was escorting a new starlet at Global, a striking brunette, while Mack was with Lucille Evans, the character actress who had become friendly with Jane.

Upstairs in the great house, Jane was being ministered to by her hair and makeup men, sent over by the studio to make sure she looked her best. They had arrived at noon and worked steadily all afternoon.

Jane had borrowed some jewels from Maud and when they were added to her ensemble, she was finally announced prepared and went downstairs to join her friends.

Everyone gathered in the drawing room had seen Jane dressed up for the cameras or a publicity event, yet tonight they stood perfectly still and stared as she stopped in the doorway before coming forward to greet them.

The metamorphosis was complete. Jane Turner, budding starlet and ambitious Hollywood extra, had successfully made the transition to star, both on screen and off. With the help of the creative men from the studio, Jane appeared not as an inexperienced hopeful, desperate for publicity, but as a recognized and accepted personality whose position in Hollywood and the minds of the public was secure.

Her dress was a black Patou velvet with a high neckline and long sleeves. It was backless and fitted tightly across her breasts and down her figure, reaching the floor in a small whirl of cloth that flared out to expose a shocking-pink satin lining.

She wore her hair up, loosely held with diamond clips, a few strands falling casually around her face, framing her perfect makeup.

Maud's diamond earrings, choker, and bracelets highlighted her appearance. In her hand she grasped a black mink stole, lined with the same pink satin of the dress.

She looked magnificent, magnetic, compelling, and yet slightly aloof, exuding the quality that set her apart from all the others who had tried for the same dream.

Jane broke the spell by moving forward. "Do you suppose I could have a cocktail? I think this is going to be a very long evening."

Everyone laughed for no reason, and Warren, visibly shaken, hurried to get Jane a drink.

"Don't forget," said David, "you promised to come to my studio for a small party after the opening. Or did you forget?"

"Of course I didn't forget," said Jane. "Aunt Maud, I told you about it, didn't I?"

"Yes, you did, dear," said Maud, not having the slightest idea what Jane was talking about, but as usual, always ready to back her up. "I think it sounds lovely."

"We'll have to go to the Mocambo for the regular party first. But I love the idea of finishing the evening at your studio," said Jane.

"I think we should be going soon," said Maud.

"Yes," agreed Mack. "You don't want to keep your fans waiting too long, Jane."

"No. I'll just finish this and we can leave," said Jane, taking her drink from Warren and looking at him. "You haven't said a word to me yet," she said accusingly.

"You look very beautiful," he said quietly. "And I love you very much."

Jane leaned forward and brushed his cheek with her lips, being very careful not to muss her makeup.

"Tonight's going to be a very big event," said Mack.

"Oh, dear," said Maud. "I'm getting very excited. Couldn't we go soon?"

"Absolutely," said Jane. "I'm excited, too." Turning to Warren, she whispered, "I always like 'big events.'" She winked at him.

Warren almost dropped his glass.

The studio had sent two limousines to Jane's house. In one, David Granoff, along with his starlet, sat with Mack and Lucille. In the other, Jane was placed in the middle, flanked by Maud and Warren. The two older people looked as if they had been assigned to protect a rare and precious gem, which was exactly what the studio had in mind when they planned the seating and travel arrangements.

After they were all settled, the cars moved along at a stately pace to the front gates, where a small crowd of autograph hounds waited for them. People rushed forward, screaming at the cars. Jane smiled and waved, but Maud looked a little frightened.

"Dear me," she said. "They act as if they want to climb right in with us."

The car continued, and Jane waved until the fans were out of sight, then leaned back against the seat. "I don't think they mean any harm," she said. "They just want to see me."

"You never cease to amaze me," said Maud. "I would be terrified if it were me they were looking at."

"It's just part of the business."

"I must admit, I don't like the idea of being an object of curiosity myself," said Warren.

"Don't worry, darling," said Jane. "They won't bite you."

The crowds around Grauman's Chinese Theatre were enormous. They spilled out from the theater plaza and lined the streets for several blocks. Uniformed policemen on horseback rode up and down the barriers, keeping watch, and foot patrolmen were stationed at intervals to hold back any overly excited spectator.

Car after car released famous faces into the glaring beams of the bright lights and the cacophony of sound produced by several thousand demanding and expectant worshipers of the film stars. As each recognizable personality made their entrance, the crowd screamed their name and cheered as the star turned, waved, and smiled happily at their adoring fans.

Ten blocks from the theater, Jane's driver, an old pro at premieres, went down a cross street, made a U-turn, and pulled up along the curb.

"Jane, what is that man doing?" exclaimed Warren, gesturing toward the chauffeur.

"It's all right," she said calmly.

"But we can't just sit here," he continued, agitated.

"Warren, please. Let me do my job," said Jane. "We know what we're doing."

Warren sighed and leaned back in his seat. "Well, if we're just going to sit, I wish I'd brought a newspaper, or at least some work to go over."

Jane picked up the speaking tube. "Do you have a newspaper?" she asked the driver.

He did, and, pushing back the glass partition, he handed it to Jane who gave it to Warren with the injunction to be a good boy.

Mack's car had gone ahead and was now in front of the theater. After the others had gotten out, Mack, looking a little shy and very handsome, stood up. The crowd cheered him, and he appeared embarrassed—which he wasn't in the least—and this encouraged the audience to even greater applause. Mack waved and reached out to shake hands with the closest fans before very graciously insisting that the other three precede him up the red carpet to the waiting microphones. He gave a short interview to the broadcasters and smiled at the newspaper photographers as they snapped their cameras and shouted out at him to turn one way or the other.

There were no other cars in sight, and after Mack had disappeared inside the theater, the crowd quieted down slightly, exchanging film star stories with the strangers around them. But there was an air of anticipation hovering over the scene. From somewhere the chant of, "Jane, Jane, Jane . . ." began.

It wasn't loud at first, only a few voices. But the chorus built rapidly until the whole crowd had joined in, the night air ringing with the sound of Jane's name.

Jane could hear the shouting, and she smiled to herself.

At this point, the driver picked up his end of the speaking tube and said, "Time, Miss Turner."

Jane quickly looked in the mirror, slightly adjusted an earring, and touched her hair.

"You look perfect," said Maud.

Jane smiled abstractly and locked her gaze forward, the excitement building inside her.

The car pulled back onto the main street and began to move slowly toward the theater. There was no one else near the entrance, walking up the carpet, or being interviewed at the podium. The stage was set for Jane Turner.

Screaming her name, the crowd was almost in a frenzy. Maud could feel the tension as she looked first at Jane's intent face and then at the waiting throngs through which they were now moving. As the fans recognized Jane, they plunged toward the car, pushing and grasping out at the vehicle. The police had to use all of their resources to hold back the mob.

Maud saw several teenage girls sobbing uncontrollably, and an elderly woman shoved through the police and pressed her face against the glass before being whisked away by an officer.

The driver knew his job. When he was within twenty feet of the entrance, he slowed down, and then, about ten feet from the red carpet, he put on a slight burst of speed and they drew up at the entrance with a flourish.

Someone cried out, "It's her! It's her!" Pandemonium broke loose. The audience waved and screamed, pushing against the barricades in an attempt to get closer.

Jane sat very erect. Every fiber of her body was tuned and ready. She raised her head slightly. *She could feel everything.* Like the night in David Granoff's studio when his lights had been on her naked body. Or in the movie studio, when the cameras were focused on her. The excitement and the adulation were all for her. She loved it.

Jane looked slightly to the left and noticed that Warren was still reading his paper, totally oblivious to the commotion around her. She raised one hand and pushed the paper to the floor of the car.

"Really, darling," she muttered.

"Sorry," said Warren, looking around and noticing the crowd for the first time. The publicity people rushed forward and opened the car door.

"You first," said Jane to Warren.

He looked at Jane, almost not recognizing her. Her face was set, intent. She seemed to have become a different person since they'd left the house. It confused him. But he nodded and adroitly slipped over Jane and Maud and climbed out of the car. The crowd didn't recognize him, and for a few moments they were confused.

"All right, Aunt Maud," whispered Jane.

Maud leaned over and kissed Jane. She didn't know why she did it, but she knew something special was happening, and she felt the need to let Jane know she was loved. Then Maud climbed slowly out of the massive limousine.

Mrs. Thomas Watson had appeared in several of the articles about Jane in the screen magazines, and her name and likeness had been in the papers when she accompanied Jane on publicity events. Thus many in the crowd knew who she was. All of the true movie fans knew that Maud Watson was always with Jane Turner, and her appearance confirmed that their idol had arrived.

Maud, in her lavender lace gown and pearls, looked distinguished and dignified, and although she didn't wave or even acknowledge the crowd, they were still glad to see her and cheered as she stood quiet and serene next to Warren.

Alone in the car, Jane waited a few more moments for the crowd's excitement to peak once again. In the rearview mirror, she caught the eye of the driver who nodded at her and gave the thumbs-up sign. She drew herself together and reached out one jeweled arm to Warren. He grasped her hand, but still Jane did not leave the car.

But the sight of Warren leaning toward the limousine and the tantalizing view of Jane's arm sent the crowd into ecstasy.

When they had reached fever pitch, chanting her name and calling out for her, Jane suddenly appeared.

It was impossible to say that she had left the car, or that she had stood up. One moment she wasn't there, the next moment she was before them. The crowd lost control. Their screams pierced the night air and blended with the popping and crackling of the giant klieg lights hurling blinding rays against the darkened sky. The newspaper men and photographers broke ranks at the podium and rushed down the red carpet toward her, snapping their cameras and shouting, their voices mingling with the cries of the crowd.

It was a collage of light and noise and confusion, all centering on one single person.

Jane stood perfectly still, allowing the sounds and sights to touch her, to pull from her the energy that she knew would send the public into an even greater state of adulation.

In her black dress and jewels, she looked regal and elegant. She was what all the young girls from small towns all over America wanted to be. She was them, and she belonged to them. Jane Turner was theirs, and they owned her. Lowering her head, Jane lifted her eyes and looked out across the crowd, drawing from inside herself the magic that they had come to see.

And the electricity and energy within her spilled forward, reaching out and taking hold of the already hysterical mob.

The publicity people and extra guards pushed back the press as Jane began to walk up the red carpet. Warren and Maud followed her closely. And with each step Jane took, the noise increased until it seemed about to blow apart the world.

But the world didn't matter. Now only Jane Turner existed. There was nothing else. She was everything. Jane Turner was a star.

"To Jane Turner . . . our newest and brightest star." David Granoff raised his champagne glass and Jane smiled at the crowd of people who had gathered at David's party after the premiere.

Everyone cheered and drank the toast. Jane thanked them, and was again surrounded by guests, as she had been since arriving at the party.

Warren and Mack stood off to one side. "Who are all these people?" asked Warren.

"The usual collection," answered Mack. "The actors I suppose you recognize, the others are artists, executives, a little bit of everything."

"I haven't seen Greta Stewart all evening."

Mack smiled. "No. And that's a mistake on her part, too. No matter how much she hates Jane—and make no mistakes, she really does hate her, she should have shown up at the premiere and the party at the Mocambo for her own sake. Jane's too important now for Greta to ignore her."

"Does she really hate Jane?"

"Of course she does." Mack looked about him. "I imagine several of the people here really hate her. Jane's made it. And many people will never forgive her for that."

Warren looked worried.

"Don't let it bother you. Jane's going to be all right. She's got several films in the works. Global has a lot of plans for her. But that's only good business. After tonight, she's worth millions to them."

"You make her sound like some kind of commodity."

"She is, and so am I. Everyone on the screen is."

Warren shook his head.

Mack smiled and clapped him on the back. "Don't look so glum. Jane knows what she's doing. And besides, she's got you and Maud around her to keep her sane." Mack took a drink from a passing waiter. "Oh, I saw an interesting chess problem . . ."

Jane slipped away from the party and went into the studio dressing room. There was a pack of cigarettes on the makeup table, and she lit one as she sat down before the mirror. Automatically, she checked her face and hair and then leaned back and relaxed, still staring at her reflection.

Her thoughts returned to the premiere. All over the country there were individuals in their homes who were aware of her this evening. Some respected her, some envied her, others lusted after her celebrity. But regardless of what they thought of her, their attention had been focused on Jane Turner.

You've made it, she thought. Now. At this very moment, the dream created by the flickering shadows in the darkened theaters had become a reality. She remembered sitting on the bed in Aunt Maud's New York house, talking to her sisters. A slight smile crossed her mouth as she thought of the words she had spoken. "I want to be a movie star," she had told them. They had stared at her in disbelief and astonishment.

But tonight it was a reality. Tonight, the face staring at her across the narrow makeup table couldn't go into any city of the country without being recognized. She had what she had wanted. Fame, success, celebrity.

There were still things to be done, though. She wasn't happy with her roles. But she was sure that would change now. Tomorrow she and Murry Edson would talk, and the parts she wanted would be offered to her.

And tonight, she had Warren. Jane's face softened at the thought of the dignified and conservative Warren Harris. He loved her. She was confident and content with his love. But until now there had been so many things on her mind, so much to do that she hadn't stopped to take stock of her own feelings toward him.

Now, with her dreams firmly in her hands, she could think about her feelings for Warren. His face came into her thoughts and, as she saw him in her mind, she realized that she couldn't imagine being without him. This stuffy, slightly graying businessman from Kansas City was the man she wanted to be with always.

She loved him. She knew she loved him. And tonight, if he asked her to marry him, she'd say yes. They'd work out their problems somehow. She could work, keep her career, and still have time for Warren.

"Hey! Are you going to stay in here all night? Some of the guests are leaving and they want to say good-bye."

Jane looked up and saw David Granoff's face reflected in the mirror. "Have I been a long time? I'm sorry. I guess I just needed a few moments alone."

"I'm not surprised. It's been a big evening. But you'd better come on out now."

Jane got up, looked at her reflection once more, and then joined the guests, looking over the heads of her friends and admirers for Warren. She couldn't see him in the crowd.

Mack had been borne away by friends and, alone, Warren began to wander about the large photographic studio, looking at David's pictures of actors and actresses that hung on the walls.

Most were standard publicity shots, but occasionally Warren found a more intimate shot in which David had tried to capture the personality of the celebrity. Warren didn't know much about photography, but he could tell that Granoff had talent. Some of the pictures were stunning.

In one corner, he suddenly came upon a print that caught his eye and held him riveted to the spot. He leaned forward for a better look.

The girl in the picture was nude, her body stretched out on a black background, her face turned slightly away from the camera. It was a lustrous and sensual shot, one that would make any man hunger for the woman posed so seductively. Any man would want this lovely young woman. The woman Warren Harris loved—Jane Turner.

Anger assailed him, slicing through his body like a knife. Rage coursed through his veins as he stared at the picture. How dare she allow this violation of her body by the cold, impersonal eye of the camera.

Warren gripped his hands tightly, his arms rigid at his sides. He looked back at the laughing and happy group of people. He could just see Jane at the center of the crowd, her head up, her eyes bright, her mouth open in happiness. There she was, surrounded by all that she wanted, all that meant anything to her.

A deadly calm came over him. His rage subsided into a constrained combination of despair and disgust. He felt defeat cover him like a shroud.

CHAPTER *Sixteen*

"DEAR ME," EXCLAIMED MAUD, seating herself in the limousine. "What a very exciting evening."

"Morning, now," said Jane. "It must be almost four A.M. What time is it, Warren?"

"A little after four."

"Mercy!" said Maud. "But it was all very thrilling, wasn't it? I was very proud of you, dear."

"Thank you, Aunt Maud." She turned to Warren. "And were you proud of me?"

"Naturally," he answered shortly.

Jane touched his face playfully. "I think we have a tired and grumpy man with us, Aunt Maud."

"That's understandable," said Maud. "I could use some sleep myself. Oh, look! Mack's car is passing us. What on earth is he doing?"

Jane looked out of the window and saw Mack and Lucille in the back of their limousine. Mack was urging the driver to go faster, gesturing with his hands as Lucille sat shaking her head and giggling. Mack looked over toward Jane and waved and blew kisses in her direction. The car swept on down the street, and Jane laughed.

"Oh, boy, Bill's going to have his hands full. It looks like Mack's had a few."

"I hope they get home all right," said Maud.

"Don't worry. Mack's not behind the wheel. And the driver will only let him go so far with his antics."

Jane leaned close to Warren. "There's going to be a wonderful sunrise. Why don't we take my little car and drive out to the beach house after we drop off Aunt Maud?"

Warren nodded, and Jane hunched closer to him for the rest of the trip. After they had seen Maud into the house, they climbed into Jane's convertible, Warren behind the wheel, and drove toward Malibu.

"You're very quiet," said Jane.

He shrugged. "I don't have much to say."

"I guess you didn't like tonight very much."

"I know you did."

"Yes. I loved it. It represented all that I've worked for."

"Then you should be very happy."

"I would be," said Jane sharply, "if you were a little happier for me. You haven't exactly been the life of the party tonight."

"I don't think I've ever been a life-of-the-party kind of guy."

"No. I suppose not. But I've never known you to be petty, either. Or to begrudge someone else their accomplishments."

"I wasn't aware I was begrudging you anything."

"Then maybe you should become aware," said Jane, twisting in the seat to face him. "This is a very special night for me, and I don't think you're being fair."

"Sorry."

"Thanks a lot," said Jane sarcastically.

"What the hell do you want me to say?"

"Nothing. You don't have to say anything. Unless you want to tell me what's bothering you."

"I don't know if I can talk about it." The cold, hard anger was beginning to build within him again. The photograph he had seen on David's wall pushed its way into his mind until it was all he could see. Without thinking, he pushed down harder on the accelerator.

Jane stared out at the night rushing by. In the distance she could hear the sound of the waves. She was hurt and angry, and couldn't understand Warren's attitude.

He took his eyes off the road briefly and looked at Jane. She was spectacularly beautiful, perhaps even more lovely now with the wind tousling her hair, than she had been at the premiere. Damn her, he thought. Damn her. Again his foot touched the gas pedal, and the little car shot forward. They were almost to the beach now, nearing the turnoff to the house. Warren was driving very fast, his face set and closed.

Jane pushed back her hair and looked over at Warren. "Kill yourself if you want to," she said loudly, "but let me out. I don't want to die."

Her words caught him unaware and, instinctively, he let up on the gas pedal. The car slowed slightly, but it was still going too fast to make the turn. Warren jammed on the brakes as he attempted the curve and the car swerved, slipping from side to side on the road. A wheel caught on the embankment and the small car slid into a ditch and stopped.

"Are you all right?" asked Warren anxiously, reaching toward Jane.

Jane didn't answer. She pulled away from him, stood up, and stepped over the closed door onto the beach. She turned back and faced him.

"What the fuck do you think you're doing?" she asked, her voice quiet and angry.

Warren climbed out of the car and joined her.

"Jane . . ."

"I've had it, Warren," she went on. "I've had enough of your little games tonight. First you won't talk to me, and then you try to kill us both. You must be out of your mind."

"That's right. Out of my mind. I've been that way since I left Granoff's studio."

"David's? What's David got to do with anything?"

"Everything. He has everything to do with it. . . . I saw the picture."

"What picture?" Jane looked at him, confused. "What on earth are you talking about?"

"The photograph. I saw the photograph he did of you."

"David has been taking pictures of me for over two years. He's taken dozens—hundreds of pictures of me. I don't have the slightest idea what you're talking about."

"Are you always nude when he takes your picture?"

Jane stared at him.

"Are you? Do you always take off your clothes for him?"

Jane looked him in the eyes. "I've only done one nude shooting. It was at the beginning, soon after I met David."

"Right off the bat, huh? Just as soon as you met."

"You know you don't have to worry about David. We've talked about him. He's a friend, that's all."

"That's very comforting. But what about all the others who've seen that picture. Did you hand out a bunch at the studio for the guys to pass around?"

"Of course not. I thought David had given all of the prints and negatives to Murry Edson. He said they'd all been destroyed."

"Apparently, David kept at least one of them."

Jane remained silent.

"It must have been very interesting to that group at the party. There you were, the newest and biggest movie star in Hollywood, and if the guests took a short walk around the room, they could see just how you started. Maybe it wouldn't have been a surprise to them. Maybe they all take it for granted that that's how you get ahead out here. Is it, Jane? Is that the way you all do it? *Is that the way you became a star?*"

Jane's eyes flashed in anger, but she controlled herself.

"I thought we'd gotten beyond all this, Warren. I thought we'd settled all your problems about my career."

"I didn't think it included naked pictures."

"Naked pictures," snapped Jane. "You make it sound like I've been making dirty films. I took those pictures because David asked me to. He's an artist. A brilliant photographer."

"Yes, but—"

"But nothing. Those pictures are very beautiful, and I'm not the least bit ashamed of them. If Murry hadn't been concerned about the press, I would never have let him destroy them. But he insisted because of minds like yours, Warren. Narrow, closed little minds that don't object to looking at blood or pain, but can't stand the sight of the human body."

"I don't like the idea of everyone seeing you like that."

"You don't like it. There are so many things you don't like: my career, Hollywood, the films I do . . . ."

"Jane—"

"Let me finish. The picture doesn't mean anything, Warren. Nothing at all. The things you read into it are from *your* mind, not mine, not David's." She walked close to Warren. "Tonight I was on top of the world. Tonight meant everything to me. And tonight I realized that I love you. That I want to be with you. And instead of something beautiful, we're right back where we were. Back to misunderstandings and accusations." Despite her anger, Jane felt sorry for Warren. His face was sad and his eyes seemed full of pain.

"Why can't you just accept what we have, Warren? Why can't you just take each day as it comes without trying to orchestrate and arrange everything to some impossible specifications?"

"I just want what is best for you," he said sadly.

"Good God, you sound like my father."

"Well, I'm certainly old enough."

She looked at him closely. "Is that what's bothering you? Is that what's behind all your anger? Because there's nothing I can do about our ages. And I can't spend all of our time together reassuring you. I chose to be with you. I chose to sleep with you because I want to. But if you keep throwing my career and my life up at me every moment we're together, then you're going to destroy whatever we have."

Warren didn't know what to say. His intellect told him Jane was right. But he would never like the idea of the nude pictures. He would never like the idea of her career. Every time another man looked at Jane, he felt threatened. His age had bothered him since they'd first met. He wasn't glamorous or exciting. He was simply Warren Harris, a businessman from Kansas City, Missouri. And he was terrified of losing her.

"I don't know what to do," he said quietly.

"Then don't do anything," said Jane. "Stop trying to do things, Warren. Just let us be. Let us have each other and care for each other. Let us have the moments and the love we share without worrying about tomorrow."

"I don't think I can stop being jealous," he said seriously.

Jane laughed. "I should certainly hope not," she answered, entwining her arms around his neck.

They kissed. And then Warren pulled back his head and looked at Jane's convertible.

"I'm afraid your car is stuck," he said.

"Is it?" she asked, her face nestled against his shoulder. "Then I guess we'd better do something about it." She raised her head and looked provocatively at him. "Tomorrow," she whispered.

Terrance Malvey and Murry Edson sat in Murry's office the afternoon following the premiere of *Handle With Care*.

"Well," said Murry, slapping down a newspaper, "we got a hit."

"Looks that way," agreed Terry.

"Then why the hell do you look so glum? This is a good day."

Terry shrugged. "You do this every time. If I had a dollar for every new star you've launched and then had trouble with, I could get out of this business."

"Just what the hell are you talking about?"

"Jane Turner. You know as well as I do that she'll be here in about fifteen minutes with a list as long as your arm of things she wants. Special hairdressers, makeup people. A new dressing room. You name it, she'll want it."

"Maybe this time it'll be different," said Murry hopefully.

"Sure it will," replied Terry.

Murry's intercom announced Miss Turner.

"Well, at least she hasn't started coming in late yet," said Terry. "Jesus. She's even early. I wonder if that's bad or good?"

The secretary opened the door, and Jane came into the office.

"Good morning, Jane," said Murry, rising and coming to greet her.

Jane smiled at Murry and nodded at Terry as Murry escorted her to a chair.

"You must be very happy today," he said, returning behind his desk. "It was a good premiere, wasn't it?"

"Yes. It was wonderful," said Jane.

"Well, there'll probably be a lot more evenings like that in your future," Murry went on. "We have great things planned for you."

Jane didn't answer.

"Terrance and I have worked out at least three more films for you. You start next week with costume fittings, and then there are several publicity things coming along. You're going to be a very busy girl."

"It sounds very interesting."

"You don't seem very excited for a girl who's the envy of the whole country," said Terrance. "Anything bothering you?"

"Not really. It's just that . . . well, I'd like your opinions about something."

"Anything," said Murry. "Just tell us. We're here to help you."

"All right. I don't know if you're aware of it, but I've been seeing Warren Harris."

"Oh?" Murry was noncommittal.

"Yes. And . . . we're thinking of getting married."

"Married!" Terry almost fell out of his chair.

"Married!" echoed Murry.

Jane looked from one man to the other. She hadn't expected them to be so surprised.

"Well, let's not do anything hasty," said Murry. "I think we should discuss this."

"All right," said Jane. "That's why I mentioned it."

"That's very wise of you," said Murry. "Yes, very wise." He looked toward Malvey, silently ordering the producer to say something.

"Well, well," began Terrance. "This is a surprise, Jane. You know we like Warren very much. And I don't need to tell you how much we care for you."

"Absolutely," said Murry. "You're very important to us. And we all like Warren. Great businessman," he finished lamely.

"Yes, well . . ." said Terrance. "I'm sure you know, Jane, that we all want what is the best for you."

"Absolutely," said Murry again.

"But," continued Terry, "I'm wondering if you've thought this through completely. After all, Warren Harris is from a different background than yours. And, of course, he is older. He has children, doesn't he?"

"Two," said Jane. "They're coming to spend the summer with me. Warren and I decided last night that it would be a good idea for all of us to get acquainted. Warren will be staying, as well."

"All together?" Murry was incredulous.

"We'll be staying with my Aunt Maud. I'm sure you agree that she's an adequate chaperon."

"Wonderful woman," murmured Murry.

Murry looked at Terrance. The two men were quickly trying to figure out just how Jane's marriage would impact on her career. Global's plans included a very elaborate film starring Jane as an alluring native girl. If it came in on schedule, it could be released as soon as September.

If Jane got married in the fall, it would mean that Global's most provocative star would be gliding up to the altar with a man old enough to be her father and suddenly becoming the stepmother of two children at the same time the studio was promoting her as a sex goddess.

"I'm sure you'll have a very good time this summer," said Terrance. "But to return to your marriage, have you thought about what effect your marriage would have on your fans?"

"My fans?"

"Yes. After all, you do have a certain image," continued Terrance. "You know as well as I do that your job doesn't stop when the camera turns off."

"I understand. But I also think I'm entitled to a private life."

"But you're America's sex symbol," blurted out Murry.

Jane stared at Murry. "I know that I have a certain—"

"Beauty," offered Terrance.

"Thank you, Terry," said Murry. "Yes, beauty. And I don't think the public is going to be able to handle you suddenly doing birthday parties and baking cakes."

"Then perhaps," said Jane slowly, "it might be a good idea to think about altering my image slightly."

Oh shit, thought Terrance, here it comes.

"I don't think I understand," said Murry, stalling for time.

"It's very simple," said Jane. "I've done virtually the same part several times, and I would like something different. Something that gives me a chance to do more than just flit across the set in a revealing dress or a bathing suit. You're afraid if I marry Warren my image will be hurt. To me, the best idea would be to give me some parts that don't keep me locked in that image. Then as my image changes, it won't make any difference who I marry."

Murry was stunned. He sat with his mouth slightly open staring at his newest star.

Terrance looked over at Jane approvingly. She had handled it very well, he thought. She hadn't screamed or cried or thrown a temper tantrum. She had used logic and sense, qualities most stars didn't even understand, let alone exercise. She had Murry right where she wanted him.

Terrance glanced at the head of Global Films. The little man was beginning to turn a bright red. It was obvious that he was furious at the trap Jane had laid for him.

When he was finally able to speak, his voice was tightly controlled. "Now, Jane," he began. "You know that we here at Global, the whole Global family, has your best interests at heart. We know what is best for you. You have just become a household word. This is no time to suddenly start making changes."

Jane looked at him inquiringly. "I would think this would be an excellent time," she said. "After all, it'll be at least a year and a half before I finish the new pictures, and by that point the public will be getting a little tired of seeing me in the same role over and over again. They'll be ready for something else."

Murry's temper was beginning to crack. "They don't ask to see Crawford do something else. They don't ask to see Cooper do something else. They don't ask to see Davis—" He stopped. Davis was not a good example. After all, she had walked out on Warner's to get the roles she wanted. He took a deep breath and went on.

"The public likes things to be consistent. They don't want change. They want to see you the way they've always seen you. What would happen if Ginger Rogers suddenly stopped dancing? Or Loretta Young became an evil character? I'll tell you what would happen. The public would hate it."

"I don't agree," said Jane calmly.

"What!" Murry exploded. "Agree? *You* don't agree. You suddenly think I don't know my own business? You think I made Global Films one of the biggest movie companies in the world by not knowing what I was talking about?" Murry stood up and leaned over his desk toward Jane. "I tell you, the public doesn't want to see Jane Turner as the happy housewife. It wants you just as you are."

"And what about what I want?" retorted Jane.

For a few moments no one spoke. Finally, Murry broke the silence.

"Jane, darling," he said. "You're a big star now. We're all very excited about your future. We have great plans for you.

But you must let us do things as we see fit. After all, we only want the best for you, don't we, Terrance?''

Malvey had been sitting calmly through the battle, and now he nodded. "Absolutely. In fact," a mischievous gleam lit his eyes, "Murry was telling me before you came in about the wonderful gifts he has for you, just to show you how much Global cares for you."

"Gifts?" asked Jane, startled.

"Yes, absolutely," agreed Murry, looking malevolently toward Terrance. "How would you like a new dressing room? We've made special arrangements for your hairdresser and makeup people to be on call for special events. And—" he seemed to be strangling, "we have even decided to give you a little bonus to show our appreciation for your work."

"That's very nice," said Jane, "but—"

"And don't forget the new car," piped up Terrance.

"Yes. Your new car," said Murry, sighing. "I hope you'll like it. It'll be delivered this afternoon."

"What good timing," said Jane. "Mine went into a ditch last night."

"Ditch?" asked Murry, stunned.

"Yes. Warren and I had a little accident."

Murry looked at her closely. "You're all right, aren't you? No scars or anything?"

"I'm fine," said Jane.

"That's good. We wouldn't want anything to happen to you." Murry got up and came around the desk. He took her arm and helped her from her chair. "Now you go along," he said. "Enjoy your time off. Next Monday you start fittings for your next film. And if I were you, I wouldn't think too much about marriage right now. You have enough on your mind without taking on additional responsibilities."

Jane knew she'd lost this round, so she obediently went to the door. But there'll be another day, she thought to herself as she smiled at Murry.

"And don't you worry about your films. Trust us. We know what we're doing."

Jane nodded and left.

Murry closed the door behind Jane and then turned back to Terrance.

"Jesus. It never fails," he moaned.

"I warned you," said Terrance unnecessarily. "Don't say I didn't tell—"

"Oh, go to hell," said Murry. "Different roles. Jesus! What comes over these broads? She's a big star and suddenly she wants to be an actress. And marry Warren Harris." He moaned again.

"She sure handled it well," said Terrance admiringly. "You've got to hand it to her, she had you going for a while. If I didn't know better, I would almost believe that Jane Turner could act."

"Now *you* sound like a fool," said Murry.

"Do you think the rooms look all right?" asked Jane. "I mean, are the flowers okay and everything?"

"Yes, dear," said Maud, giving Jane a pat on the shoulder, "the guest rooms all look lovely."

Jane stamped her foot. "Warren makes me so mad. He hasn't told me a thing about what the children like and what they don't like. I've asked and asked, and all he says is that Susan is shy and David is noisy. What kind of description is that?"

"It might be all he knows," said Maud practically. "You really should be getting dressed, or you're going to be in your robe when they arrive."

"My, God," said Jane, suddenly animated. "You're right. But what should I wear?" Jane ran toward her room and began scrambling through the massive, well-filled closets. Louise was nearby and came to help. Maud followed.

"Just pick something comfortable, dear," advised Maud.

"Comfortable!"

"Of course, dear. Children are very active, and you can handle them easier if you move fast."

"I don't think I'll be chasing Warren's children around the house. Oh, I do want to make a good impression on them. I want them to like me."

"I'm sure they will, dear. Just be yourself. Have they seen your pictures?"

Jane shrugged. "Warren says no, but what does he know?"

"Just keep calm. Don't work yourself into a state. It's bad for your acids. We have everything planned. There is plenty of room for everyone here, and on the weekends we can go to the beach house. And while you and Warren are working, I can take them on all the usual tourist jaunts."

"Dear Aunt Maud," said Jane, putting her arms about her. "You are wonderful. I hope it won't be too much for you."

"Of course not, dear. In fact, I'm rather looking forward to it. I've never been to any of the other studios since I've been here, and there are a lot of other sights to see. By the way, don't you have to work today?"

"No. I told them I had an appointment so they arranged to shoot around me."

"My. That is star treatment," said Maud with a smile.

Jane grinned back and held up a light green linen* suit. "What do you think of this?"

"It's lovely," said Maud.

"Maybe," said Jane. "But I've heard that green is bad luck. It's rather a strange color, too."

"It's like the sea, very calming."

"The sea? Oh, no. I don't want the children to think I'm swimming at them. What about this one?" She picked up a severe black suit.

"Don't you think that's a little serious?"

"Oh, you're right," said Jane, dropping the suit on the floor. "Damn it. Everything's wrong."

"Nonsense," said Maud, stepping forward and selecting a simple, fawn-colored dress. "This one will be perfect."

"Do you really think so? All right. But what about my hair?"

"It looks lovely as it is," said Maud, studying Jane's blond hair which was flowing loosely over her shoulders.

"Oh, no," said Jane. "I can't leave it down. That's too sexy. I'd better put it up. Maybe a tight bun—"

"You'll look like a schoolteacher," finished Maud. "Really, Jane, you must stop worrying about your screen image. Even if they have seen your pictures, these children are not going to expect you to greet them in an evening gown, tons of eye makeup, and a long cigarette holder."

"I bet they do. And that's just what I'm trying to avoid. I don't want to look the way I do on the screen."

"Then what about a nice dirndl. Or perhaps some pants and a sloppy shirt?"

"Aunt Maud!"

"I was just trying to be helpful. Put on this dress," said Maud with finality. "I'll expect you downstairs in a few moments, and we'll wait for them together in the drawing room."

"All right," said Jane meekly.

David and Susan Harris, along with their father, arrived an hour later. Jane had calmed down and was sitting with Maud when they heard the front doorbell. In a few moments they were all together.

David was sixteen and trying hard to be sophisticated. Contrary to his father's belief, he had seen Jane's films several times along with his friends and had been fascinated with her shimmering image. He had often stayed awake late at night thinking about her. But now that the film goddess was before him, looking much like any other woman, he was a little disappointed. He made a little bow when Warren introduced him, said hello, and then was silent.

Susan was a slightly overweight fourteen-year-old. Her hair was nondescript and uninterestingly arranged. Her dress was obviously expensive, but much too young for her. She looked at Jane wistfully, captivated by the actress's beauty.

Maud took charge immediately, rushing the children off to their rooms and inquiring if they were hungry or tired. She talked so much, the children didn't have a chance to think about being shy.

Alone, Warren and Jane looked at each other for a few moments. It had been several weeks since they had been together. Warren had had business to take care of, and then he had waited for his children to get out of school so that he could bring them to California.

"Hello, darling," said Jane, lifting her face to his.

Warren kissed her and ran one finger down her cheek. "Hi there," he said quietly. "Have you missed me?"

"Desperately," said Jane, pushing her body toward his.

"I've missed you, too," said Warren. They kissed again, and then pulled apart slightly.

"You know," he said, "I'm not sure I'm going to like this whole thing."

"Now Warren," replied Jane, moving away from him and lighting a cigarette. "We've been all through this. It just doesn't make sense for you to take a house and find someone to take care of David and Susan, who, incidentally, I think are charming. I want to get to know them, and Aunt Maud is delighted with the chance to show them around. And you know it's the only way you can spend the summer here. If they go back to Kansas City, you'll have to keep traveling back and forth."

"Most of the summer they're usually in camp."

"But, still—"

"Oh, I know what you mean," said Warren. "I'm glad the kids are here. I haven't seen much of them in the past few years, and it'll be good for us to be together. The only drawback of this whole arrangement is us."

Jane knew exactly what Warren was talking about. When they had decided that Warren's children should come and spend the summer with Jane, it seemed to make sense for Warren to stay in Maud's house as well. But they also had to realize that they couldn't be sneaking back and forth between their bedrooms all summer. For their time alone, they would have to make other arrangements.

"Now don't worry," said Jane. "We can go out to the beach house occasionally, and I'm sure we'll find plenty of time to be together. We just can't share the same bed in this house."

Warren smiled. "You always come right to the point."

"You know you agree with me. What if Aunt Maud, or even worse, David or Susan should see us scurrying down the hall half-dressed? It just wouldn't be nice."

Warren exploded with laughter.

"Don't laugh at me," said Jane, although she was delighted to see that Warren was beginning to have a sense of humor.

"I can't help it," he said. "I'm just picturing myself in my underwear rushing by Maud."

"That would be the least of your worries. Aunt Maud would probably say, 'Oh hello, dear. Would you like a cocktail?' But your children are something else again."

Warren put his arm around Jane. "I agree with you, darling. You're absolutely right. But I still retain the right to feel like that man who is starving in the midst of plenty."

"Which man?"

"I was afraid you were going to ask me that," said Warren. "I'll look it up later," he finished, bending down and kissing her.

CHAPTER *Seventeen*

IT WAS A GOOD SUMMER for Jane. She wasn't happy about her new movie, *Tragic Lady*, the story of a widow who makes her living as a bar hostess in modern day New York. But she went to work each morning as usual while Warren traveled to his new office in Los Angeles. As planned, Maud took the two youngsters to see the sights, and each evening at dinner they talked about their exploits.

Warren and Jane often took David and Susan to the beach, where Warren was delighted to have the chance to spend time with his children and get to know them better.

David got over his disappointment in Jane very quickly and was soon treating her like a buddy. Susan spent as much time with Jane as possible, studying her hair and makeup and timidly asking Jane's help in improving her looks. One morning, Jane took the young girl to the studio and had her grooming crew give Susan a complete make-over.

The cosmeticians spent several hours working on Susan. She got a new hairstyle and clothes from the costume department. And at the end of the day, she was thrilled with her appearance.

But when they got home, Warren wasn't so pleased. He didn't like the idea of his daughter being caught up in all the glitter and tinsel of Hollywood. It took Jane awhile to calm him down, but eventually she was able to convince Warren that even if he didn't approve of his daughter's new look, it was at least time that she had clothing suited to her age. Maud immediately took on the commission and had several exciting afternoons rampaging the better Beverly Hills shops.

In the third week of August, Jane finished *Tragic Lady*, and the family group headed to the beach for an uninterrupted week.

"Susan is going to be a very lovely young woman," commented Maud, who was sitting on the sand along with Warren and Jane, watching the young people near the water. "She's lost some weight, and her new bathing suit looks very nice on her. She has a nice tan, too."

"Which is something you're not likely to get," said Jane, looking at Maud's beach costume which consisted of a loose beach gown, several light silk scarves, and an enormous hat around which a length of chiffon was draped, hanging down over Maud's face. "You look like a beekeeper."

"In my day, ladies didn't let their skin get touched by the sun," said Maud sternly. "And I don't think it's a good idea to change things too quickly."

"I agree with you," said Warren. "About the sun and about changing things too fast. I don't want Susan growing up too soon."

"I'm sure she'll be fine," said Jane. "In a couple of years she'll have all the boys panting after her."

"I sincerely hope not," said Warren.

"Jane! What a vulgar expression," lamented Maud.

David raced over and asked Jane to toss him the beach ball. Warren volunteered, but David said he wanted his friends on the beach to see that he really knew Jane. Laughing, she got up and went to the admiring group of young men.

"I thought this was a private beach," said Warren, looking at all the people sitting not far away.

"It is," answered Maud. "Supposedly all these people belong to the houses you see on the cliff. I guess the others are their guests."

"I'm surprised Jane hasn't been mobbed by autograph seekers."

Maud sighed. "I always worry about those people. You never can tell just how far they'll go to get close to her. But it doesn't seem to bother Jane at all."

Warren watched Jane talking with the fascinated teenagers. It was obvious that they were all enchanted by her as she threw the ball in the wrong direction and giggled, just as they had all hoped she would.

"I guess you know," he said, "that I'm still trying to convince Jane to quit Hollywood and go back to Missouri with me."

"I thought this summer was to see if you couldn't live in California instead of Kansas City?" asked Maud, interested.

"Yes. But I'd still like to have one more try at getting her away from here."

"And if it doesn't work?"

"Then it'll have to be California. But I still don't like it for the kids. Or for us, either, for that matter."

"As far as your children are concerned, Warren, they can get into just as much trouble in Kansas City as they can here. Why, remember the 1920's and all those gangsters? That wasn't Hollywood or even New York. I can't imagine a duller place in the world than Chicago, but there they all were, shooting at each other, and apparently enjoying it enormously."

"I see your point," said Warren. "I guess I'm trying to make the kids an excuse for the fact that I'm still worried that as long as Jane is in the movie business, I'm going to play second fiddle to her career."

"I think that with a woman like Jane it won't matter what she's doing or where she's living. If she wants to do something, she'll do it. And if she loves you, she'll always find time to be with you." Maud smiled at Warren. "It's very difficult, isn't it? I mean, it's hard to understand someone like Jane. I admit that if I didn't know her mother, I wouldn't have a clue about her. But Jane is very much like Maggie. They both have something extra, something special in them that drives them. I don't know whether it's bad or good." Maud pulled out her knitting and began arranging her yarns. "But it's there. I often wish I had some of whatever it is. Then, on second thought, it's much more comfortable being undriven."

Warren laughed. "I'm sure you're right. But since Jane has

just finished a film, and I'm going to take the kids back next week, it seems like a good time to ask her to come along."

"We can but try," said Maud, concentrating on her work.

The day before Warren was to leave for Kansas City, Jane had an appointment with Murry Edson. She walked into his office promptly and found Murry sitting behind his desk with Terrance Malvey, as usual, in a nearby chair.

"Jane, you look beautiful," said Murry, giving her a kiss.

"Hi, Jane. You do look wonderful," said Terry.

"Thank you," said Jane, sitting down.

"I just saw the rushes for *Tragic Lady*," said Murry. "Excellent, Jane, excellent."

"Thank you," said Jane again.

"Yes," agreed Terry. "I thought you really brought life to the character."

"It wasn't hard," said Jane. "After all, I have played similar women before."

Murry laughed uncomfortably. "Now what can we do for you, Jane? Nothing wrong, I hope. Dressing room all right? Your car in good shape?"

"All of those things are fine."

"Good, good," said Murry, rubbing his hands together. "I understand you're doing some more publicity shots. Good idea. We can always use more pictures of you. And I hear the *Saturday Evening Post* is going to do a story on you."

"Yes. They called publicity last week."

"Wonderful," said Murry, who seemed bound and determined to ignore the fact that Jane had not smiled since she walked into the office. "Wonderful," he repeated, before lapsing into quiet.

There was a brief silence. Jane looked at both men, then spoke. "I want better roles," she said flatly.

Murry didn't take his eyes off Jane, nor did he answer.

"Well, we were just talking about your next film, weren't we, Murry?" said Terrance. "We both agree that it should really be a blockbuster."

"Oh?" Jane was interested, but suspicious.

"Yes," agreed Murry. "And we have just the thing. I believe we sent you the script last spring. We wanted to do it sooner, but decided that you shouldn't follow *Wanton Woman* with another costume piece. That's why we scheduled *Tragic Lady* first. But now it's time for *Island Woman*. It should be great."

"I remember it," said Jane. "It's a piece of shit."

"Jane!" exclaimed Murry.

"For the entire movie I wander around in a little sarong, speaking in broken English."

"Now, Jane," said Terrance. "It has a lot of possibilities. Did you read the scene where you are about to be sacrificed to the great god JuJuBe?"

"I threw up on that scene," said Jane.

"Jane, dear," interposed Murry, "*Island Woman* can be a very important film, full of deeper meanings. The simple villager's life versus the threats of civilization. Your doomed affair with the sailor from America—"

"Which I am supposed to pronounce Ah-muh-ee-ka," said Jane witheringly.

"You can hardly expect a simple native girl to have perfect diction," said Terrance. "After all—"

"After all, nothing," said Jane emphatically. "This whole piece of trash is just another excuse to get my clothes off in front of the camera. I want to do something else for a change. I'd like to do a scene without my breasts falling out of my costume."

"Jane, please!" Murry was shocked.

She stood up. "I tell you, I don't want to do this movie."

"And we're telling you it's perfect," said Murry, also standing. "Now be a good girl and trust us. We'll talk some more about your roles after you've gotten back to work."

"That's a good idea," agreed Terrance. "I know you actresses. You're not yourselves when you're out of harness. Once you're back on the set and working, you'll like *Island Woman*. You'll see, it'll be a great picture."

Jane stared at the two men. Nothing she had said seemed to register with them. Turning abruptly, she walked out of the office.

Driving home, her anger grew until she was seething. She pulled up at her front door and rushed into the house where she found Warren waiting for her.

"Jane, what on earth is wrong?" he asked, seeing the expression on her face.

"That son of a bitch," said Jane between clenched teeth. "That dirty bastard son of a bitch."

"Jane!" Warren was shocked.

"Who, dear?" asked Maud placidly as she walked into the room.

"Murry Edson and that little pet snake of his, Terrance Malvey. Today we discussed my next film. It's another piece of garbage, just like all the others. I can't believe them. They make me so angry." Jane grabbed a cigarette and sank down onto the sofa.

"Well," she continued bitterly, "they're not going to get the best of me this time. I've always been the good little girl around Global. And I'm not going to be so good anymore. Just you watch. I'm going to make their lives a living hell from the first day of shooting. I'll be late. I'll throw temper tantrums. I'll have a bad cold. That's it. I'll have a cold . . . maybe even pneumonia. That'll fix those bastards."

"Language, dear," said Maud, sitting next to Jane and taking up her knitting.

"Maybe this would be a good time to get out," suggested Warren. "You could come back to Kansas City with me and—"

"Excuse me, miss," said Hardgrave, coming to the door.

"Yes, Hardgrave?"

"Miss Hudson is here to see you. She says it's very important."

"Elizabeth's here? Now?" asked Jane. "She couldn't have picked a worse time."

"Tell her to come back later," said Warren.

"Yes sir," answered Hardgrave. "But, begging your pardon, miss. She seems to be very agitated."

"I'd better see her." Jane sighed. "Ask Miss Hudson to go into the library. I'll be there in a moment."

"Very good, miss." Hardgrave departed.

"I wonder what Elizabeth can want?" mused Jane.

"Forget about Elizabeth," said Warren. "What do you think of the idea of coming to Kansas City?"

Jane appeared to be lost in thought for a few moments, and Warren spoke to her again. Finally she smiled at him.

"Warren, I'm sorry. I don't mean to ignore you. It's just that I have a lot on my mind right now. We'll talk later, after I've seen Elizabeth." Jane hurried out of the room, leaving Warren staring after her.

"I guess it was a bad idea, anyway," he said, mostly to himself.

When Jane walked into the library, she found Elizabeth sitting in a wing-back chair in front of an empty fireplace. She was wearing an old polo coat, and in her hands was a twisted and torn hankerchief. She stood up quickly as Jane came in.

"Jane," began Elizabeth.

"Elizabeth. I'm glad to see you. But I'm afraid you've come at a rather bad time. Warren and his children leave tomorrow, and I've just had a difference of opinion with Murry, and—"

"Jane, I need your help," interrupted Elizabeth.

Looking at her friend, Jane could see that she was very upset. She took Elizabeth's arm, helped her back into her seat, and sat down across from her. "Elizabeth, are you all right? What's happened?"

"I . . . I'm not sure how to tell you. It's so awful."

"You know you can tell me anything. What's wrong?" Jane leaned forward.

Elizabeth looked at Jane for a moment, and then she began to cry. "Jane. I'm so afraid," she began. "So very afraid."

"You must get hold of yourself," said Jane. "Would you like a drink?"

Elizabeth nodded, and Jane went to a tray and poured a small glass of brandy. Returning, she handed it to Elizabeth who swallowed most of it immediately. She looked up at Jane.

"I suppose you think I'm a terrible fool," she said.

"I don't think anything," answered Jane. "I don't understand what all this is about."

"It's very simple," said Elizabeth, struggling for control. "Ralph's come back."

"I see," said Jane, not knowing how she was supposed to react.

"Yes," said Elizabeth, finishing her drink and placing the glass deliberately down on the table. "He came back last night."

"I see. And are you glad?"

Elizabeth laughed. "No. I'm not glad." Her laughter stopped suddenly and her eyes stared straight ahead, as if she were looking at something only she could see. "I'm scared," she said.

Elizabeth got up and walked over to the bar. She poured herself another drink, and then looked back at Jane.

"I was with Senator Mark Richmond," she blurted out. "I know you know about us."

"Yes," said Jane.

"I'm very frightened," said Elizabeth.

"Well, I'm sure that if you tell Mark everything he'll—"

"That's not the problem."

"Then explain to Ralph. I don't know who you're trying to appease."

"You don't understand. When Ralph walked in last night, I was in bed with Mark. At first Ralph didn't know who he was." Elizabeth stopped and remembered. "He thought it was funny . . . until he recognized Mark."

Jane felt a sinking feeling in the pit of her stomach. It was the same kind of feeling that she imagined she would have if she were to see a horrifying accident on the road or watch an execution at the federal penitentiary. She knew something bad was coming, and there was no way to ward it off. She couldn't stop Elizabeth's next words, and Jane was sure deep inside her body that it was going to be terrible.

Elizabeth seemed lost in thought once again as she filled her glass to the brim. Then she continued as if she'd never stopped. "It was horrible. When Ralph recognized Mark, he decided that it would be a good idea if Mark gave him some money to keep his mouth shut. He wants a lot, Jane. He told Mark to come back at midnight tonight with cash, or he'll tell the press about our affair."

"I see," said Jane. "And you need money."

"No. I don't need any money," replied Elizabeth. "Mark will take care of all that." She shrugged. "He hasn't any choice."

"Where is Ralph now?"

"At the apartment. After Ralph made his demands, Mark left but Ralph stayed all night. I didn't want him to, but he wouldn't leave. He's been there all day, drinking. It's been terrible. I called the studio and told them I was sick. I couldn't face anyone. But this afternoon, Ralph got really drunk and wanted to . . . you know. . . . When I wouldn't, he started hitting me, and I ran out and came here." Elizabeth drank deeply from her glass. "What shall I do, Jane? What can I do? I'm so afraid."

Jane thought for a few seconds. "I think you'd better call the police."

"The police? I couldn't," said Elizabeth. "The press would hear about it in no time. It would be all over the papers. That would ruin Mark, Jane. You know that."

"Then the studio. Call Murry Edson. I'm sure he'll know what to do."

"I can't, Jane. What if they blame me? What if they decide I'm no good or that I'm a danger to them?"

"Murry Edson doesn't worry about danger when one of his players is in trouble. At least, not when they're making money for him. Your first picture did very well, and I know they have high hopes for your future."

"High hopes. That's all, Jane. I'm not an established star like you are. They won't protect me like they would you. I can't let them find out anything. Promise me you won't tell Mr. Edson anything about all this, Jane. Promise me."

"All right," agreed Jane, slowly. "Then that only leaves us one thing to do."

"What's that?"

"You'll have to stay here tonight, away from that apartment."

"But what about Mark? He'll be going back to the apartment tonight and I won't be there."

"I'm sure he would agree that you have no business anywhere near Ralph." Jane touched Elizabeth's arm. "Mark is a senator. I'm sure they're used to dealing with all sorts of people. He'll give Ralph just so much rope, and then your ex-boyfriend will know exactly who's really in charge."

"I guess you're right."

"I'm sure of it. Just as I'm sure that you should stay with me tonight, and tomorrow when you go home, Ralph will be gone, and you and Mark can—"

"Go on where we left off?" asked Elizabeth. "You know better than that, Jane. After tonight Mark won't want anything to do with me. And I don't blame him."

"Don't start worrying about tomorrow," said Jane. She smiled. "Remember Scarlett O'Hara."

Elizabeth didn't smile.

Jane stood up. "I'll have Hardgrave show you to a room, and then we'll have dinner—"

"Oh, please, Jane. I really don't want to see a lot of people."

"All right. You can have dinner in your room. I'll come up to see you later."

Jane pulled the bell for Hardgrave and turned back to Elizabeth. "Don't worry, Elizabeth. It's going to be fine."

After dinner that night, the children rushed off to finish their packing, with Maud's help, and Warren and Jane walked out to the pool area.

Warren had decided to forgo any discussion of his hopes that Jane might move to Kansas City. She had seemed upset and distracted at dinner, and he didn't want to add to her confusion.

"You look very lovely tonight," he said.

Jane smiled at him. The Chanel evening robe she wore matched her blue eyes and made them look enormous. "Thank you," she whispered.

"You've had a confusing day, haven't you?"

"I admit, I was very angry when I came back from my meeting with Murry."

"And what did Elizabeth want?"

"She's having a . . . personal problem."

"I see. Are *you* all right now?"

"Of course. I'm always all right when it's just the two of us."

"Have the kids been too much?"

"Not at all. You know better than that."

"I hope not. They think you're wonderful."

"I like them, too," said Jane. She grinned. "And I'm very, very fond of their father."

"Just fond?" asked Warren. "I would have hoped for a more emphatic set of feelings."

"Just what did you have in mind?" asked Jane.

Warren didn't answer, simply taking her in his arms. They kissed, and Jane leaned her head down on his shoulder. "I always feel so safe with you," she said.

"I'll always keep you safe," he answered. "As long as you'll let me."

Jane and Warren strolled around the pool, talking of unimportant matters.

"I'm sorry you have to go back tomorrow," she said.

"So am I. But I can come back soon. I just have to make sure the kids get back all right and start school."

Jane laughed. "I think that's wonderful."

"What?"

"Well, all the time I've known you, you've talked about your children, but you've never mentioned anything about taking care of them. There was always someone to do it for you. And now, you're discussing getting them away to school as if you'd done it every year since they started."

"I guess you're right. It's been good for us to be together like we have this summer, to become interested in each other. I've never had the time to spend with them I should."

Before Warren could continue, Hardgrave appeared at the door. "Excuse me, miss, sir," he began.

Jane pulled away from Warren. "Yes, Hardgrave? What is it?"

"It's Miss Hudson, miss," the butler went on. "She is asking for you."

"Good God!" exclaimed Warren. "Is Elizabeth still here? You didn't tell me that, Jane."

"It's nothing serious."

"But what's wrong?"

"I promised her I wouldn't say." She looked back at Hardgrave. "Tell Miss Hudson I'll be along in a few moments."

"Yes, miss." Hardgrave left, and Jane and Warren followed him slowly to the door.

"So much for our evening alone," said Warren.

"We'll have many in the future," said Jane, leaning against him slightly. "Many evenings of just you and I. How soon did you say you'd be back?"

"Next week soon enough?"

"Not nearly," said Jane as they entered the house.

Jane said good night to Warren and went to Elizabeth's room where she found her friend pacing back and forth, a cigarette in one hand, a very dark drink in the other.

Elizabeth rushed at Jane. "Do you know what time it is?" she asked frantically.

"Almost eleven," said Jane. "Have you had any rest at all?"

"No. But I'll be all right. What do you think is happening?"

"I don't know. They were supposed to meet at midnight?"

"Yes."

"Then we have at least an hour before we can expect to hear from Mark. Does he know how to find you?"

"Yes. I called him at the hotel."

"What did he say?"

"He told me that he was going to meet Ralph as planned and that he'd call me afterward. But Jane—"

"Yes?"

"He didn't seem to want to talk to me. I guess I should have expected that, but it still hurt."

Jane patted Elizabeth's hand. "I'm sure he was just thinking about other things. He'll be fine after he's gotten Ralph off his back."

Elizabeth shrugged. "I wish I could believe that. . . . Jane?"

"Yes?"

"Will you stay with me until he calls?"

"Of course I will," said Jane. She leaned back and lit a cigarette, preparing for a long evening.

The two women sat together for the next two hours. Occasionally they talked, but mostly they were quiet. Elizabeth chain-smoked and often asked Jane the time, and Jane tried to keep her friend calm. But as the night wore on, Elizabeth became more and more distraught. Midnight passed, then one A.M., and there was still no word from Mark. Finally, as the clock approached two A.M., Elizabeth could stand it no longer.

"Jane, something must have gone wrong. Something must have happened," said Elizabeth. "I'm going to call Mark's hotel."

"All right." Jane stood by as Elizabeth dialed the number and asked for the senator's room. After a few moments, Elizabeth hung up. "There's no answer," she said.

"Maybe he's at the apartment?" suggested Jane.

Elizabeth brightened. "Maybe you're right." She dialed her home number and let the telephone ring many times before hanging up. She turned to Jane.

"Something's wrong. I know something's wrong. What should I do? I can't just sit here like this."

"I think you'd better wait to hear from Mark."

"I can't, Jane, I just can't." She walked purposely to the closet and grabbed her coat. "I'm going to the apartment."

Jane sighed. "Then I suppose I'd better go with you."

"Would you, Jane? Thank you."

Jane got up and went to her room. She changed into pants and a shirt and gathered up a loose jacket, then rejoined Elizabeth at the top of the stairs. Together, they crept quietly down the darkened staircase and through the still house to the front door. Once Elizabeth started to speak, but Jane forestalled her. When they got outside, Jane explained that she hadn't wanted to wake up anyone.

"They all have a busy day tomorrow," said Jane. "Warren and his children are leaving, and I know Aunt Maud is exhausted."

Elizabeth nodded, and they climbed into Jane's new little sports car.

"What about the gateman?" asked Elizabeth.

"His job is to keep people out," said Jane. "Not me in."

"But won't he think it's strange that we're leaving at this hour?"

"He's not paid to think," said Jane as they pulled up at the gate.

The guard was visibly surprised, but quickly unlocked the gate and they passed through.

Despite the lateness of the hour, Los Angeles was still an active and brightly lit city. Partygoers were returning from their evenings out. The nightclubs, which closed at two, were beginning to give way to the after-hours spots along the Sunset Strip. Elegant couples on their way into the most popular places passed by hungry street people made homeless by the depression.

Leaving the bright lights behind, Jane drove on until once again they were surrounded by darkness as they reached the lower-middle-class residential area where Elizabeth lived. The streets were eerily silent. Occasionally they heard a dog bark or a car pass them, but mostly they were alone. Jane could almost feel the quiet as it wrapped itself around the two of them. It seemed an eternity to her before she pulled up at Elizabeth's place. It was completely dark.

"Does Mark have a car?"

"He usually takes taxicabs," said Elizabeth.

"The house looks dark."

"Yes. But the apartment is in the back. The light wouldn't show out here."

"Well, we'd better go see," said Jane practically.

Together they walked up the drive to the back of the house. When they reached Elizabeth's door, they stopped. There was no light showing.

"It doesn't look like there's anyone here," said Elizabeth. "What do you think has happened?"

"We won't know unless we go in and see," said Jane flatly. She started forward, but Elizabeth caught her arm.

"Wait, Jane. I'm afraid."

"Don't be silly," said Jane. "We'll go in and turn on some lights, and then you'll see that everything's all right."

Elizabeth nodded, and once more they started into the apartment, Jane leading the way. The door wasn't locked, and Jane pushed it open and looked into the darkened living room. There was no sound. The room lay in black stillness.

Jane made her way to a lamp and turned it on. The dim bulb cast an eerie glow across the living room.

Elizabeth closed the door and stood by it. "It doesn't look as if anyone's been here at all," she said.

"Someone has," said Jane, pointing to the overflowing ashtray.

Jane went into the bedroom and turned on a light. It was also empty.

"I don't understand," said Elizabeth, following her. "What do you suppose happened?"

"I don't know," said Jane. "But . . ."

She glanced about the room once more, and her gaze caught a slight smudge on the door leading into the bathroom. She walked to it and tentatively reached out her hand. With one finger she touched the spot. It was sticky.

"What did you find?" asked Elizabeth.

"I'm not sure," said Jane. "You stay here."

Slowly Jane pushed open the door. At first, the bathroom seemed as clean and untouched as the rest of the apartment.

Then Jane noticed that the shower curtain was pulled at an odd angle, as if something was holding it. She moved forward. The only light in the bathroom came from the bedroom and spilled shadows across the white tiles.

Jane grasped the curtain in one hand, then released it, looking back at Elizabeth, standing in the open doorway. She took hold of the curtain once again and ripped it back quickly. The sound of the hangers sliding over the metal rod crashed through the silent rooms.

Jane stood perfectly still, her hand still gripping the curtain, her body rigid as she gasped in horror at the sight before her. She couldn't speak or turn her eyes away.

"Jane, what is it?" asked Elizabeth. "Jane! Answer me." Elizabeth's voice rose as she started into the room.

Jane forced herself to speak. "Don't come in, Elizabeth," she said hoarsely. "Stay where you are."

"But I want to know what you've found," insisted Elizabeth as she pushed forward. She shoved past Jane and looked down, following the direction of Jane's paralyzed gaze.

Below her, the unmoving and lifeless eyes of Mark Richmond stared up at the two women.

CHAPTER *Eighteen*

ELIZABETH'S SCREAMS split the quiet night. Over and over again, the girl's voice reflected the horror that coursed through her body. She couldn't stop screaming.

Elizabeth's panic startled Jane back to action. She pulled her eyes from the sight of Mark Richmond lying in the tub, a pool of blood staining the porcelain near his head, grasped Elizabeth and pushed her back into the bedroom. She placed her on the bed and tried to calm her.

"Quiet," said Jane urgently. "Do you hear me? You must be quiet. You'll wake up the neighbors."

Elizabeth responded slightly, but she was still incoherent and hysterical. Jane rushed into the living room and brought back a glass of brandy, which she helped Elizabeth drink. Sitting next to her, Jane held her tightly until she was under control.

Elizabeth looked toward the bathroom and began to cry. "My God, Jane. Oh, my God. He's been killed. He's been murdered. I saw the blood, Jane. I saw the blood." Elizabeth's voice once more rose in panic.

"Stop it," ordered Jane. "We've got to be calm."

"Maybe he's alive," suggested Elizabeth. "Maybe he's not dead—"

"Elizabeth—"

"Please, Jane. Maybe he's still alive."

"Very well, I'll go and see." She went back into the bathroom and looked again at the body. She bent down and felt for Mark's pulse. His skin was still slightly warm, but it was clear that no life remained. Jane pulled the curtain back over the body and returned to Elizabeth.

"Well?" asked Elizabeth. "Can we help him? Is he still alive?"

"No. I'm afraid not."

Elizabeth started to cry quietly, dropping her head down on her chest.

Jane held her for a few moments, then gently suggested that they should call someone.

"Who?" asked Elizabeth.

"I think the best idea would be to call Murry first. Then we can call the police."

"It's all so horrible," said Elizabeth. "What do you think happened?"

"It's hard to tell. Obviously Ralph did it, but I can't imagine why."

"I can't either."

"I'll call Murry. You'd better come with me."

Elizabeth nodded numbly and stood up. She followed Jane into the living room and sat down, listening uninterestedly as Jane put through her call to Murry.

Jane had no trouble reaching Murry. The servant who answered the telephone had worked for the Edsons some time and knew when someone important was on the line.

"Murry, it's Jane Turner. I'm afraid there's a problem, and I need you."

"Where are you?"

Jane gave him the address.

"I'll be there shortly. Don't do anything until I get there."

Jane hung up. "He'll be here soon," she said.

"But he didn't ask what it was all about?"

"No. But I'm sure he knows that I wouldn't have called at this time of night if it wasn't important. He'll know exactly what to do."

"I hope so," said Elizabeth. "I could use a little more of that brandy."

Jane looked at her critically. "I don't think that's a good idea. You're going to need all your wits about you."

"I guess you're right," said Elizabeth.

The two women lapsed into silence and were quiet until they heard voices outside. Jane went to the door. Opening it, she saw Murry Edson, accompanied by Terrance Malvey, making his way up the driveway. She went out to meet them.

"Murry, thank you for coming," said Jane quietly.

"I figured it must be important."

"Where the hell are we?" asked Terry. The producer looked sleepy, and his clothes were creased and rumpled. Murry Edson, on the other hand, was neatly dressed in a business suit, as if for a day at the office.

"This is Elizabeth Hudson's place," said Jane.

"And just why are we at Elizabeth's apartment at three in the morning?" asked Terrance grumpily.

"There's been an accident," began Jane.

"To Elizabeth?" asked Murry, suddenly animated.

"No, she's fine," said Jane. "I think you'd better come inside."

The two men followed Jane into the living room, where they found Elizabeth still seated where Jane had left her. Frightened, she looked up at Murry and Terrance. She didn't speak, obviously expecting Jane to do all the talking.

Jane closed the door and indicated that the men should sit down. She took a chair and looked unblinkingly at Murry.

"I'm afraid there's been rather a terrible accident here."

"What kind of accident?" asked Murry.

"A killing," said Jane flatly. "Senator Mark Richmond has been shot. He's in the bathroom."

Murry continued to stare at Jane, but Terrance gasped audibly. "What? Senator Richmond? Killed here?" He gaped.

"Yes," continued Jane. "Neither Elizabeth nor I were here when it happened. We came in a little over an hour ago and found his body."

"I see," said Murry. "Terry, go look in the bathroom," he instructed. Terrance left the room and Murry turned back to the girls. "All right. What's it all about?"

Jane briefly told Murry about Elizabeth's visit the night before, and the situation between the singer and the two men.

As she was talking, Terrance came back into the room. He

was a bit green, but under control. Terrance and Murry exchanged glances, and Terry nodded.

When Jane had finished her story, the group was quiet. Murry had his head down and, at first, Jane thought he might be ill. Then she realized he was thinking. She could almost feel his mind working, weighing and dismissing alternatives. Jane could have sworn that in those few minutes Murry had checked every possibility and could have given her the immediate and even long-range outcomes of the tragedy. When he looked up again, his words were to the point.

"Jane, I think you'd better go back home as soon as possible. I will go with you. Terrance will stay here with Elizabeth until she calls the police. Then I think he should also leave."

"Leave!" Elizabeth spoke for the first time. "You can't all leave me alone here. You can't."

"You will simply call the police and say that you arrived home and found the senator's body, which is true," said Murry.

"I can't stay here alone tonight!" Elizabeth was almost shouting. "I can't."

"Don't worry, Elizabeth," said Jane. "I won't leave you." She turned back to Murry. "I won't let her stay here by herself tonight," she said flatly.

"Jane—" began Murry.

"I mean it, Murry." Her eyes didn't flinch.

Murry realized he wasn't going to change Jane's mind. "Very well. Elizabeth, you and Jane will leave here together and go back to Jane's house. Is your car there?"

Elizabeth nodded.

"All right. You stay with Jane until early morning. Can you come back here alone in daylight?"

"Yes . . . I can do that," said Elizabeth miserably.

"Good girl. You'll drive back here by yourself and call the police and tell them that you stayed with Jane last night and then came back here to get your things because you had an early call at the studio. Do you?" asked Murry.

"What?" asked Elizabeth, confused.

"Have an early appointment at the studio."

"N—no. I don't have any appointments at all today."

"Fix that," said Murry to Terrance.

Terrance nodded. He knew it was simple to insert Elizabeth's name on a meeting roster or a makeup test schedule. He could do it early, before anyone else was around.

"Now," continued Murry, "the place should look just as it did when you arrived. What have you moved or touched?"

"Very little," said Jane. "Elizabeth had a drink. I'd better wash the glass."

"What about cigarettes?" asked Terrance.

"Yes," agreed Jane. "We've both been smoking."

"The lipstick will show," said Terry. "We've got to get the butts."

"That ashtray was full," said Jane, indicating the one she had noticed when first coming into the apartment. "Other than that, the place was very neat and orderly."

"Ralph must have straightened up before he left," added Elizabeth. "When I went to Jane's, things were somewhat messy."

"I see," said Murry. "Jane, I think you'd better use a cloth to wipe away your fingerprints."

"I doubt that I can get them all."

"You don't have to. It stands to reason that you've been here before. I'm just concerned about any of your fingerprints on things that you wouldn't have touched before tonight. Have you ever taken a shower here?"

"Why, no."

"Then I suggest we clean off the outside of the shower curtain. You did touch it, didn't you?"

"Yes."

"That's the kind of thing I mean," said Murry. "All right. Let's get to work."

The four moved quickly. Elizabeth bluntly refused to go into the bathroom again, but Jane resolutely cleaned the areas of the shower curtain her hand might have touched. When they were all finished, Murry sent Jane and Elizabeth on their way and took one more look around with Terrance.

"Jesus. This is a nice mess, isn't it?" asked Murry.

Terrance got a silly grin on his face. "A fine mess you've gotten us into, Ollie," he said, smirking.

Murry looked at him like he'd lost his mind.

"Sorry," said Terry. "I've always been partial to Laurel and Hardy."

"This sure isn't a comedy," said Murry.

"No. But it could be a circus when the press gets hold of it."

"We've just got to see if we can keep Jane and Global out of it."

"Jane should be all right. But I think it's going to be rough on the studio . . . and on Hudson."

"We'll have to deal with her as it falls. We'd better meet first thing in my office to decide what our options are."

"About Elizabeth?"

"About the whole fucking mess," said Murry, viciously.

"All right." Terrance followed Murry to the door. "Have you got everything?"

Murry nodded. "Yeah. Let's get out of here." He turned back for one last look at the living room. "Jesus," he muttered. "Why the hell couldn't Richmond have been screwing someone over at Paramount?"

"She's where?" bellowed Murry Edson.

"At Jane Turner's house," replied Terrance. "I just heard about it."

"Oh, God," moaned Murry. "Is stupidity catching? What does Turner think she's doing. I want her as far away from this whole thing as possible."

"Well, it's a little late now. Apparently, right after Elizabeth got to her apartment, she called the police. They questioned her and then released her. She went straight to Jane's."

"Is Turner here?"

"Not yet. She's still at home. It seems that Warren Harris and his children are going back to Missouri today. She's seeing them off."

"If she keeps doing things like this, she might as well go with them," said Murry.

"Nothing would make Warren Harris happier, from what I hear."

"Well, we'd better get over there and see what's going on."

Murry called for his car, and he and Terrance sped away from Global toward Jane's Beverly Hills house. As they approached the gates, they could see masses of reporters and sightseers.

"Jesus! It doesn't take long, does it?" asked Terry.

At the house they were met by the imperturbable Hardgrave, who escorted them into the drawing room where they found

Jane, Warren, and Maud sitting together. It was obvious that Warren and Jane were having a difference of opinion.

"Jane, I want you out of this," Warren was saying. "I won't leave you here with that girl upstairs and all those press people outside, yelling for you. It's disgusting. Both you and Maud should leave. I think Maud should go back to New York, and you should come with the children and me to Kansas City."

"I can't, Warren," said Jane simply. Looking up, she saw Murry Edson pushing his way past Hardgrave who had intended to announce him. Terrance was right behind Murry.

"What on earth do you think you're doing?" asked Murry. "Where is she?"

"If you mean Elizabeth," answered Jane, "she's resting."

"Of course I mean Elizabeth. If I'd thought that you intended to have her back . . ." Murry stopped, realizing that he was about to say more than he should in front of Maud and Warren. "I mean," he began again, "I don't think it's a good idea for you to keep Elizabeth here with you."

"I was just telling her that," said Warren. "In fact, I was trying to convince her to leave with me."

"Leave!" Murry was astonished.

Terrance moved in smoothly. "You know, Murry," he interjected, "a little vacation might not be a bad idea for Jane. She has been working hard," he went on, ignoring the fact that Jane had just come back from a week off.

"Absolutely," agreed Warren. "My children and I are leaving today, and I think Jane should come with us."

The three men discussed the advisability of Jane's removal from Hollywood as Jane and Maud sat quietly on the sofa. Neither of the women spoke until Jane finally decided she had had enough.

"I think, before you all finish, you should know that I have no intention of leaving," she said.

Everyone turned and looked at her.

"I'm serious, Murry. If you feel I need a vacation, which incidentally I don't, then I'll take it. But I'll do it right here at home. Where Elizabeth is going to stay until this whole mess is over."

"Jane, I don't think—"

"Jane, don't be ridiculous—"

"Jane, I'm ordering you—"

All three men started talking at once, then stopped. Warren began, appealing to Maud for help.

"Maud, surely you don't think Jane should stay here. You know how awful this thing will get."

"Jane must do what she thinks is right," said Maud with finality. "I, of course, still have several engagements and committee meetings in Los Angeles, so it is simply not possible for me to leave at this time." Maud rose from her seat. "And that reminds me, I have a meeting of a British war relief group this afternoon. I'd better go get ready." After smiling at each of the guests, she left the room.

The men watched her leave and then turned back to Jane and began talking once more. But Jane stopped them.

"Enough!" she said loudly. "Get this straight, gentlemen. I'm not going anywhere. Elizabeth is one of my best friends, and I have no intention of leaving her when she needs me."

"That's very noble, Jane," said Terrance. "But—"

"Nobility has nothing to do with it," interrupted Jane. "It is simply a statement of fact. She tried to talk to her parents this morning on the telephone, and they didn't seem interested or want to get involved. She doesn't have anyone else. And if you're concerned about my image, well, it might be time that my fans saw that I was a grown-up."

The men were silent.

"Now, I think I'd better go see how she is. I'm sure you'll excuse me." She paused on her way out of the room. "Murry, am I on vacation or do I show up at the studio in the morning?"

"If you're going to stay in town, you might as well come to work," said Murry with disgust.

Jane smiled. "Thank you."

When Jane had made sure that Elizabeth was as comfortable as possible, she walked back into the hall and found Warren waiting for her at the top of the stairs.

Jane smiled at him and took his hand, leaning her body close to his. "This isn't exactly the send-off I'd planned for you," she said.

Warren looked down at her. "I didn't think it was."

"I know you're angry, Warren. But try and understand—"

"You won't leave Elizabeth or any of the rest of the craziness of this place."

"I *can't*."

"No. I suppose not. I think I've shown you that I'll try anything to keep us together. But do you really expect me to consent to my children living in a place where their step-mother's best friend is a murder accomplice?"

"Elizabeth didn't have anything to do with the murder. She was with me last night. You know she was here."

"Oh, I don't think she actually held the gun and pointed it at Mark Richmond's head, but . . ."

Jane looked at him inquiringly.

"Yes. I know all about it. It's in the papers. All over them as a matter of fact."

"I saw the wound," said Jane quietly.

Warren held her close. "You shouldn't have been there, Jane. You shouldn't have been anywhere near it. And you shouldn't stay to suffer through the aftermath. It's going to be terrible."

"I know," she said.

"Then please, come with me."

She smiled softly at him. "You know I won't leave, Warren." She lifted one hand and gently caressed his cheek. "But you'd better gather up Susan and David and start on your way. You don't want to miss your train."

"I don't want to leave you alone like this."

"Alone?" Jane grinned. "Just you wait. In a short while this house will be full of people. Everyone will want to see me. Besides, you did say you'd be back next week, didn't you?"

Warren looked at her. "Yes, of course," he answered.

Jane kissed him once and watched as he walked down the steps.

Over the next few days, everything seemed to happen at once. Jane found herself in the center of a tangled and constantly unpleasant situation. Friends, co-workers, and virtual strangers stopped to speak to her at the studio, offering advice, sympathy, or just trying to hear something the press had missed.

They hadn't missed much. Reporters besieged the house. Global had to send out guards to keep order, and Jane was transported to and from work in a chauffeured studio car.

Elizabeth never left the house, and rarely even her room. She was distraught and very frightened. Each day she seemed to withdraw more into herself. At Jane's urging, Murry had sent a doctor to Elizabeth. He prescribed large dosages of tranquilizers, which the young woman unwisely mixed with the brandy she always kept near her.

Jane didn't know what to do to help Elizabeth. Each morning she visited her before she left for the day, and after she returned home from the studio, she went to Elizabeth's room and attempted to talk to her, telling her little events of the day, trying to bring her out of her depression.

But Elizabeth often seemed to be in another world. Her emotional state combined with the sedatives made her virtually unreachable. It wasn't until nearly two weeks after the death of Mark Richmond that Elizabeth showed any signs of animation.

Jane came back early from work, bringing the afternoon papers with her. She went directly to Elizabeth's room and found her friend wearing an old robe, sitting in an armchair in front of the fireplace. She held a drink in her hand, but didn't seem to notice it as her gaze stayed resolutely on the dry hearth before her.

"There's some news," said Jane. "I think you should know about it."

Elizabeth looked at Jane without speaking. Jane sat down in a chair facing her and held the newspaper out. "They've found Ralph," she said as Elizabeth took the paper from her and stared at the front-page photograph of her ex-lover being escorted into the county jail.

"He was captured near Ojai, California," continued Jane. "He had almost ten thousand dollars on him . . . and a gun."

"I never knew Ralph to have a gun," she said. "I wonder where he got it."

"I suppose all of that information will come out later," said Jane. She hesitated. "There's something else," she began.

Elizabeth looked up from the paper she was studying.

"Farther down on the page."

Elizabeth looked at the bottom of the front page. There was a picture of Mark Richmond's wife and children at a memorial service in Washington, D.C. Mrs. Richmond stood very erect, her face covered by a heavy veil. One of the children had tears on his face.

For several seconds, Elizabeth couldn't remove her gaze

from the picture. She slowly lowered the paper, her eyes filled with sadness. "Oh, Jane, he was so sweet. So very sweet. He always treated me so well. . . . We had such good times together."

Jane didn't speak. She couldn't think of what to say to help her friend.

"It's all my fault, Jane," Elizabeth went on. "All my fault. I should never have left the house. I should never have let him meet Ralph. I should never have—"

"Stop it," said Jane. "Stop it, right now. It's over—all over. Once something is over, you can't do anything about it. You can't change what is finished, Elizabeth. There's nothing you can do for Mark Richmond now. It's a terrible tragedy, but you'll only make things worse by burying yourself along with him. You haven't left this room for days. You can't keep this up. You've got to start living again."

"Oh, Jane, it hurts so bad, so very bad." She broke down in tears and Jane took her in her arms and held her as the sorrow and terror of the recent experience rushed forward and consumed Elizabeth.

Jane comforted her friend until she began to quiet down, then helped her to the bed and covered her with a light blanket. When Elizabeth was asleep, Jane went to her own room and sat down on her small balcony, looking out over the pool area below. In a short while, Maud knocked softly.

"Jane . . . are you here?"

"Yes, Aunt Maud. On the balcony."

"Good. I'm glad to see you resting. Are you hungry?"

"No, thank you. I really don't feel like eating."

"You can't starve yourself, dear. I think this thing is wearing you out. I know it doesn't sound nice, but I could wish that your friend hadn't brought her problems to you."

"She didn't have any other place to go."

"I understand, dear. And I must tell you that I think you've been very brave and strong through all this."

Jane smiled. "I didn't have much choice."

"I know." Maud returned Jane's smile. "The fact that you see that makes you the person you are. I'm very proud of you."

Jane didn't answer.

"How is Elizabeth?"

"I think she'll be better now. I showed her today's paper. It had pictures in it of Ralph's arrest and Mark's memorial service. Maybe I shouldn't have, but I wanted to try and break through to her."

"Did it help?"

"I think so. I hope so."

"Well, that's good. But I'm afraid that the really rough road is still coming."

"You mean the trial?"

"That will be bad enough. But I was thinking about the newspapers you've been keeping from her. The columns, editorials, radio broadcasts, and all the rest of the media that have directly blamed her—and Hollywood—for Mark Richmond's death. And neither Murry nor any other studio person has tried to contact her since that horrible night. I don't know what the studio is doing, Jane, but I've been in this world long enough to know that you can't ignore all of those newspapers or that Murry doesn't seem very concerned about her."

"I can't talk to her about all that. She hasn't asked about the studio at all, *or* about the papers. But I agree with you, the press is crucifying her. You would think she was the first woman to ever have an affair with a married man."

"Not all affairs have such tragic results."

"No. Of course not. But surely they can't think that Elizabeth intentionally set out to destroy Mark Richmond."

"I think, besides the fact that the press sees it as a great story, those peculiar church ministers will grab any opportunity to attack someone different from themselves. They're all going to keep it going as long as possible."

"I'm afraid you're right. Warren said it was going to be terrible."

"Well, you know I often agree with Warren."

"Are you suggesting I take his advice and run off to Kansas City?"

"There are worse fates."

Jane smiled. "Name one."

Maud wasn't smiling. "I just don't want what is happening to Elizabeth to ever happen to you. I don't imagine you'll ever get involved with people like Ralph Mason. But it doesn't seem to take much to start a cycle of hate that can't be stopped. Have you really read those columns? Really paid attention to what they're saying about her? That sweet, innocent little girl is actually a dangerous temptress. They've called her everything from Jezebel to Salome. It's horrible, Jane, horrible."

"I know."

"And where is Murry Edson during all this? Where is the studio? You see them every day. What have they said about Elizabeth?"

"Very little."

"And do you know what they plan to do about her?"

"No one has said. I've seen Murry a couple of times, but he hasn't mentioned Elizabeth."

"Then what's going to happen to her?" pursued Maud.

"I don't know, Aunt Maud. I don't know!" Jane's voice rose.

"I'm frightened, Jane."

"Of what?"

"Of what celebrity and fame and all the rest of it can do to a person. Of how fragile the whole thing is. I've never seen anything so exciting turn into anything so destructive. I've never seen such viciousness and hate. A man has been murdered. A *good* man. And now there's a girl whose whole life is probably destroyed. I don't understand any of it. But I do know that I don't want you to have to experience anything like what Elizabeth is going through."

Jane was silent.

"Please understand, my child. I do want you to do and have whatever you want. But nothing is worth the kind of pain I'm seeing around me now."

Jane stood up and walked to the edge of the balcony. "So you think I should just pack up and leave."

"I wish you would. You've arrived, Jane. You're a big star. What else do you have to prove to the world? What else do you have to prove to yourself?"

"I don't know." Jane turned and faced Maud. "But I know that I can't run at the first sign of trouble. And I know that I'm not finished yet."

"I see. Then there's nothing else for me to say, is there?"

"No . . . I guess not."

Maud got up and started for the door. She turned back and looked at Jane. "But you will be careful, dear, won't you?"

"Yes, Aunt Maud. I promise I'll be very careful."

• • •

"Hello, this is Elizabeth Hudson. I'd like to talk to Murry Edson, please." Elizabeth idly twisted the phone cord as she waited be to connected. In a few moments, Murry's secretary was again on the line.

"I'm sorry, but Mr. Edson is in conference. Is there anything I can do to help you?"

"N—no. I guess not. Would you just tell him I called?"

"Yes, of course," was the crisp answer.

"Thank you." Elizabeth hung up the telephone and turned to Jane who was standing near her. "Mr. Edson is busy. But I left a message."

"Yes, I heard you," said Jane. "Well, I guess you'd better go now. The studio lawyers are downstairs, along with one of the men from publicity."

"At least they haven't forgotten that I'm alive," said Elizabeth as she gathered up her gloves and jacket. "Do I look all right?"

"You look fine," said Jane, studying her friend. Elizabeth wore a simple navy blue dress with a matching jacket. She was pale, but seemed to be in control of herself.

"I wish I could go with you," said Jane.

"You know that's a terrible idea," said Elizabeth. "It's bad enough that you've let me stay with you for the past several weeks. To show up at Ralph's trial would be disastrous for you. I'm sure Mr. Edson told you that."

Murry Edson had said almost exactly those words to Jane when he told her that Global lawyers would accompany Elizabeth to the trial. She hadn't been charged with anything, but Murry emphasized that he wanted to make sure Elizabeth was protected.

"Besides," continued Elizabeth, "I will have the lawyers and publicity man to hang onto. But I wish I didn't have to go."

"You're a very important witness," said Jane. "There's no way out of it."

"No, I guess not," agreed Elizabeth as she started out of the room.

"I'll be home early tonight," said Jane. "As soon as you're through with all this, I think you should think about a vacation. Why don't we look through some travel folders this evening?"

"All right. A trip sounds nice."

The two women went downstairs and met the waiting representatives from Global Films who were to escort Elizabeth to the court house where Ralph Mason would go on trial for the murder of Mark Richmond. Jane gave Elizabeth a hug and stood in the doorway as several of the men climbed into a small car. Elizabeth seated herself between one of the lawyers and the man from publicity in the back of the limousine, and they drove off.

Even from a distance, Jane could hear the sounds of the press calling out to Elizabeth, asking questions and attempting to stop the car for a picture as it reached the gates.

Jane went back into the house and walked to the dining room. She picked up the morning paper and sat down at the table. Hardgrave brought her a cup of coffee and a plate of food she didn't really want, but she knew if Maud came down and discovered she hadn't eaten, she would have to explain. That would require more effort than eating.

The trial was headline news. For a brief period, the murder of Mark Richmond had been relegated to the back of the papers. But with the opening of the trial, once again it had made its way onto the front page. And once again, the editorials were lamenting the untimely death of a future statesman, and the perfidy of Hollywood and all it stood for.

Jane threw down the paper in disgust. It wasn't fair, she thought. None of it was fair. Everything about the whole situation had been horrible, and now, since the beginning of the trial, they had had to relive that awful night over and over again.

Ralph had discovered an ambitious attorney who wanted to shift the blame away from his client and focus it on the decadence of the movie world, as personified by Elizabeth Hudson. He had done his work well. He had constantly hammered away at the jury that Elizabeth had thrown Ralph over for Mark Richmond, that her overpowering ambitions and lust had destroyed Ralph and driven him to acts of violence that were not a part of his personality. He based Ralph's defense on the idea that he had returned to his home and found the woman he loved in the arms of another man.

It was obvious to every observer that the defense wasn't going to totally stand up. Perhaps, the district attorney had reasoned with his assistants, if Mason had killed Richmond on the spot, he might have had a chance. But the fact that the crime happened the following night, combined with the blackmail Mason was accused of, left the murderer with little to excuse his act.

The gun had belonged to Mark Richmond. He had brought it with him for protection. However, there had been a struggle, either because Mason had asked for more money or for some other reason that wasn't clear, and during the fight, Mason had wrested the gun away from Richmond and killed him. Ralph had then dragged the body into the bathroom and cleaned up around the apartment. There was the suggestion from some quarters of the D.A.'s office that Ralph had hoped Elizabeth might actually be blamed for the shooting. But the defense attorney dismissed this idea based on the fact that Ralph still had the gun with him at the time of his capture.

It was all confusing and very messy. And, not for the first time, Jane wished it were all over and done with.

As she sat at the table, she tried to put the events of the past weeks into some order. Richmond's death, Elizabeth's near collapse, the newspapers, Murry's avoidance of Elizabeth. And Warren. He called every night, but he hadn't come back since taking his children home. He said he was involved in business.

Jane had a feeling that he might be trying to force her to come to him. He knew the pressure she was under and, perhaps, Jane thought, he was hoping his absence might make her leave Hollywood.

There had been moments in the past weeks when she had wanted to do just that, to pick up and leave California and go to Kansas City.

But she hadn't acted on her impulses. She wouldn't quit. Each day she had gone to the studio and done her job. And a job was about all it was, too. God, how she hated *Island Woman*. She felt like a fool, stumbling around the make-believe island set on the back lot. She didn't know how much longer she could keep it up.

She was tired. Not just a physical tiredness, but an emotional exhaustion resulting from her constant efforts to further her career and still balance her personal life. She was tired of trying to keep everyone around her happy and satisfied with her.

Jane got up and walked over to the large mirror in which the opulent dining room was reflected. She stared at herself as if she'd never seen the face that looked back at her. Just who the hell are you? Jane wondered. You're Jane Turner. You've got money, success, fame, an adoring public. . . . You're a movie star, the envy of millions of women, the fantasy of millions of men.

But it isn't enough. There's no substance to it. Jane knew she loved her career, her work in the movies. She knew it was what she wanted. But it wasn't complete.

She left the mirror and went back to her seat. Picking up her fork, she pushed the cold eggs around on her plate. I still don't control it, she thought. I'm on top and I still don't control my career. And until I do, I can't control my life. There must be an answer. I know there's an answer. Something I've left undone.

CHAPTER *Nineteen*

"COME THIS WAY, Miss Hudson." The Global public relations man hurried Elizabeth down the long corridor outside the courtroom. "I think we can get out the back," he continued, urging her forward. Around them were several policemen, the lawyers assigned to keep watch over Elizabeth, and a crowd of reporters anxious for a statement.

Flashbulbs exploded, and the newsmen's voices crashed around Elizabeth. "Give us a statement. Is it true that you and Mark Richmond were thinking of getting married? Have you talked to Mrs. Richmond? Were you having an affair with both men at the same time? Who designed the dress you're wearing today? Have you sold your story to the Hollywood News? Did you plan Richmond's murder with Mason? Will you marry Mason if he gets off? What's your next picture? Have you talked to your family?"

Elizabeth was terrified of the press, almost as frightened now as she had been in the witness chair answering the questions of the defense attorney.

He had been determined to paint Elizabeth Hudson in as black a light as possible and didn't restrain himself in his effort to convince the jury that Ralph Mason had been the unwilling victim of a dangerous and unprincipled woman.

Elizabeth had answered his questions hesitatingly and without conviction. Her confusion and fear had translated itself to the jury and the spectators as guilt and complicity. She may not have had a hand in the murder of Senator Richmond, but she was certainly a bad woman.

Outside the building, Elizabeth faced a barrage of interested spectators. Some blamed her for Senator Richmond's death . . . others saw her as a wicked and designing tramp. One woman cried out to Elizabeth that she was a slut and tried to spit on her. But despite their voiced disgust, the public couldn't get enough of her. Elizabeth Hudson was a celebrity, a woman in the limelight, a woman around whom there was a juicy scandal. They wanted to touch her, see her up close, tell their friends that they had been near her.

"Jesus, they're like animals," said the lawyer, closing the car door.

"Get us out of here, quick!" ordered the public relations man.

The driver skillfully drove through the crowd, and in a few moments the car was moving at a normal speed down the street.

The lawyer leaned back in his seat and lit a cigarette. "Jesus, am I glad that's over." He sighed. "What a mess."

"You're right, there," agreed the other man. "How do you think it went?"

The lawyer shrugged.

"You don't have to be nice," said Elizabeth. "I know I didn't do well on the stand. I couldn't help it. Their voices were so loud and they confused me. I didn't know what I was saying."

"God knows we talked about it enough before you went up there," said the lawyer.

"Yes. But I forgot everything when the defense lawyer started to ask me questions. And I didn't think Ralph would be there."

"Where the hell did you think he'd be?" exploded the PR man. "My God, he's the one on trial."

"I know," said Elizabeth meekly. "I just didn't think about it."

"I see," said the lawyer.

"Do you think I'll have to go back?" asked Elizabeth. "To testify some more, I mean."

"I doubt it," the lawyer replied caustically, "I imagine the defense got all they wanted out of you. And you weren't much help to the prosecution."

The three were silent for a few moments, then Elizabeth turned to the PR man. "I called Murry Edson's office this morning. But he was in a meeting. Do you know what the studio has planned for me? Should I come back tomorrow?"

He was hesitant as he answered, "There's no rush—"

"Oh, but I'd like to get back to work," said Elizabeth. "I think I would feel so much better."

"Yes, I'm sure. But Murry thinks you should let things settle down a bit before being seen in public too much. You know what the press is like."

"Yes, I guess so," she agreed. "But I'd like to come back as soon as possible. Will you tell him that for me?"

"Of course," he agreed.

At Jane's house, both men got out and walked Elizabeth to the door. She invited them in, but they declined and, after she had thanked them profusely, they climbed back into the car and drove away.

"Well, that was pretty bad," said the lawyer.

"At least she didn't say anything about the studio."

"Speaking of which, what's Global going to do next?"

"I had a meeting last night with Murry and Terry and a lot of other people. Global has taken a lot of bad press over this thing. And they're afraid of her. 'Too volatile' is how Murry describes our Miss Hudson. So, as soon as possible, Global will announce it's shelving her next picture—production problems or something. Later on we'll buy out her contract. And that's that."

"You know, I feel sorry for the girl."

"Well, there's nothing you can do for her."

"I guess not. But couldn't the studio—"

"Listen, you've been a lawyer out here long enough to know that a beginner like Hudson can't make mistakes. At least not the size of this one. All of her publicity, her image, has been built around the sweet girl-next-door bit. And then the public finds out she's been shacking up with a senator and a part-time pimp? No way. She's done for. Are you sure she won't be called back to testify?"

"Pretty sure," said the lawyer.

"Well, make sure. We want to make that announcement

about her picture as soon as possible so we can get away from the whole damn thing.''

"What if she doesn't want to quit?"

"Shit. By the time that dumb broad figures out what hit her, she'll be yesterday's news, gone and forgotten. No one will care what she's doing."

"Nice business we're in," said the lawyer, looking out the window.

"No worse than any other. You can strike out at AT&T, too, you know."

"I guess so." The lawyer looked at his watch. "Still early. I'd like to get in some golf. Could the driver drop me at the Hollywood Country Club?"

"No problem. I wouldn't mind playing a few holes myself, but I gotta get back."

"What's your handicap?"

The discussion of golf took up the rest of their ride.

It took five days for the Global lawyers to get a definite commitment from the trial attorneys that they would not be recalling Elizabeth. Global's public relations department announced the shelving of her picture a few hours later, in time to make the early editions of the papers.

Elizabeth had put in constant calls to Murry and her musical producers. But no one was ever in. She was completely cut off, and couldn't understand what was going on.

Jane didn't have any success at finding out about Elizabeth's position, either. Murry couldn't very well refuse to see Jane Turner, but he could be evasive and noncommittal about Elizabeth's future.

The morning the newspapers carried the information that production problems had halted the filming of her latest picture, Elizabeth came down to breakfast early. She had stopped spending all of her time in her room, and each day she prepared herself for the studio and then waited for the call that never came.

Jane knew Elizabeth was worried. And she also knew that each night, Elizabeth was taking pills to help her sleep and continuing to drink heavily when she was alone in her room.

Elizabeth sat down at the table and picked up one of the several papers delivered to the house, idly glancing through the columns. Greer Garson was making another film. *Gone With the Wind* was still a major smash all over the country. There was a lot happening in her industry.

At the bottom of the page was a short notice.

> Global Films announced today that due to production difficulties, their new musical, *A Bright Day*, would be shelved for the present. Readers will remember that this was to be Elizabeth Hudson's first starring role. Murry Edson, president of Global, admitted that, at present, they had no plans for Miss Hudson who was recently involved in one of Hollywood's more infamous scandals. Mr. Edson commented that Miss Hudson was in need of a rest, and that, at present, they had not discussed any future projects with the singer.

Elizabeth read the item three times, then deliberately laid the paper aside and tried to push the story out of her mind.

Although she didn't say anything to Elizabeth, Jane also saw the piece, and as soon as she got to the studio she barged into Murry Edson's office, carrying the newspaper.

"Just what does this mean?" asked Jane, shoving the paper onto his desk.

"I don't know what you're talking about," answered Murry.

"Oh, yes you do," said Jane. "The item this morning about shelving Elizabeth's picture. What's going on?"

"Jane, my dear," said Murry, putting down his work. "I'm sorry you're upset. I know you have to work today—"

"Do you? Do you know that, Murry? Well *I* don't know that. I'm not sure at all that I'll be working today."

"Really?" he asked, walking from behind his desk.

"Yes, really. I want to know about Elizabeth Hudson. I want to know what this item in the paper means. And I want to know what you intend to do for her in the future."

"That's quite a large order," said Murry. He smiled, but his eyes were hard and unblinking.

"Not too large," said Jane, seating herself as if she intended to stay a long time.

"I don't think this concerns you. Let Elizabeth's agent handle things."

"You know as well as I do that he dropped her as soon as this whole mess began. She hasn't got anybody but me. I've seen her every day. I've watched her suffer a little more each time one of the newspapers writes about her. She's terrified, and the only thing she's got to hang onto is her career. With this announcement, you've taken *that* away from her."

"I simply felt that at the present time it was a good idea to halt production on her next picture. As you yourself said, she's had a lot of bad publicity. No matter what she does now, she'll be killed by the press. So . . . it stands to reason that it's best to wait until things calm down. Then . . . if Elizabeth is ready to work, we can think about something for her."

"Do you mean that?" asked Jane. "You're not dropping her? You're going to bring her back?"

"After she's had a good rest, we'll see."

"Will you tell her that?"

"Of course. I'll call her very soon."

Jane looked at her employer for a few moments. "Well, all right. Thank you very much," said Jane.

"You know my door is always open to you, Jane. Always open," said Murry as he leaned forward and gave her a kiss. "You're very busy these days, aren't you? Publicity says they can't get enough of you. There's something tonight, I hear."

"Yes. I have to go right from work. It's a screening for British war relief."

"I suppose Mrs. Watson will be there as well."

"Naturally. She's more active than anyone I know in the committees."

"Mrs. Watson is a great woman," said Murry. "But I don't want to keep you. Shouldn't you be on the set? I know you're filming today."

"Oh, yes," said Jane with a bitter laugh. "Today is the day I'm sacrificed to the great god JuJuBe."

Elizabeth Hudson was alone in the great house. It was very quiet and in almost total darkness. Jane and Maud were out, and the servants, after having served her dinner, had retired to their part of the house.

Elizabeth had spent most of the day in her room, alternately looking at the newspapers and drinking brandy. Now, after having eaten almost nothing of Mrs. Hardgrave's excellent meal, she went into the drawing room. She wore a long dinner robe borrowed from Jane. It was a little snug, but Elizabeth had simply left buttons open where it was uncomfortable. In her hand was a large drink.

She moved to the piano and seated herself. Carefully, she struck a chord. Then another. She began singing, her voice harsh due to neglect and alcohol. She stopped and started again. It was an old song, one she had learned in Toledo. The familiar melody was very comforting to her. When she finished, she took a deep swallow of her drink and idly touched the keys. She had taken a tranquilizer earlier that day, but now she thought it was wearing off. Her hands shook slightly as she tried to play.

Nerves, she thought. I wish I weren't so nervous. She stood up and went to her room and took two more of her pills. In a few moments she felt much better.

Her eyes caught the newspaper lying on the bed, and she picked it up and turned automatically to the item about her picture. Although she knew it by heart, she read it once again. Strangely, it didn't seem to touch her anymore. She had pressed against the pain so many times since that morning that nothing seemed to have much effect on her. It was as if the world had somehow moved on and left her standing along the side, watching.

Elizabeth caught sight of herself in the full-length mirror. Jane's robe was slightly too long for her, but the additional length seemed to her to make it more elegant. She moved slightly, back and forth, letting the folds of the gown sway gently around her body. She heard music. The sweet lovely strains of the song she had performed in her first film came back to her. The room was filled with the sounds of the orchestra, and she began to dance, turning and twisting about. She felt beautiful.

Her foot caught in the robe, and she stumbled slightly, falling toward the mirror. She caught herself, sinking awkwardly to her knees and looked up. Her face was right in front of the mirror, and her reflection stared back at her, hard and uncompromising. Instead of the sweet and lovely girl of her imagination, Elizabeth saw the tearstained and ravaged face of a woman whose life was over.

Raising one hand, she touched the mirror. "That can't be me," she said. "I can't look like that. That isn't me." Her voice was a pleading call in the empty room. "No," she uttered. "Oh, please, no. Don't let that be me. . . ."

She pushed away from the mirror and crumpled onto the floor, her whole body convulsed with her sobs. Over and over again, she cried out against the reality that had pushed its way through her alcoholic haze. Over and over again, she fought to find the gentle girl she remembered beneath the destroyed and desperate woman.

There was nowhere she could turn. No one she could call out to for help. No place for her to hide. She thought of her parents and remembered their rigid and moralistic dismissal of her after Mark's death. Mark, she thought. Dear, dear Mark. The picture of his body, crumbling and decaying beneath the earth, came into her mind, and she almost screamed aloud with the pain. She thought of her career and remembered the newspaper item that effectively ended all her hopes. There was nothing left.

She crawled to her feet and found the brandy bottle. She drank from it quickly, thirstily, then lowered the bottle to her side and simply stood, a figure of dejection and defeat.

She raised her head and gathered the collar of the robe closely around her throat. I must leave here, she thought. That's it. I must leave here. Holding the robe with one hand and carrying the bottle with the other, Elizabeth walked purposefully out of her room and down the darkened staircase of the silent house. She rushed out the front door and stood on the steps. It was a bright, clear night. Elizabeth stopped and let the softly scented air sweep over her. It was a delicious feeling.

Smiling to herself, she went to the garage and found Jane's new Ford convertible. She walked unsteadily to it, climbed into the driver's seat, and started the engine. She drove carefully down the drive to the gate.

Since Maud and Jane were still out, the guard was on the watch and looked surprised at seeing Elizabeth drive up in Jane's car.

"Open the gate," ordered Elizabeth.

He looked at her and noticed the bottle. "I don't think that's a good idea, Miss Hudson. Wouldn't you like to go back to the house? Or perhaps if you need to go somewhere, I could call you a taxi."

"I don't need a taxi, you fool," said Elizabeth. "Can't you see I'm in a car?"

"Yes, ma'am, but—"

"Open the gate. I insist on it."

"Just a minute, ma'am," said the guard. He tried to think fast. Obviously, Miss Hudson was in no condition to drive. But he was afraid to stop her. He decided to call up to the house and talk to Hardgrave. The butler would know what to do. He went into the gatehouse, and Elizabeth saw him pick up the telephone.

The fool is calling someone, she thought. They're going to try and trap me.

She climbed out of the car and quickly slipped to the gate, pushing one side of it back, letting it swing wide open. Then she returned to the car and started slowly out.

The guard saw her and rushed out of the gatehouse, calling to her, "Miss . . . Miss!"

His voice frightened Elizabeth, and she pressed the gas pedal. The car shot forward, scraping the side of the gate, and then whipped onto the road, swinging crazily back and forth. The guard continued to call after her as she drove away.

Elizabeth didn't know where she was going. But she knew she had to get away. If she didn't escape, they would kill her. Just as they'd killed Mark. Just as they'd killed her career. She pushed the little car faster and soon was driving up the canyon road. Above her, she could see the glittering stars. The sky looked clean and bright.

Elizabeth pulled off the road and stopped. A car following her quickly swerved to avoid hitting her, its driver calling out obscenities in her direction. But Elizabeth didn't pay any attention. Her gaze was riveted on the stars. Slowly, she took a deep drink from her bottle. They were so pretty, she thought.

Below her, the city was stretched out, its lights shining mockingly up toward her. She looked at it with disdain. What a terrible place, she thought. A horrible, horrible place. They're not going to keep me. They're not going to trap me. I'm going to get away.

Urgently, she started the car again and backed up. But one of the wheels slipped on the soft embankment, and the car swerved slightly. Elizabeth couldn't understand what the problem was. She tried to go forward, but the car was still embedded in the shoulder.

My God, she thought. They're trying to keep me here. They're holding me. Elizabeth pressed the accelerator hard, and the car leaped suddenly forward. It hesitated slightly at the edge, and then once again gained momentum as it plunged over the cliff and hurled down the side of the mountain.

Surprise was Elizabeth's first reaction, then terror as the lights of the city began rushing up toward her. They were laughing. She could hear them laughing as they sucked her in.

"*No!*" she screamed. "I have to get away. *I have to get away.*"

The car twisted and crashed against the side of the mountain as it fell deeper and deeper toward the bottom. "Oh, no," sobbed Elizabeth. "Please don't. Please don't keep me here."

She never saw the final light that exploded around her and then subsided into darkness.

When questioned by reporters, Murry Edson said that Elizabeth's death was a tragedy, and that she had been very talented; Global had had high hopes for her. Murry also announced that Elizabeth's body would be transported back to Ohio for burial, but that there would be a short memorial service in Hollywood to which her friends and co-workers would be invited.

The crowds were thick outside the chapel. The press pushed forward, taking pictures and trying to get interviews. It was difficult to keep them out of the building.

Jane sat with Maud and Mable Cramer. Bill, Mack, and Lucille Evans were in the pew behind them. The room was surprisingly full. Several contract players had come, along with a great many musicians Elizabeth had met during her short time in California. These were the people that perhaps she had been most comfortable with. They had understood her without really even trying, simply because they shared the common bond of their love for music. The Global executives were all there, as were many of the publicity people and creative artists. Sam Withers sat alone, his face stark and angry. He could accept the death of Elizabeth Hudson, but he could never forgive the loss of her talent.

After the minister had said a few words about life and its insecurities, the choir sang a hymn, and it was all over.

Jane said good-bye to Mable, and then she and Maud slipped out the back way. They were followed by Mack and Bill, with Terrance and Murry bringing up the rear. Jane had invited Bill and Mack back for lunch, but had not included the others.

"Well, Jane," said Murry, catching up with her, "it's a terrible tragedy. A terrible tragedy."

"Yes," said Jane briefly.

"It's so sad when a young girl dies like that," said Maud.

"It was an accident," said Murry. "A terrible accident."

"Was it, Murry?" asked Jane, stopping and looking at him. "Hardgrave told me that Elizabeth didn't receive any phone calls, on the day she died."

"Oh?"

"I thought you intended to call her and tell her everything was all right. Maybe if you'd made that call, she wouldn't have been driving around in the middle of the night. Maybe she wouldn't be dead."

"I meant to call her," said Murry. "But it was a very busy day. I had a lot on my mind."

"And Elizabeth Hudson wasn't important enough. She wasn't a big star, making you a lot of money. So you didn't bother to call her."

"I did my best for Elizabeth. As I do for all the people at Global."

"Until you're finished with them," said Jane flatly.

"I don't think we'd better talk anymore," said Murry. "You're tired. You've been under a strain for a long time. You'd better take a few days off work."

"It's been a lot harder on Elizabeth," snapped Jane.

"Jane!" Maud was horrified.

"She's tired," said Murry sympathetically. "Elizabeth made entirely too many demands on her. If she hadn't died—"

"What?" asked Jane. "What would have happened?" Jane looked at him accusingly.

"I know she was your friend, but you have to face facts," said Murry slowly. "Elizabeth Hudson could never have survived in this town. What happened to her was inevitable. Maybe she wouldn't have died, but she would never have been able to make it here. She didn't have what it takes. For your sake, I think it's better that it happened now than for you to have gone on trying to help her."

"How dare you?" Jane's eyes flashed with anger. "Who gave you the right to pontificate about people? To decide who can and can't make it. You bastard." Jane slapped Murry once across the face, then again, and again, her hands flailing out at him. "A young woman just died, and you dismiss her like an unacceptable servant." Tears coursed down her cheeks. "You bastard! You dirty, lousy bastard." She became completely hysterical, crying and lashing out toward Murry. The dam of constraint broke, and all of Jane's sadness over Elizabeth and her own frustrations broke through.

Mack rushed to her and held her tightly, calling to Maud for help. She put her arms around Jane.

"Jane, dear, you're tired. That's all. Just very, very tired."

Murry had lunged back, away from Jane's attack, but now he moved forward again. "Jane . . . I—"

Jane pulled away from Maud and Mack. "Don't talk to me," she said, her mouth hard. "I don't want to hear anymore. I don't want to ever hear anything again." Her voice cracked, and she broke down completely in Maud's arms.

"You'd better take her home. I'll send a doctor," said Murry.

"Yes, of course. I'll take her right now," agreed Maud, leading Jane to the waiting limousine, looking at Mack and Bill over her shoulder.

They nodded and followed to Maud's house. When they arrived, Hardgrave informed them that Mrs. Watson was upstairs with Miss Turner. Mack and Bill went into the drawing room to wait. The doctor arrived, and they saw him pass through the hall on his way upstairs. In a short time he left, and Maud joined them.

"She's resting," said Maud, sitting down on the sofa.

"Would you like a drink?" asked Bill.

"Perhaps a little sherry. It's been a difficult morning."

"What did the doctor say?" asked Mack.

"Exhaustion. He gave her a sedative to make her sleep. He said she should take some time to have a good rest. Everything's been too much for her." Maud took her sherry. "We'll have lunch soon. Oh, dear, I wish Maggie were here. I'm so worried about Jane."

Mack smiled. "I'm sure she'll be all right. She *is* tired. It's been a rough time for her."

"I wonder if she'll ever go back to work?" said Maud. "I must admit that up until now I've been rather in favor of her giving up her career and marrying Warren. But I hate for her to leave like this, with such a bitter taste in her mouth about the whole thing. It takes away all the nice things that have happened to her in the past."

Mack laughed. "Maud, you've got it all wrong. Jane isn't going to quit. And she isn't going to leave Global. She won't quit as long as she's able to walk, crawl, or drag herself onto the set."

"But upstairs just now she was adamant about giving up the whole business. And you heard her after the service."

Mack stood up and went to the bar. Pouring himself a drink, he waved the bottle at Bill, who declined. He returned to the sofa and sat down, looking seriously at Maud.

"I wish I knew how to explain this," he said. "I wish I knew the word that would make you understand what it is that makes a woman like Jane Turner click. Ambition, ego, a lust for power . . . they're all part of it. But not all. There's something inside her, something in her guts that won't let her quit. For want of a better phrase, I guess you'd call it star quality. The certain extra energy that comes to life when the camera rolls. That little touch of magic that makes the camera want her—makes it love her. And she knows she has it. Anybody who's really good knows they have it. Jane Turner is a movie star, Maud. And there'll never really be anything else in the world for her."

"Something that drives her," Maud said quietly to herself, remembering her conversation with Warren.

"What?" asked Bill.

"Nothing," said Maud. "I know you're right, Mack. But I wish with all my heart that you were wrong."

Bill moved over and sat down next to her. "Poor Maud," he said. "I don't think anyone realizes that this hasn't been a bed of roses for you, either. After all, this is your house and to have Warren and Jane acting out their romantic woes all over the place, and then having Elizabeth going to pieces right under your nose, is bound to be unsettling."

"Oh, Bill," said Maud between giggles and tears, "don't make me laugh or . . . or feel sorry for myself."

"Bill has always had a way with words," said Mack.

"At least I hope Jane will go away for a little vacation. She needs a change. Of course, she can't go and visit her mother in Europe right now, it's too dangerous. And in this country, she'll be recognized everywhere. I suppose we could just go to Malibu and hide away at the beach house. But that sounds rather depressing."

"I agree that she should go away. And you should, too," said Bill. "Has she finished her picture yet?"

"I don't really know. If she hasn't, there can't be that much left."

"Then right after it's completed, we'll think of somewhere for you to go."

They heard the doorbell, and Maud looked up unhappily. "I do hope that isn't more reporters. I'm so sick of all those pushy people."

"Can't be," said Mack. "The guard would never let them get this far."

In a few seconds, Hardgrave appeared in the drawing room and announced Warren Harris. Maud jumped up and rushed to him.

"Warren. I'm so glad to see you. You don't know how happy I am that you're here."

Warren kissed her. "Hello, Maud. I'm sorry to surprise you like this, but I didn't know when I would get here so I didn't want to say anything. I hope you don't mind."

"Of course not. You couldn't have come at a better time. Jane needs you."

"How is she? I spoke to her last night and she didn't sound very good."

"She's no better today," said Maud. "She's sleeping, but she should be up for dinner. You can see her then."

Warren nodded and greeted Mack and Bill.

"It's been some time since we've seen you," said Mack.

"Yes," said Warren wearily.

"You look tired," said Maud. Warren's clothing, usually immaculate, was crumpled, and he needed a shave.

"I flew here," he said. "It wasn't too bad, but I couldn't get a berth and had to sit up most of the night."

"I didn't know it took all night to get here from Kansas City," said Mack.

"I wasn't in Kansas City," replied Warren. "Do you suppose I could have a drink?"

"I'm sorry," said Maud. "I'm becoming a terrible hostess. Mack, would you or Bill get Warren a drink?"

"I'll do it," said Bill.

They all waited until Warren had tasted his drink and appeared to relax somewhat. Then Maud very casually asked how his children were.

He smiled. "Fine. I know you've been wondering why I've been away so long. . . ."

"Jane said you had a lot of business to take care of," said Maud.

"Yes."

"And I thought that perhaps you and Jane were—"

"Having a problem? No more than usual. I did have some business to take care of, but not the usual things. I've been to Washington."

No one knew what to ask, so they remained silent.

"Our government seems to think this thing in Europe will grow."

"I know that Roosevelt would like us to get into it," said Bill. "But I didn't think we were making plans already. After all, we haven't been attacked by anybody."

"No," agreed Warren. "But Mr. Roosevelt feels it's important to be prepared as much as possible."

"But what is the government doing?" asked Maud.

"I don't know everything," said Warren. "But, for example, two senators, Burke and Wadsworth, have a bill requiring compulsory draft. We've never had that in peacetime before."

"I didn't know about the bill," said Mack.

"You will soon. It should pass Congress very quickly."

"I thought you were a die-hard Republican," said Maud.

"I am," said Warren. "And I told the president that."

"The president? Did you meet with Roosevelt?" asked Mack.

"Yes. He offered me a job in case we get into the war."

"What kind of job?" asked Maud.

"Nothing special. Just an advisory position on some business matters in case we enter into it."

"I'm sure you're underestimating your position," said Maud. "Or you're not allowed to tell us about it. Which we all understand."

Warren smiled at Maud. "Well, anyway, that's why I've been away so long. We had a lot of meetings, and I couldn't leave until things were settled."

"Settled?" asked Maud. "Does that mean that the president is sure we're going to fight?"

"You know I couldn't answer that if I knew, Maud. And I don't know."

"Well, I'm afraid we'll all know soon enough," said Mack quietly.

"Yes," said Maud. "But I must change the subject, Warren."

"To Jane I hope," he answered.

"Yes. It's been terrible for her." She began explaining all that had happened. Warren knew the bare facts from his telephone conversations with Jane, but she had never told him how devastating the entire experience had been on her; she'd never betrayed her own sense of sadness or frustration at the events unfolding around her. Maud elaborated, pointing out Jane's steadfastness to Elizabeth and her battles for her friend.

"But she is completely exhausted," finished Maud. "The doctor was with her earlier, nothing serious. But he had to give her a sedative. We've been sitting here trying to decide what to do. Right before you came, we had almost settled on a trip, but we don't know where to go."

"I do," said Warren.

"Where?"

"Kansas City," said Warren simply. "I want her to see it anyway, and she—and you, I hope—can come to my house. My children are away at school, but they'll be back for the holidays. I'd like you both to stay at least through Christmas. And if I'm lucky, maybe Jane will want to stay forever." Warren had obviously made some plans.

"But Warren, I thought you all had agreed to live here."

"Jane knows that I'll come here if I must. But I think she should at least see my home. And this is a perfect time."

"Yes," said Maud.

"Perhaps you would like to come out, too," said Warren, turning to Mack and Bill.

"It's certainly something to think about," said Bill.

Warren stood up. "Well, you're welcome." Looking back at Maud, he continued, "Do you mind if I stay with you for a few days? I didn't have time to get a hotel."

"Naturally, you'll stay here," said Maud. "Hardgrave will show you to your room."

"I've already given him my bag," said Warren, grinning at her.

Maud smiled back at him.

"And if you'll all excuse me, I'd like to go and clean up, maybe take a little nap. All right?"

"Of course," said Maud. "Mack and Bill are spending the

day. We'll be out by the pool this afternoon, going over my books. I don't seem to be able to keep all my relief committee accounts straight. I don't know why they think I should handle the money."

"Because you're an honest woman," said Warren, leaning over and giving her a kiss.

"Of course I'm honest. But that doesn't mean I can add or subtract. Fortunately, Bill does both beautifully."

"Good luck, Bill," said Warren.

He nodded to the group and left.

As soon as he was out of earshot, Maud turned to the others. But before she could speak, Mack began.

"I think it's a good idea," he said with finality.

"You do?" asked Maud.

"Absolutely. Look, Jane is a mess right now. She needs to get away to someplace uncomplicated. Warren loves her. He'll take wonderful care of both of you. And frankly, if they really do plan to stay together, he needs to find out that Jane isn't going to be happy away from here for long."

"Kansas City is going to love her," said Bill, smiling.

"And that's another thing," said Mack. "She'll get all the attention without all the hassles. You can be damn sure Warren isn't going to let anyone ask the wrong questions or put her on the spot about Elizabeth or anything else."

Maud looked thoughtful. "Oh, I agree that it'll be good for Jane. In fact, awhile back I tried to suggest that she marry Warren and move to Missouri. It's just that I never imagined *myself* in Kansas City."

"You know she'll never go without you," said Mack.

"I suppose not," said Maud.

"Besides," Bill laughed, "you'll fit in anywhere."

"I'm not sure that's a compliment," said Maud, standing up. "Will you two try to come for a few days?"

Mack looked over at Bill. "We'll have to think about that. We've never traveled together, you know. It might be bad for my career."

"You can come on separate trains," said Maud desperately.

"Kansas City may not be ready for us," said Bill.

Maud had a slight smile on her face. "When I get finished with them, they'll be ready for anything," she said slyly.

CHAPTER *Twenty*

As THE SLEEK Twentieth Century Limited train pulled into the Kansas City station, Maud looked out of the window and called to Jane.

"I don't see Warren anywhere. I do hope he's here."

"I'm sure he is," said Jane calmly as she checked her hair and makeup in the mirror of an elegant leather case. It was the size of a small suitcase and contained a variety of creams and lotions, along with Jane's makeup and hair supplies.

"Do I look all right?" asked Jane, studying her reflection critically.

"You look lovely, dear," said Maud. "I like that dress."

"It's nice to wear things that are a little heavier again. I was getting rather tired of the same climate. Kansas City is cold."

"Of course it is, dear," said Maud. "I think it was very wise of you to buy all those new clothes."

Jane smiled and closed her case. Lifting it off her lap, she straightened the doe-colored suede skirt which she wore with a matching jacket and hat. Her blouse was of pale beige silk, and a mink scarf was tossed around her neck. She lowered her veil to cover the upper portion of her face and stood up.

Maud gazed at her serenely. She looked better already, she thought. It hadn't really been hard to convince Jane to come on this trip. After a few discussions with Murry Edson, and one private meeting between him and Warren, the head of Global had reluctantly given Jane several weeks off from work. But she had to be back immediately after Christmas.

Warren had come ahead to prepare everything, while Jane and Maud had indulged themselves in an orgy of shopping and then booked rooms on the train for a leisurely trip.

Maud knew that Jane was still not completely herself. There were moments when she had a frightened and tense look on her face. And once on the train, Jane had cried out in the night. Maud had heard her and gone into her room, but Jane had immediately fallen back to sleep. Maud had never said anything. She assumed that Jane was haunted by the death of Elizabeth Hudson. But she was also sure there was something else that she didn't know about.

The train stopped, and Maud immediately got up from her seat.

"Well, here we are, dear," she said, suddenly beginning to flutter. Jane knew the signs. Whether Maud was traveling or not, the minute she got anywhere near a station, she began to get excited and a little dizzy.

"Fix your hat," said Jane.

"Oh, dear, you're right. My hat." She looked in the bathroom mirror and adjusted the rakish black feathered pinwheel which she wore with a black wool suit. Returning, she picked up her sable coat and said, "I should go back to my room to make sure I haven't left anything."

"I'm sure that Maria will take care of everything," said Jane. Maria had almost forced Maud to go and sit with Jane for the last few miles of the trip in order to straighten out the mess Maud had made in her own room.

"Yes. But she gets confused sometimes. Where is Louise?"

"She's helping Maria," said Jane. "She finished my packing early. They'll take care of everything, don't worry."

"Yes, of course." Maud smiled. "Well, dear, shall we go?"

Jane stood up, and the two women made their way through the corridor to the nearest exit. The porter nodded smilingly at them as they passed him, and the conductor solicitously hurried forward to help them down the steps. Maud went first, carefully protecting her hat, and after she had reached the platform, Jane followed.

It took only a few seconds for the photographers and reporters to spot Jane and rush forward. Flashbulbs popped and questions were hurled at her. Jane smiled graciously, answered a few questions about her picture plans, and posed provocatively on the steps of the train. In a few moments, Warren came running toward them.

"God, I'm sorry," he said. "I don't know who told these guys you were coming. *I* certainly didn't. Let's get you out of here."

Mindful the press's attention was still focused on them, Jane calmly smiled at Warren and took his hand, kissing him on the cheek. Maud also greeted Warren, and then the two women allowed him to lead them through the massive station, followed by the reporters, to a waiting limousine.

"What about our luggage . . . and Maria and Louise?" asked Maud.

"One of the men from my office is at the train. He'll see to everything," said Warren. "I'm really sorry about all that press business."

"I don't know why," said Jane, surprised.

"I was just hoping you wouldn't be attacked your first day here," he said.

"They were very nice," said Jane. "How are you, Warren?"

"Fine. Much better now that you're here. There are a few social things lined up for us, but mostly I just want you to rest and enjoy yourself."

"I'm sure it's going to be wonderful," said Jane.

"Yes," murmured Maud, "wonderful."

Warren's house was a large rambling structure in the Country Club section right outside Kansas City. Surrounded by old trees, it was made of brick and, with the ground covered with snow, looked like it had been created by Currier and Ives.

Inside it was comfortably furnished and overseen by a housekeeper who had been with Warren for years.

After settling in, Jane took a long bath and changed into an evening robe of deep rose wool. She put her hair up and wore small diamond earrings. She looked very lovely as she joined Maud and Warren for dinner. There were no guests, and immediately after the meal, Maud excused herself on the pretext of exhaustion in order to leave the couple alone.

Jane and Warren moved into the pleasant living room where a blazing fire cast bright shadows over the polished furniture. Easy chairs flanked a large sofa, and low lamps cast a cozy glow over the scene.

Warren poured himself a snifter of brandy and offered one to Jane, who refused.

"It's wonderful seeing you sitting there," he said. "Seeing you in this house."

"Thank you. It's nice to be here."

"I hope your room is comfortable."

"It's lovely," said Jane. "And where did you get all of those flowers at this time of year?"

"Even Kansas City can provide things if you know where to look for them." He smiled.

"Don't start being defensive about Kansas City already. I've only been here a few hours."

"And I hope you'll want to stay a long time."

Jane reached out and touched his arm as Warren sat down next to her.

"Don't expect too much, Warren. You know that I still have a job."

Warren shrugged. "People have changed their minds before."

She started to speak, but he stopped her.

"Don't bite my head off," he said with a laugh. "I'm not trying to start an argument. I gave Hollywood a try, and fair's fair. Now you should give Kansas City a try."

Jane smiled. "I've always hated logic," she said. "How are David and Susan?"

"Furious that they can't be here to meet you. But they'll be home from school in a week, and I'm sure you'll see more than enough of them."

"I'm looking forward to it," said Jane. "But what about you? How are you?"

"Me? I'm fine," said Warren.

"I guess what I'm really asking is what's going on with the situation in Washington. You never did fully explain that to me."

"There's nothing to explain," said Warren. "I just went to meet the president about what this country would do if we got into the war."

"And will we?"

"I hope not." Warren turned away and set his glass down on the coffee table. "But that's nothing for us to worry about now. I just want to look at you and count my blessings."

Later that night after Warren had walked Jane to her room, he went down the hall to his own room and prepared for bed. But in a short while, a soft knock at the door interrupted him. He opened it to find Jane, wearing a soft negligee of black silk, standing in the dim light from the hall.

She smiled at him, a twinkle in her eyes. "I thought I'd help you count your blessings," she said.

Warren backed up for her to enter, and then quickly closed the door behind her. "You look very beautiful," he said. "But I thought we had agreed in California that it wasn't a good idea for us to meet like this when we were staying with others."

"That was because your children were there. I just didn't like the idea of one of them getting up in the middle of the night and seeing you stumbling down the hall in your pajama bottoms."

"I don't stumble."

Jane ignored his comment. "The children aren't here now."

"But Maud is."

"Aunt Maud could hardly be described as a child. Now, are you going to stand here arguing with me, or are we going to make love?"

"Well . . ." Warren appeared to be considering the matter.

"What!" Jane said incredulously.

He laughed, picked Jane up, and carried her over to the bed, placing her carefully on the turned down sheets and leaning over her. "I love you," he whispered.

Jane reached up and encircled his neck, drawing him down to her. "I love you, too, my dear, dear love."

He touched her breasts, pressing slightly, and Jane moaned. "Oh, yes, darling."

He pushed the straps of her gown down over her shoulders and leaned forward, kissing her exposed breasts. She slipped out of the negligee and lay naked on the bed, her eyes half-closed in anticipation, her nude body shining and lovely.

Warren quickly removed his clothes and lay next to her. They embraced, their hands exploring, touching familiar places, slowly arousing each other. Warren pressed his face between Jane's breasts, and then ran his tongue around her hardened nipples. Jane began to move her body, rubbing it against him, as he slipped further down on the bed and placed his face between her legs. Jane gasped as she felt his tongue slip in and out of her.

As he continued, Jane writhed in passion. She twisted around until she was lying opposite him, and as he continued to excite her, she slipped her mouth around his penis, sucking, licking, devouring him. Their bodies rolled back and forth over the bed as their hunger drove them to a frenzy of desire.

Jane pressed herself up to his mouth, urging him, leading him. Her hands grasped his buttocks and gripped tightly as her tongue licked his groin.

When their sexual tension seemed explosive, Warren pulled away and turned around, his body pressing down on hers, and they kissed. Their tongues searched each other's mouths. Then Warren pushed himself up and looked down at her. She was beautiful.

Her eyes never left his as he slowly entered her and began to push. Jane's legs encircled his back, pulling him tighter to her. He licked her breasts, kissed her mouth, her neck, her eyes.

"Oh, you're so wonderful, my dearest love," she whispered. "You feel so good in me. So very good." Jane watched his face. The excitement, almost madness in his eyes increased her desire. His strength covered her. His love consumed her.

Their bodies jammed together, and Warren's breath grew faster as his rhythm increased. Jane met each thrust of his body with her own. She wanted him. She wanted all of him.

Warren had never felt so strong. Never felt so powerful. There was nothing but the two of them, and he muttered soft words of love and passion as he plunged deeper and deeper into her.

Jane gasped. It felt as if he would split her body as the fire between her legs swept up through her whole body.

They reached their climax together, and Warren's body became rigid as he stabbed again and again into her. Then they held each other tightly, as if time had stopped and would never start again.

Warren was a dearly loved citizen of Kansas City and, consequently, Jane and Maud were entertained opulently and constantly. Jane gave several interviews to the local papers and graciously appeared at fund-raising events and charitable functions in addition to the dinners and parties planned by Warren's friends.

She sailed through each day and evening, being charming at the social events and smiling blindingly whenever a camera was in view.

For Maud, it wasn't quite so simple. The Kansas City hostesses knew all about Mrs. Thomas Watson and were frankly more impressed with her social connections than with Jane's star status. The local matrons vied to outdo each other in their entertaining and often assumed such correct manners around Maud that she inevitably felt like she was in a particularly oppressive church service.

But despite her own boredom, she was convinced that the visit was good for Jane, so she continued to be overpoweringly gracious to the wives of men who raised cows, sold cows, butchered cows, or simply ate cows. And in private, she gave serious thought to becoming a vegetarian.

The children arrived, and Maud and Jane enjoyed them tremendously, entering into all their projects and activities. The best times for everyone were the few evenings they stayed home alone, playing games or just talking about the children's plans, Christmas, or Maud's fabulous tours of Europe before the war in 1914.

In the middle of December there was a large party at the country club, a traditional dinner dance considered one of the most important parties of the holiday season.

"What are you wearing tonight?" asked Maud as she went up to dress.

"Black," said Jane.

"Oh dear. Then we're going to look as if we're in mourning. I'd planned to wear black, as well."

"You go ahead. I have a white dress I've been saving for a special occasion. And I imagine tonight is a perfect time for it."

"You don't mind?"

"Not at all."

"Good. As you said, tonight is a special occasion, so I think I'll bring out all the diamonds. I wish I had my tiara. Would you like to borrow anything?"

"Probably. You can help me decide when I'm dressed."

"All right, dear. I'd better get started. I don't know why, but it seems to take longer and longer for me to look twenty-nine." Maud started to her room.

"Aunt Maud," said Jane.

"Yes, dear?" She turned back.

"Thank you for staying here so long. I know you don't like it very much."

"Darling. You look rested and beautiful and very happy. For that I'd stay in the downtown section of hell. Which, incidentally, is what Mrs. Skylar's drawing room reminded me of the other night," continued Maud, bringing to mind a recent hostess.

"She adored you."

"Perhaps. But I had the distinct impression that she would have liked to have me stuffed and mounted on her wall."

Jane laughed.

"Aren't you coming up?" asked Maud.

"In a few moments. You go ahead. I bet I'm still ready before you are."

"Nonsense. Everyone knows you Hollywood stars are never on time."

Alone, Jane walked about the familiar living room, touching various objects, enjoying the peaceful atmosphere. The fire burned brightly, and through the windows Jane could see children building a snowman across the street. Cars moved slowly down the street, their drivers waving at neighbors as they passed. It was a warm, secure community where businessmen played golf together and their wives played bridge and discussed their children and their maids. They were all successful, but no one lived ostentatiously. Each couple went away for a few weeks in the winter, and during the summers there were family vacations. They had known each other most of their lives, and even the newest inhabitants appeared to have lived in Kansas City for years. There was nothing to fear, nothing to worry about. Nothing to become enraged about or fight about. It was charmingly uneventful. Jane knew she couldn't ever live here.

The realization made her a little sad. It would be so easy, she thought. And so very impossible. There was no future for her in Kansas City. She took a long, lingering look at the comfortable room, and then went upstairs to dress. Warren had called an old friend of his, a widowed lawyer who was now retired, and invited him to act as Maud's escort for the party. The man had unassailable dignity and at first seemed a little cold when he arrived at Warren's. But soon he and Maud discovered friends in common in New York and thoroughly enjoyed themselves, discussing all the people they both knew who were dead.

The entrance of Warren's group at the country club was the unofficial indication that the evening had started. Maud and her escort walked up the short staircase first, followed a few seconds later by Jane and Warren.

Maud had, indeed, brought out the big guns for this occasion. She wore a deep black velvet dress by Worth and had decorated it with a diamond necklace, earrings, bracelets, and an enormous, square-cut ring. To keep her warm, she had thrown a magnificent cape of black velvet, completely lined in mink, over her shoulders.

"Really, Aunt Maud, you look just like a Russian empress," said Jane.

"Nonsense. I don't know any Russians," said Maud as she swept into the room.

If Maud was impressive, Jane's appearance was devastating. With Warren at her side, immaculate in white tie and trying not to look too proud of the woman he loved, Jane glided into the room, using her well-rehearsed trick of suddenly appearing. She took the other guests, who had been trying to appear as if they weren't waiting for her, by surprise. One moment she wasn't there, the next she was. And while the ladies of the country club were still mentally totaling up the amount of money it must have cost to outfit Maud, the men had the first chance to admire Jane Turner.

She was magnificent. Her white sequined sheath hugged her body tightly and glittered in the festive lights that illuminated the room. Her dress dipped almost to the waist with a loose cowl collar, and her back was totally bare. Her hair was swept up onto her head and held with a diamond pin, a few blond wisps allowed to fall around her face. Her arms were covered with long, white gloves, and she wore a pair of astonishing diamond earrings. One hand grasped a long ermine scarf.

There was a murmur of appreciation as the two women made

their entrance. Warren and his friend escorted the ladies to a table for ten, at which the other guests were already seated. The faces were familiar to Jane and Maud, including that of Mrs. Skylar who verbally hurled herself at Maud.

"My dear Mrs. Watson, how very nice you look. Is that dress by Worth? I must see if my little dressmaker can't make me something like it."

"You must," said Maud, seating herself, and privately thankful that a dinner partner separated her from Mrs. Skylar. The woman was totally undaunted and leaned either backward or forward around the hapless gentleman in order to continue the conversation.

"I always say that black is so safe," said Mrs. Skylar. "Don't you agree?"

"Well, I certainly—"

"And appropriate. No matter where you're going, black is simply perfect."

"With the possible exception of a wedding," interposed Maud.

Mrs. Skylar laughed affectedly. "Oh, now dear Mrs. Watson. You're pulling my leg."

"What an appalling thought," said Maud under her breath.

"I was telling my husband not long ago—that's him over there. But of course you've met, haven't you? At my little dinner party. I *do* hope you enjoyed yourself that evening."

"Very much," said Maud.

"I received your gracious note. Where *do* you get your stationery? I simply can't keep up with my correspondence."

"Really?" asked Maud.

"And of course, it's so important. But you must have friends all over the world to whom you write."

"Not quite," said Maud who felt herself sinking under the flood of Mrs. Skylar's discourse. And constantly turning and leaning back and forth to answer was giving her a stiff neck.

"I understand Miss Turner's mother is in Europe. How exciting for her. But of course, it's not the same there anymore, is it? I mean, with all the changes. I remember when Orlo, that's my husband, and I went, right after the last war they had. Well, it was devastating . . . just devastating. But nevertheless, it was still better than today. You must be very worried about Mrs. Turner."

"It's Mrs. Austen now," said Maud quietly with what she thought might be her last breath.

"Oh, of course, Mrs. Austen. I *did* hear something about her remarrying. Is her new husband nice? Does he have money?"

For one of the few times in her life, Maud couldn't think of a thing to say.

Warren came up behind her. "Would you like to dance?"

"Desperately," she replied.

"You'll have to forgive Mrs. Skylar," said Warren as he steered Maud around the dance floor. "She has a tendency to speak her mind at every opportunity."

Maud privately thought it would be difficult for Mrs. Skylar to speak something she obviously didn't have. But ever polite, she merely smiled and said sweetly, "Everyone's been so kind."

"Naturally. They all like you very much," said Warren.

"Well, we've certainly been beautifully entertained," said Maud. "I know Jane has enjoyed it very much."

"She looks beautiful tonight, doesn't she?"

"Exceptionally. And very rested. That's your doing, Warren. You've been very good for her."

"Thank you. I hope I can continue to be. Do you think she likes it here?"

"We really haven't talked about it," said Maud evasively, terrified that she might commit Jane to something.

"Well, I plan to talk to her soon," said Warren. "I hope she likes it enough to make Kansas City her home."

Maud looked at him quickly, and then away. "Well, I'm sure you two will do what's best." She looked around the room. "What a good orchestra," she commented.

Always quick to point out Kansas City's superior points, Warren amiably discussed the music for the rest of their dance.

When he led Maud back to the table, there was a great deal of well-intentioned ribbing from the other men about Warren's keeping the two visiting ladies to himself and how they were going to steal Maud away from him.

Everyone laughed and Maud joined in, thinking what a nice place Kansas City was and how she'd slit her wrists if she had to stay much longer.

The holidays were beautiful, filled with tradition and

pleasant social exchange. But as the days wore on, it was obvious to Maud that Jane wasn't herself. She became distracted and when spoken to sometimes didn't seem to hear. Often she called Mack long distance and talked to him for a long time and then went to her room.

Maud didn't want to interfere, but she was concerned and, finally, on the day after Christmas, she decided to speak to her.

"Jane, dear," called Maud as she knocked at the door. "May I come in?"

"Of course," said Jane.

Maud walked in and found Jane lying across the bed on her stomach. She had on two-piece lounging pajamas, and her hair was held up by a bright red band across her forehead. Her knees were bent and her mules dangled off her feet. She looked to be about sixteen years old.

Maud stood near the bed and looked down at her. "Dear. Are you all right?" she asked.

"Why, yes," answered Jane, looking surprised. "Did you think something was wrong with me?"

"Well, you seem a little strange. The children have been asking for you, and we all wondered if you were feeling well."

"I'm fine," said Jane, smiling at Maud and patting the bed next to her. Maud sat down on the edge and rubbed Jane's back. "Do you want to tell me about it?"

"There's nothing to tell, really. Where's Warren?"

"He went to the office hours ago."

"Did he think there was something wrong with me, too?"

"I guess not. He didn't mention it."

Jane smiled. "Good."

"Now Jane," began Maud. "I've known you too long not to know when you've got something on your mind. What is it? You've been bothered by something ever since we left California. I know Elizabeth's death upset you very much, but that wasn't the only thing on your mind, was it? I've seen it in your eyes all along. Have you resolved it yet?"

"No. Not really. I just keep coming back to the same thing."

"I don't understand," said Maud.

"Never mind. I wish Mack were here. I really need to talk to him."

"But you've called him almost daily."

"Yes. But it's not the same. I need more time with him. And I need to see him face to face."

"It's a shame they couldn't come here for a few days," said Maud wistfully. "But I guess they were just too busy."

"You really like Mack and Bill, don't you?"

"Very much. They're very charming young men. And very well mannered."

Jane got off the bed and wandered to her dressing table. She picked up a brush and lightly touched her hair. Looking at Maud in the mirror's reflection, she asked casually, "Do you think we could leave here soon?"

Maud looked at Jane. "Are you ready to leave?" she asked. "I thought perhaps you were beginning to enjoy it. Everyone here loves you. And Warren—"

"Yes, Warren," said Jane. "Damn it. It's so confusing and difficult." She put down the brush and came back to Maud. Kneeling on the floor, she rested her head in Maud's lap. "I do love him so very much, Aunt Maud."

"I know you do, dear," said Maud, stroking Jane's soft hair. "I know."

Dinner that night was a boisterous affair. The children had spent the day visiting friends and were loudly telling about their adventures. Warren had felt Jane's unsettledness and was trying to ignore it by talking about plans for the future, even discussing a possible trip to Mexico at Easter. When dinner finally broke up, Maud suggested that David and Susan come with her, and she would teach them how to play the game of Monopoly she had given them for Christmas. It was a relatively new game, and she had had it sent from New York.

Jane and Warren went into the living room and sat down together before the fireplace.

Warren continued to talk. "I think a trip to Mexico during Easter would be perfect. The kids would love it, and I think you would, too. I haven't been there for a long time. Maybe Maud will come along and—"

Jane turned to him and gently placed her hand over his mouth. She smiled at him. "Don't, Warren. You forget I'll be working at Easter. In fact, I should probably be working right now."

Warren took her hand and kissed it gently, and then stared at the fire. "I guess I didn't want to face this." He smiled. "Even grown-ups don't like to face unpleasant things."

"You know I only came for the holidays."

"Yes. But I guess I thought you were enjoying yourself so much that you'd want to stay."

"And give up my career and all the rest," finished Jane. Warren smiled ruefully and nodded.

"I can't, Warren," she said simply.

"Well, you have to give me credit for trying."

"It's been a wonderful visit, Warren. But I can't stay here for the rest of my life. It's simply not me."

"You'll never convince me that Hollywood is really you. You're too good for all that. You're too special and kind and real to ever be a part of that place."

Jane grinned at him. "You make it sound like some kind of purgatory. It's where I do my work."

"Which you hate. You said so yourself. You said how much you hated the roles you were playing."

"I have."

"And you saw what happened to Elizabeth. I don't want that to happen to you, Jane. I don't want you to go back out there and be destroyed by the whole system."

Jane turned away from him. "I won't be." Her voice was low, but determined.

"I wish you'd stay here. I want to give you a home, protect you. I'd try very hard to make you happy."

"Oh, you do make me happy, Warren. Really you do. I love you. But I have to go back."

He shook his head. "I guess I'll never understand. But I can't very well kidnap you," he said thoughtfully. "Although the thought has crossed my mind."

She kissed him. "That's a very nice thought," she said. "It might be rather fun."

"Well, it looks like we're moving to California," said Warren resolutely. "After all, I made it through last summer. It won't be so bad. And the kids loved it."

"And you hate it," said Jane. "Warren, please understand. I do love you. But Maud told me once that people couldn't change to make other people happy. If they did, they wouldn't be the person they were meant to be. You love it here. It's your home and your life. Everyone you know and love lives here."

"Except you."

"I want you to think very carefully before you pick up and move your life to Hollywood. I want you to be happy and I don't want you to eventually resent me because I took you away from the people and the things that are dear to you. This place is your home, Warren. But it isn't mine."

"Jane, a place is just a place. The important thing is for us to be together."

"I hope you're right. I'd love to be Mrs. Warren Harris of Beverly Hills, California."

Warren put his arm around her. "Who knows, maybe suddenly you'll get sick of the whole thing and we'll come back here."

Jane sat up. "Warren, you can't base a relationship, or a life, on maybes. I can't be anything but what I am."

"I love what you are. I'm not complete without you."

"And I'm not complete without you, either. I love you, Warren. I'll always love you."

"I won't be able to go back with you. I have to stay with David and Susan until they return to school, and I have some business to take care of."

"I understand," said Jane. "I have something to work out, myself. Come when you can. I'll be waiting for you."

"When do you think we should get married?" asked Warren.

"Soon, I hope, darling," she answered, nestling once again into his safe and comforting arms.

Twenty-One

ON JANE'S RETURN TO HOLLYWOOD, she was met at the train station by Murry Edson, several publicity men, an enormous number of newsmen, and many photographers. Everyone greeted her as if she'd been away for years rather than a few weeks, and the attention confused Jane. It had become a normal part of her life to be surrounded by reporters, but she thought that this display of interest was somewhat excessive and couldn't understand it.

Mack and Bill had promised to be at the house waiting for her, and as her car drew up they came out to greet her. Hardgrave also joined them and went directly to the third car in the procession in which Maria and Louise were in charge of the luggage.

"Jane, it's good to see you," said Mack, giving her a big kiss. "You look wonderful."

"Thank you. It's good to see you, too. Hello, Bill."

Bill greeted Jane, and then went to help Maud out of the car.

"Oh, thank you, Bill," said Maud as she alighted. Spying her butler, she cried, "Hardgrave! How nice to find you here."

Hardgrave, who couldn't imagine being anywhere else, bowed to Maud and said good afternoon.

"Hardgrave," continued Maud, "you can't imagine how I've suffered without you. My tea was never right and—"

"Really, Aunt Maud," interrupted Jane. "Warren's housekeeper was perfectly capable."

"I know, but it is good to be back with people who know how one likes things without having to be told. I want one of Mrs. Hardgrave's special dinners tonight. She's quite well, I trust."

"Very well, madam. Thank you for asking."

"And you?"

"Very well."

"And I suppose the maids are fine."

"Everyone is in good health," said Hardgrave with finality, feeling he had given his employer enough information.

"Lovely, lovely," said Maud.

Murry Edson, who had followed Jane and Maud, climbed out of his car, spoke to Mack, more briefly to Bill, and then led the way into the house, which was filled with flowers.

"Good heavens," exclaimed Maud. "Who died in here?"

Murry looked shocked and Jane, immediately realizing that it was he who had arranged for the welcoming bouquets, said, "Oh, Aunt Maud, they're beautiful." She turned to Murry. "I bet you did this. How very kind of you."

"Nothing is too good for Global's leading lady," said Murry. The returns on Jane's latest pictures had been extraordinary, and theaters all over the country were demanding more Jane Turner movies. "But I must be stern with you," he said playfully. "You must be back at work in two days."

"Two days," said Maud. "But the poor girl has just gotten off the train. She needs a little rest."

"We have a schedule to keep. I think you'll find everything perfect for you, Jane. We negotiated a new contract with your agent while you were away, and I think you're going to be very pleased with your new agreement. But I do need you to start right away."

"I'll be there," said Jane. "What do you have in mind for me?"

"We can talk about that at the studio."

"All right."

"I have to leave now," said Murry. "But I'll see you soon."

After Murry left the others went into the drawing room and

sat down. Maud pulled off her hat and tossed it on the table behind the sofa and leaned back luxuriously. "I've always liked trains," she said, "but it is nice not to be swaying and rocking all the time."

"Mack, you should have seen the reporters at the station," said Jane. "I expected some, but it was really excessive. Was that Murry?"

"Partly. But some were there on their own."

"Why? I know they come whenever somebody in the movies arrives. But this seemed different."

"Well," said Mack, "don't forget you're a big star now. Everything you do is news. And frankly, Jane, I think some of them came just to let you know they liked you."

Jane looked surprised.

"Oh, I know, the press rarely has any heart, but after you left town, people began to talk about how brave you'd been through the whole mess with Elizabeth. They respect the fact that you stood by her and tried to help her."

"Nothing is kept secret in this town very long," said Bill. "Word got round that you put yourself in a precarious position to help a friend, and the reporters respected that. So they wanted to let you know. The others in the crowd were people in the business who had heard what you did—"

"I didn't do anything," interrupted Jane.

"You tried," said Mack.

"And failed. If I'd done anything, Elizabeth would be alive right now."

"You can't possibly blame yourself for Elizabeth's death," said Maud. "You did all you could."

"I wish I could believe that. I keep thinking that there must have been something. You know, after Elizabeth died all I could think of was that terrible notice in the paper that said Global had shelved her film."

Maud looked questioningly at her. "I don't understand."

"I do," said Mack. "And Jane's response is a natural reaction. That was the part of Elizabeth's life you could understand. You couldn't, no one could, understand what she felt for Ralph or for Mark Richmond. But that announcement was about her career. And it seemed to end it."

"Murry told me that they would find something for Elizabeth."

"Murry is a liar," Mack said flatly. "Elizabeth was finished. She didn't have a chance of coming back after that scandal. You'd think she was Fatty Arbuckle and several other people all rolled into one. No studio can run the risk of trying to buck public feeling."

"So Global just threw her in the garbage," said Jane.

"Really, Jane," said Maud. "I've been in the wilds for weeks and now I have to hear about garbage."

Bill laughed. "Maud, why don't we go into the kitchen and see if we can't convince Mrs. Hardgrave to feed us. I have a feeling these two need to talk."

"That sounds like a good idea," said Maud, rising. "And then I think I'll take a little nap."

"Well, I don't think I'll join you there," said Bill.

"Really, Bill, you're too absurd," said Maud as they left the room.

Jane and Mack watched them leave, and then Mack looked at Jane closely.

"After all our telephone conversations, I know something's on your mind. But all you ever talked about was how I got started in the business. Suppose you tell me what you want to know."

"Yes, I'd like to, if you wouldn't mind."

"I'm all yours."

"It's going to sound selfish. So selfish that I didn't want to admit it to myself, much less someone else." She stopped and stared at Mack, but he didn't speak, and she continued hesitantly. "It's just that you know I haven't been satisfied with my roles for some time. You were right when you said that the announcement of Elizabeth's film being shelved was something I could understand. But it didn't stay in my mind because of what it meant to Elizabeth. I couldn't forget it because I was thinking of myself. I thought of myself when Murry dismissed Elizabeth so casually. I thought of myself when I saw how quickly everyone forgot about her. Through her funeral, I was thinking about myself. I'm ashamed. But I can't help it."

"But what about you?"

"What if it happened to me?"

"You're not likely to become involved in one of the most sensational murders of the year."

"No . . . but I'm going to get older, Mack." Her voice was quiet.

"We all are," he said dryly.

"Don't you understand? In a few years, it could be me who reads about her picture being shelved or who can't get through to Murry on the telephone or who doesn't have anyone to turn to. Look at the roles I'm playing. I don't do *anything* that doesn't concentrate on the way I look."

"You're a very beautiful woman, Jane. Naturally—"

"And how long is it going to last? What happens when I get older? What happens to my career then? Mack, I'm in my mid-twenties. How long do you suppose it'll be before the public gets tired of me? How long before I get dumped and forgotten like Elizabeth? Is her future what I have to look forward to?"

"Jane, I—"

"I've wanted to be in pictures since I was twelve years old. And once I start losing my looks, I might as well be back in Kansas."

In spite of himself, Mack started to laugh.

"What's so damn funny?"

"Nothing. Except you've got to admit your dialogue could use some work."

"It's perfect for one of my films," said Jane.

"Then why don't you demand better parts? You've got a lot of clout now, Jane."

"I've tried. I told Murry I wanted better parts last fall. And I got nowhere. All they wanted to talk about was that *Island Woman* mess. Really, Mack, you should see me in this thing."

"I have. Or at least I've seen some of the rushes. I must admit that it's really a dog of a film."

"Thanks. I needed that," said Jane. She moved closer to Mack and grasped his hand. "Mack, I'm really scared. You've been a good friend. And you know this business. Tell me what to do."

"Have you talked to your agent about the situation?"

"Constance? Hell, as long as she gets her ten percent she wouldn't care if I danced naked at a Rotary banquet. All she says is keep doing what the studio wants."

"What do you want from me?"

"Help, damn you," said Jane. "I want you to tell me what to do."

"I'll try. But you have to make your own decisions."

"I've made a decision. I want better parts. I want a career that's based on something besides the way I look. I want some kind of insurance against being tossed away."

"Jane, we'd all like that kind of insurance."

"You have it. If things don't work here, you can always go back to New York and do stage work. Hepburn has insurance. She tells her studio what to do. So does Davis. They're not limited to roles that only show off their figures."

"They don't have your figure," said Mack dryly.

"That's not the point. I want to do the kind of roles they do. Parts that require more of me than just a good diet. If I don't prove that I can do more than just flit across the set in a tight dress, I'll be finished out here in five years. And I couldn't stand that, Mack. I can't let that happen." Jane was almost hysterical with ambition. Her voice was loud and strident. "I've got to have parts that make me into something more than a sex symbol."

"Do you think you could handle them?" asked Mack quietly.

"What on earth are you talking about? How do I know what I could handle. I've never tried."

"That's the point, Jane. Hepburn started on the stage, and Davis has worked hard at her craft. They're actresses."

"And what am I?"

"A very beautiful woman who's had everything handed to her because she's beautiful. The things you're talking about require more than just a great face. You have to be able to act, to become different characters."

"And you don't think I can do that."

"I don't know. *You* don't know."

Jane looked thoughtful.

"Jane," continued Mack. "You know as well as I do that if you really thought you could handle something more difficult, you wouldn't be talking to me. You'd be bellowing at Murry and Terry and anybody else in authority over at the studio. You wouldn't be worrying about your future or any of the rest of it. *You* want big parts and you want to try and do things that are more challenging. But frankly, I don't think that you're sure you can handle them. It isn't just Murry Edson holding you back, although I admit that he's not one to try and mess with a proven product, but it's you as well. You're chicken, Jane. All this talk of yours about wanting to do more interesting things is just a sop to your conscience. In reality, you're going to keep on doing exactly what you've been doing as long as you're too scared to do anything else."

Jane was furious. "How dare you?" she screamed. "How dare you talk to me like that? I've got as much guts as anybody in this business. There isn't anything I wouldn't try. There isn't any part I wouldn't go for."

"And there isn't anyone, including yourself, who would take you seriously if you announced a change in your career. I understand what you want, maybe better than you know. But you have to prove yourself."

"How?"

"You won't like this."

"Tell me!"

"Jane, listen to me. You've got magic, everything it takes to be a movie star . . . and you just might be an actress as well. But you need to find out just how much talent you have and how you can handle what you've got." Mack stopped for a second, then continued. "I think you should start really working at your craft. Take some acting lessons. Learn what acting is all about. Then at least you'll be able to make the most of your abilities, regardless of how great or how limited they are."

"I see." Jane was quiet. "But I thought acting lessons were just a lot of nonsense."

Mack laughed. "A lot of them are. And they're no good for many people. But in your case, you've got all this energy and excitement in you, and you don't know how to let it all go. You know instinctively what to do in front of a camera, you know how to move and look to capture the audience. Those things are talents, Jane. But you have to know how to control them, and how to direct them where you want them to go. Acting lessons can't give you talent, but from the right person you can gain confidence and learn the techniques and insight you need."

Jane stood up, and at first Mack thought she was going to hit him. Then her mouth lifted into a wide smile. "Just why the hell haven't you suggested this before?"

"Oh, Lord," moaned Mack.

"I think it's a wonderful idea." She gave him a hug. "But where shall I go? Who should I study with?"

"There's an old Russian, Olga Brinski. You met her a long time ago at my place, I think."

"I'm not sure I remember her."

"She's from Moscow, but she taught in New York for several years. She insists that she was never warm in Russia and couldn't stand the winters in New York, so she moved out here. I personally think she came here because she feels she can be superior to everyone else. In New York there are teachers from all over Europe, and people didn't make much of her. But out here she's very important. She is good. And she knows her stuff. But she's a real terror."

"I can handle her," said Jane.

"I hope so. But I should warn you that one of her pet hates is beautiful women. She must have been attractive in her youth, but that's long gone. She rarely takes a good-looking woman as a student."

"Shall I wear a mask?" asked Jane sarcastically.

"No. You don't have to go that far. Just don't try to rely on your beauty to get you by. If she takes you, chances are she'll be very hard on you. This isn't going to be easy."

"I can take it," said Jane firmly.

"I know you can."

"How do I find her?"

"I'll give you the address and talk to her before you meet her."

"Thank you. Do you study with her?"

"Occasionally. It might not be a bad idea to take Maud."

"Aunt Maud? What for?"

"Olga is always impressed with respectability. She'll like Maud."

"Well, I'm sure Aunt Maud will love it."

"And one more thing. If I were you, I wouldn't say anything to Murry Edson about this."

"Why not?"

"You never can tell how he's going to react. Besides, there's no reason to tip your hand before you have to."

"I won't say a word. I'm not sure I want to talk to him, anyway."

"Who does?" asked Mack.

• • •

Madam Olga Brinski lived in a small house, one of a series of semi-detached villas in a little section right outside Hollywood. She had a little plot of grass in which she unsuccessfully grew roses, and there were vines growing up around the doors and windows. The cottages were built of wood, but inside Olga had recreated the atmosphere of her native Russia as closely as possible.

The rooms were dark almost to the point of total blackness. The walls, painted a deep rose color, were covered with religious icons and paintings depicting martyrs going through a series of painful tortures, while heavy drapes of ruby-colored velvet effectively blocked out the sun. The furniture was massive, and there were a great many pieces of it so that moving around the rooms was an effort. Every tabletop or surface was filled with framed photographs, some hung with black crepe, or objets d'art. Two small, unattractive dogs whined and barked at each visitor.

Maud and Jane had both dressed carefully for the interview. Jane had attempted to play down any glamour that might be attached to her with a simple light suit, while Maud, feeling the occasion required a little more formality, was in black with numerous strands of pearls and a hat with a large feather.

They were shown into the overcrowded living room by a tiny old servant who hissed at them to sit down, that madam would be with them shortly.

"Cheerful place, isn't it?" asked Maud, looking at a depiction of the violent crucifixion of St. Peter.

"Aunt Maud, I'm so nervous," whispered Jane.

"I know what you mean, dear," said Maud. "School-teachers always upset me, too."

"I am *not* a schoolteacher," proclaimed a loud, deep voice.

Maud and Jane looked up to find a woman who could be anywhere in age from sixty to one hundred and ten. She was short, very slender, and slightly bent. Her face was a study in the art of stage makeup circa 1900. Olga's eyebrows were finely penciled lines that made her look as if she were continually asking a question, and her cheeks and lips were heavily rouged with a vivid shade of scarlet. Her hair was completely gray and placed chaotically on top of her head. Her dress was long, shapeless, and black with a huge collar and

sleeves to the wrist. Over this forbidding garment she fought
off the California chills with a heavy black shawl, decorated
with fringe at least a foot long. Around her neck were several
lengths of jet and crystals which clanged together whenever
she moved, and her clawlike fingers were covered by rather
dirty rings.

But Jane and Maud forgot the eccentricity of her outfit when
their attention was grasped and held by Olga's vivid eyes which
stared out at them from her sunken cheeks. The eyes were
blue. Not a warm, bright blue like Jane's, but a hard, cold,
forbidding blue that seemed to reach out and examine the
observer's innermost secrets. Jane and Maud stood respect-
fully, and Jane went forward to greet the old lady.

"How do you do," said Jane in her whispery voice. "My
name is Jane Turner. I believe Scott Mack told you about me.
This is my aunt, Mrs. Thomas Watson."

Olga looked at Jane for some minutes and then turned her
gaze to Maud, nodding at her as she advanced into the room
and took possession of a thronelike chair. She indicated with a
regal gesture that her guests could be seated, and Jane and
Maud sat down as one person on the horsehair sofa.

No one spoke and finally Maud, whose sense of social
conventions had never yet failed her, swung into conversation.

"How nice to meet you, Madam Brinski," said Maud
happily. "I believe we must have some friends in common. I
know Mrs. Fisk, of course, and I've met Helen Hayes and
Judith Anderson. Once when I was in England I had tea with
Mr. Shaw and Beerbohm Tree. Mr. Shaw ate a great many
pastries and . . ." Maud's voice trailed off as it became
obvious that Olga wasn't interested in Maud's theatrical
reminiscences.

Maud took a deep breath and started again. "The weather is
very nice, isn't it?" she suggested.

"You must protect from the drafts," said Madam Brinski
with finality.

"Yes, of course," said Maud, looking down at her light
dress as contrasted with Olga's heavy shroud.

"The chill is bad for the voice. Already I can see that your
niece has a cold."

"Do you, dear?" asked Maud, turning to Jane.

"No, I don't," replied Jane.

"Oh, of course," said Maud. "You see, madam, Jane has always had a very soft voice, and many people think she might be ill when she is perfectly well. Isn't that true, dear?" asked Maud, inanely.

Jane decided she had better get to the point of their visit. "I would very much like to study with you, Madam Brinski. Scott Mack has told me so much about you and about how you've helped him."

Olga didn't answer immediately, her eyes boring into Jane.

"You are very pretty," she said finally. "I, too, used to be very pretty. I was once a favorite of Czar Nicholas," she finished in a proud voice.

"Somehow, I thought she would be," murmured Maud under her breath.

Olga didn't catch what Maud said, but she looked at her suspiciously.

Jane spoke quickly. "Madam Brinski, I don't know what your procedure is for accepting new students. I mean, I don't know how I qualify—"

"Qualify? What is this, qualify?" asked Olga. "Are you a show animal? No. Of course not. You want to be an actress. I understand you have had a little success in the films."

"Why, Jane is a major star," proclaimed Maud indignantly. "She is constantly mobbed by the public, and her picture has been on the cover of *Life* magazine."

Olga shrugged as if this were nothing to her, which in fact it wasn't, and continued. "But now, Mr. Mack tells me you want to study the craft of acting."

Jane wondered what she'd been saying the past few minutes, but rather than upset the woman, agreed instantly that that was exactly what she wished to do.

Madam Brinski nodded. "I do not take girls who just want their pictures in the newspapers."

"I've had my picture in the papers," said Jane. "I want to learn to act."

"I see. Your voice needs work."

"I don't know if I can speak any louder—"

"It is not volume that matters," replied Olga. "It is projection. Even if you speak very softly," Madam Brinski dropped her voice dramatically, "you must be heard in the last row of the balcony. That is, of course, when you are doing plays." Madam moved her voice back to normal level. "When you are in the films, it doesn't matter so much what you do . . . about anything," she finished.

"I'd like to become the best actress I can," said Jane.

"Very well. Normally I do not take young girls with beauty. They are too flighty, too absurd. But Mr. Mack has spoken for you, so I will give you a try. It will be very hard and," she paused, "I am very expensive." Madam Brinski then mentioned a figure that caused Maud to sit bolt upright in her seat and stare at the teacher.

"That will be fine," said Jane calmly. "When may I start?"

"You will start tomorrow morning."

"But I have to be at the studio all day. I'm making a new picture," said Jane.

"Very well. Then you will have to work here in the evenings. I have several students who must do other jobs to pay for their lessons. They also come in the evenings. You will work with them."

"I had hoped to have lessons alone," said Jane.

"Impossible in the evenings. I cannot disturb my regular work."

"Very well," agreed Jane. "I'll work with the other students." She and Olga discussed schedules, and Olga instructed her to wear loose clothing so she could move easily. When all the details were settled, Jane and Maud rose to go, but Olga stopped them.

"Wait," she ordered. "We will have tea."

Maud, who had been roasting in the overheated room, could think of several things she would enjoy, but tea was not one of them. Ever gracious, she reseated herself and smiled benignly on the teacher and student.

In a few moments the wheezing maid struggled into the room, carrying a large tea tray which she set down before her mistress. Then hurrying out, she returned with a tray of tea cakes with pink and blue frosting. Maud glanced at them and felt they looked toxic, but she took one and murmured, "How nice," at her hostess.

Jane didn't seem to notice anything out of the ordinary. She munched the cakes and drank the tea without blinking. Maud credited her with either an iron stomach or a complete lack of sensitivity.

Jane and Maud listened as Madam Brinski talked about herself, her dogs, Russia, the horror of films, herself, how terrible the communists were, her house, her maid, and, finally, herself. She didn't stop, or for that matter even seem to take a breath, for almost forty-five minutes, and Maud, upon whom the rich cake, endless monologue, and oppressive heat in the room were working, began to doze off. She leaned her head back against the rough fabric of the sofa and unfortunately managed to catch the feather of her hat in a large arrangement of dried flowers which rested on the sofa table.

When Jane and Olga finished their tea and conversation, Jane stood up to leave and Maud, snapping back to consciousness, found that although she was capable of rising, her hat stayed where it was.

After tossing her head around several times like a frisky colt, a performance that caused both Jane and Olga to stare at her, Maud finally confessed that she had become entwined with the lovely arrangement of dried flowers. She admitted that it was very stupid of her, and as Jane went around and extracted the feather, Maud apologized profusely.

Madam Brinski bid them farewell from the living room; she didn't like going into the hall when the door was open, in case there was a draft. After nodding pleasantly at the old maid, they were once again outside.

"Really, dear," said Maud as she climbed into the waiting limousine, "what a very peculiar woman."

"She's supposed to be a very good acting teacher."

"Well, if you want to go there, I'm sure it's fine. Just promise me one thing."

"What's that?"

"You won't pick up any decorating ideas from her—or ever invite me along again."

"Good morning, Jane, dear. It's good to see you here again." As usual, Murry Edson came out from behind his desk and greeted her with a kiss before leading her to a chair.

"Good morning, Murry," answered Jane.

"Well, well, well," continued Murry. "You've had a nice rest and now you're back. I trust you enjoyed yourself in Kansas City very much?"

"Yes. It was lovely."

"Good, good. Terrance will be here in a few minutes. He has a new script for you to look over, and we would like you to start as soon as possible. I guess you heard that *Tragic Lady* is a great success."

"I heard it was doing well."

"Yes. It was a shame you missed the premiere. And I've been looking over *Island Woman*. That should be another hit."

Jane didn't answer, and for several minutes Murry talked about what had been happening at Global while Jane was away. Terrance arrived and, after greeting Jane affectionately, he sat down, holding a script.

"So, what have you got for us?" asked Murry, who knew exactly what Terrance was carrying.

Terry held up the new script and tapped it with one hand. "Something good for you, Jane. Something I think you're going to enjoy. It's all about a girl in the old west—"

"Another costume piece?" asked Jane incredulously.

"A perfect story for you," continued Terry. "This girl is exciting, and a heroine. She was captured by the Indians when she was a baby, but eventually she falls in love with a handsome cavalry soldier and saves his whole regiment. It's called *Half Breed*."

"I see," said Jane.

"Both Terry and I are very excited about you doing this," said Murry. "We think it's a perfect thing for you to follow *Island Woman* with. After all, in that you were a native girl. In this you're an American, and you fall in love with a soldier. Very good with all the trouble in Europe, you know. Patriotism and everything."

"Is this the only thing you could come up with?"

"Now be fair," said Murry placatingly. "After all, you haven't even read it yet. Take it home and go over it. I think you'll find that it's perfect for you. We'd like you to start costume fittings and makeup tests this week. Can you read the script by tomorrow and let us know if there's any little thing that bothers you? I'm sure we can take care of it."

"Naturally," said Jane.

"Oh. And we have a little present for you," said Murry, standing and going to his window. "Come here."

"The last car we gave you . . . well, the less said about that the better. Now look there."

Jane looked. Parked directly below Murry's office was a bright yellow Cadillac convertible. "It looks very pretty," said Jane.

"It's all yours. And while you were gone we redecorated your dressing room, and you have a new trailer, as well. You'll see, you're going to be very comfortable. Won't she, Terry?"

"You're going to be very comfortable."

"Thank you very much," said Jane.

"Here are the keys to the car," said Murry, handing her a small gold key ring. "Now suppose you go on home and look over the script. You'll have a meeting with Earnest Kahn—you see we still kept your favorite director—tomorrow and then you can get started."

Jane nodded, took the script Terrance held out, and walked to the door. She turned and smiled at them once. "Good-bye," she said.

"She's up to something," said Terrance as soon as the door was closed.

"I think so, too," agreed Murry. "What do you suppose it is?"

"Hard to say," said Terrance. "I just hope she's not going to be a lot of trouble on the set. Remember how she was during *Island Woman*? Jesus. I don't want to go through that again. Nothing was ever right for her."

"Nothing is ever right for any of them," spat Murry, sitting back down at his desk. "This would be a great business . . . if there just weren't any actors in it."

Twenty-Two

JANE WAS AS NERVOUS her first night at Olga Brinski's as she had been on her first day of shooting. She dressed carefully in a simple navy blue dress and kept her makeup very light. As she was leaving the house, she found Mack and Bill in the drawing room, visiting with Maud. The men got up as she came into the room.

"Well, hello," she said. "I didn't know you two were here."

"We just arrived a few minutes ago," said Bill. "Maud is trying to convince Mack to roll bandages or some such thing."

"Not in the least," said Maud. "I simply want him to appear at a fund-raising event for me."

"You didn't ask me," said Jane. "I think I'm insulted."

"This meeting is for women," said Maud. "I'm saving you for when I go after the men."

Jane shrugged and smiled at Mack, who asked where she was going. Jane told him.

"Not like that, you're not, my girl," said Mack.

"Why? What have I done wrong?"

"Well, several things. To begin with, you look like you're on your way to a tea party, not an acting class. You're going to work."

316

"I can work in this dress," Jane said defensively.

"I doubt it. That skirt's too tight. And," continued Mack, "I might also ask how long you think it will take for someone in Olga's neighborhood to recognize you and call the papers. If you want to go study and be left alone, you'll do something to minimize the chances of anyone knowing who you are."

"Like what?" asked Jane.

"Well, for one thing, take off *all* the makeup, put a scarf over your head, and wear a pair of slacks and a loose shirt."

"What?" Jane was appalled.

"Isn't that what you usually wear to the studio?"

"Naturally, but—"

"Well, you're going to work tonight. So dress that way and try to keep a low profile. You'll be happier if you do."

"The other people there will recognize me immediately, anyway," complained Jane.

"That isn't important. They won't bother you."

Jane looked questioningly at Maud. "I'd do what Mack says," said Maud. "He's usually right."

"Not always," whispered Bill.

Mack punched him playfully as Jane, ignoring their antics, went back to her room. When she returned, she was dressed as Mack had suggested and her face was free from makeup. In addition, she was wearing a large pair of sunglasses.

"That's much better," said Mack. "Now you're not so obvious. But don't you have a somewhat less ostentatious pair of sunglasses?"

"I'll get some tomorrow," said Jane with resignation. "Can I go now?"

"Absolutely. And you'd better hurry. Madam doesn't like to be kept waiting."

Jane gave Maud a quick kiss, wrinkled her nose at Mack and Bill, and left the house.

"I do hope she's going to be all right," said Maud, watching Jane leave. "I met Madam Brinski, you know, and I thought she was very strange."

"Jane'll be fine," said Mack. "This is going to be very good for her."

"Well, I'm sure you know best. Now, what about spending an afternoon with the ladies before the fund-raiser? You could stir up interest, sign some autographs, maybe . . ."

As Maud's voice droned on, Mack groaned softly to himself.

When Jane arrived at Olga Brinski's, she found the house ablaze with lights and heard the sounds of loud voices coming from the living room. She knocked and was admitted by the maid who directed her without speaking to the class.

Olga sat in her usual chair, nodding at a young man with untidy hair who was rendering a passage from a play with which Jane was unfamiliar. Jane slipped through the room, found a chair, and turned her attention to the other members of the group, none of whom had taken notice of her arrival.

There were four women and three men, including the one speaking, and they all looked alike. The women wore saggy skirts, loose blouses, or sweaters, while the men were dressed in sport coats, ties that were not firmly knotted, and baggy trousers.

They listened intently to the young man and when he finished, the group all sat back in their chairs and waited for Olga to speak. She made several comments about the reading, then announced there would be a slight break before the next recitation.

The students coalesced like quicksilver, suddenly becoming much more at ease. They laughed and talked to each other, and Jane felt ridiculously alone. In the last few years she had become used to being the center of any group she approached. Now, she was an outsider without the attention she had become accustomed to.

Madam Brinski beckoned Jane to her side. "We are on time for these classes," she said grandly.

"I beg your pardon," said Jane. "I was detained. It won't happen in the future."

Olga nodded. "I will introduce you to the others."

"Oh," said Jane, slightly alarmed. "Is that necessary?"

Madam Brinksi raised her eyebrows even higher than usual. "Do you expect to sit in a room with people and not know them? Do not be preposterous."

In a few seconds, Olga had called the class to order and introduced their newest member, Jane Turner. "Miss Turner," continued Olga, "is in films. But she has come to our class in the hope of studying some of my methods. I trust that you will make yourself known to her as time goes on."

The others turned and stared at Jane. Naturally, they had

heard of her, and all but two of the group had seen at least one of her films. She was an internationally recognized movie star and, despite themselves, they were impressed and intrigued. They all wondered how long it would be before she began demanding star treatment.

Jane smiled at them, and then Madam Brinski once more took the attention of the students and demanded the next reading. For the next three hours, there were readings, breathing exercises, and movement lessons, all done under the constant supervision and continuous monologue of Madam. She pointed, exclaimed, encouraged, and attacked her students with an energy that Jane had never seen equaled. By the end of the evening, Jane felt a combination of exhaustion and exhilaration she had never experienced.

Before allowing them to leave, Olga assigned various projects to the students. Jane was given a simple poem to learn and recite at their next meeting. She didn't understand why she should learn a poem, but she was too frightened, excited, and worn out to argue.

For the next few weeks, Jane worked each day at the studio, fulfilled her publicity engagements, studied her script for *Half Breed*, and still made time to learn the material assigned to her by Madam Brinski.

It was becoming easier and easier to go to Olga's. Standing up the first time and performing before the students was one of the hardest things Jane felt she'd ever done. Much more difficult than appearing in front of the all-seeing camera, or a group of fanatical fans. These few people were working hard for something, and their intensity frightened Jane. She had gotten through her poem, her voice halting and so soft it was virtually impossible to hear. Olga had asked for comments from the others, as usual. But they hadn't said much. Then Olga had personally lit into Jane, ripping apart her performance. Jane was devastated and angry, and had sworn to herself that she would never again go back to the classes. But Mack had convinced her to return, and now she looked forward to the three meetings each week.

Warren and Jane talked on the telephone as often as possible, Jane often interrupting filming to take a call from him, or Warren asking to be excused from important meetings just for the chance for a few words. He had returned to Washington after Jane's visit to Kansas City and was still there. He wasn't sure when he'd be able to get away.

Jane missed him terribly, but she couldn't ask him to leave his responsibilities any more than he could ask her to walk out on her latest picture to come to the capital.

They talked about everything in an effort to feel close to each other, and relatively minor events of the day were important topics in their conversations. Warren was a little taken aback when Jane first told him of her plans to study acting with Olga Brinski. He couldn't understand the need for her to participate in what was obviously a beginner's course in a craft he thought she'd been performing for some time. But he enjoyed her descriptions of Olga and their class exercises. And as Jane made friends with the other students, he likewise found himself concerned about the lives, ambitions, and hopes of several young people he'd never seen.

Jane was often in Warren's thoughts. He tried to picture her each day as she went through her usual appointments and plans. Often he just wanted to escape from Washington and catch the next flight to California. But he was deeply involved in work pertaining to the possible inclusion of America in the European war. Matters that required a great deal of energy and foresight.

Many of Warren's business associates considered his presence in Washington a betrayal of everything he stood for. Warren Harris was an important Midwest businessman. His theater holdings were small when compared to his other interests: land, factories, lumber. He, along with a few other men of equal stature, virtually controlled the financial and even political climate in their states.

They all hated Roosevelt with passion and energy. But even with all their power, they had been incapable of stopping their electorate from voting for the man in the White House.

Harris had to admit Roosevelt had been smart in his selection of the men who were now advising him. He had gone over party lines, relying on the patriotism of prominent Americans, to make them join him at this time. Roosevelt wanted America in this war. He wanted his country to fight and help England. But he knew he needed more than his own party to prepare the country to face the conflict that he was convinced was coming.

And each time Warren went to a meeting, with each document he read, each committee he sat on, his growing suspicions, that Roosevelt was right were confirmed. Something terrible was coming. The future of the world was in jeopardy. And each night as he looked out across the nation's capital from his hotel suite, he saw the shadows of war drift closer and closer to his homeland.

At those times, he thought about the people he knew and cared for. His friends in Missouri, his children, Maud. But mostly, he thought of Jane and his promise to always protect her.

It was three months after Jane left Kansas City before Warren could get a break and come to California. He arrived unannounced and went directly to the studio, where he tracked Jane down on Stage Four and stood off to the side as she completed one of the final scenes in *Half Breed*. "Jane," complained Earnest Kahn, "try to be a little more sympathetic at this point. You are in love with the guy, you know. He's damn near dead with an arrow in him, and you don't seem to care."

"I'm doing the best I can," snapped Jane. "You try being sympathetic with these stupid lines. It's all I can do not to laugh out loud."

"Just what the hell is wrong with the lines?" asked another voice, and Warren turned to see a man he didn't recognize striding toward the set.

"You ought to know," said Jane angrily, "you wrote this trash."

"I wrote a sensitive story of a young woman who—"

"You wrote, or I should say typed, a piece of garbage. And I for one am sick and tired of constantly trying to cover up for your inadequacy."

"*My inadequacy*!" exploded the writer.

"Look, you two," said Earnest, "we have to finish this scene today. We're already way behind schedule on this picture, and the front office isn't going to stand for any more delays. Let's try and get it done without any more problems."

Jane raised her chin slightly. "Would you like to invite

Murry down here to see just what he'll stand for?" she asked. "If you want me to finish this ridiculous parody, then get the goddamn dialogue fixed."

"The words will work if you just do them as they're written," explained the writer. "You don't have to act all over the place."

"It is not possible to act with this kind of script," said Jane viciously.

"Just how the hell would you know?" asked the writer.

"Why, you insignificant little scribbler," said Jane, moving toward him. "How would you like to find yourself barred from this lot? Or perhaps out of the business completely? If you think for one minute that I have to put up with—"

"Jane, please," interrupted Earnest. "Please! We must get back to work. You," he looked at the writer, "go back to your place off the set."

The writer didn't answer, just turned on his heel and disappeared.

Earnest stood and watched until he was out of sight, and then looked back to Jane. He kept his voice calm. "Now Jane, we've been through several films together. I admit this isn't Tolstoy—"

"It isn't even Ethel M. Dell," said Jane with emphasis.

"Do you think I like this picture? But it's what we've got. It's a job, and we've got to get it done. I'm sorry the script isn't to your liking, but we've been changing lines since we started filming, and we just don't have the time to do any more work on it. We have to take it as it is."

Jane started to interrupt, but he held up one hand and continued.

"As far as your acting is concerned, I must agree with the writer that you're overdoing it a bit. I've told you for the last two months not to try and put things into this character that just aren't there. I've gotten the impression that you're trying out various techniques on us. You haven't played this woman the same way two days running since we started. Now just do an old friend a favor, Jane, and put away whatever textbook you've discovered and let's get this goddamn picture finished."

Jane stared at him for a moment. "Very well," she said quietly. She walked back to her place, Earnest returned to his chair, and the scene continued. When the scene was finally over, Earnest called, "Cut, print," and everyone started to relax. Jane didn't speak to anyone. She moved quickly off the set and went to her dressing room without a glance at either Earnest or the writer or anyone else connected with the production.

Warren followed her and knocked on the door of her trailer. There was no answer, and he knocked again. Louise opened it slightly.

"Miss Turner doesn't want . . . why Mr. Harris. I'm sure she'll be glad to see you."

Warren could hear Jane's voice behind Louise. "Warren? Is Warren here?"

She rushed to the door, a robe covering her costume. When she saw Warren, her face lit up with a smile.

"Warren, how wonderful. Why didn't you tell me you were coming? When did you arrive? Come in here."

Warren went into the trailer as Jane dismissed Louise. In a moment they were alone.

"Are you finished for the day?" he asked.

"Yes, thank God," she said wearily. "What a dog of a film. If this keeps up, I won't be able to get a job anywhere in another year."

"Really?"

"Don't look so happy about it. I'll survive," she said. She threw her arms around him. "Oh, it is good to see you. Kiss me."

Warren kissed her softly at first, then more passionately. He pulled back. "Don't you think we should—"

"Don't worry. They know when I want to be left alone. No one's going to come near me for a while. They know better."

"Does that include me?"

"Don't be ridiculous." Jane smiled. She slipped out of her robe, letting it fall to the floor. Her costume was mostly ripped pieces of buckskin, and it emphasized her figure, making her look untamed and alluring.

"I don't know about the picture, but that costume is probably going to be a hit. I'm surprised the Hay's office hasn't come down on you. You look almost too sexy to me."

"Do I?" she asked, running her fingers along his cheek. He took her hand and kissed the palm. "At least for the public," he said, pulling her into his arms. They kissed, and Warren moved his lips down over her neck.

"Oh, how nice," she murmured. "How nice. I've missed you so much, Warren. So very much."

He stepped back and looked at her, holding both of her hands in his. "I've missed you, too," he said.

"Then hold me," she said. "Hold me close."

Warren put his arms around her and, for a few moments they stood basking in the warmth of each other. Jane lifted her face to his and they kissed, deeply and passionately. Warren reached up to unfasten the top of her costume. His fingers fumbled with the catch. Jane laughed.

"Let me do it." She reached behind her, easily released the garment, and then held it in front of her, moving seductively around in front of Warren, gliding the material back and forth over her breasts.

He watched her carefully, then smiled. "There's something to be said for making love to a movie star."

"What?"

"You never know who she's going to be next. I wonder how many men would like to spend one night with a Roman temptress and the next with an Indian girl."

"Well, all these women are just for you," said Jane, dropping the cloth and pressing her breasts against him.

Warren touched her nipples and leaned down to kiss each of her breasts. She pulled at his suit coat and helped him undress. When he was nude, she slipped out of the rest of her costume. Naked, they embraced. He picked Jane up and carried her to the chaise longue where he placed her gently on the soft, satin pillows. She lay back and looked up at him.

"I do love you, Warren," she said.

"Yes," said Warren as he bent down over her and began kissing her neck. He moved his face down her body, consuming her skin with his lips. She moved restlessly under his touch, yearning for him, reaching out for him. Jane grasped his arms and pulled him onto her, raising her hips to meet him.

"You are my only love," said Jane softly, "my very only love."

Warren knew that he could be called back to Washington at any time, but he hoped to stay in California as long as possible. He needed to set up a larger office in Los Angeles than the one he had and get settled. He and Jane also wanted a place where they could be alone, and after a very long discussion, Maud suggested that he sublet her beach house. That way he would have his own home where Jane could visit without raising any suspicion.

Naturally, Jane couldn't move in and live with Warren; if the press found out there'd be a major scandal. But as long as her home was still officially with Maud, she could move around fairly easily.

Jane and Warren also decided they would be married during the summer when his children would be with them. Then they could take a honeymoon to Mexico, leaving David and Susan with Maud, who had decided to stay with Jane as long as Maggie remained in Europe. All of the plans seemed to fall into place, and Jane was very happy, while Warren resolutely put aside his worries about the changing world situation and tried to live each day as it came.

When Jane finished *Half Breed*, she found that her next script was for a movie titled *Laugh A Minute*. In this piece Jane had to play the dumb, sexy blond girl friend of a small-time hood whom she is eventually able to reform. Jane was astonished at the script and disgusted with the whole idea. But rather than fight the studio before she felt ready, she merely demanded a short vacation and held her peace for the time being.

Jane's classes with Madam Brinski had been helpful and interesting, but rather than increase her confidence, Jane found that often she was simply overwhelmed by what she still had to learn.

David and Susan both wrote to their father asking permission to join friends on a trip to the World's Fair in New York for the first two months of the summer, and come to California for the month of August.

Warren was immediately against the idea of his children traveling to New York without him. But Jane convinced him that they were old enough to accept some responsibility on their own, and in a few days he agreed.

In June, Jane took her two week vacation, and she and Warren never left the beach house. Maud went to Pasadena to stay with some ladies from New York who were visiting, and the only people to see Warren and Jane were Mack and Bill. They came out often, Bill lugging supplies that he was sure Jane had forgotten to order. Mack and Warren settled down at the chess board, while Bill and Jane talked and swam in the ocean.

Late one afternoon as Jane and Bill were walking back to the house, he stopped and looked at her accusingly.

"You don't seem to be very interested in what I've been saying," he said.

"What?" asked Jane. "I'm sorry. My mind must have been wandering."

"Obviously. Here I've been informing you of all the gossip about Greta Stewart, and you haven't even said one dear me."

"What has Greta been up to?" asked Jane.

"Very little, actually. You know Global has declined to pick up her option this time. They haven't been able to find anything to do with her. She has announced that she is looking at several different projects, but hasn't yet made a decision."

"What are they?"

"Who knows? Probably three bellhops and a bartender, if I know my Greta."

"What about her career?"

"What career? Since she wasn't a hit as the bitch in *Dawn to Dusk*, she wants to go back to playing frail, young damsels in distress. At her age it's ludicrous. I hear Warner's offered her a part as Bette Davis's mother for some picture, but she turned it down flat. And, incidentally, left very insulted."

"I'm sorry for her," said Jane simply.

"Don't be. She wouldn't waste any pity on you. Of that you can be sure."

"That doesn't mean I have to act the same way," said Jane.

"No, I suppose not. Sometimes I wonder why I like you . . . you're such a decent sort of person. How long are you and Warren going to stay holed up out here?"

"Until I have to go back to work or he has to go back to Washington. I still have several days left of my vacation, and if there are any problems with my next epic, I might be able to stretch it out a little."

"Have you talked to the studio at all?"

"No. Why should I?"

"It just isn't like you to not want to know what's going on."

"I was in Kansas City for almost two months without talking to the studio."

"That was different. You weren't feeling well, and you were upset about Elizabeth. Now you're right outside town and don't seem very interested in what Murry and his minions are up to."

Jane shrugged.

"How are the acting lessons?"

"I took some time off from them, too. I don't know if I'll start again or not."

"Why?"

"Oh, Bill, it's just that they take so much time. And those classes are hard work. I'm not sure I'm getting anywhere. Each time I go, I just find something else I don't know. Besides, my new picture isn't going to require me to do anything special. It's just another dumb blond role."

"You're too good for that stuff," said Bill.

"Why, thank you. I don't think anyone's ever said that to me before."

"I know several who think it. We're just waiting for you to get the right part."

"So am I. But I doubt it'll ever come."

"Not unless you work and fight for it."

"I've tried, Bill. I've argued and screamed. And I still don't get anywhere."

"Do you know what part you want?"

"No."

"Well, that might have something to do with it. If you don't know what you want, you can't go after it. Have you read a book called *Another Life*?"

"No. Is it new?"

"Not really. It was on the best-seller lists a few months ago. It's only been nominated for practically every award there is," he said disparagingly.

"I'm sorry," said Jane. "It's just that, with classes and work and Warren, I don't have a lot of spare time to read."

"Well, make time for this. I happen to know that Murry has an option on the book. I'll send it to you."

"You're coming back Saturday. Why don't you just bring it then?"

"Because I want you to get started on it so we can talk when I get here."

"Yes, sir," she said meekly.

"You'll have it tomorrow."

"All right. Is there something special in it for me?"

"You'll see," said Bill. "Now, I guess we'd better get back and break up the chess tournament. The movie star has to work tomorrow, and he's terrible if he stays out too late."

"You know, you're a decent sort of person, yourself," said Jane, smiling at him.

"Well, don't tell anybody. I'll never be invited out again," said Bill.

Jane was sitting up in bed with *Another Life* the next evening when Warren leaned over and gave her a kiss.

"You looked totally absorbed," he said. "What is that?"

"A book Bill sent me."

"Oh, *Another Life*. I've been meaning to read that."

"Well, you can't have this copy," said Jane, still reading.

"Hoity-toity," said Warren, going into the bathroom. When he came back, he climbed in next to Jane and brushed her hair with his fingertips. She set the book down on her lap and smiled at him.

"Hello," she said.

"Hello, yourself." Warren stretched and pulled the covers up around his neck. "This feels good. It's cold this evening."

"Would you like another blanket?"

"I'm fine next to you. Are you going to stay up late?"

"I'd like to finish this chapter. You don't mind, do you, darling? I can go into the other room if the light bothers you."

"I can put up with just about anything as long as you stay right where you are."

Jane smiled and went back to her reading. She finished the chapter, but as Warren slept peacefully next to her, she continued until finally, at nearly five A.M., she closed *Another Life*, and set it down. "Of course," she whispered to herself. "That's it. That's right." She crept out of bed and slipped into the kitchen. Dialing Mack's number, she waited through several rings until she heard Bill's sleepy voice answer.

"Bill, it's Jane. I'm sorry I woke you."

"That's all right. Is there something wrong? What's happened?"

"I've finished the book." There was no need to say which book.

"Yes?"

"Oh, Bill, you're so right. I can play that part. I can do it. It's wonderful."

"I thought you'd like it," said Bill. "Now can I go back to bed?"

"Sure. But don't you dare miss Saturday. Come early. We have a lot to talk about."

"Yes, Jane. Saturday. I've got to hang up. If I stay up much longer I won't be able to go back to sleep, and then I'll wake up the movie star, and then we'll both have hell to pay."

"All right. Good night . . . and thank you. Thank you very much."

Jane hung up and went back to the bedroom. She crawled in next to Warren and snuggled close to his body. A faint smile crossed her face. Now I know what I want, she thought. And I can't wait!

The next morning, Jane called Olga Brinski and asked for an immediate appointment. The old lady was hesitant, but finally agreed, and Jane arranged to go to her home that afternoon. She left Warren with a fishing pole and several sandwiches, and sped off to Los Angeles, arriving at Olga's a few minutes early.

Madam Brinski was with someone, and Jane had to wait in the hall, but soon the student left and Jane hurried into the living room where, despite the summer heat, Olga was shrouded in her usual black dress with a long shawl. The curtains were still closed, and the room was close to one-hundred degrees.

"Madam Brinski," said Jane. "I must speak with you."

"So I understood from your telephone call. Just what is the problem?"

"It's not a problem, really. I need to ask you a question. Two questions."

"Very well. Begin."

"Have I got any talent?" blurted out Jane.

Madam Brinski stared at Jane for a few seconds. "What a peculiar question."

"It's an important one," said Jane. "Actually, I think it's one that most of your students would like to ask, but no one ever does. I have no choice, I need to know."

"Sit down," ordered Olga. "Take a deep breath and explain what this visit is all about."

"It's about a book," said Jane.

"A book?"

"Yes, madam. This one." Jane pulled her copy of *Another Life* from her bag and held it out to the teacher.

"I am familiar with the story," she said, not taking the book.

"All right." Jane took a deep breath and looked straight at Olga Brinski. "Can I play Helen?" she asked.

For several minutes there was silence in the room. Madam Brinski had an enormous clock on the fake mantel, and Jane could hear the ticking. It seemed the loudest sound in the world. After what Jane thought of as an eternity, the old woman smiled. Jane had never seen Madam Brinski smile, and it came as a shock to see her lips curl back in pleasure. For a moment, Jane was terrified that Olga was going to laugh at her.

Olga's smile grew larger as she muttered to herself, "Of course. Of course. That's it. That's what was haunting me." Madam Brinski looked straight at Jane.

"I read this book several months ago, before you came here. But since you began your studies, each time I have seen you, I have also seen someone else. I saw it the first day you came here. But I could not think whom I was seeing." Olga leaned forward and placed one of her old hands over Jane's. "Of course, you can play Helen," she said, her voice low and dramatic. "You *are* Helen."

Jane was close to tears at Olga's words. But she was still unsure. "But can I? Can I handle the part? Am I good enough?"

"What do you think?" asked the teacher.

"I think this is something I want very much. It's the part I've been waiting for. But I'm afraid. I need to hear that you think I can do it."

"Very well. If you really want to play Helen, you will have to work very, very hard. It will not be easy. You have come a long way since your first lessons, but no actress is ever finished learning. Helen will take effort and time. . . . It could not be done in a few weeks like most of your films have been. But if you truly want this, I say you can do it. And I will help you."

Jane felt that if she spoke she might start sobbing, so she merely nodded and stood up.

"When do you want to begin?" asked Olga.

"Soon, Madam Brinski," said Jane, gaining control of herself and turned to practical matters. "I have one small detail to take care of first. May I call you next week?"

After Jane had gone, Olga called to her maid.

"Bring me some tea," she ordered. "I suppose you were listening."

"Yes, madam."

"And what do you think?" Madam Brinski's maid had been with her almost fifty years and often offered her opinion on the students.

"Is right," said the maid simply.

Olga nodded. "Go get my tea."

The maid left and Olga smiled to herself. "Is right," she said quietly.

On Saturday Jane was outside, waiting for Mack and Bill as they drove up to the cottage. As soon as she saw them, she ran to meet the car, embracing Bill as he climbed out of the driver's seat.

"It's wonderful," she exclaimed. "Absolutely wonderful."

"I thought it was nice," said Bill simply.

"*Nice!* It's perfect!"

"All right, all right," said Bill. He leaned over and kissed her. "Now say hello to the movie star and then we can talk."

"Hello, Mack," said Jane obediently.

"Hello, Jane," he answered with mock seriousness. "I can see that I'm not wanted here," he continued, grinning at them. "Where's Warren?"

"Out trying to convince some poor fish to jump onto his hook."

"Then I'll join him," said Mack. "Maybe I could recite something that will make them bite."

"It always works on me," said Bill.

Mack laughed and walked toward the beach as Bill put his arm around Jane, and they went into the house. Jane talked nonstop about *Another Life* and her meeting with Olga Brinski. "Isn't it wonderful, Bill? She thinks I could do it."

"That's wonderful," he said sincerely.

"Now sit down," said Jane. "I want to talk about Helen."

"Jane, at this point I really think you need Mack. He knows a lot more about it than I do. Do you think we should pull him away from his fishing pole, or shall we wait until lunch?"

"I guess we'd better wait. Warren is bound and determined to catch *something* besides old shoes. And if Mack comes in, he'll feel like he must, too. I'll start lunch and you can help."

"You know better than that. I'm the worst cook in the world. And I can't set the table because I can never remember what goes where."

"Well, at least you can keep me company."

"That I will do with pleasure. But I don't want to talk about the book again until Mack is with us. I don't want to say the wrong thing and mess you up."

"You couldn't do that."

"Hey," said Bill. "Remember, I'm not in your business. I just live around it. And we don't want to make any mistakes on this one."

"You're a love," said Jane. "All right. No talk about the book until Warren and Bill are here. Tell me the latest gossip."

"That I can *really* do," said Bill. "Have you heard about Greta?"

"Of course not."

"Well, this is too good. The old girl is getting married."

"Again?"

"That's right. She's marrying the president of Wopee Cola. I understand the stuff can rot out your stomach in less than a month, so she should fit in nicely with the product."

"You must be joking."

"About the drink or Greta?"

"Greta, you fool," said Jane.

"Not a bit. He's a few years older than Greta, which is an accomplishment in itself, but—"

"I thought she only liked, well, you know, men that—"

"Greta likes them hung and hungry," said Bill flatly. "But these days she can't afford her usual taste, she was living pretty high there for a while. And without any new films starting up for her, she's probably worried about the tax man and paying for all those ex-boyfriends."

"Well, I hope she'll be very happy."

"You said that as if you'd just had a drink of Wopee Cola," said Bill.

"I'm doing my best," said Jane.

"So is Greta. But don't worry about her. She'll be back."

"Do you really think so?"

"Absolutely. Miss Stewart is a dyed-in-the-wool, real live bitch of a movie star. And the only thing that'd keep her from in front of a camera would be if she couldn't find the set—which, incidentally, happened one day—but that's another story."

"You really think, though, that she can make a comeback? After all, she's made a lot of enemies, and her last pictures have all been failures at the box office."

"It doesn't matter. I may not be in your business, but I've lived with the movie star long enough to recognize the types. Some of you will never quit, no matter what happens to you."

"Do you include me in that group?"

"Certainly."

Jane looked stricken. "Am I really like Greta?"

"Don't panic. In many ways you and she are identical. You both have the same drive and ambition. But you have a lot more sense . . . and a lot more heart. And you have something else, too. At least, I think you do."

"What's that?"

"Talent," said Bill, "real talent. God knows, none of your parts have given you much chance to show it. But there have been moments . . ." Bill stopped a minute, then continued. "In *Dawn to Dusk*, there was that time when you turned and looked at Mack, right before he left you. It was amazing. And even in *Wanton Woman*, which I must admit is probably one of the all-time film dogs, when you did your speech about killing the Christians, there was something there. Something that makes both Mack and me and several others think you might be a real actress under all that sex appeal. And that is something Greta certainly is not."

"Murry Edson doesn't seem to think I have any talent."

"Then I guess you'll just have to show him he's wrong, won't you?" asked Bill, grinning at her.

CHAPTER *Twenty-Three*

"I DON'T KNOW whether to be grateful to you, Bill, or angry," said Warren. "For the last three days, Jane hasn't stopped reading. I'm delighted to see her so excited, but I'd like to have it directed at me."

"Don't be so selfish," said Jane, adding "darling," as an afterthought.

"See what I mean?" said Warren.

The four friends had finished lunch on the terrace and had moved inside out of the glare of the afternoon sun. The doors and windows were open, allowing the faint breeze to gently move across them. Bill and Mack were on the sofa, while Warren was in his favorite chair near the fireplace, and Jane was curled up on the floor beside him. The men all had after-lunch drinks, while Jane held a large glass of orange juice.

"She won't even tell me what's going on," complained Warren. "I wish somebody would tell me what it's all about," he finished plaintively.

"It was really Bill's idea," said Jane.

"What is? I'm afraid I'm as much in the dark as you are, Warren," said Mack. He looked at Bill. "What's going on?"

"I didn't want to jump the gun. Besides, I wanted Jane to

make up her own mind and then talk to you both. I promise I haven't said anything I shouldn't."

"He's been wonderful," said Jane, looking kindly at Bill.

"Will somebody please explain," said Mack.

"It's really very simple," said Jane. "I'm going to try for the part of Helen in *Another Life*. Global has an option on it, and I intend to make them pick it up and produce the picture for me."

Mack looked blank for a moment. Then his face lit up. "That's perfect," he said excitedly. "Why didn't I think of that?"

"Probably because you were too busy casting yourself as Russel when you read it to even bother about the female lead," said Bill.

"Who thought of this?" asked Mack, ignoring Bill.

"Bill did," said Jane. "He sent me the book and encouraged me to read it and said I would know why when I finished. He was right. And I've talked to Madam Brinski, and she agrees that I can do the part."

"It's a rough role, Jane," said Mack. "Really rough."

"I understand. But I want to play it. What do you think?"

"I think it's a wonderful idea," said Bill. "Good for both of you."

"Bill thought of it," said Jane.

"Show-off," said Mack, looking over at his lover who grinned back impishly at him.

"Are you going to play Russel?" asked Jane.

"I'm not sure. Murry asked me about it, but we haven't finalized anything. I want to, though."

"And that brings up another problem," said Jane. "Did Murry mention anyone for the part of Helen?"

"When I asked, he just waved and said nothing was settled."

"Which means he has something up his sleeve," said Jane. "Maybe he plans on bringing out someone from New York."

"It's possible," said Mack.

"Will someone please explain the whole thing to me," asked Warren. "I think I have a right to know what's going on. After all, I rent this place from Maud, so that should give me some consideration."

"Absolutely, love," said Jane. "What would you like to know?"

"Well, for starters, who is Helen and why does everyone want to play with her?"

Bill choked, and Mack and Jane laughed.

"You really should read something other than the *Wall Street Journal*. Helen is the woman in *Another Life*, a book you may have seen," Jane explained.

"I have noticed it," said Warren. "But you wouldn't let me borrow it."

"I'll loan it to you tonight, and you can start reading."

"All right, I will. But why don't you tell me the story? I'd like to be up on what you're all talking about."

"No fair," said Jane. "You must read it for yourself."

"I think Warren has a good idea," said Mack. "If you tell the story of Helen and Russel, it might give you more insight into the characters."

"Really?" asked Jane.

"I agree," said Bill. "Tell us the story, Jane."

"All right." She laughed. "I know it's ridiculous, but suddenly I feel as if I'm at school, doing my first piece."

"I just want to know what the book is about," said Warren, lessening her nervousness.

"It's the story of a young woman," began Jane.

"A very beautiful young woman," interrupted Bill.

"Quiet," said Mack.

"All right," said Jane, beginning again. "A very beautiful young woman. She's caught between her ambitions and her inability to accept a better life. She was born poor and because she's beautiful she raises herself up to money and comfort. But a part of her character is still in her background. She can't escape what she was. And her fear of becoming like the people she grew up with or her mother drives her so hard that the very fear itself makes it impossible for her to be content. She's in love with a man of birth and breeding, but she doesn't feel she fits in with his family and friends. And the more he tries to help her, the more she's convinced his family hates her. Finally, he leaves her, and as she ages, she returns to her old neighborhood and becomes just like all the people she's always despised."

"It's a great story," said Mack.

"Wonderful," agreed Bill. "And one that you can play,

Jane. But it sure isn't going to be like anything you've ever done before."

"You really want this role?" asked Warren.

"More than anything," said Jane. "More than I've ever wanted anything in my life."

Warren was thoughtful for a moment. "Then go get it," he said quietly.

Jane looked up at the man she loved and smiled at him. She knew what an effort it had taken for him to say those words. He had to be aware that a difficult part in a picture would take much of her time and keep her from being with him as much as he would like. But he had said go ahead. He was a wonderful man. She reached out and touched his arm, and then turned back to Mack and Bill. The same thought came into their minds simultaneously. Bill voiced it.

"I guess the next step is Murry Edson."

"I start rehearsals for *Laugh A Minute* a week from Monday. I'll see him then."

"I hope you're ready to do battle, Jane," Mack warned. "I'll help as much as I can, but Murry doesn't like listening to actors."

Jane smiled slightly. "He'll listen to this one," she said softly.

"Well, Jane, I hope you had a good rest," said Murry, smiling at her.

Jane answered that it had been very nice.

"Well, we should start rehearsals next week. We hope to have *Laugh A Minute* in the can by the end of the summer."

"There's something I want to talk to you about," said Jane.

"Of course, of course. I'm always interested in hearing what my stars have to say. You know I saw the rushes of *Half Breed*. It should be a blockbuster. We'll have a big premiere this fall, sometime in late September or early October."

"Yes," said Jane. "But there's something else."

"Anything. Anything at all," said Murry. "Oh, here's Terry. You know I always like his advice on important matters."

Terrance Malvey came into the room, greeted Jane, and sat down.

"Jane has something to say to us," said Murry. "Now Jane, tell us what's on your mind."

Jane had decided that the direct approach was the only way to handle Murry. She raised her chin slightly and looked directly at him.

"*Another Life*," she said flatly. "I want to play Helen."

"I see," said Murry, leaning back in his chair and tapping the ends of his fingers together.

"You certainly got right to the point," said Terrance.

"I've read the book. And I've thought about the character a lot. I can play this role. I know I can."

Murry looked at Terrance, his eyes full of meaning which Terrance couldn't mistake.

"Well, now Jane," said Terrance. "Helen is a very difficult part. We've been considering several actresses from New York. Someone with stage experience; someone a little more seasoned than you. You're a fine performer and a great star, but the part of Helen, in my opinion, isn't really right for you."

"Because the part needs an actress?" asked Jane. "I think I can do it."

"But Jane," said Murry. "Helen spends part of the movie dressed in terrible clothes. She's poor. Even when she's rich she doesn't have very good taste. And then she's poor again. And gets old. It's all very depressing. I wouldn't even have considered buying it, except that Terry insisted it would be a good prestige thing for us to have. But Global can't risk a big name like yours on a picture that's bound to make the audience unhappy. You have a certain image. You can't appear on the screen looking like a sharecropper. The audiences expect you to be chic and elegant and beautiful. You can't suddenly change your image. It just won't work. It could destroy you . . ." Murry leaned his arms on his desk and looked sympathetically at her. "I'm sorry, Jane. This part simply isn't for you. After you've finished *Laugh A Minute* we'll look around for something you might like better. But you must trust us. We know what's best for you."

"Shit," said Jane softly.

Murry almost fell out of his chair. "Jane!"

"I mean it," she said quickly. "You know what's best for me," she continued brutally. "And yet I keep appearing in roles that could be played by any showgirl on Broadway. I haven't changed or grown since I started here. Hell, I could do my movies without even waking up. They're all the same.

Over and over again, I'm either in a ridiculous costume or the foil of some stupid comic. Dressed up and dumb. Well, I'm tired of being dumb, Murry. Both on the screen and off. I want to play Helen. If you want me to test for it, I'll test. I'll do anything you ask for that part. But I intend to have it."

"Test!" exclaimed Terrance. "Really, Jane, you don't have to test for movies anymore. You're a big star."

"I know that. And you know it. But what we don't know is if I'm an actress. I think I am, and I want to act in a part that amounts to something."

"Jane, we've had this discussion before. We still think we know what's best for you."

"Are you going to give me a chance at Helen?" she asked, rising from her chair.

Murry looked sorrowful. "No, dear. I'm sorry to disappoint you. But I just don't think it's a good idea."

"Then who is going to play my part in *Laugh A Minute*?"

"Why, you are," said Murry, confused.

"Oh no I'm not. I'm not walking onto any set until you agree that my next picture will be *Another Life*."

"Absolutely not," said Murry. He stood up and faced Jane across the desk.

"Then find yourself another girl," said Jane.

"May I remind you that you have a contract with Global?" asked Murry. "You can't walk out on us. We start work on *Laugh A Minute* next week, and you'll be there."

"Don't hold your breath," said Jane. "I'm not trying to be unreasonable. I'll do this stupid film *if* you'll guarantee me that my next picture will be *Another Life*."

"*No!*" shouted Murry. "No deal. You'll make *Laugh A Minute*. And you'll start next week," he exploded. "No star dictates to me. This is my company, and I do the ordering. You are not going to play Helen and that's final."

"And you can go straight to hell," returned Jane. "I'm walking, Murry, and you'll have to move a lot faster than your short little legs can carry you to catch up with me. You can take your company and your orders and your stupid movies—and hang them on your Christmas tree!" Jane turned around and left the office, slamming the door behind her.

"You have a contract," Murry screamed at the closed door. "You'll never work again. I'll see to it. I'll stop you from

working. I'll sue you for everything you've got. I'll . . ."
Jane could hear Murry's voice until she was out of the building.

She climbed into her car and drove to her agent's office. Jane
and Constance Steiner had never become close. Their relationship was easy, if not particularly personal. Jane hadn't bothered
much about the business end of her dealings with the studio.
Maud's accountant in New York took care of her financial
matters, so she knew Constance couldn't be doing anything
really illegal, and she trusted the agent to make deals and settle
contracts, which Constance had done with regularity and to her
own personal satisfaction. Constance had often maintained,
particularly when she had been drinking at one of the cocktail
parties she loved to attend, that she wished she had more
clients like Jane Turner.

"A sweet girl," Constance always said. And, to the agent's
friends, this meant that Jane didn't show up at the office every
day, making demands.

Constance Steiner had kept her position in Hollywood by the
simple expedient of never bucking the system. She always held
out for a little more money or slightly better billing, just to look
good, but both she and the studios knew that Constance would
give in when they needed her to.

Jane walked into the office of Constance Steiner Associates
and startled the secretary, who'd never seen her before.

"I'm Jane Turner. I'd like to see Constance."

"Yes, Miss Turner. Of course, Miss Turner," stammered the
girl. She quickly buzzed Constance, announced Jane, and told
her to go right in.

Jane found her agent sitting behind a massive desk in front
of a window that looked out at the Capital Record Building.

The walls of the office were covered with pictures of clients
and several abstract paintings. The furniture was impersonal
and looked uncomfortable.

The woman herself was equally uninviting. Constance was
in her mid-fifties, had untidy brown hair, inexpertly dyed, and
wore bulging suits that had probably cost a lot when purchased, but were now old and out of shape. She smoked
continually, using a long holder which she waved about to
make her points.

"Well, hello, Jane. Nice to have you back in town. Did you

have a nice vacation? I haven't talked to you since you left. How have you been? Have you started *Laugh A Minute* yet?"

Jane sat down and took a cigarette from the box on Constance's desk. "No, I haven't started work. Yes, it was a nice vacation. And it looks like it might continue."

"What on earth are you talking about?" asked Constance.

Jane briefly told Constance about her scene with Murry Edson. She left out nothing, including the fact that she had told Murry to go to hell. Throughout her recital, Constance stared at Jane, her eyes getting larger and her mouth wider with each blow of the battle.

"So," finished Jane. "I'm on strike." She smiled happily.

Constance didn't speak for a few seconds. Then she went to pieces. "Are you out of your mind?" she cried, jumping up from her desk. She rushed toward Jane, her eyes wild. "Have you completely gone out of your senses? You're not Bette Davis. This isn't Warner's. My God! Global won't stand for this kind of thing. I want you to get back there and apologize immediately and make things right. I don't care how you do it. Make a date with Murry if you have to. But I want you on the set of *Laugh A Minute* next week, and I don't want to hear any arguments."

"I gather," said Jane, who had remained calm throughout Constance's diatribe, "that you don't approve of what I've done. What do you think about my playing Helen?"

"I don't think anything about it. If Murry doesn't want you to play the part, then you don't play it."

"Just whose side are you on?" asked Jane dangerously.

Constance ignored the warning in Jane's voice. "That is not the point. You girls are all alike. Jesus Christ. You get a few pictures under your belts and think you know more than anybody else. Well, let me tell you something, honey, this town will be here long after you're gone and forgotten. And it will still be run by people who know more than you do. Now if you have any sense, you'll get the hell out of my office and go back to work."

Jane stood up. "I'm going," she said.

Constance looked victorious.

"But not to the studio. And to clarify your thoughts, I don't think I know it all. But I do think I know what's best for me. I fully expect Hollywood to be here after I'm dead and gone. But

I won't be forgotten if I get to do something that is important enough to be remembered. And I'm going to see to it that I do something that important." Jane turned and walked to the door. Opening it, she looked back at Constance and smiled sweetly.

"Oh, Constance?"

"Yes?" responded the defeated woman.

"You're fired."

It didn't take long for the columnists and the radio commentators to find out about Jane's strike against Global Films. Her loyalty to Elizabeth Hudson during the murder crisis paid off for her by putting most of the reporters on her side.

Every movie magazine immediately wanted an interview with Jane, and all of the gossip and movie columns in the papers did articles. Most of them were slanted in her favor, citing Jane's determination to excel as an actress. Made to look like the bad guy, Global was held up as an example of the misuse of studio power and the horror of the all-encompassing control the studios exercised over the lives of their players. Hedda and Louella both said Jane was brave. Walter Winchell was concerned about her ability to actually perform as an actress, but he gave her credit for trying. Adela Rogers St. John was vehement in her defense of Jane. The ever-emotional Alexander Wollcott called Jane a present day Joan of Arc.

Daily, the reporters surrounded Maud's Beverly Hills home, just as they had during Elizabeth's crisis. They called out to virtually every car that passed, trying to get some inside information about either Jane's or the studio's latest move.

Murry Edson said, "No comment," to every question, and the Global publicity department tried to suggest that Jane had never gotten over Elizabeth's death and, consequently, was in need of additional rest. But no one believed that for a minute.

Jane spent most of her time by the pool of Maud's house. Warren came over every night, but he never stayed, and Jane was afraid to go to the beach house without Maud, for fear that the reporters would follow her there. She and Warren would be defenseless against them away from the protective gates and guard of the Beverly Hills house.

Global contacted Constance Steiner and discovered that she no longer was acting for Jane. It was decided during a very long meeting in Murry's office that they would wait for a time and see if Jane would come to her senses. They knew she wouldn't want to sit idle for long.

But Jane wasn't sitting. Maud contacted the Los Angeles branch of her New York law firm and had one of their representatives meet with Jane. The lawyer, David Martin, was familiar with the movie business and he recommended a new agent, Marty Beckman, and a personal publicity representative, Virginia Hovas. By the third week in July, Jane and her new advisors were working together to plan her future. Marty called Global and met with Murry Edson, who still refused to budge from his position; Jane would come back to work on his terms. Marty politely refused the offer and, along with Jane's other new advisors, decided to hold a carefully planned and rehearsed press conference around the pool at Maud's house. Surrounded by her new representatives and with the protective presence of Maud Watson, Jane would give her side of the conflict with Global and answer questions about her decision to leave the studio.

Hardgrave and several satellite waiters with trays of cocktails and opulent food circulated around the reporters. Forty newsmen and women were very mellow by the time Jane and her group walked out of the French doors onto the patio almost thirty minutes late.

Although it appeared that Virginia Hovas preferred to lead Jane directly to a chair set aside for her to answer questions from, Jane stopped along the way and greeted many of the press people by name, remembering particular stories they had written. The reporters were astonished. Almost no one ever remembered their names and, unless the stories were about themselves, stars never seemed to read anything. But here was Jane Turner, pausing to chat and appearing to know exactly who each of them was, ignoring the urging of her publicity woman.

Jane had always had a wonderful memory for names and, with a little help from Bill and Virginia, she had learned about most of the people who would be at the conference. Her entrance was a carefully orchestrated maneuver designed to put everyone on her side. It was working.

She looked beautiful in a simply tailored black silk dress, cut high at the neck, and with long sleeves. Her makeup was restrained and, against the bright glare of the sun and the light clothes of the others, she stood out like a beacon. The chairs were arranged so that she had her back to the sun so she wouldn't have to wear sunglasses, and when she took her place, she looked out at the blinking mob and smiled brightly.

A woman from the Associated Press started the questions by asking what her status with Global was at the moment.

"I'm afraid we're not very close," said Jane. "But I hope we'll be able to work things out in the future."

"Who do you have with you?" asked a man from *Movie Star Monthly*.

Jane introduced her companions, ending with, "And I'm sure you all know my aunt, Mrs. Thomas Watson, from New York."

Most of them did, and the few who had never seen her had certainly heard about her. Wearing a large hat and strands of pearls over a printed blue afternoon dress, Maud looked exactly the way every club woman in America was supposed to look, which was exactly what Jane had hoped for. She put the conference on a slightly different plane by taking the opportunity to speak out for British war relief, and inviting all the press to a gathering of her ladies' club which would be meeting that week with Scott Mack as the guest of honor. The press waited patiently for Maud to finish her commercial, and then returned to Jane's recent breakup with Global.

"What are your plans for the future?" asked a woman from the *Los Angeles Times'* entertainment section.

Jane explained that at present they were still hoping things could be worked out with Global, but if not, she had several things she was considering. When a decision had been made, they would be the first to know.

The conference continued for over an hour. Jane was gracious, cool, and very friendly. Maud, sweltering under her elegant hat, longed for a cocktail, but she and Jane had decided not to drink in front of the clicking cameras.

When it was finally finished, Hardgrave and his helpers again hurried forward with more cocktails. Maud looked thirstily at them, but followed Jane obediently through the crowd, smiling and nodding to familiar faces. She felt as if her smile was permanently in place, and even after she and Jane reached the upstairs and filed into Jane's room with the advisors following them, she found she was still grinning idiotically. Maud and Jane sank down on opposite sides of Jane's bed, and Maud pulled off her hat.

"Dear me," she exclaimed. "That was exhausting."

"Do you think it went well?" Jane asked Virginia, who had sat down in a chair near the window.

"Beautifully," said Virginia, looking out at the pool area. "And if your butler gives them one more drink, I think they should certainly be on our side."

Jane laughed. "Well, we certainly practiced everything long enough. We spent longer rehearsing that hour than I have on some of my movies. What do we do now?"

"We wait," said her agent. "Wait and see what Global does. It's their move now."

"And what do you think they'll do?" asked Jane.

"Well, they only have two choices. They either have to reinstate you and give in to what you want. Or they can let you out of your contract. They're in a bad position right now. *Half Breed* cost them a lot of money. It's due to be released this fall. But it's going to be rather awkward for them to have a big premiere for a movie starring an actress they don't own. They won't want to release the movie unless they have you back. And they can't have you back unless they work things out with me," finished Marty.

"But what if you can't come to terms?"

"Something *has* to happen," said Marty. "If they agree to our terms, then you go back to work. If they release you, then we go with the best offer from another studio. You're important now, and we'll be hearing from Warner's and MGM and Paramount and all the rest. As a matter of fact, I got a call from Republic this morning."

"Republic!" exclaimed Jane.

"Don't worry. I didn't take the call. They were just hopeful that you were panicked and might slip and sign with them. I think Global will come around, it'll just take awhile. You know we've asked for quite a lot."

"Really?" asked Maud. "I thought Jane just wanted to play Helen in *Another Life*."

"Well," Marty grinned, "since Jane had walked out anyway, and hired me, I thought we might as well go for the moon. We've asked for a considerable raise, a limit to two pictures a year, and approval of all scripts, in addition to her getting Helen."

"Dear me," said Maud.

"We won't get all the money I asked for, and we may have to do a contract for five pictures in two years, but we'll get Helen and script approval and at least part of the money."

"The money isn't important," said Jane.

Marty groaned. "Please don't say things like that around me."

"How long can they hold *Half Breed*?" asked Virginia.

"Awhile. Maybe into late fall. Jane can probably count on being off at least another couple of months."

"Then we'll have to think of something for her to do," said Helen.

"Oh," said Jane, thinking of Warren. "I might have a few plans of my own."

Warren Harris was easily the calmest person throughout the whole conflict between Jane and Global. He knew Jane wouldn't ever quit working, but her forced vacation fit in perfectly with their plans to get married. He and Jane were privately very grateful to the studio for holding on to its position and giving them a chance for a real honeymoon.

David and Susan arrived the next week, and Jane and Warren planned to have their ceremony at Maud's house with only a few close friends with them.

When Jane told the news to Virginia Hovas, the public relations lady was delighted, both with Jane's happiness and the chance for the additional publicity the wedding would create. But Virginia was disappointed when she found that Jane refused to turn her wedding into a media event. Jane was adamant. It would be a simple ceremony and immediately afterward, Jane and Warren would leave for Mexico.

But the plans were abruptly canceled when, a few days later, Warren was hastily called back to Washington. The president was involved in preparing the eight-point Atlantic Charter, which he planned to release with the British prime minister, Winston Churchill. Warren's advice and input were necessary. Warren had been afraid of hearing from the government, and he and Jane were terribly disappointed.

Maud immediately offered to take care of the children, but

Warren didn't know how long he'd be away, and finally decided that they should go back to Kansas City. He would take them home and then go on to Washington.

David and Susan had been staying with their father at the beach house, and the night before they were to leave, Jane came out for dinner. After the meal, Warren and Jane walked to the beach together.

"I guess you know how sorry I am about all this," said Warren for at least the fifth time.

Jane took his hand. "Stop worrying. We just should have scheduled the wedding sooner. It's not your fault. You can't very well ignore the president."

"No. But I was looking forward to our wedding."

"So was I. And I was particularly excited about the wedding night," said Jane with a little grin.

"I guess we won't even have that," said Warren sadly, "since the children are here."

"We'll have time when you get back," said Jane.

"I'm beginning to wonder if we'll ever have time just for us. Everything always seems to go so fast."

Just then David ran out and told them that Mrs. Watson had called and invited the children to her house for the night. She would take them to the station the next morning in plenty of time for them to meet Warren and catch their train.

A little later, as Jane and Warren waved the kids off from the driveway, he turned to her.

"I always said Maud was a remarkable woman. Are you sure you don't mind David driving your car?"

"Not in the least," said Jane. "Besides, you gave him so many instructions, it'll probably take him hours to get to Maud's."

"I just wanted him to be careful."

"Sometimes it doesn't pay to be careful," said Jane, running her fingers over his shirt.

"Maud isn't the only remarkable woman in your family," said Warren, smiling down at her.

"How would you like to go for a swim?" asked Jane.

"All right."

Shortly they were in the water, splashing each other and playing like children.

"Darling," said Jane moving close to Warren. "Don't you think these suits are a little 'careful'?"

"Much too careful," agreed Warren. Underwater, they helped each other out of their bathing suits and then swam naked through the warm waves of the ocean. It was an incredibly sensuous feeling for both of them. The water, lapping against Jane's breasts, made her nipples harden and sent shivers of excitement through her body. She dived underwater and slipped up to Warren's body. She touched him, running her hands over his buttocks, kneading and gripping it tightly. Warren reached down and pulled Jane up, lifting her upper body out of the water. He kissed her breasts, her stomach. The feel of her smooth skin drove him to the point of desire.

"Let's go inside," said Warren.

Jane nodded and, ignoring their discarded bathing clothes, they grabbed their towels and ran to the house.

Inside they dried each other and then embraced, lowering their bodies onto the pillows in front of the fireplace. They kissed, their mouths passionately crushing together as if each wanted to devour the other.

"You're so beautiful," said Warren, looking down at Jane. "So very beautiful."

"My darling, darling, Warren." Jane encircled his neck with her arms and drew him closer to her. "I love you so much."

She wrapped her legs around his body and pulled him closer to her. Slowly and gently, he entered her and began moving back and forth. Jane moaned slightly and tightened her grip on him.

Warren ignored her urgency as her hands grasped him, and her body moved faster beneath him. He maintained his slow rhythm, bringing her again and again to the point of climax and then retreating. For Jane, it was magnificent agony as she twisted about on the pillows, her body aflame with desire for him.

He seemed to grow larger and larger within her with each thrust. His body controlled hers and his movements directed her passion. It seemed he would never stop, never let her release the overwhelming desire inside her.

"Please," she murmured. "Oh, please, my darling, darling, Warren."

He looked down at her and their eyes met. She stared up at the triumphant and strong man she loved. He possessed her, controlled her, adored her. She was everything to him, and now he completely absorbed her body and her mind as he drove deeper and deeper into her, filling her body with his love and his desire and his strength.

Jane lifted her body to meet his, trying to draw him in, attempting to control the ecstasy created between them. Warren touched her nipples and ran his tongue over her throat and between her breasts. She was completely mesmerized by him, totally dedicated to their passion.

Warren began to move faster, his body thrusting harder and harder into Jane. She met his passion with her own, and the night exploded around them as they came together as one. For a few very special moments, the outside world couldn't touch them.

Twenty-Four

JANE WAS NOT COMFORTABLE with her enforced rest. She spent a lot of time studying and working with Madam Brinski, but without a commitment to do Helen, it was hard for her to concentrate on the character. Her days began to stretch out dully before her until one afternoon Virginia Hovas dropped in to talk to her.

Maud joined them, and they settled themselves by the pool. Virginia brought up the reason for her visit immediately.

"Jane, I know you don't have enough to do, so I'd like you to think about making some personal appearances."

"She can speak at my committees for British war relief," volunteered Maud.

"Good idea," said Virginia. "There are a lot of things you can do, all of which could be very important. Visit some hospitals, maybe entertain some soldiers."

"I'd like to do that," said Jane. "But I can't sing or dance."

"You can wear a tight dress and talk your way through a song," said Virginia. "You'll be a great hit."

"I don't want to sound precious," said Jane. "I don't mind doing the publicity things, I'm used to them. But if I'm going to do things with hospitals and servicemen, I want to really get involved. Not just do surface stuff that's good for the press."

Maud patted Jane's hand.

"Don't worry about it," said Virginia. "When you do this sort of thing, everyone gets something out of it. The places you visit get you, and you get the press."

Jane looked troubled.

"Look," said Virginia, "I know what you're thinking. It's all a bunch of hype. Well, the fact is it's only hype if you let it be. No one tells you how great your commitment should be. Frankly, Jane, you've got quite a bit of energy, and it won't hurt you to spend a little bit of it doing things worthwhile. You've got a famous name. Use it to help someone else. And get yourself some good press at the same time."

Jane smiled. "I was doing fine until your last sentence."

"Think about it," said Virginia. "I've got to go. I'll call you tomorrow." She left, and Jane turned to Maud.

"Does it all sound terribly sordid?" she asked Maud.

"Well, dear, I've always admitted I don't understand your business. I think you know what is right. And I think you'll do the right thing."

Jane's first appearance was at a Navy base outside San Diego. She had groaned inwardly when Virginia told her about it; the idea of facing several thousand sailors was scary. But Virginia just smiled and told her it was an excellent way of getting started. She was to sing a couple of songs, talk to the audience, and then tour the base hospital.

Jane had found someone to coach her on her songs, and a small group of musicians were gathered to accompany her.

She wore a very conservative suit for her arrival in San Diego and her meeting with the Navy brass assigned to welcome her. But for the show, she dressed in a revealing evening gown under a full-length satin coat. Her hair was piled onto her head, a few wisps falling around her face, and her makeup was elaborate and glamorous.

The public relations man from the Navy awkwardly informed her that many of the men had been away from their families for some time, a large portion of them had just gotten back from sea duty, and it was possible that they wouldn't be as dignified as other groups she appeared in front of.

Jane thought about her screaming fans back in Hollywood and dismissed the warning. She was sure these boys couldn't be any more volatile than the people who lined up daily outside the gates to her house.

She walked onto the stage with a smile and an air of excitement. The crowd greeted her with catcalls and applause, and she bowed and went into her first number. When she had finished, the audience was polite, and Jane suddenly realized that she was enjoying herself. She looked down at the first rows of enlisted men behind the officers and saw the fresh, bright faces upturned to her. She winked at them, and they responded by going wild.

Walking to the front of the stage, Jane invited one of the sailors up to join her.

After a scuffle, one blond, blue-eyed man who appeared to be about nineteen climbed over the edge and stood bashfully next to Jane. She smiled at him, asked his name, and then commented that it was very warm that day.

He agreed, perspiring freely in his excitement.

Jane asked him if he would help with her coat, and when he nodded, she turned her back and let the satin slip down her body. She handed the coat to the sailor and turned back to face the audience. Her dazzling, black-sequined gown was cut low in the front and fitted her body like a second skin. She looked spectacular.

The audience went wild. Jane kissed her helper on the cheek, sent him back to his seat, and went into her second song. The show was a vivid success, and Jane's only difficult moments came when she visited the hospital and saw the sailors who had been hurt in training accidents. There were even men there who had been immobilized since the war of 1917. At first, Jane was shy under the stares of the bedridden patients and held back.

But Maud whispered that this was the time when Jane had to make a choice between hype and real interest in what she was doing. Jane looked at Maud's serious face and nodded. With the same courage with which she had faced the important moments in her life, Jane took a deep breath and walked slowly through the wards, smiling and touching the sailors with warmth and affection. She gave autographs to a few, signed several casts, held the hands of a few elderly men, and never once betrayed horror or fear toward the mangled and diseased bodies before her.

When they had reached the outside once again, Maud smiled at her, but wisely refrained from making a big deal out of what Jane had done. Instead, she simply patted her arm and said, "That was very nice, dear. Do we have to eat with the officers?"

Jane continued making personal appearances for a variety of organizations and causes, becoming very adept at judging her audiences and handling different crises. Her popularity grew, and she was in constant demand. She was selective about her engagements, and often frustrated Virginia Hovas by giving up major press occasions for simpler events where she thought her presence would be more valuable.

But Jane knew that her life couldn't continue this way. The time away from the studio was becoming interminable. There were moments when she didn't think she could stand it. She wanted to be back at work so badly it was eating her alive. No matter how hard she worked with Olga or how much time she spent on volunteer activities, every fiber of her being longed to be back in front of the cameras.

"All right, what the hell are we going to do?" asked Murry. He looked around his office at the gathering of executives and assistants who had met to discuss what was now known as The Jane Turner Problem. "I want answers," he proclaimed, hitting his desk with one fat fist.

"Have you thought about talking to Warren Harris?" asked Terrance Malvey.

"I called him several weeks ago," said Murry. "He said he never interferes with Jane's business."

"That's the only thing of hers he hasn't interfered with," said one of the assistants.

"If I want jokes," exploded Murry, "I'll get Abbott and Costello, or Gracie Fields. Not an almost out of work production man."

"Sorry," the man murmured and lapsed into silence.

"In case it interests any of you 'executives,'" continued Murry, "New York is not happy at the moment. They want Jane Turner back in the Global fold. And I don't think I need tell you that when New York is unhappy they usually do something about it. And let me make this very clear. *Mine* won't be the only head that rolls around here if the money men decide to start cleaning house."

"What is Jane doing now?" asked Terrance, ignoring Murry's diatribe.

"The same thing she's been doing since Harris left town. Making a wonderful name for herself around town, visiting hospitals and military installations. Hell, she's even christened a ship. It wouldn't surprise me if she started getting some stupid citizen's award. The press loves her."

"Has she had any other offers?" asked another executive.

Murry shrugged. "Rumors, nothing definite."

"Have you talked to Jane?" he asked.

"I've tried," said Murry. "But I didn't get anywhere. Her *new* agent has instructed her to just sit quietly and let him do the talking. Jesus, that man can talk."

"So?" asked an assistant. "What happens if we just let her go?"

Murry sighed. "I'll tell you what will happen. Jane's agent will make a deal with another studio. They'll buy out her contract from us and suddenly have a big star in their stable. In the meantime, we'll have to release *Half Breed* and give her *and our competition* a lot of free publicity. This does not take into consideration the loss of future profits projected on Jane Turner properties. New York will have a fit over the whole thing, and we'll all be out on the street."

"Well, that about covers it," said Terrance.

"What exactly does she want?" asked the first executive.

"In the beginning, all she wanted was Helen in *Another Life*. Now she, or her agent, wants ten thousand a week, a maximum of two pictures a year, and script approval on all projects."

"Jesus!" The executive whistled.

"What'll she settle for?" asked Terry.

"It's hard to say," answered Murry. "I imagine we can make it three films a year, and I'm sure we can get the money down. That's one thing in our favor, Jane never cares much about the money. She's always wanted the power."

Terrance looked surprised.

"Oh, yes," said Murry, "you probably didn't think I understood. But I know these women. They usually want something other than the movies themselves. With some it's the fame, others the money. Once in a great while you get one who wants power. Jane Turner is like that. And that's why she'll never quit. She could get tired of the fame or make enough money. But that lust for power never stops. Some people think women like Jane Turner have star quality because they have to be in front of the camera. Because of some chemical thing they have with the lens. But don't let them fool you. What Jane Turner has and wants more of is power. Power over the camera, over the viewer, over us. And she'll never get enough. She'll keep fighting for more until she drops." Murry looked thoughtful. "I suppose it's some form of chemistry. But it's sure as hell what makes her a star. You watch Jane on the screen, watch Davis, or Gable, or Garbo. You'll see power. But it's our job to make sure their power stays on the screen and not behind the scenes."

Terrance looked at his boss with respect.

"Enough philosophy," snapped Murry, conveniently forgetting that he was the one doing all the talking. "I want to know what the hell we're going to do."

"Let her play Helen," suggested an executive.

"And risk ruining a big star in a movie that audiences are going to hate? Are you crazy?" bellowed Murry. "We might as well dump her as let her play that part. It could kill her career. To say nothing of the precedent. If we let Jane Turner dictate to us, we'll have every two-bit actor on the lot running in here and making demands. Joey the clown will want to do Hamlet, and Greta Stewart will insist on being Rebecca of Sunny Brook Farm."

"We dropped Greta," reminded Terry.

"All right, all right. It doesn't matter. There's always another Greta Stewart. Right now it seems to be Jane Turner who's the problem. At least Greta never thought she could act. She was just a bitch." Murry sighed as he remembered easier days.

Terrance looked thoughtful. "I think he's right," he said, nodding at the executive. "I think we ought to let Jane test for Helen."

"What?" asked Murry, astonished.

"I didn't say play. I said test. The one thing I've always noticed about Turner is that she's fairly honest. At least as honest as any of them can be. I say test her and send the results to New York. Let them make the decision. That way you get it off your hands. If they agree to letting Jane play Helen and it's a flop, then they have no one to blame but themselves. If she survives, then you get the credit for letting her take the chance. She agreed to do a test. Let's let her do it."

"And if it's no good?" asked Murry.

"Then she'll sink with it," said Terrance flatly.

Murry was quiet for a few moments, his head down as he thought out the various ramifications of Terrance's idea. Watching him, Malvey remembered the night they had gone to Elizabeth Hudson's apartment. Murry had the same expression on his face as he had when he'd weighed his options in relation to Mark Richmond's murder.

Finally, Murry broke the silence. "Do we have a script?" he asked.

"There ought to be something," said Terrance. "The writers have been working on and off since we got the book."

"All right. But I want to make it very clear that this isn't to go out of this room. We don't tell anybody. I don't want it in the columns that Jane is preparing to do the role of Helen. And I don't want the place surrounded by press. It'll look like we've given in. You tell her agent that we'll let Jane test for the part of Helen, as long as he agrees to keep it strictly quiet."

"What about the crew?" asked Terry.

"Don't tell them what's going on. Closed set. Tell only the director, makeup and hair people. Everybody else gets locked in. We'll do it at night when there won't be as many people around."

"That's still a lot of people to keep quiet," said another executive.

"See to it." Murry waved his hand.

"When do you want to do it?" asked Terry.

Murry looked at his desk calendar. "Let's see. This is the twenty-sixth of September. Let's do it next week, October second. That'll give us time to make sure we have a script and get set up. But let me warn you, if I see anything in the press, some of you guys are going to find your asses out on the street."

"Do you think you can depend on Turner to keep her mouth shut?" asked Terry.

Murry nodded. "Oh, I think so. She may be a bitch, but

she's not a fool. She's not going to want anyone to know if she falls on her face."

"Which way do you think it'll go?" asked an executive.

"For her?" asked Murry. He leaned back in his chair and surveyed his executives. Then a slight smile crossed his face. "Frankly," he said, "I don't give a damn."

Late one night, Jane arrived for her test at the appointed time, wearing comfortable clothes with her hair pulled back and large sunglasses covering her eyes. In the limousine with her were Marty Beckman and Virginia Hovas, along with Olga Brinski.

Murry had a fit when he learned that the acting teacher was to be a part of the group. But he couldn't think of any acceptable reason for keeping her out, and that made him even madder.

He and Terrance waited on the set with Earnest Kahn, the director, and the carefully selected crew which included Jane's usual hairdresser and makeup man. After formal greetings were exchanged, Jane left for her dressing room while the others sat down and talked about inconsequential matters.

Olga Brinski stood off to one side with her hands folded over her waist, impassively surveying the preparations going on in the studio. Her expression indicated that Global Studios did not measure up to her lofty standards.

Seated in front of her makeup mirror, Jane stared at her reflection as Roger and Paul began their work. She reached out for a cigarette, and her hand trembled. Warren's face came into her mind, and she wished that he were with her, holding her, protecting her. But she was alone now. Surrounded by technicians, creative artists, and the studio's business leaders, Jane had never felt so alone.

When the artists were finished, Jane put on the simple dress chosen as her costume and then walked slowly out onto the minimal set, which consisted of two easy chairs set against a stock background. Jane briefly closed her eyes and envisioned the house that Helen and her husband lived in, drawing a sense of her character from the environment.

The scene selected for the test was one of the most challenging in the story. It was a dramatic moment in which

Helen argues with her husband and then watches him leave her, knowing she has nothing left.

Earnest Kahn set up the shot, and they began rehearsal. Jane constantly looked toward Madam Brinski for guidance and reassurance, much to the director's annoyance. After nearly an hour, Earnest had had enough.

"Miss Turner," he began, "do you suppose your coach could wait in the locker room? After all, the players are on the field now."

Jane looked at him blankly, and Madam Brinski appeared as if she were about to burst. Jane smiled slightly at Earnest. Here was something she could handle. The scene terrified her and she knew it wasn't going well, but a director giving her problems was a familiar part of her life. Looking at him steadily, she replied, "I don't think you remember to whom you're speaking."

Kahn was only stopped for a minute. He had worked with Jane too many times not to know exactly what he was doing.

"I think I know," he said casually. "But since you've been away for so long, perhaps you don't remember that on a movie set the director is the boss."

"I remember," said Jane. "I'm just not sure I've ever agreed with that policy."

"Agree or not, the rules haven't changed. *I'm* running this test. And I don't want to have to fight for your attention."

"Go to hell," said Jane simply, examining her nails.

"Miss Turner!" Kahn bellowed. "Will you please shut up and let us get on with rehearsing this scene?"

"*I* didn't stop the rehearsal," said Jane. "But since you did, I don't like the way my hair is moving."

"Will somebody get the goddamn hairdresser?" screamed Earnest.

Paul hurried up and began adjusting Jane's hair while she stood impassively, waiting for him to finish. She was grateful for the short break. She didn't know what was wrong, but somehow it just wasn't working. She couldn't get to that part of herself that would make Helen come alive. She knew it was there. But now it seemed to have escaped from her control. The fear that she wasn't good enough made her more nervous and awkward, and her tension blocked her ability to respond to her character.

When Paul was finished, Jane turned back to Kahn and assumed her offhand manner. "I think I'm ready now," she said.

"Good," said the director, smiling viciously. He turned to the crew and announced, "Miss Turner is ready now, we can proceed. I'd like to do this scene once again before we film. Feed Miss Turner her lines, please."

The extra stationed off camera whose job it was to read the part of Russel shook out his script and began reading in a monotone. Jane picked up her cues automatically and followed all of the blocking Earnest had set up for her. She moved around the set as instructed and spoke every line clearly and distinctly. She was technically perfect, and absolutely wooden. There was no emotion in Jane's Helen, no breadth that would bring the character to life.

Murry, sitting next to the director, moaned softly. "Jesus, she's terrible. I knew she'd be terrible. Jesus H. Christ. What the goddamn hell am I going to tell New York?"

"I'd also worry about what you're going to say to the writer if you let Jane do this role," said Kahn. "I thought she'd be better. I don't understand what's wrong." He shrugged. "I guess it's just too much for her. I suppose we might as well have a break and then do a take."

Murry nodded miserably and Earnest called out that there would be a short rest and then they would film.

Jane nodded and walked off to her dressing room. She was followed immediately by Paul and Roger. In a few seconds, Virginia and Marty joined them.

"God, Jane," said Marty. "You've got to do something. There's no fire, no life. Are you feeling okay?"

"I'm perfectly fine," said Jane as she lit a cigarette.

"Jane," began Virginia. "I think if you want to secure this part you've got to—"

"Would you please step out of the way?" ordered a deep voice. Jane's advisors turned and found Olga Brinski standing at the foot of the short flight of steps leading up to Jane's dressing room. The old lady began pushing through them. "You heard me, step aside," she said. Once she had gained entrance, Olga placed herself in a chair and looked at Virginia and Marty. "Leave us," she said, waving her hand at them in a dismissive gesture.

The advisors looked at Olga, glanced at Jane, and then shrugged and started down the stairs.

"And close the door behind you," said Madam Brinski.

Turning to Jane, the old teacher looked her over carefully. Jane returned her stare and then sat down and faced her mirror.

"I know I'm terrible," said Jane softly.

"Yes," replied Olga. "Terrible. If you'd been passably all right, I wouldn't be here now. Terrible I can live with. Great I can live with. I can't live with mediocrity. It's death. The average actor is mediocre. He can do everything and nothing. Tonight you are terrible. Perhaps you will yet be great."

"How? I'm working very hard."

"Perhaps. So do many salesclerks. But they are not artists. How strange, if you think about it."

"What?" asked Jane.

"The similarity between you and Helen, the character you play this evening."

"I don't think we have anything in common."

"Really? I do. Helen is losing the only man who ever meant anything to her. She is losing him because she's not strong enough to change and become the person she needs to be to hold him. She's not capable of growing and moving herself out of her background into something better. No matter where Helen is, no matter how much money she has, she'll still be common."

"Are you saying no matter what I do, I'll never be an actress?"

"No. I'm saying that while Helen finds it impossible to change, to be anything more than she is and consequently loses everything, you're standing out before those people tonight, facing the possible loss of what you want. When that barbarian Murry Edson looks at you tonight, he sees Jane Turner, movie star, sex symbol, whatever that is. He doesn't see an actress. From our work, I was under the impression you were strong enough to change. To not lose everything you wanted because you can't stop being Jane Turner. Because you can't stop letting the camera do your job for you. Because you're afraid to stop relying on your face and your body to carry you through. And like Helen, in a few years, you'll find yourself without anything. Because you can't change and adjust . . . because you can't grow. What Helen is losing is not so very different from what you're going to lose. You both are losing your chance to have the life you want. Helen is too weak, too common, to meet her challenge. Apparently, so are you."

"I'm not weak," said Jane, her voice sharp.

"Then stop thinking about the camera and think about Helen. Think about what she's losing and imagine how you'll feel if you lose as well."

"I won't lose," said Jane.

When Earnest was ready to begin filming, he sent for Jane. She came out of her trailer, followed by Olga. Jane was a little pale under her makeup, but her hands were steady and she was able to smile at the technicians as she took her place.

The cameraman found his angles, the sound man checked his readings, and the lighting man adjusted a few overhead lights. Each person in the studio was a professional who knew his job. They slipped quickly into gear as the machinery of movie-making began to roll. Even before the director called for quiet, there was an almost tangible air of silence in the room.

The director took his seat near the camera and told Jane that they were ready. She nodded, and Earnest signaled to the box boy who ran forward and slammed the box labeled: "Turner Test, take one." Earnest called out the magic words, "Lights! . . . Camera! . . . Action!" He thrust his finger at the contract player who read his dialogue, and everyone waited for Jane to begin.

For a moment it appeared that Jane had frozen. She didn't answer, didn't respond, but just as Earnest Kahn was about to call cut, her voice came softly across the set.

"I don't think you've ever loved me," said Jane. "Not once. Not in all the time we've been together. You've never really thought about what it is to love a woman like me."

The cuing actor read his lines, and the scene continued. Days later, Earnest Kahn and Murry Edson would still be arguing about what happened that night on Stage Three. Earnest maintained that Olga Brinski had said or done something to Jane during the break. Murry insisted that it was simply that once Jane had heard the sound of the camera working, she had fallen under the spell of movie-making. It was an argument that was to recur often among anyone who watched the test being done.

Moving slowly, Jane had taken control of the set, the scene, and her character. Her actions were intense, and her voice ripped across the stage and grasped the imaginations of all who watched her. They were mesmerized by her, caught and held by her performance.

In the last moments of the scene, the script called for Helen to laugh at her husband as he walked out on her. But as soon as he left, her mood was to turn abruptly to one of abject despair.

Jane's laugh was strident as she ruthlessly taunted Russel with the line, "You'll live without my love?" But after she knew he was gone, Jane turned to face the camera, her face a mask of loneliness and defeat as she repeated, "You'll live without my love," in a voice from which all hope was gone.

For several seconds, time stopped in the studio. No one moved. Earnest finally called, "Cut," and the technicians began their usual tasks. Jane stood perfectly still, her face locked in the emotion she had portrayed.

Murry muttered, "Jesus," under his breath, but it was more a prayer than an exclamation.

Earnest stood and walked toward the set. As he approached, Jane looked up at him and smiled slightly, her eyes asking a question.

When Earnest reached her, he took her hands in his and leaned down to kiss her. "Bitch," he whispered.

Murry decided against sending the film to New York, reasoning that he was capable after all of making a decision without their help. By the next morning, Jane's new contract had been settled. There had been a small battle over Jane's right to choose or approve her scripts, but by careful wording of the contract, the studio had at least the appearance of some say in what Jane was to do. And by Marty's lessening the money demands and agreeing to Jane's appearance in a minimum of five pictures within a two-year period, everything was finally arranged.

Half Breed was scheduled to premiere on December 6 at Grauman's Chinese Theatre, and Jane would begin actual filming on *Another Life* the week after. For the next several weeks, she was to rehearse, be fitted for costumes, undergo the extensive makeup tests required for a part in which she had to age almost thirty years, and to generally prepare for what she hoped would be the start of a whole new direction in her career.

Within three days of the contract settlement, there was a large press party given on Stage Three at which Murry, Jane, and all of the Global executives along with Jane's business partners were gracious and friendly to almost a hundred reporters and photographers. They were all anxious to hear about the agreement between Global and Jane, and while their questions were answered practically by Jane's agent and happily by Global's public relations men, Murry kept saying that Jane was a great girl and he was happy to have her home. Jane smiled, but said little. Her mind was on other things.

That morning, Warren had arrived from Washington, and she couldn't wait to see him. As soon as Jane could get away, she drove to the beach to meet him.

As Jane walked into the house, she saw him sitting on the deck, staring out at the ocean. He looked tired, and his hair was a little grayer. But he was still the man she loved, and he was home.

She slipped up behind him and bent forward to kiss him on the top of his head. He looked up and smiled at her and took her hand, pulling her down onto his lap. They embraced and held each other without speaking, relishing the closeness of each other.

"Oh, my darling, darling, Warren," said Jane.

He kissed her, gently at first, then more passionately. He stood and carried her into the bedroom and laid her gently on the bed. She was the most beautiful woman he had ever seen in his life. And she wanted him—only him.

Jane reached out her arms to Warren, and he lowered himself to her. Their bodies touched, and even through their clothing there was heat and passion. Warren pulled away from Jane and began to undress her, slipping her light blouse off her shoulders and unzipping her skirt. Jane sat up to help him, and in a few moments she was nude.

"Now you, darling," she whispered.

Naked, they reached out for each other again and together they dropped down onto the bed, Warren covering Jane's body with his own. He kissed her lips and then moved his mouth across her face and down to her breasts. Jane's body twisted in excitement as he touched her.

"Oh, it feels so nice. So very nice."

Warren continued to explore her flesh, touching, kissing,

licking her body, driving her to a delicious state of desire. She pulled him closer, her hands slipping down to his buttocks, kneading his flesh.

They whispered words of love and passion to each other as Warren moved up to kiss her mouth once again and slowly began to enter her. Jane gave a start of surprise and delight at first feeling him, and as he pushed harder and stronger, she thrust up to meet him, calling out his name.

Their movements grew to a frenzy. Warren lifted his head and looked at Jane. Small beads of perspiration had formed on her upper lip, and her eyes were closed. Her beauty moved Warren to a greater sense of desire. He couldn't get enough of her.

Jane's nails dug into Warren's flesh as they crashed together faster and faster, becoming one in a blasting climax. Their bodies were so tightly locked it seemed they would never be separated, their voices uttering words of wonder and love as they slowly eased their way off the peak of their lovemaking. Gently, Warren slipped his body from Jane's and lay beside her, holding her tightly against him.

She turned to face him. "That was wonderful," she murmured, stroking his hair. She kissed him lightly.

"I love you," said Warren.

Jane smiled softly at him, her eyes echoing his words.

"You look tired, darling," she said. "Why don't you sleep?"

"I don't want to stop looking at you."

"Don't worry. I'll be here when you wake up."

Warren began to doze, and Jane pressed her body close to his, as if trying to protect him. She touched his face. "Sleep, darling," she whispered. "I'll be here. I'll always be here for you."

Twenty-Five

J ANE T URNER HAD IT ALL. She was rich, famous, sought-after. She loved and was loved in return by a man she respected and whose devotion to her was unquestionable. Her contract with Global insured her the opportunity of growing and expanding as an actress. And she was surrounded by friends whose encouragement and support were unfailing.

Over the next weeks, Jane spent her days working harder than she had ever imagined possible, preparing for the role of Helen. The evenings were filled with the quiet camaraderie of the people she cared the most about. And always, there was Warren. Holding her, laughing with her, walking on the beach, grinning in a chef's hat as he attempted to grill a steak, surprising her with small, silly gifts. Each moment seemed to bring them greater happiness and contentment as the love and comfort and security of their relationship grew deeper and stronger.

The premiere for *Half Breed* was a big event for Global. Not only was the film expected to be a major money-maker, but the premiere itself would be a public celebration of the studio's settlement of its dispute with Jane Turner.

The press, public, and especially the public relations people of Global, went all out for the occasion. For days in advance the newspapers had described the opulent decorations and celebrities that could be expected at Grauman's, and the studio sent out stills and releases in record numbers. The guest list included every important star in Hollywood, and the event was expected to receive unprecedented press coverage.

Jane Turner was a heroine to many of the Hollywood crowd. She had survived the scandal around Elizabeth Hudson, had outmaneuvered her studio, and she was becoming recognized as a compassionate and tireless performer who would take the time after an exhausting work day to visit hospitals and military installations, bringing laughter and beauty into the lives of people to whom she was the essence of glamour and allure.

She was a star who had weathered her first storms, and members of the movie industry virtually fell over each other in an effort to honor her.

The evening would begin with the premiere, at which all of the major radio stations and press people would be included. At the end of the film, Jane would appear on the stage for the first time. A huge party was planned to follow at the Trocadero nightclub.

Maud was near hysteria on the afternoon of the great night, and constantly rushed into Jane's room to ask questions or make suggestions about matters that had long been settled. Finally, Jane stopped her.

"Aunt Maud," she said, "what on earth is the matter? You've been through all this before."

"I know, dear, I know. It's just that I'm a little nervous today. Aren't you excited?"

Jane shrugged. "I'm more interested in getting started with *Another Life* than I am in pushing a picture I hate."

"You may hate the picture, but you can't deny that it's going to be a wonderful evening. Why, I heard on the radio that the crowds have already started lining up outside the theater. And every newspaper has mentioned it. I must admit," continued Maud, "that it's nice to see something in the papers besides the war in Europe. It's so depressing. I just wish I could do more."

"As it is, Aunt Maud, your days are completely filled with meetings and fund-raising. I don't see how you could add anything more."

"Perhaps you're right. Anyway, I think it's wonderful that,

for tonight, we can forget all about the tragedy and pain, and concentrate on something glamorous and exciting."

"If it would make you happy, I'd have a premiere every night," said Jane, smiling at Maud.

"Well, I don't think you have to do that. But I would like you to borrow some jewels tonight. I think you should look very special."

"All right. When Roger and Paul finish with me, we'll come in and pick out some things."

"Good, dear. Now you must rest. I'll be around if you need me."

"You always have been," said Jane, giving her a kiss.

As usual, Jane arrived at the theater a few minutes late, accompanied by Warren and Maud. Mrs. Thomas Watson had dedicated thought and time to her apparel and had finally selected a dress from Molyneux's collection of all-black evening gowns. With it she wore an impressive diamond necklace and several lengths of pearls, in addition to bracelets and her square-cut diamond ring. On her head was a festive black creation that boasted a collection of feathers held in place by a diamond pin.

Warren and Maud were the first out of the car, and the crowd waited breathlessly for Jane to make her entrance.

Jane absolutely glistened as she suddenly appeared before her fans and looked up to find a thirty-foot cutout of herself as the heroine in *Half Breed* rising above the theater entrance. Jane had chosen a dress of clinging white silk in the style *Vogue* dubbed as "hardhearted chic." The material was cut low at the neckline, and she was bare to the waist under her arms. The skirt of the gown slipped seductively over her hips and legs, ending in a slight flare at the bottom. An enormous diamond pin was placed at the bottom of her cleavage, and diamonds sparkled at her ears and on her bare wrists. Over one arm she carried a white ermine scarf. Her hair was elaborately arranged, and her makeup was dramatic. She looked wonderful, and Warren smiled slightly to himself as he watched her accept the accolades of the mob. As in the past, they started chanting her name, and the rhythmic shouting continued as Jane walked up the red carpet to the waiting microphones.

Always with Maud on one side and Warren on the other,

Jane swept through the entire evening without a hitch, even appearing not to notice when Murry Edson belched loudly as they danced together at the Trocadero. It was nearly four A.M. when they finally sank into their limousine and headed back to the house in Beverly Hills.

"Well, that's over," said Jane, leaning back and taking out a cigarette. She looked at Warren. "Are you tired, darling?"

"Oh, I'm fine. If I stay around here long enough, I may get to like these things."

"But you doubt it," finished Jane with a smile. "Don't worry, dear. You won't have to go to another until I finish *Another Life*. Unfortunately, I have one next week."

"Really?" asked Maud. "What's it for?"

"Walt Disney is releasing *Dumbo*. I like Walt, and I hear it's a charming picture."

"It sounds lovely, dear. Maybe I'll go with you."

"Not that I have anything against Walt Disney," said Warren. "I've picked up a lot of his pictures, but are you sure I don't have to attend?"

"Absolutely," said Jane as she and Maud laughed. "You can stay home and play chess with Mack."

"If I weren't going," added Maud, "I'd play Monopoly with you. I must admit that I find the game absolutely fascinating. All that buying and selling things. I do think that if any lady could have been in business when I was a girl, I could have been a regular J.P. Morgan, only nicer," finished Maud.

"I like you just as you are, dear," said Jane. "You're staying with us, aren't you?" Jane asked Warren. "I would love to get up and find you at the breakfast table in the morning."

"Maud has very kindly asked me to stay over," he answered. "And, of course, I said yes."

"Oh, dear," said Maud.

"What's the matter?" asked Jane.

"Well, it's just that I didn't expect you to be so very tired. I thought you'd be exhilarated after the evening. You know how you are after a day at the studio. It seems to take you forever to calm down."

"I don't think I understand."

"Well, it was your mention of breakfast—"

"Are we out of orange juice?" asked Jane with a smile.

"In California!" exclaimed Maud. "No, it's just that you might have breakfast a little earlier than you planned."

"Why would I do that?" asked Jane.

Maud took a deep breath and blurted out, "Because I'm giving you a surprise breakfast at the house. A party to celebrate your premiere and getting the role of Helen and settling your contract and everything." Maud looked at Jane a little guiltily. "I've only invited people you like. Honestly I have."

"How many people do I like?" asked Jane, looking at her aunt.

"About a hundred," said Maud quietly. "I'm sorry, dear. It's just that it seemed like such a good idea at the time. A champagne breakfast with everyone . . ." Her voice trailed off, and she glanced toward Warren for support. But he continued to look out the car window.

Jane also looked at Warren, and then back at Maud. She smiled. "I think it's a wonderful idea," she said. "And you were very sweet to think of it."

"Are you sure you don't mind?" asked Maud anxiously.

"Positive. In fact, the more I think about it, the better I like it. We haven't had a party for our friends for a long time. This is a wonderful chance to get together." Jane's face did seem to brighten as the thought of the party sank in. Her tiredness disappeared, and she became as excited as a young girl facing her first formal dance. She took Warren's arm and whispered to him, "I suppose you knew all about this?"

"Are you sure you like it?" asked Warren.

"I love it."

"Then yes. I even helped make up the guest list." He looked bashfully at her.

"Coward," said Jane, poking him. "What would you have done if I hadn't liked the idea?"

"Let Maud take the blame," said Warren simply, winking at Mrs. Watson.

"You two are amazing. I love you both very much."

Maud leaned close to Jane, and Warren held Jane's hand as the car started up the drive.

"Oh, my God," said Jane, sitting bolt upright.

"What's the matter?" asked Maud, alarmed.

"My makeup, my hair. I must look terrible." She called out

to the driver to slow down, and, quickly looking in the mirror, began straightening up her face. When she had finished, she told him to continue. As they drove up at the entrance, she found the house ablaze with lights and could hear the sound of an orchestra playing.

"My Lord, you did go all out, didn't you?" asked Jane.

Maud giggled, and they walked into the house, where Jane was greeted by a wonderful collection of the people she liked best in the world. Among the guests were stars and celebrities Jane had met and become friends with, including Clifton Webb, Mr. and Mrs. Walt Disney, Fay Bainter, Meryl Oberon, and a few of Maud's New York acquaintances. Of course, Scott Mack and Bill were there, along with David Granoff and one of Jane's early costars, Wayne Marshall. Maud had even remembered Mable Cramer, who was dressed as if she were planning to come out of a cake before the evening was over. Warren and Maud hadn't forgotten the extras and crew people Jane had a good relationship with or the hairdressers and makeup people she liked. Amazingly enough, they had even convinced Olga Brinski to make an appearance.

Jane was immediately engulfed in a whirl of dancing and storytelling that seemed as if it would go on forever. She loved every minute of it. Often she looked up and found Warren's eyes, and they smiled at each other before being caught up once again in their conversations.

At one point, Jane realized she hadn't seen Warren for some time. She wondered what had happened to him and went into the hall to search for him. She met Bill, who was listening to an old character actress as she told of the days when she had worked with the Daly Company in New York. Jane stopped and asked them if they'd seen Warren, and Bill told her that he and Mack had gone off to the library to play chess.

"Now?" squeaked Jane. "You must be kidding."

"No. They even convinced Hardgrave to bring them each a private bottle of champagne and plates of food. By the time they come out of there, they should be drunk, full, and completely unaware there's a party going on." Bill's companion tugged on his sleeve and he said, "Excuse me, Jane. Hettie here has just gotten to the part where she plays opposite Otis Skinner and I don't want to miss it."

Jane smiled and went to the pool area where Maud had little

tables set up and live camellias floating on the water. The scent was almost overpowering. Hardgrave offered her a glass of champagne, and Jane saw Mable Cramer coming toward her.

"Hello, Mable. I'm so glad you're here. It's been a long time since we've seen each other."

Mable smiled. "Things change," she said. "You've done it, haven't you?"

Jane looked questioningly at her for a second, then grinned. "Yes. I guess I have."

"Well, I'm proud of you, honey. And I think Miss Goodie Two-Shoes would be, too."

"Miss . . . ? Oh, Elizabeth. There are times," said Jane quietly, "when I can't really believe she's dead."

"You know the number she sang in that one movie of hers?"

"You mean, 'You'll Always Be Mine'?"

"That's the one. They made a record of it."

"But who . . . how?"

"I guess the studio took it off the sound track. Someone gave it to me last week. I play it every once in a while." Mable shrugged. "Memories of lost innocence."

"I'll have to get the record," said Jane.

"I'll send it to you. Well," said Mable, lifting her glass. "Here's to you, honey. All the best."

"No," said Jane. "Not to me. Let's drink to Elizabeth."

Mable smiled softly, and the two women silently lifted their champagne and drank. When they had finished, they hugged each other for a moment and then Mable drew back. She smiled brightly and looked out over the guests. "I'd better circulate. There're plenty of good-looking men here tonight. Maybe I'll get lucky."

Mable walked away, and Jane was quickly caught up in a conversation with David Granoff and Clifton Webb. In a few moments she was laughing again.

As Clifton began telling her an outrageous story about someone he'd worked with, Jane leaned back and thought about the people around her. This was her family. These were the people who counted in her life. She felt joy and excitement and great affection as she thought about the dear friends who had come to honor her.

It was close to eight when Hardgrave and his helpers began serving the coffee. But the party was still going strong. It was a magical gathering. The sun had come up brilliantly, and the guests had toasted it with champagne and cheers before sitting down to eggs Benedict and fresh fruit, telling each other how terrible they looked in the bright light of day.

Jane was seated with Bill and David and several others when Warren came out onto the patio and walked quickly to her.

"Darling," said Jane. "How nice of you to come out of that room. Have you left Mack there? Good heavens, can't he come out as well?" asked Jane gaily.

"Mack is fine," said Warren quietly.

Jane noticed the expression on his face and immediately asked if something was wrong.

"I wonder if you could excuse yourself for a few moments," he asked.

"Of course," said Jane quickly. She stood up and took Warren's arm. There was something in his face that frightened her.

He looked past Jane at Bill and asked him to come also. Bill stood quickly, and after they had excused themselves, the three went into the house. The other guests looked at them in wonder, then returned to their food.

"It's Mack, isn't it?" asked Bill, his face white under his usual tan.

"No," said Warren briefly. "I don't mean to be mysterious, but I want to wait until we're all together."

Jane took Warren's hand, and together they went into the library. The radio was on, which surprised Jane as it seemed to be doing battle with the musicians who were still playing near the pool. Mack sat near the radio, his face intently listening to the announcer. Maud sat across from him, but she wasn't looking at anything, her face was set, closed. Jane couldn't understand what was happening.

"Warren, what is all this about?" she asked, her voice becoming sharp. "I don't understand. Did you bring us in here to listen to the radio? Is it something about the premiere?"

"No," said Warren. "It's not about the picture. I'm sorry to take you away from the party. But—" Warren's voice cracked, and Jane thought for a moment he was going to break down. She stared at him. "Warren, tell me. What is all this?"

"Listen, there's something else," said Mack urgently.

Bill had gone to Mack's side and now inquired angrily, "What the hell is going on?"

"Just listen, damn it," said Mack.

There was static from the radio, and then the announcer's voice.

". . . We have confirmed that at dawn this morning, December seventh, planes from the Imperial Japanese Air Force attacked and bombed the American military installation at Pearl Harbor, on the island of Oahu, Hawaii. We do not yet have accurate information on the full extent of the damage, but losses of both lives and ships are said to be high. The president is aware of the situation and has asked all Americans to keep calm during this national emergency. I repeat, this morning, the Japanese Air Force attacked . . ."

The voice droned on, but to everyone in the library, it seemed that time had totally stopped. No one moved. It was as if they hoped that by remaining still they could push back the last few moments, not accept the horror shoving itself into their consciousness.

Jane whispered, "Oh, no . . . oh, no." Her voice was that of a child whose favorite toy had broken and lay in pieces before her. She felt herself begin to sink under the shock, falling farther and farther into darkness. She gripped her hands tightly, her nails cutting into her palms. She couldn't let go. Not now. Not this minute. Jane took a deep breath and her self-control returned. Suddenly, she was completely calm—a calm created from utter helplessness.

She looked at Warren and with a steady voice asked, "What do we do now?"

Her practical question seemed to bring the others back to life. Warren smiled at her. "I knew you'd be all right."

"Only for the moment," she answered. "I have a feeling I'm going to have a nice bout of hysterics shortly."

"Well, just hang on for the time being. We have to make some decisions."

"Yes?"

"To begin with, there are the guests, and . . ." He looked across the room. "I think Maud needs you."

Jane looked at Maud. She hadn't moved since they had first come into the room.

"Of course," said Jane. She started toward Maud and then

turned back to Warren. "Will they come here?" she asked. "Will we be next?"

"I don't know," said Warren. "It's possible. I think you'd better take Maud up to bed. I'll go and speak to the guests. Do you think I should tell them what's happened?"

Jane thought for a second. "Yes. They might have things they need to do. Yes, tell them. I think Mrs. Edson has a nephew who's stationed at Pearl Harbor. You might want to speak to her first."

Warren nodded. "I think Bill and Mack should stay here," he said.

The two men looked surprised.

"Your house is in the mountains," explained Warren. "It's too good a target. You're safer here."

"Warren's right," agreed Jane. "We have plenty of room."

"All right, thank you," said Mack.

"I'll take care of the guests," said Warren and left as Jane went over to Maud.

"Aunt Maud," she said gently. "Do you want to go and lie down?"

Maud didn't answer, but she stood and let Jane lead her from the room.

Alone, Bill and Mack sat next to the radio and listened sadly as the announcer continued his description of the destruction.

For the rest of that terrible day, the news continued. Along with Warren, Mark and Bill, Jane listened to the radio, rarely speaking. They heard that over 2000 people had been killed and nineteen ships either sunk or damaged. Their hearts were torn a little more each time additional news of the holocaust was broadcast.

In the late afternoon, a cable arrived for Maud from Maggie Austen. In it she announced that she and her husband and Mary would be coming back to New York on the next available boat. Maggie asked Maud to meet them in New York and to bring Jane with her.

Jane knew that the cable, offering as it did a particular assignment and responsibility, would help Maud overcome her deep despondency about the attack on American soil. She hurried up to her aunt's room and read the cable aloud. Soon Maud began to function again, making plans to return east, assuming that Jane would accompany her. Jane was noncommittal about the trip, but Maud was too absorbed in her own arrangements to notice.

Mack and Bill insisted on going back to their own house, but Warren stayed with Jane and Maud. He called Washington and left Jane's number, expecting them to call him back soon.

The next morning, Jane called the studio. Murry Edson and his assistants had been working since the night before, trying to sort out the situation and make plans. He informed Jane that they would proceed as planned with all of the film schedules, although certain adjustments would have to be made due to the absence of many of the leading men who were going into the army, and the possible limitations of certain materials. But everything was still so confused that Murry couldn't give Jane any specific information other than they were still working and had no intention of stopping.

He also mentioned that there had already been an enormous number of calls requesting Jane for personal appearances to sell bonds or support various fund-raising committees. Murry told her that as soon as the publicity department had gone through the requests, they would give her a schedule of the ones she would be expected to attend.

Jane thanked Murry and then called publicity and informed them that she wanted to be made aware of any war-related requests for her services. She would make the final decision as to which engagements she would accept.

Publicity wasn't happy, but they didn't have much choice but to comply, and that afternoon a large box of telegrams, phone messages, and letters arrived for Jane to look through.

Everything seemed to be happening at once. The house was in complete chaos and the hours sped by under the unspoken threat of another attack from the enemy. Warren tried unsuccessfully to get a call through to his children, but Washington did reach him and the president requested that he be in the nation's capital as soon as possible to take up his duties. Maud was chaotically trying to explain the current state of her work for British war relief to members who would be staying in California and now working for the American war effort, while at the same time reminding Hardgrave of all the last-minute details of her departure.

Late that afternoon, Jane, Maud, and Warren sat down in the

drawing room with trays of food. Maud had wanted to sit outside and enjoy the warm air since she was leaving California, but Warren warned against it. There was still the threat of Japanese planes.

"How horrible," said Maud. "To think they could just fly over here and attack our house. It seems so unreal."

"War is very real," said Warren. "And this one will probably go on for quite a while."

"Well, at least we'll be safe back in New York," said Maud.

"That's on a coast, too, Aunt Maud," said Jane.

Maud looked abashed. "I know you're right. It just seems different somehow."

"I think we'd better talk," said Warren.

"What about?" asked Maud. "I thought everything was settled. We're leaving the day after tomorrow. Fortunately, we were able to get train reservations. Mrs. Hardgrave is going today and she can start opening the house. Hardgrave and Maria will travel with Jane and me. I think everything will be fine. We naturally hope to see you in New York as soon as you can get away, Warren. When do you leave for Washington?"

"Day after tomorrow," said Warren. "In the afternoon."

"You're flying?" asked Maud.

"Yes."

They were quiet for a few minutes, then Jane said, "Aunt Maud, I think you should know that I'm not going with you."

"What on earth are you talking about?" asked Maud. "Of course you're going." Then her face lit up. "Or are you going to Washington?"

"No," said Jane, looking at Warren. "I'm not going to Washington, either. I'm staying here."

"Here!"

Warren sat with his head down. He didn't meet Jane's gaze or react in any way.

"But that's impossible," said Maud. "Your mother expressly asked that you join us. Besides, you can't stay out here all alone. Think of the danger. How do we know those terrible people won't suddenly decide to bomb California?"

"Aunt Maud—"

"Warren, can't you talk some sense into her? We can't both just go and leave her here. Why, Jane, there won't be any servants in the house."

"The maids will be here, and Louise. I'll get the studio to find me a cook this week."

"But—"

"Aunt Maud. What would I do in New York? My life is here. You and Warren both have jobs to do in the east. I have one to do here. Murry says we're going ahead with *Another Life*, and I've had a lot of requests for personal appearances. Don't worry about me. I have Virginia and Marty and all the people at Global. I'll be fine."

"Warren . . ." began Maud again.

He finally looked at them, a rueful grin on his lips. "I've been rather expecting this. And I don't see what we can do about it," he said. "Jane has to make up her own mind about what's right."

Jane kissed him on the cheek.

Maud looked thoughtful. "I would like to stay with you, dear, but—"

"No, Aunt Maud. I'd love to have you here, but you know that Mother will need you now. She and Laurance will probably take government jobs or something important and someone has to run the house. I'll be fine. Honestly I will."

Maud still didn't look convinced. "But . . ." Her voice trailed off as she realized she was fighting a losing battle. She looked at Warren and Jane, and then stood up. "I'd better make sure that Maria has everything under control. I'll speak to you later." She left, and Warren and Jane were alone.

"Thank you," said Jane.

"What for?"

"For understanding. For not trying to change me."

"I gave that up a long time ago. But just for the record, I'd be a lot happier if you were going with Maud. Or better still, marrying me and coming to Washington."

"You know I can't, Warren. It isn't just my career now. As a performer I have some value to all those charities and soldiers. You're going to do your work to help the war effort. I have to do mine, too. I know it's not as important as yours, but I do have to do it."

"I'm sure you'll make it very important. But I'll miss you."

"Oh, my dear, dear Warren," said Jane, leaning close to him. "I do love you so very much. You're the kindest, gentlest man I've ever known. You're the strength I turn to when I feel down, and the love I count on when I'm afraid. What we have is ours, Warren. And nothing will ever be able to change it. Not war, or careers, or even distance." She smiled at him. "It looks like you're stuck with me. And when this whole thing is over—"

"Hey," said Warren, smiling at her. "I thought you were the one who always insisted on taking one day at a time."

"In this case, I'll make an exception. When this war is over, I expect you to make an honest woman out of me, Warren Harris."

"I'm looking forward to it," he said.

Jane slipped into his arms, and the couple sat quietly as the day began to fade.

Maud was finally packed and ready to leave. She refused to let Jane see her to the station because of the confusion her appearance would create. So Jane stood on the steps of the big house and watched as Maud fluttered about the car, instructing Hardgrave and Maria to check and change the arrangement of the luggage. When she was satisfied with things, she went to Jane and put her arms about her. The two women held each other for a few moments, and then Maud pulled back.

"Oh, dear. I'm afraid I'm going to cry," she said.

"If you do, then I will, too, and we'll both look terrible."

"You will take care of yourself, won't you, dear? And call often and write, and if you can get away you'll come to New York?"

"Yes, of course."

Maud looked at Jane, her blue eyes shining brightly in the brilliant sunlight. "I'm very proud of you," whispered Maud. "Not just because of your achievements, but because you're a fine young woman."

"Thank you, Aunt Maud."

"We'll get through this, dear. We'll all get through this thing." Her voice was determined. "Just you wait and see if we don't."

"I know we will. But I'll miss you, Aunt Maud. It won't be the same here without you."

Maud smiled mischievously. "That's what they all say, dear."

Laughing, Jane helped Maud into her car and then stood

back. As Hardgrave drove away, Jane could hear Maud's voice calling out the open window. "Take care of yourself, dear. And thank you. I've had a wonderful time."

In the afternoon, Warren returned from the beach house, where he had been packing his belongings. His chauffeured car pulled up at the front door, and Jane ran out to meet him.

They embraced, and Jane laughed. "I seem to be spending the entire day standing on these steps, saying good-bye."

"Shouldn't you have gone to the studio?"

"I told them I couldn't make it. It's just costume tests, they can use my stand-in."

"Did Maud get off all right?"

"With the usual confusion. I'm going to miss her." Jane's voice grew serious. "I'm going to miss everything. We seem to be coming apart. Nothing is ever going to be the same, is it, Warren?"

"I'm afraid not, darling. But we'll survive."

"Aunt Maud said almost the same thing."

"You see? And Maud is never wrong."

Jane smiled at him.

"You'll be all right?"

"Yes, I'll be fine. Just missing you every moment."

"That's all I wanted to hear."

"I love you, Warren, darling. Nothing will ever change that."

"No matter what happens," he said. "We'll always have each other."

For a moment they simply stared at each other, not knowing what to say, each reluctant to be the first to say good-bye.

Warren's driver called out, "Mr. Harris. I'm afraid, sir, we'll have to leave if you don't want to miss your airplane."

"Yes," said Warren over his shoulder.

Jane's eyes filled with tears, and she put her arms around his neck. "Oh, my very special darling," she whispered.

They held each other tightly. Warren kissed her and turned and went quickly to the car. Jane watched until his car was out of sight, and then walked slowly back into the house.

Closing the door behind her, Jane leaned against it. There were no sounds in the house. A heavy and oppressive silence had settled over each room. The quiet made her feel closed in and trapped. She moved through the drawing room and out onto the patio, anxious to avoid the tight sense of solitude.

Staring up at the bright blue sky, Jane felt terribly alone, her whole body filled with an empty and aching loneliness.

The sound of the telephone ringing through the silent house startled her, and she flinched. It continued to ring, and Jane remembered that she had given the servants the rest of the day off after they had seen Maud on her way. Jane walked back into the house and went into the library.

Picking up the receiver, she heard the voice of one of the studio assistants explaining that some additional color tests were needed. Would it be convenient for Miss Turner to come to the studio early the next day?

Jane agreed, made the arrangements, and hung up. Still sitting in the chair, her hand on the telephone, a slight smile crossed her face. Of course it would be convenient, she thought. It would always be convenient to go to the studio.

After all, it was what she'd always wanted.